REPU TATION

DR. REBECCA SHARP

a novel

Published by Dr. Rebecca Sharp
Copyright © 2018 Dr. Rebecca Sharp

Cover Design:

Sarah Hansen, Okay Creations

Printed in the United States of America.

Visit www.drrebeccasharp.com

To every woman who's ever had a story told about you.
('You're too fat.')
To every woman who's ever had gossip and lies told about you.
('You're not strong enough.')
To every woman who's had her life belittled and turned into a work of fiction.
('This is all your fault. You're pathetic.')

They're all lies, darling. Ignore them.
Keep your head high and your standards higher.
You are beautiful. You are strong.
You are not responsible for someone else's failure.
You are not responsible for someone else's flawed moral character.
You are not responsible for someone else's hate.
When the cruelest words want to cut you down, be brave.
Be true. Be unapologetically you.
You are enough.
You. Are. Better.

The idea of my life as a fairytale is itself a fairytale.

- Grace Kelly, Princess of Monaco

PROLOGUE

Blake

Do you know what it's like to have people judge you by what you say? How about what you do or don't do? Or even by what you wear?

Do you know what it's like to have people twist your words or actions?

Do you know what it's like to have people say things – *make up stories* – about you for their own benefit, even if that benefit is to hurt you?

Do you ever feel like you do *all you can* and still have a target on your back?

I do.

People have all kinds of ideas about fame.

Being famous doesn't make me different.

Being famous doesn't make me special.

Being famous just makes my target bigger.

Shinier.

Easier to take down.

"Blake Tyler wins 9th Grammy at only 25!"

ROCKSTAR.

Rock. Star.

You came from Earth - from the dirt and stones and nothingness - and were rocketed up to the stars, set ablaze along the way for everyone else to enjoy your glow. Every night. Every place. You were on display. Every bright and burning piece of you was seen. All. The. Time.

"How does Blake do it? *Love Struck* sells 2.5 million copies the first week!"

I'D BARELY FINISHED high school when Heart Break caught fire and exploded me to the top of more charts than I'd seen in all my math and science classes combined. SATs and ACTs quickly became AMAs and VMAs.

It was unnerving since I'd always been shy. I didn't think I'd ever get used to the kind of soul-sucking fame that someone had yet to diagnose as a more dangerous addiction than heroin. Turns out, my naiveté only seemed to make the world love me even more; how ironic that elusiveness was the most potent ingredient in the recipe for popularity.

"America's sweetheart named one of Rolling Stone's Greatest Songwriters of All Time!"

I FOLLOWED MY FAME - WILLINGLY, excitedly, and with an innocence that can only spell eventual disaster. But that was the real me. *America's sweetheart. Believer of fairy tales.*
Perfect.
Princess.
Popstar.
That was my reputation – and reputation was everything in this town.

But I wasn't perfect. And my life wasn't a fairytale. *In fact, it had taken me a decade to forget about my chronic, incurable disease.*

I'd had ZP since I was a kid. It did all sorts of things to my body, including, but not limited to chills, heat spells, sleeplessness, chest pains, nausea, and bouts of indescribable aches in unmentionable places.

I guess I should mention that ZP isn't actually a disease - then at least there might have been hope for a cure. No, ZP stood for Zach Parker and before he'd become my disease, he was the god-next-door that set my soul on fire.

Zach was my neighbor, if that word still counted with a solid two football fields of farmland between our two houses, complete with growing corn, a small island of trees, and a stream small enough to babble. And to add icing to the cake, Zach was my older brother, Ashton's, best friend. He was the gorgeous football star who should have had 'Superman' written on the back of his jersey. Instead of a cape, he wore a cap - the one from the University of Alabama was his favorite. *Go Tide.* He was the man of steel with a heart of gold and a smile that could light up our whole hometown.

Whether I fully realized it then or not, I'd attached myself to him in ways that didn't come apart without some sort of amputation.

The loss of my heart all started the day I met him – the day he convinced me not to run away. *One chunk gone.* Then there was the time he let me steal all of the eggs from his

3

chicken coop because I didn't want the baby chicks to die. Once I calmed down, he gently informed me that unfertilized eggs don't hatch. *Another chunk missing.* Piece by piece until the day I lost my glasses, tripping as I rushed out to the school bus pick-up. I broke out into tears when Jensen Nabors, the biggest and meanest third grade bully, found them and proceeded to hold them (and me) hostage while he made fun of me for being blind without my four eyes. Zach, who was two years older, pushed him to the ground and threatened worse if he ever made fun of me again. And when Zach put the frames back on my tear-streaked face... Well...

My heart became his to keep and his to lose.

I'd loved Zach Parker with every fiber of my eight-year-old body, and every cell that had grown in it since only magnified the obsession. *That's what happens when you have a viral disease; it changes your DNA and how every molecule in your body is made.* And from that moment on, breathing Zach Parker was written into the cells of my lungs, feeling Zach Parker was written into the cells of my skin, seeing only Zach Parker was written into each inky blue cell of my eyes. And *loving* Zach Parker? Well, that was engraved into the demanding cells of my heart - deeper and deeper with each and every beat.

But to Zach, I was just a friend on good days and the annoying little sister he never had on bad ones. And after eight years, I learned that sometimes it's the things that feel good in the moment that hurt us the worst in the end.

When Zach realized he had my heart, he promptly tried to return it. At that point, it was too late. My own heart was a foreign object to me. What was I supposed to do with this thing that hadn't been mine for almost a decade?

I didn't know how it worked, but there was no mistaking that it was broken.

"Blake + Matt McCoy confirmed couple status with appearance at the Grammy's!"

Now, almost another decade later and with the whole world watching, I was *still* fumbling with the stupid thing. I wanted to give it to someone who knew how to take care of it, someone who *actually* wanted it - so pitifully so that I completely missed how they were all just after my limelight and not my love.

"Blake Tyler spotted in close quarters at Met Gala with actor Xavier James. Is she done with McCoy?!"

I came home and *tried* to focus on my music, writing in the hammock in our backyard, staying out late into the tranquil Tennessee nights, and staring up at the stars that could identify with the struggle of my soul: *to not be swallowed up by the vast darkness of everything around me.*

"McCoy is gone and looks like Xavier has himself a new bae - or Blay!"

"The only competition for Blake Tyler is the one between her number of awards and her number of ex-boyfriends!"

THAT's the thing about stars – they shine like a bright beacon amid the stifling masses of blackness. They sparkle and twinkle and put on a show. But at some point, everyone wishes so hard on them that they can't hang onto the sky anymore.

And that's where most people get it wrong. You don't wish on a falling star, you wished *for* it - for its magical plummet.

They love you when you shine, but they only wish on your fall.

"Blink and Blake has another beau!"

I HADN'T DONE anything wrong. But the press isn't a courtroom where you have the luxury of being innocent until proven guilty. *Player.* No, the tabloids thrive on guilt. *Serial narcissist.* They thrive on breaking shiny things... *spotless things...* like a reputation hiding a broken heart.

"Swedish DJ, Levi Janssen, and Blake Tyler announce relationship with impromptu live collaboration of his song 'Always' at Webster Hall."

THAT's the thing about reaching *this* level of fame. Everyone thinks you're put on a pedestal - nice and tall and stable.

You're not.

I was a superstar walking on stilts... on a very thin tightrope. And I was pretty darn clumsy.

But aren't we all when it comes to love?

Which is how even doing the right thing put me so precariously close to being ruined.

"Forget 'Always,' someone let Levi know that he'll be lucky if he lasts two days with BT."

MY REPUTATION... everything that was real about me that I *thought* people truly believed... was being torn to shreds. Sputtering. Flailing. Falling.

And I'd do anything to try to get the world to stop questioning the person my heart hoped they still believed me to be.

Anything.

Including re-infecting myself with the disease that - through what felt like extensive broken heart surgery nine years ago - I'd barely managed to recover from.

Blake Tyler.

Superstar.

Sad story.

CHAPTER ONE

BLAKE

Track 01: Reputation
"They said, 'you've gone too far this time.' The thought never even crossed my mind.
On my knees, I'd beg you to stay. Turns out knees are just a pit-stop on the fall from grace."

A LOT CAN HAPPEN IN A DECADE.

I slipped off my shoes and crossed my legs as I stared at the wall in my manager, Bruce's, office. A decade in photos, news articles, magazine interviews, and award letters that tracked every move of my brightly shining star from the moment it had been rocketed into the orbit of fame.

I saw myself - the homegrown little girl from Tennessee who liked sweet tea, every flavor of chewing gum, reading James Patterson novels, and sleeping in a tree house under the stars - standing in a place that I never in a million light years thought I would be. From acres of land and freedom to roam to a personality cult where personal space is non-existent.

#superstar

#famous

Sometimes I sat here and felt like I didn't know that girl with all the make-up, holding her guitar up in front of a screaming crowd of seventy-thousand fans with the biggest smile on her face. Sometimes, I still felt like I was on the outside, trying to look in.

"Hey, girl! So sorry I'm late!" Taylor said as she crashed in through the door, holding a million bags and coffee travel cups in both hands.

Petite, with an asymmetrical mahogany bob that was in complete disarray, and a brilliant white smile, Taylor Hastings was an organized mess who was single-handedly responsible for keeping my life - *and me* - together. She was my PR manager-slash-publicist-slash-best-friend-slash-keeps-Blake-sane. She was my person – my go-to for everything. We'd known each other since middle school and I didn't care that she didn't have a degree in any of the things that she did for me; the fact that she'd come out on top (Prom Queen, Homecoming Queen, Class President and Valedictorian) *and* managed to stay friends with everyone in our class was enough qualification for me. 'Popular' made the best PR.

I also may have been slightly freaked out when my debut studio album shot to the top of the charts within a few weeks after my seventeenth birthday and before you could flash a camera, I was opening for the likes of Justin Bieber, Ed Sheeran, and Maroon 5.

Taylor had been my tether back to home and reality when fame tried to rebuild my world on fantasy. *She was the anchor that kept my boat from being swept away with the storm.* And over the past eight years, we clung to each other while we navigated the entertainment industry.

Well… I wouldn't call it an industry. Most days it felt more like the Hunger Games. I'd been picked as tribute and every song, every album, every performance was one more step to see whether I was going to make it out alive.

May the octaves be ever in your favor.

"God, you're such a bag lady!" I teased, standing to take my Chai Tea latte from her hand. "Calm down; Bruce isn't even here yet."

"Seriously? I *just* got off the phone with him like an hour ago," she gasped, dropping one armful of stuff. "I swear. Sometimes, I think he forgets that you're - oh, only the biggest pop star in the world. Like no big deal, dude. Just keep Blake Tyler waiting." She rolled her eyes and I couldn't stop myself from laughing at her dramatics.

Bruce Pillars was my manager and for all his awkward quirkiness, he was considered the best in the business which is why I'd hired him at the very beginning even though four years of college would have been cheaper than what he billed. He was direct to the point of insult, abrupt to the point of rude, but knowledgeable to the point of premonition. He also had the habit of being perpetually late.

"Sorry, just anxious to get this over with," she mumbled grumpily.

I winced, burning my tongue on the steamed soy milk that was still too hot to drink.

"Everything ok?" I asked with concern, setting the damaging liquid back on the coffee table, and crossing my legs on the black leather couch. I began to pull my straight blonde hair back into a ponytail and when she didn't respond, I added, "I know you've been crazy busy getting everything ready for round two of the tour. I feel like I haven't seen you."

It was in the middle - the intermission - of my *Lovestruck* album tour. The first leg had been our European shows; two weeks ago, we'd landed back in the US to regroup and re-organize and spend the holidays at home before we would start our trek through most major US cities at the beginning of the New Year. I'd been in a bubble of photoshoots, interviews, and promos for the past two weeks in New York City, all the while trying to find elusive inspiration for my next album that I was supposed to be writing.

Busy was good.

Busy meant ignorance and ignorance meant bliss.

It had been a whirlwind and I was more than ready to go home and relax with my family for a few days before the craziness started all over again. And then Bruce had called this morning and asked for an emergency meeting before our flight home to Nashville this afternoon; he never had emergencies.

Not when it came to me.

"It's... alright," she replied hesitantly, with a tone that had completely changed to something much more somber. "How are you? After Levi?"

And my blissful ignorance was coming to an end.

My eyes fell, staring blankly at the lid on my tea.

Levi Janssen was one of the hottest DJ's out of the Netherlands. I met him right before the start of my European tour and we clicked. Of course, I thought it was fate that I was heading overseas, my tour aligning with some clubs that he was scheduled to DJ at. So, we'd jumped from a few casual dates to basically a three-month vacation together.

Spoiler alert: It hadn't gone well.

But I tried really hard to make it seem like it had; I tried really hard because I refused to believe that it wasn't. Pictures of the two of us all over each other in Madrid, Berlin, and Copenhagen graced the cover of every tabloid - especially the ones from Berlin where we both had on matching t-shirts with huge red hearts on them and our names inside. They'd been a gift from a fan and I'd looked the gift horse in the mouth.

The press would never know just *how* much Levi liked to talk about himself. *He loved himself more than he could ever love me.* They also missed how touchy he was. *And I don't mean with me.* I know that Europeans tend to kiss each other in greetings and such, but I'm pretty sure they don't kiss friends that are girls *that* way in front of their *girlfriend.*

"I'm fine," I sighed. "Sorry... that was so stupid of me."

With a frustrated groan, my head tipped back on the couch and I stared up at the ceiling. "He was so stupid of me." *Ugh.* I shook my head. "I have no idea what I was thinking. What's wrong with me, Tay?"

Like she had an answer.

Like she had an answer that we had time for.

Tay was the one left to clean up the pieces of another one of my quickly failed relationships. My life was starting to sound like a new version of 'Mambo Number Five.'

One. Two. Three, four, five.

A little bit of Matt telling me lies… A little bit of Xavier getting some on the side… A little bit of Levi's promiscuity…

This one – Levi – had been foolish. I was hurt and upset after I'd broken up with actor Xavier James and the press painted me as the bad guy. *Again.* Two months after I'd broken up with designer, Matt McCoy. It didn't matter that I'd dumped Xavier because he was sleeping with his co-star or that I'd ended it with Matt because I'd caught him sexting with one of his models. *I* was the famous one. *I* was the one that broke up with the 'next James Bond'. *I* was the one who left the rising fashion star in 'an attempt to damage his career out of jealousy.'

Being infamous made the press far richer than plain-Jane famous ever would.

"I mean I did try to tell you he was a douche canoe," she murmured wryly and I stuck my tongue out at her. "It's ok…" The way that she said it told me that it wasn't.

"How bad was it?" I cringed asking. "Don't lie. You suck at lying."

She'd flown home right after I dumped him to start preparing for the US leg. Meanwhile, I was in London, the second to last stop in Europe, when the news broke over here. Too depressed about in my third break-up for the year – *not because Levi ended up being a douche, but because I couldn't understand how I kept ending up with all the players* – I crawled into a hole, ignored social media, and made it through three Patterson novels before we flew back home. This state of black-hole ignorance had continued right up to this moment.

Was there such a thing as a douche magnet? Because my picture should show up in the definition.

The way her face scrunched suggested that it was about as bad as the whole Brangelina breakup. *Probably even worse.*

She took a sip of her coffee, staring at me over the lid like it was some sort of shield.

"*Tay…*"

"Alright, it was bad, B," she huffed, slamming her cup down on the table. "Honestly, the first half of this break was still dealing with the shock waves. Fielding calls and reporters. I've had a dozen interviews cancelled and ticket refunds are rising. I-I don't know why. Or why now. But it is literally exploding everywhere."

"Seriously? I wasn't even with him for that long!" Animated, I jerked up to stare at her, flailing my arms. "And he was a self-centered ass! Yeah – of course the public doesn't know that but—ugh!" I huffed, falling back against the seat.

"I'm on your side, babe, but all the world sees is you going through boys faster than Oprah goes through free giveaways. And that woman gives away a lot of free shit…"

"Whatever. I'm swearing off boys," I promised as I toyed with the edge of my shirt. "Heart. Break. My heart is taking a break. I'm done."

Go ahead, stick a fork in me.

"I don't think that's going to help," she said, reaching into her bag and pulling out her laptop. "The damage is already done."

"What do you mean?" My brow furrowed.

"B…" She flipped open the screen and shoved it onto my lap. Eyes widening, I scrolled through the word doc of what I assumed where headlines that she copied.

14

"Another Break-Up for Blake?"

"Love Struck? More Like Love Struck Out…"

"America's Sweetheart Or America's Heartbreaker? Is Blake Tyler The Girl That We Thought She Was?"

I HATED how my heart jumped in my throat. *Bye, bye, Bliss.* I slammed the screen shut.

"I'm sure that they're over it by now. It's been a month since I dumped Licentious Levi."

At least my nickname game was still going strong. Then again, so was theirs…

The stories were ridiculous, but not as ridiculous as the fact that the words still hurt.

"Those were from last week." *Good Lord. Does anyone have a life? Would anyone care to have a life besides mine?*

My eyes narrowed on her, unwilling to believe it.

"I'm sorry, B, but that's why we're having this meeting."

"I thought this was about the tour?" I handed her back the laptop.

"It is. It's about the tour because we've noticed substantial changes in ticket sales and the overall tone of publicity for every event since you broke up with Loser Levi. The headlines, his comments, the responses from all your exes… they all add up. I've done what I can without slandering each and every one of them for the disgusting shitheads that they are – because we are above that," she said as though she needed to remind both of us, "but it's not enough."

Not enough? It's not enough that I give the world my everything and they still want to take more?

My life was revving at the limit of what I was capable of and still, the press… the media… continued to push with a lead foot on the gas to see just how far and how fast I could go before I crashed and burned.

"How is it—" I broke off, burying my face in my hands. "I don't get it, Tay. What am I doing wrong? How does it always seem so right and yet I still end up with a player or a narcissist? Why do they have to love *me*?"

"You're too good, B. Too trusting," she said with a shrug (like she hadn't warned me about this before.) "And that has nothing to do with your fame. It's just you. And it's easy to take advantage of."

Logically, it made sense that they'd want me for what I had. And *that* was breaking me. Because in a world of fake, at least the relationships I made should have been real.

Like lighthouses in stormy seas, they should have been a beacon of safety and stability.

Instead, they were turning out to be mirages in the middle of the desert sand of stardom.

And my mouth was becoming so dry it was getting harder and harder to breathe.

"You're making me sound like a ho." I rolled my eyes at her, trying to lighten the conversation before I started bawling.

That cracked a small smile on her face. "Hey," she put her hands up, "I just said you were easy. That's all."

My offended gasp that bordered on a laugh was interrupted.

"Ladies!" The door burst open and Bruce strolled inside. A short, balding man wearing a suit that should fit much better for the amount of money that I paid him and glasses that looked too small for his round face, eyed us both quickly before walking behind his desk.

"Finally." I heard Taylor grumble underneath her breath.

Bruce's narrow eyes darted to her as he paused his paper rifling. "Have you brought Miss Tyler up to speed?"

After eight years, he still called me Miss Tyler no matter how many times I asked that he *please* just call me Blake.

"I was just starting to, Bruce. I showed her a few of the headlines."

Starting to? There was more?

"We have a serious problem, Miss Tyler." He turned to me with a curt nod to acknowledge his statement.

I rubbed my palms together before linking my fingers and squeezing them tight to keep them stationary. I hated this feeling - the feeling of being punished for something that I didn't do. I may have won Entertainer of the Year - *two years in a row* - but I'd been unofficially the Worst Boyfriend Picker since the beginning of time.

Yes, I did break up with them. *That's what you do with guys who hurt you.* But playing the blame game wasn't my style. I wasn't going to turn around and point fingers and shine the spotlight on their lies, their cheating, and their general callousness. *It wasn't who I was.*

I was just a girl trying to find my Prince Charming - *while the whole world watched.*

Were they really going to hold that against me?

"And what's that?" I asked quietly. "My ex-boyfriends?"

"Your reputation," he said tightly, seating himself in his high-back chair with an exaggerated movement. "It's sinking faster than the Titanic if the Titanic had backed up after the first hit only to run into the iceberg again."

Well then.

"Tell us how you really feel," I mumbled wryly. Catching his disapproving stare, I bit my tongue and apologized, "I'm sorry. I just can't believe this. Since when are my relationships the public's business? Can't I just make my own mistakes in peace?" I sucked in a huge breath. "Sorry. So, what do we do? How do I fix it? Should I make a statement? I've been M.I.A. from social media for a little now; coming back with a sort of explanation could mean something."

An explanation that would let me wallow in my self-consciousness in peace.

"As much as your fans love you, sometimes they are more fascinated by a star that explodes than one that shines." He paused and adjusted his glasses like it would make the small frames fit better. "The press is on a witch-hunt, Miss Tyler, and we need to put an end to it before the burns to your image get any worse."

"Burning witches? Even if I'm not one?" I couldn't believe what I was hearing - how serious this was becoming. All over stupid boys.

He nodded curtly, opening up his laptop on his desk and punching a few keys. "That's how this world works. They'll burn anything in the hopes of creating a firework." He clasped his hands in front of him and, in all our years of working together, I'd never seen him as serious as he was in this moment.

"I know who you are, Miss Tyler. But the world only knows what they've been given. And right now, they're being told that what you've given them is a lie. At this level, it's no longer about your talent, your fame, or your music. At this level, people feel like they know you from the image that you've created. At this level, *your reputation is everything.*"

I reached in my bag and pulled out a piece of gum, shoving it in my mouth before I chewed a hole right through my tongue.

"What do I do?" I whispered. "I... I told Taylor that she's in charge of making me stay away from any and all boys until the tour is done."

"We don't have the luxury of that kind of time," he informed me with the calmness of the weatherman saying there was a thirty-percent chance I'd no longer be famous or America's favorite by tomorrow morning. "We need to give them something now. We need to give them what they want."

"And what's that?" I asked like I wasn't afraid to know.

"You. In a relationship that they can believe in. In love. And on tour."

Steve Harvey announcing the wrong Miss Universe had been less shocking than what he'd just said. And so, I waited patiently for the stuttered correction.

Silence.

"E-excuse me?" I finally squeaked out when it was clear that I hadn't misheard him. Reaching for my tea, I gulped down two huge mouthfuls.

"What Bruce is trying to say," Taylor inserted, "what he and I have been discussing over the past few days, is that your fans need to see you in a happily-ever-after and they need to see you fall into it now. You have to start this next leg of the tour with a boyfriend, B, and the world needs to see you fall in love with him."

"H-how am I supposed to fall in love with someone - even pretend to - that I haven't met? I-I'm not an actress. Just because I go on stage doesn't mean that I'm putting on a show. I'm performing, but it's all me out there - my hopes, my fears, my feelings, and my heart." My arms flailed in every direction as I spoke, mirroring the frantic nature of my thoughts. "They already think me a heartless liar, why would I become the exact thing they accuse me of?"

"Because they won't believe the truth, Blake," Taylor said, grabbing one of my hands. Her palms were just as sweaty as my own. "More than that, they don't *want* the truth. They want a lie that fits their idea of the truth. I know this isn't how you normally… ever… do things, but sometimes the end has to justify the means."

Just because that was a saying didn't make it true.

Letting out a nervous laugh, I pulled my hand from hers and ran it through my hair that was quickly becoming dislodged from the elastic that held it together. *I couldn't believe what I was hearing.*

I didn't know how to be in a real relationship, let alone a fake one.

"Tay, I'm a worse liar than you and considering the world doesn't believe me when it comes to my very real ex-boyfriends, I can't fathom how they would believe a fake relationship with someone that I just met," I insisted. "Like you might as well just hook me up with Matt-freaking-Bomer – even *that* would be more believable… and he's gay!"

There was no way - *no way* - that this was a good idea.

Bruce cleared his throat and I watched his eyes flick to Taylor. I looked back and forth between the two of them, watching the invisible battle wage over who was going to deliver the next blow to me - whatever that was.

Great. Blake-the-Punching-Bag.

"What? What is it?" I demanded. "Just tell me."

"Miss Tyler," Bruce began, clearing his throat again even though there was nothing in it to clear. "We aren't suggesting a relationship with someone that you don't know. We're suggesting a relationship with someone that you do and have known for a long time."

'Clueless' wasn't even the right word for me. I looked to Taylor saying. "Who is he talking about?"

She sighed deeply and, just like the time in ninth grade when she promised me that I was not going to like the ending to *A Walk to Remember*, I knew I was in trouble.

"Next week you and I are going home for Christmas. You. America's Sweetheart. The Southern Belle with a heart the size of Texas." Dread began to eat its way through my cells like acid as she continued, "We think the world would jump at the chance to see you with someone that you knew before you were famous, someone that you liked before you were a star. They'd want to believe you found love with a childhood sweetheart. That's the kind of relationship that will have them rooting for you instead of against you."

My face burned as I looked at her. We'd known each other for too long for me not to know where this was going - to whom this was going. I felt like my longest and best friend had just stabbed me in the back.

No, not stabbed.

She carved a letter into it as though she were the masked legend of Zorro.

Z. Zach. Zach-asshole-Parker.

"No, Tay…" I whispered, betrayal dripping from my words.

She knew what she was asking of me. She knew how I'd loved him and she knew how swiftly and callously he'd broken my heart. She'd slept over my house almost every night after that party, trying to cheer me as I bawled my eyes out. She'd stepped in front of me when Ash flipped out on me that night, forcing him to leave me alone.

She'd been the first one to listen to every lyric that I'd written about my love and loss - each of which ending up on my debut album, *Heart Break.*

I'd loved him for so long that for months, I truly didn't know how to live without being able to see him or talk to him - even if he'd never felt the same.

She'd helped me to stay strong when I swore that my guitar knew only how to play sobs instead of songs. And now, she sat there asking me to rip back open the horrible scar down the center of my heart in order to save face and save my dream.

She rubbed her hands together and stared me down, handing me my heartbreak on a silver platter.

"You need to be in a relationship with Zach Parker. And you need to convince the world that you've fallen in love with him."

"Are you joking?" I asked breathlessly, feeling the invisible band around my chest squeezing tighter. I felt like I just got out of convincing myself that I *wasn't* in love with him.

"This is no joke, Miss Tyler," he said sternly and heat bloomed in my cheeks.

"No, it's not. This is my life, my heart, Mr. Pillars. If there is any joke going on here, it's on me," I replied harshly.

Zach Parker had my heart before I knew I'd lost it.

Before I knew what love was.

Before my life became not my own and fame rewrote my stars.

Zach Parker was my Achilles heel.

"Blake…" Taylor's hand reached for my shoulder and I didn't have the strength to push it off. "I know, babe. I know what happened. But it was a decade ago. Do you think… maybe you've both moved on since then?"

One would hope.

I must have looked like I was waiting for another option – *any* other option – because she continued, "I tried. I tried to get interviews. I tried to give statements. I even reached out to a few news places, but no one wants to hear it. They don't want to hear your side when the other side is selling so well. You know me… you know that if I'm suggesting this I've thought about every other option to try to reason with them."

"Not dating sends the message that they are right and that we are punishing you," Bruce interjected, reaching up to adjust his glasses again. "Dating makes a statement that you can't be bullied, but a random person is too risky. Too much like what they've already seen."

"Zach was all I could think of," Tay ended, regretfully. *I knew that feeling. All too well.* "I'm sorry."

My head moved back and forth between them like a volley, both bombarding me with reasons why this was the only way.

I shook my head. "Even if I could…" I trailed off trying to swallow the lump in my throat. "How am I supposed to convince him? When am I supposed to convince him? I never see him. I don't even know—"

"He's going to be home for Christmas, too. I already talked to Ash." My assertive mess of a friend looked at me calmly and I knew that she had the whole thing figured out already – she always did.

"You told my brother about this—"

"No. Of course not." She slid her laptop back into her

bag. "But you're going to have to; he's part of the band. Along with your parents. Because they're going to see and they're going to need to know that it's not real."

"He won't go for it," I resorted to the last and probably most truthful pitfall of their entire plan.

I'd wanted Zach before. I could pretend something that I'd already felt. Zach, on the other hand, had never wanted me and never would; he'd made that painfully clear. *And the last thing I needed was to hear his rejection for a fake relationship when I was still haunted by his rejection for a real one.*

"We'll make him an offer that he can't refuse," she replied simply and stood, reaching down to calmly collect her department-store-sized collection of bags. "We should get going. Better to be early to the airport. We have a busy week ahead."

"I trust you'll let me know what you decide," Bruce said calmly; if they gave out ranks for emotions, he would have a black belt in impartiality. "But I would be remiss if I didn't inform you, Miss Tyler, that there is no explanation you can give to make this better. This tour is no longer about you or *Lovestruck.* This tour is about saving your *reputation.*"

I stood, pulling down my oversized sweatshirt over my yoga pants and gave him a quick nod. "Have a good holiday," I replied, standing abruptly and heading for the door.

Was it worth it?

I stood outside in the hallway, waiting for Taylor to catch up.

Was saving my reputation worth the open and public dissection of my heart?

CHAPTER TWO

BLAKE

Track 02: Sixteen

"Cause when you're sixteen and all you wanted was to be wanted.
Wish I knew what I know now. I should have looked before I fell."

9 YEARS AGO

THIS WAS the biggest moment of my entire life: the moment when I would kiss a god.

Zach... Zeus... We'd been learning about Ancient Greek mythology, but I think the textbooks spelled it wrong.

He certainly looked like the statues in the book. All big and cut and strong. Like if the un-tool versions of Zac Efron and Justin Bieber had a love child that was actually cool while still being incredibly hot. *That* was my Zach. He had a Southern twang that made my toes curl, especially when he sang, and a smile that made... other parts of me... curl even tighter. To top it all (melt-my-bones hot, talented, and stereotypically popular) off, he was sweeter than Southern sweet tea - which said a lot when you lived just outside of Nashville in Franklin, Tennessee.

We take our sweet tea *very* seriously down here.

How did that make him a god?

Besides the above-mentioned reasons…

Well… how else do I explain why, when he walks by, I can barely breathe?

And like any god would, he looked down on me like a mere mortal. At least nowadays. And it wasn't just because I was only fifteen (for a few more months) and he was a senior. There was a time when he was nice and attentive and a friend. But I was younger and I didn't look at him the way that I do now. Now, I couldn't take my eyes off of him while he hardly looked at me. And even though I knew I'd loved Zach for a long time, it was only recently when I craved everything that word could mean. And that's when the space between us began to grow larger. Insurmountable.

For a while, he treated me the same as my brother. If Ash was annoyed with me, so was Zach. If Ash ignored me, so did Zach. If Ash teased me, so. Did. Zach. And that's why looking down on me was preferable because at least it meant he was looking.

"Baby Blake… are you wearing make-up? Are you old enough for that?"

"Baby Blake, put some clothes on. You look like you just went shopping in the toddler section."

"Baby Blake, why are you playing guitar so late? It's past your bedtime."

His taunts were casually cruel. Maybe if his voice wasn't so calm and indifferent as he spoke… maybe then I could've read more into why he said what he did. Instead, he was always the jaw-dropping, gorgeously perfect god of disinterest when it came to me - the mortal… the little sister.

I wondered if he knew that he was all I thought about at night.

So, I began to push, and every time I did, he pulled away.

I wasn't deterred though. If there was one description of me that he and I could agree on, it was 'fearless'. *I'd had to be in order to grow up and keep up with the two of them.*

So, I pushed harder - completely unaware of Newton's Third Law of Motion and how it came into play. I learned the hard way that every time I pushed, *he pulled back with an equal and opposite force.*

I tried everything in the book. I tried flirting when my brother wasn't looking; that was met with a blank stare in his delicious honey eyes. I tried new clothes to *highlight* my long not-quite-filled-out form; I might as well have worn a grocery bag for all the difference it made: his eyes still scanned my body like a barcode that registered 'Not Interested.'

In fact, my attempts only made it worse. The past year or so, indifference had turned into sour annoyance.

"Are you trying to practice flirting with me, Baby Blake?" He smirked. *"You need help, but not from me. I can tell you though - don't do what you just did. It's borderline pathetic."*

"I'm not trying to practice, jerk," I shot back in defiance and mortified defense. *"I'm trying to flirt with you!"* Maybe a shot at the truth would change something.

It hadn't.

"I'm not a cradle robber. Find someone your own age, kid," he sneered and stalked from our kitchen, leaving me to explain to my brother why his best friend had up and left while he was in the shower.

Since then, even my breathing in his presence had become an offense.

That conversation sent me back into a dark hole where I wallowed, writing in my diary, writing angry and then apologetic letters to him that I never sent. Finally, six months ago, I renewed my efforts with a subtler attempt. For my birthday, I asked for a guitar and music lessons. Maybe a similar hobby might pull me out of the little-sibling-zone.

He hardly said a word about it, let alone allowing it to grow as something between us. *Another failure.*

Ever fearless – *or maybe just foolish* – I didn't give it up. I realized that I couldn't. It felt like each strum of the pick was retaliation. I sang my hurts, my feelings to the guitar instead of him.

At least, it couldn't talk back.

Those diary entries, letters, poems - all to Zach - had now been set to music. A depressing and pleading soundtrack to my love.

But if there is one thing in this world that is the strongest instigator of action, it's fear. In my case, fear that my time was running out - that my chances to show Zach just what he was missing out on were dwindling. If he could just *see* me, something told me things would change.

Tonight was their senior prom. Graduation was in two weeks and after that was Zach's combined graduation and eighteenth birthday party. One week later, he and Ash would be heading further south to the University of Alabama – both of them on football scholarships. *I should have known his favorite hat would be bad news for me.*

Every breath was like a ticking time bomb to when my time would run out. I *knew* what would happen at college. I knew what girls he would find there. He'd find them and forget about Ash's lanky little sister that got left behind.

In a stroke of pure luck, I'd overheard him and Ash talking last weekend about their plans for prom night. They both had dates already, but I wasn't worried about Alexa. Sure, she was a blonde bombshell. Sure, she wore short skirts while I preferred to steal Zach's old t-shirts. Sure, she was the cheer captain and I was just a quiet nerd, jotting down lyrics and humming melodies as I got lost in my own head. But I was the one who'd been here the whole time. I was the one who had grown up with him. I was the one who knew how important music was to him and how *not* important football was becoming even though he took the scholarship.

I was the one who understood him.

He was the one who didn't understand that what he'd been looking for was right in front of him this whole time.

But I was determined to make that crystal-clear tonight.

Their plan (and mine) involved our treehouse that sat between our two houses; I'd passed it on my way over to Zach's house an hour ago. Built in the thin strip of trees between our two properties, the tiny room sat high above the ground with a giant open window that looked off into the horizon and a metal roof that turned raindrops into a melody.

The three of us (with some help from our dads) built it. The biggest reason I loved it was because Zach and I had spent a lot of time together working on it since Ash wasn't big into manual labor; he'd rather just boss us around. That was when he'd looked on me kindly - and I'd fallen further.

The treehouse had gone unused for some time now; teenagers had cooler places to hang out. But when we were younger, we practically lived in the thing - even when Ash tried to insist that there were 'No Girls Allowed.'

Yeah, I scoffed, *not tonight*.

Unfortunately – or fortunately – Zach was only allowed to bring his date back to his house where his parents could keep an eye on things. And so, the treehouse had been resurrected to serve a more sophisticated purpose.

Sneaking out from his house to spend the night in the treehouse was a piece of cake.

You already knew this, I reminded myself as my body cringed.

I already knew that he and Alexa had slept together. I'd cried for weeks - *and wrote three songs* - after Tay broke that news to me. Pain is certainly productive.

They thought they were clever. I thought I was cleverer. *(And yes, that is a word when you are almost sixteen.)*

At fifteen, that should have been the first indication that I was *not*.

It hadn't been hard. Childish? Yes. But not hard.

I'd snuck into Zach's house through the basement doors that connected to the back patio. His family had a finished basement complete with a family room, bedroom, a sewing room for Zach's mom, Trish, and a bathroom. That guest bedroom was where Alexa would be 'sleeping.' It was also the farthest spot from Zach's room on the second floor.

From my dark corner of the sewing room, I listened for the two soft taps as Zach knocked on Alexa's door just before I saw his shadow slip smoothly through the hallway and out the patio doors like Peter Pan was after it.

My heart pounded against my chest, screaming *'Bad. Idea. Bad. Idea. Bad. Idea.'* - if I'd cared to listen to it.

I didn't.

Hormones and teenage crushes and all that.

My bare feet padded over to the door, half-expecting Alexa to throw it open any second and send caution to the wind. Hardly breathing, I listened but didn't hear anything on the other side.

Youthfulness blurs the line between foolishness and fearlessness. And while believing it was the latter (when later I'd realize it was the former), I reenacted an event that had happened to me countless times in the past. (Although I'd always been the one in her position.) I propped the sewing chair underneath the door knob, making it impossible to open, and trapped her inside.

What was she going to do? Scream for Zach's parents? Yell to let her out so that she could go sleep with their son?

Yeah. I didn't think so.

I felt a twinge of guilt as I let myself out of the basement, glancing back but still hearing nothing. *Maybe she'd fallen asleep.*

Sorry, Alexa.

Zach Parker is the other part of my soul. Find your own god.

My feet flew over the familiar terrain, the chill of the spring night air not even touching me as I slowed when I reached the thick of trees. Branches cracked underneath my bare feet and I bit my lip to keep from whimpering.

"Alexa?" I heard Zach's hoarse whisper from above.

There was a bright light and I quickly darted right underneath the treehouse, my back pressed against one of the support trees, as a flashlight flickered out of the window.

"Yes," I whispered steadily even though my chest was heaving – and it had nothing to do with the sprint over here.

The light instantly shut off. He knew the trees weren't dense enough to hide any light out here from either house, which meant that maneuvering in utter darkness was a complete necessity unless he wanted to risk being caught.

"Come up," he whispered back roughly. Something changed in his voice. Maybe he'd hidden some alcohol up there.

Steady, Blake.

I took a deep, slow breath, oxygenating my anxiety. *This was it.*

Turning to look up the ladder, I stubbed my toe on the side of it, tears balling in my eyes as I bit down on my fist to stop my cry. It was cloudy so there was no moon (or moonlight) out tonight which meant I was lucky to be able to see my hand in front of my face. Honestly, it would have been a miracle if Alexa had made it out here without hurting herself; *she* hadn't made this trek, oh, only a thousand times before.

At the bottom of the ladder, I pulled my hoodie and track shorts off. I wasn't taking any chances. I'd tried everything in the book so the only thing left to do was throw the stupid thing at him. And that meant removing as many obstacles beforehand as possible.

Alexa. Clothing.

I held back a pathetic curse as my sleeve got caught on my

charm bracelet that I'd forgotten to remove. It only had one charm: a guitar with my initials on the back. Ash had given it to me for my birthday last year. I unclasped the hook and hung it, along with my clothes, on one of the rungs before climbing up to the side entry in only my bra and boyshort underwear. They were plain cotton – nothing sexy like I'd wanted, but when you can't drive, options are limited. The bra was too big because I'd bought it at first hoping my boobs would grow into it and then settling for the fact that at least my boobs *looked* bigger wearing it. Now, it rubbed uncomfortably against my tight nipples.

The ladder led up to a small latch door in the side of the treehouse. I was shaking so badly by the time I reached the top, I'm surprised that I didn't slip and fall right back down. Through the opening, I could see that the window was propped open, the dimmest light from night just filtering through. Zach was standing, facing out the window with his hands on the wooden sill. His silhouette darkened even more with the outlines of his muscles, tensing as he stood. I allowed myself just a second to look – to look and not be afraid that he would notice, to look and not worry who was around or could show up at any second… to look at him like he'd turn and look at me with the exact same burning inside that never went away.

Swinging my legs over the edge, I stepped into the treehouse; I stepped into the ring, my body prepared for anything at this moment.

Slowly, he turned towards me and my heart stopped, waiting patiently to see if he would notice my ruse as I stood completely encased in the shadows along the back wall. His eyes felt like spotlights along the length of my body and I thought I heard a growl - *or was it the wind through the trees?*

"Cold?" he asked.

I bit my lip, afraid to even whisper. *Did this mean he didn't realize it was me?*

31

He stalked carelessly over the makeshift bed that was on the floor; he was coming for me. *Finally.*

And he didn't stop until he was practically on top of me, breathing down on me like a lion about to devour his prey. I'd been close to him before but never like this. I could taste the anger and desire that flickered over his shadowed face. I should have known then and there that the game was up — that there was no rational way he didn't know who I was. I had no excuse for why I thought this would actually work.

I was crazy.

Love made me crazy.

Our breaths turned into steam in the cold night air. I expected the curtain to fall and my charade to crash and burn. Instead, his face drifted closer, like the sea coming for the shore. I licked my lips, my need to kiss him stronger than anything I'd ever felt before.

Was it always like this?

Was this even right?

Maybe something was wrong with me to want him so much.

"*Fuck.*"

His lips crushed over mine. He was burning and sweet - like the brandy that he and Ash and I had snuck a taste of a few Thanksgivings ago, *only better.* I'd never kissed a boy - *really* kissed, that is. His tongue traced along the seam of my lips unlocking them and sinking inside. With each lick against my tongue and stroke of exploration, he wiped away pieces of my innocence - pieces that I was only too happy to give.

Licking… Sucking… I had no idea what I was doing, but whatever it was, I threw everything I had into it. My tongue met his. I traced along the inside of his teeth; I always wanted to taste the smile that made my knees weak and the difference between seeing it and tasting it was the difference between a glass of wine and a bottle of Jack.

He stepped further into me just as I began to sag against

him, my body in overdrive with sensations it couldn't process. I shivered as the damp wood hit my back and his hot hardness hit my front. The hard ridge of his erection jammed against my stomach and triumph exploded inside me.

I'd won. He wanted me.

But why wasn't he touching me? I wanted him to touch me. My hips rocked forward, wanting to feel more of everything that he had to give and searching for *something* that I wasn't quite sure about.

"What are you doing here?" he hissed. His fingers gripped my chin as the words cut right through the haze of desire.

His kiss had erased all thoughts... all fears... that he was going to send me away. Heck, his kiss erased all of me except what was made to respond to him.

"W-what do you mean?" I whispered huskily. In truth, I barely recognized my own voice at the moment; there was no way he could, *right?*

Wrong.

Crazy and wrong.

"You think I don't know it's you, Baby Blake?" I choked on air.

My heart rocketed out of my chest and then dropped into my stomach.

Oh God. He knew. He knew it was me. What was he going to do? Was he going to send me away? Was he going to tell Ash?

Why was he still pressed against me?

I swallowed painfully and he repeated, "What are you doing here?"

"T-trying to seduce you." At this point, even lies wouldn't be able to help me.

The warm breath blowing over my skin from his harsh laugh felt like acid eating away at my exposed heart.

"I told you, I'm not a fucking cradle robber," he sneered.

"I'm not a child!" I insisted - *like a petulant child.*

"No?" His thigh shot up higher between my legs, my core

33

pressing uncontrollably against it to relieve the now-burning ache. "Because you have no tits," he began. And then I felt my left nipple being pinched between his fingers. *How did he manage to make pain feel good?* "And you sure as shit don't know what the hell you're begging for."

I winced with how much it hurt. But my hips also rocked against his leg because it also made something inside of me feel really, *really* good.

"Do you even know what you're doing? Riding my leg like that?" he growled. "Do you even know what you're searching for?"

Tears began to leak down my face. I hoped that he at least wouldn't see those.

"N-no," I answered honestly. "I want you to show me."

"Jesus Christ," he swore and I felt him pulling back.

"Please, Zach," I begged as my hand rose up to the corner of his shoulder and his neck. "*Please*, I need you—"

"*Fuck,*" was the word that cut me off and crushed his mouth back onto mine.

His hands found my wrists and pinned them to either side of me. This kiss was deeper. It was anger and resignation all rolled into one. It took. *It stole.* Too bad everything I had already belonged to him.

A burn that I'd never felt before seared through my body, centering, coiling in that most sensitive part of me that began to move against his leg in a rhythm that I didn't learn, but I still *knew*.

"Is this what you want?" he growled into my mouth.

At first, I thought I was easing the pressure, but that was wrong. Like any other drug, it only seemed to make things better until you realized that you were addicted to something - searching for something so much more.

I whimpered like the little girl he thought that I was. There was a knot that was twisting and tightening over and over again and only pressing myself against him promised to release it.

"Is this what you came here for? To fuck my leg, Baby Blake?" he said angrily against my lips, shoving his leg harder between my thighs. "Well, take it. Take whatever it is you want from me."

I sucked in hard little breaths that never exhaled as the knot tightened stiffer and stiffer.

"*Fucking come, Blake,*" he demanded of me.

Me.

Not Baby Blake.

Me.

My strangled cry echoed out into the wind that shivered through the trees. I couldn't breathe as indescribable pleasure washed over me, engulfing everything in its path. I had no words, no thoughts, maybe even no body left – but I was too paralyzed to confirm that; all I knew that it was both too much and not enough all rolled into one.

My very first orgasm consumed me just like every other thing about Zach had - from my bones right down to my soul.

The gentle tapping of raindrops on the tin roof was the first thing that registered – like little knocks of reality on the door of my mind. Then I felt Zach, still pressed up against me, breathing just as raggedly as I was.

"Zach…" I whispered. *What did I say now? I had no plan for this.*

"You got want you wanted," he said with a voice that chilled me quicker than the breeze blowing through the window, "now get the fuck out."

He stepped back what seemed like three feet with just one movement. My legs gave slightly with my full weight unceremoniously dumped back onto them. I reached behind me for the wall before I fell (literally) for him.

"Zach," my voice broke on his name, just like my heart broke from his tone.

"You have five seconds to get the fuck out before I call your brother," he warned. "Don't *ever* pull this shit again."

My heart was being ripped apart. I could feel it – the tearing into pieces.

I bit into the soft flesh of my fist to stop myself from sobbing. Grabbing my bra from the floor I quickly snapped it on, the underwire cutting into my boob because it wasn't seated even remotely right.

I climbed down the ladder, not even registering the rain. Picking up my clothes, I ran back home like I could outrun the pain that I knew was licking at my heels. The spring shower soaked through me and camouflaged my tears. Rapidly wiping my face, I realized that in my fairytale-ending flee, I'd left my charm bracelet in the woods – one more thing I'd mark as 'lost' that night. Finding my bed in a blurry mess of agonizing rejection, I climbed under the covers.

Fact: The rainstorm breaking through the sky was no match for the heartache breaking through my heart.

***

2 Weeks Later - Zach's Graduation Party

TIME PASSES QUICKLY when your heart isn't beating.

The past two weeks had flown since the night in the treehouse. My one attempt to corner and talk to him about it had gone about as well as a red cape in front of a raging bull. I was still reeling.

Even now, approaching the giant white tent that the Parker's had set up in their yard for the graduation party, I knew I was only invited because my whole family was; Zach would be as excited to see me as you would about waking up to see poison ivy on your arm.

I toyed with the idea of sulking at home, but anger, sadness, and complete and utter desperation collected into one final Hail Mary idea that had me grabbing my guitar, throwing on some ripped jeans and worn out Dave Matthew's tee, and stalking towards the party.

There were all sorts of activities and things set up to do – one of those things was a small stage set up where Ash and Zach's band could play later tonight.

I'd walked around numbly for a while until Taylor showed up, perfectly dressed in cute summer shorts and gingham shirt. I looked down at my own haphazard attire and wondered if I should have tried to look at least a little more put-together. I listened to her blabber on about all the seniors who were going to colleges that she wanted to go to. *We weren't even juniors yet.* I didn't know what the summer was going to hold, let alone college that was two years away.

She rambled because she knew my thoughts were taking me to a place that I would probably regret later on; I loved her for the attempt, but I was already there.

"I'm singing for him, Tay," I interrupted bluntly right after she finished with the pros and cons of going to Vanderbilt.

"I was afraid you were going to say that." She looked at me worriedly.

"I have to. You can't stop me."

"I figured from the look on your face – the one that says even a natural disaster can't stop you from going up on that stage," she said wryly. "You know how much I love your honest-vomit." That was the word she designated to refer to my compulsive need to spew out my feelings regardless of the consequences. My brother was loyal to a fault whereas I was honest to the point of self-destruction; if I felt something for someone, I had to tell them. And no matter how many times the habit had come back to bite me, this was the one part of me that never seemed to adapt. "But I don't think it's going to change anything."

"I have to try." My fist tightened against the neck of my guitar.

She pulled me into a tight hug. "Do what you gotta do, B. I'll be right here…"

Breathe, Blay.

I caught a few stares as I maneuvered my way through the crowd, basically ignoring anyone who tried to talk to me. If I stopped, I wasn't sure my nerves would let me start again.

Walking right up to the mic, I bent down and plugged in my acoustic electric guitar into Zach's amp. I plucked a few strings to make sure it was in tune - even though I'd checked it too many times this morning.

Flicking on the mic, I finally looked out into the crowd. Like lights turning on as the sun begins to set, more and more eyes turned in my direction and nausea rolled through me like a wave. I'd never played any of my songs for anyone before - aside from my teacher and Tay. *Never.* Why would I? They'd all been written for him.

Clearing my throat, I spoke because it was preferable to vomiting, "H-hello, everyone." I forced a weak smile as now it seemed like *every* eye in the acre radius was on me. *Including his.*

I had yet to find him, but I'd know the feeling of his gaze anywhere – like sunburn on my skin, scorching me, making me itch and ache, and damaging me one cell at a time.

"If you don't know me, I'm Blake Tyler. Ash's… sister." *I refused to say 'little.'* "I wrote a song," I continued, my eyes scanning every head. And then I found him. Mahogany hair and honey eyes that looked anything but sweet when they fell on me. "And I'd like to play it for you."

Even though it was all and only for him.

Glancing at the frets, I tried to ignore my own as my fingers clumsily found the chords and began a song that would make me infamous.

"In your eyes, I am the sunrise.
Always there and taken for granted."

My voice wasn't strong or confident as it tripped over each word. Yet, somehow, it still sounded right. Somehow, I still hit every note, pulled along by the thread of truth.

"In your eyes, I am the sunrise.
Easily ignored, too familiar to be enchanting."

I couldn't look away from him even though his stare threatened to rip my vocal chords if I didn't stop.

"Here I am, day after day.
My heart, it rises for you.
So, don't walk away,
My heart, it rises for you.
Don't turn me away."

It was plea set to melody. I'd never wanted anything so badly – for him to see me and want me. It was all I thought about when I'd first written the words, and singing them now, for him, was like tearing them from the beats of my heart all over again.

"Don't turn me into a sad little story
And leave the mess of my heart
That had the nerve to adore you."

All those bad things that you think can happen when you sing your heart out on stage? Yeah, they all happened. The silence. The stares. The snickers. The cameras coming out to capture my humiliation. The mocking pity in Alexa's eyes as she looked at me with a sneer. And the angry confusion and embarrassment in my brother's hard gaze.

Yeah, it all sucked.

But the look on Zach's face killed me. The blank stare of anger morphed into indifference with a dash of disbelief.

'*Pathetic*' was written in the tight line of his mouth. He chugged the rest of what I assumed was beer in his cup and shoved it into my brother's chest before stalking off towards the house. Not before he put his arm around Alexa's smug shoulders and took her with him.

I stared a hole through the back of his head, willing him to turn and come back to me.

Spoiler alert: he didn't.

He left a few days later.

And I knew my heart would never be the same.

CHAPTER THREE

BLAKE

Track 03: Kansas City Shuffle

"All the world wants is drama. They've pulled out all their tricks. No choice left but bait-and-switch. This is the only fix."

PRESENT

BEING famous meant that eyes were always on you. Being famous meant that your every move was watched, everything you said was documented and written in stone, and that you had zero time for yourself. Being famous meant that your life was constantly *for* someone... everyone... else. There was an unimaginable love and an unfaltering obligation. But there was also a seed of regret – wishing it could bloom into a solitary life where actions and choices were all your own.

Being famous was like being a parent... to six billion children.

All kicking, screaming, and desperate to follow you into the bathroom and publicize every last shred of your privacy... and your sanity.

No matter what I looked like - sloppy clothes, fancy

clothes, makeup, gas mask… they could still pick me out. *My fans. Blake's Babes.* Not only could they pick me out, but I could pull a full-blown Britney Spears and shave my head and half the world would follow suit. I could see the hashtags now… #yolo #blakedown

Unfaltering obligation to stay sane.

Even people who weren't my fans looked at me as they walked down the aisle of the plane searching for their seats, whispering to their travel partner or immediately reaching for their phone to text their friends.

And yes, it was obvious when they were not really calling someone, instead faking it in an attempt to secretly take a picture of me. Yes, it was obvious when they pretended to hold their phone nonchalantly down by their leg even though it's angled up and their finger is pressing furiously on the side button to snap a pic.

I didn't mind photos. I enjoyed the photos. I enjoyed talking to my fans. I enjoyed being a person and not some untouchable creature that only deserved to be admired from afar. They could have just asked.

"We already have our tickets to see you in Nashville at the end of your tour!" A frazzled mom gushed as I signed two United napkins for her to give to her daughters.

"Oh, I'm so excited!" I said with a smile even though my mind was around a thousand miles up in the air thinking about what said tour was turning into.

"Thank you so much!" she said, clutching the napkins to her chest as the line began moving again, taking her back down the aisle to her seat.

They always booked Tay and I in first class even though I told them I was fine to ride in coach. *Maybe in coach, no one would be looking for me.* Bruce insisted that - *again* - it was all part of my image. Plus, 'did I really want my entire flight to be disrupted with requests for photos and autographs?' I laughed to myself. The sad excuse for a barrier between first class and coach was *zero* deterrent to stop Blake Tyler's Babe Squad; the *Babes* were relentless.

I plastered a small smile on my face, patiently waiting for Tay to finish unpacking all of her in-flight essentials (Kindle, blanket, neck pillow, and tiny Moscow Mule cocktail kit) so that I could talk to her; needing time to process, I hadn't said much on the ride to the airport.

What I did mind, I thought as I listened to the muted conversations around us, was when people thought I lived in my own little celebrity bubble where their words, when said just a few feet from me, couldn't get to me - *couldn't hurt me.*

"Did you see the hot flight attendant back there?" I heard two teen girls gossiping in a half-whisper.

"Wait until the end of the flight, Elle. Blake Tyler's sitting right over there which means she'll probably date him and dump him before the plane lands. Then you'll be able to swoop in and pick up the pieces."

"Shh, Andrea! I think she heard you! God, you're such a bitch." They both broke into muffled laughter.

Heat rushed to my face and I turned away from the aisle, trying not to let them see how their words stung or the way I had to swallow down the sudden urge to cry.

At the end of the day – and written on my grave – was that I cared too much. I didn't want to admit what another break-up cost me. I was the superstar. The celebrity. The sweetheart of the nation who hadn't let fame go to her head. I was *the* It-Girl.

And the headlines lately were a giant slap in the face. *'Too many boyfriends.' 'Too many dates.'* And how I *'can't make them stay.'*

Slap.

Slap.

Slap.

I was tired of reading what people say. Yes, I dated them all. *Guilty as charged.* But I wasn't trying to play with their hearts.

Maybe Bruce and Tay were right… Maybe this was a lot worse than

I thought. I was the Princess of Pop whose castle had crumbled overnight.

"Ok," Tay said with a huff, finally relaxing back in the seat. "I think I'm good."

"You'd think after all the flights we've taken that you would have this down to a much finer science," I grumbled, reaching in my purse for a piece of Trident, pulling out all four boxes of gum that I had stashed in there. A sad testimony to my nervous habit.

"I do have it down to a science; it just takes time," she said with a sweet smile, getting her cocktail kit ready as the other *female* first-class attendant came over and asked if we wanted anything to drink.

"I can't believe you're on board with this," I began softly.

She reached over and squeezed my hand. "You know I wouldn't be if I thought there was any other way."

"Yeah, well, for the record, if the Titanic is sinking, then you're Rose for relegating me to the frigid ocean when there was *definitely* room for two on that board," I said with a strangled laugh.

"Seriously. How am I going to do this?" I popped another bubble.

How was I going to survive this?

"Well, asking him would be a good start," she said flipping open the cover on her Kindle.

"Nope." I reached over and grabbed the thing from her hand. "Don't even think of disappearing on me right now. What do you mean, 'ask him?' Like 'Oh hey, Zach. Remember me? The girl who dry humped you in the treehouse and then sang a lame-ass song about you at your own graduation party?' I swear, Franklin is the only town in the whole US where I'm not famous - *I'm infamous.*"

She rolled her eyes. "Well, I wouldn't say *that.*" Tay took her drink from the attendant, continuing as she added in her fixings, "Look, that was like... ten... nine years ago; that's a long time. Now, you are world famous. People would literally do anything to meet you - let alone go on tour with you - and I think that's what you need to focus on: that you aren't the only one benefitting here. Opening for you for *Every. Single. Show.* in the States is huge. Like career-making huge."

I took a deep breath, sighing back into my seat as the plane began to lift off the ground.

"Yeah," I agreed, "but he still has to pretend to fall in love with me. God, he couldn't even pretend to like me when we were younger. And now, I haven't seen him in so long - at least two years. Was this *really* the best plan you could come up with?" I groaned.

"B, trust me, I wouldn't have dared to mention the Z-word if it wasn't," she paused as the captain announced, *'Our flight time is two hours and forty minutes to touchdown in Nashville where it's a brisk ten degrees outside.'*

"But we are in damage control here," she continued with a sigh, "and he's the only person with the background and situation who is most likely able to pull this off. So, take off your rear-views, put on your big girl panties, and remember that you are offering him not only the opportunity of a lifetime, but also a chance to let the world think he's hooked up with the hottest pop-star on the planet."

"Oh, God," I moaned, burying my face in my hands. *This was such a bad idea.*

"It's simple. You ask Zach. Even if he says no, once you tell your brother, he won't let Zach pass up the opportunity; it's the break that will get ZPP launched and Ash will be *all* over that," she said with such dramatic emphasis that I almost wanted to ask what she meant. "I hate to say it, but you're really not giving him an option. So, just make it as business-like as possible and it won't be that awkward."

Tay didn't know - she didn't know what Zach did to me. Talking to him had always been a perpetual tongue-twister that I could never get right no matter how she coached me.

45

No, I could do this, I pep-talked myself, closing my eyes as Taylor went back to the latest Fifty Shades book on her Kindle.

It had been exactly two years since I'd seen him; I didn't want Tay to know how *exactly* I remembered these things. My brother and Zach had come home for the holiday. They'd moved back after graduation - not back to Franklin, but into downtown Nashville. My brother, using his business degree, had been dabbling in several start-ups in the city as well as being the quasi-manager for Zach's band, the Zach Parker Project. And Zach, well, he'd left football when he'd left Alabama and immersed himself in the music scene.

Two years ago, my mom called me after one of my recording sessions and told me that Ash was bringing Zach to the house for Christmas Eve dinner. After blaming my momentary shock on a poor cell connection, I brushed it off like it was going to be no big deal. It had been a long time. *I should have known better.*

I walked into my parents dining room for Christmas Eve dinner with the confidence of being famous and currently dating one of the stars of the TV show, *Vampire Journals.* (It also helped that I'd crimped my long blonde hair, done my makeup, and wore a tight, fancy number that had been a Grammy-option reject.) It was a confidence that faltered when I saw Zach for the first time since their college graduation. *He was still as devastatingly gorgeous as the day he devastated me.* Fueled by the need to rub my current fairytale in his face, I sat at the table and went on and on (*and on*) about Jake, only to have Ash snicker at me and ask why, if the guy was so great, hadn't I written a song about him yet?

I was dumbstruck. He'd meant it lightly (because I did *sometimes* write songs about my boyfriends), but only after the words came out did he realize it sounded like he was bringing up their high school party - *and my song to Zach* - again. My face burned as my mouth opened and shut like I was a goldfish waiting to be fed something that would make the moment less humiliating.

After the long moment of silence to mourn the last shreds of my self-confidence, Ash mumbled an apology and started a conversation about how ZPP was really picking up popularity with a lot of larger venues in Nashville – and Zach jumped right in, just as eager to forget that moment. I barely spoke the rest of the meal, once again, humiliated about my feelings for Zach right in front of him.

That was my fear. That this request was going to be one more humiliation.

Closing my eyes, I immediately returned to the ending of that memory.

"Seriously, Ash? What the fuck man?" Zach's tight and irritated voice rasped.

I'd walked back into the dining room to grab the rest of the plates and overheard Zach and my brother talking in the living room next door.

"Chill, bro. It was just a slip. It's fine," my brother said with a laugh.

"Yeah, well, when your little sister writes a goddamn love song about me, it's not just a slip."

"Christ, I would hope she's fucking over that by now," Ash grumbled, *"the way she's going on about what's-his-name."*

"Another reason why we should go," Zach said tightly.

"It's all over the news. There's no way she made up the damn boyfriend just to get your attention even though that's sure as shit what it sounded like."

I wanted to punch my brother – partially for throwing me under the bus but mostly because he was one-hundred-percent right. Not that I made Jake up. But that I brought him up for Zach's attention.

"Let's go," Zach replied. *"I can't be around her anymore."*

I jerked back, the plates in my hands clattering against one another just as sure as if he'd struck me. My stomach rolled with the need to vomit and I just prayed I didn't drop the plates as I ran back into the kitchen with black spots still clouding my vision.

That night, I jotted down the names of every song that ended up on the Lovestruck album, bits and pieces of verses and refrains flashing in front of my eyes.

He was the reason for them all. And he was the reason for the teardrops on my guitar.

I jerked my eyes to the window, hating how I went back to that December all the time...

Well, not all the time, but more than I should.

A small patch of turbulence shook me back to the present and I chewed nervously on the now flavorless piece of gum.

Remember, Blake, you have two more Grammys under your belt since then. Another platinum album. A star on the Boulevard. You are better than this stupid crush. Stop letting it cripple you.

Grabbing my iPad from my bag, I pulled my hair back into a ponytail and out of my face. Out of the corner of my eye, I saw that Tay was already napping. Popping in my earbuds, I threw on some classical music to focus my thoughts on what exactly I was going to say. There was no winging this one; there was no way he could say no.

'Hey, Zach. Here's the deal... I'll make you famous if you save my reputation.'

Or maybe: *'Hey, Zach. So, I was wondering if you would consider being my fake boyfriend while I'm on tour? In exchange, I'll let your band open every show. By the way, you know how I wrote that song for you one time? Yeah, well, this whole album may or may not be about you...'*

'Hey, Zach. If I bribe you with everything that you've ever wanted, do you think you could love me then?'

I was pathetic.

***

"WE'RE ALL SO excited that you're ending your tour in Nashville," my mom, Alison Tyler, gushed as we checked on the lasagna that was heating up in the oven. I'd confined myself and my anxiety to the kitchen leaving Taylor to set the table while we waited for my brother and Zach to get here.

"Yeah, it was originally shoved in the middle of the schedule, but then we bumped it to the end," I replied, grating some parmesan cheese into a bowl and sneaking a few bites for myself. Cheese and Christmas cookies were my weaknesses.

"And everything's been going ok?" she asked, concern seeping into her warm, caring voice, and I immediately knew where this was going - as if I needed one more reminder about my failing love life.

I loved my parents - and my brother - more than anything. I'd never played up the 'small-town girl' or 'all-American family' catch-phrases; they were just the truth.

My mom always called me before every performance (no matter what time it meant she had to wake up) and my dad always made sure that I took time off between touring and recording to come home, regroup, and eat a whole pot of his famous chili. This place was my rock, my safe space, no matter where in the world I was or what I was doing. They brought me back from the lights and the fame and the all-too-real and all-too-fake dichotomy of the entertainment scene.

"I know better than to believe the tabloids, but I thought you really liked that DJ," she said quietly. I'd called her from Europe to tell her about the breakup but I hadn't really told her why, too frustrated with myself - yet again - for picking another dud.

"He was a jerk," I mumbled, softly, setting the grater in the sink before I couldn't help but add, "They all are."

"I'm sorry, honey," she empathized, putting an arm around my shoulder. "You'll find somebody. I know you will." *Yeah, ok.* "Maybe finding him on tour isn't the best thing. I know how much you love tours and performances and meeting all your fans, but I also know how much it takes out of you and sometimes I think you forget that you are only twenty-five. And human. You don't have to always be what they want; it's ok to just be you."

I bit back a groan as she pulled me close. *If only she knew what I had to do tonight.* And no, I hadn't forgotten that I was only human - it was the world who apparently did - who thought I'd become this heartless black widow, eating up boyfriends like they were Grammys.

My head jerked with a nod as I picked up the bowl of cheese and headed for the dining room, needing Tay and a change of topic.

Instead, I walked through the swinging door to find myself face-to-face with that god who'd created a fire inside of my soul and burned my heart to the ground.

I'd stood on stage in front of tens of thousands of people. I'd walked up and accepted Grammys after being told that I was too young to deserve them. I sang my heart out for millions of people all over the world and yet, I'd never felt nervousness like this moment. I was standing there naked about to sing the sappiest love song in the entire world to the one boy who never wanted me - *at least that's what it felt like.*

Where the hell did Taylor go? She was supposed to warn me.

Max and Muffin, my parents two cocker spaniels, came tearing into the room yapping and jumping up on Zach's legs and mine. I heard his chuckle just before he saw me. After all this time, he had become a stranger whose laugh I could recognize anytime, anywhere.

"Zach... hey," I greeted him a little too breathlessly. But I was a little too surprised - and he was a little too gorgeous.

Ripped jeans and a shirt that clung to him like it was painted on brought back memories of summertime when even Mother Nature herself got all hot and bothered admiring a topless Zach Parker. He hadn't lost the solid build from his football days. If anything, his frame matured into smoother, wider expanses of male that I wanted to lick like he was ice cream about to melt away.

His whole body tensed at my greeting. Lean, sculpted muscles outlined by the washed denim and a plaid button-up made him look like Hercules masquerading as a farmer.

Eyes that were still the color of honey and molasses stuck to me, leaving a sticky sweet trail of goosebumps over everything that they touched. I hadn't gone all-out when getting dressed after showering the plane off of me because I knew that would have been taken the wrong way. Instead, I settled for a comfortable, stretchy pair of jeans and a bulky, dark red sweater that laced up the back.

Perfect for keeping in all the heat he'd just ignited in me. *With a frustrated and shadowed stare, no less.*

It was probably a good thing for my ovaries that he didn't want me; they might explode if he looked at me like he actually did.

"Blake," he said with a low, gruff voice. The edge in his tone was almost as chiseled as his jawline. *Greek god. Definitely.* I hoped that my sweater could hide my shiver.

"How are you?" I asked with a nervous smile. "How's your family?"

His hands shoved into his pockets as he replied, "Fine," glancing around as though he were waiting for back-up.

Ass.

"Blake!" Taylor's sing-song voice preceded her around the corner. "Your brother is—" she broke off as she walked into the room and saw Zach and I locked in awkward silence. "Oh, you already know," she continued with a sheepish grin. "Hey, Zach."

I glared at her for not being here to do the *one* thing I asked her to do - the one thing that was her job. *Prepare me.*

CHAPTER FOUR

BLAKE

Track 04: Stand Still, Look Pretty

"First it was the boys who played me like a toy.
Now my heart is on a string, your puppet it's forced to be.
Not that I have a choice, but I don't wanna just stand still, look pretty."

THANKFULLY, DINNER THIS YEAR WENT WITHOUT INCIDENT —
no talk about my (ex) boyfriends and no mention of any songs
written for anyone in particular. Ash carried most of the
conversation, updating my parents and me on ZPP who'd just
finished recording their first full-length album. Ash was neck-
deep working to get their name out there and gain more
exposure for it.

I tried to politely participate in the conversation but it
didn't help that Tay kept looking from me to Zach like she was
expecting me to get down on one knee and propose to the guy
or something.

"Don't tell," I whispered to Max as I gave him a bite of
leftovers from the plate I was about to wash and put in the
dishwasher. He greedily ate them before running off through

the dog-door to go outside, apparently unable to decide what he was more excited about - human food or being outdoors.

"Let's go, lady." Taylor nudged me in the back. "We don't have all night."

Biting back a groan, I let her lead me outside towards Ash and my soul-lighter, the screen door slamming behind us. The boys were enjoying a beer out by the fire pit – a poor source of heat in the frozen night, in my opinion.

The screen door slammed closed behind us. It was an incredibly clear night out - Orion's belt perfectly visible in the black sky. *That was me. Always shining. Always seen. When the truth was that I was burning up inside.*

"Ash," Tay called as we approached them, "your mom wants your help inside for a sec."

My brother turned and mumbled something, but Zach stayed facing the flames. I felt Ash brush by me and when I turned, Taylor was gone, too. It was just Zach and me. Alone.

"Zach," I said, clearing the lump out of my throat, "can I talk to you for a minute?"

I saw him flinch slightly, not realizing that I'd come out with Tay. He let out an audible sigh that would have translated into a 'no' given the chance. But, while he felt uncomfortable around me, he was too respectful to flat out refuse my request. At least at this point. If I started singing, he might change his tune.

His hands came up to pull off his old Alabama hat, running one through the waves underneath, before replacing it. My stomach clenched watching the subtle show of frustration and the way his shirt tightened over his body. *God... Bama and time had done a number on Zach.* Bigger. Harder. Leaner. *Larger.* That was the word. I may have become the biggest popstar in the world, but Zach, well, he had become larger than life.

I licked my lips, taking in the subtle details that I'd been too nervous to notice earlier. His hair was a little longer, the rich brown locks curling out from underneath his hat. His shirt really seemed like it should have been purchased a size bigger, the way his biceps were outlined.

The flash of his movie-star-perfect smile appeared for a split second as he let out a harsh laugh.

"You going to stand there ogling me all night or was there something you wanted to say, *Baby Blake?*"

I winced. He was only half-turned to look at me, the fire melting the honey of his eyes to gold; it wasn't warm enough though to melt the scorn from his voice.

My stomach rolled at the derisive nickname. I could practically hear the unspoken words *'Please don't sing another fucking song to me again,'* on the night breeze.

I closed my eyes and the flashbacks started – me, standing there, on that makeshift stage in the humid, summer air...

Crossing my arms over me (even though I wasn't cold *at all)* I replied, "I-I have something that I want to offer you." His eyebrows raised warily. "I mean, to the band."

He turned to face me. Now, I had his attention. Of course.

"I was wondering if you would be interested," I paused to clear my throat. *There was no going back from here,* "in having ZPP open for the rest of my US tour?"

His eyes widened and now it was his turn to stare. Shaking his head, he laughed again. "Is this a joke?"

Oh, how I wished it was.

I took a step back, offended, crossing my arms even tight over my chest. "What do you mean? N-no. This isn't a joke."

His broad shoulders shrugged; he thought I was taunting him with this to get back at him for all of the humiliation I suffered because of him.

I wished. But no.

"I mean—Shit." He wiped his hand over his mouth, forcing my tongue over my lips again because it wanted to taste him. Did he still taste like honey? "Seriously?" he asked again.

I nodded, adding, "I'm very serious right now."

And that's when his eyes narrowed on me, reading my mind just as expertly as ever. "What's the catch?"

My gaze dropped to the ground, attempting to kick around dirt that was too frozen to move.

"*Blake…*"

My eyes jerked back to his. "I need you to do something for me."

"What?"

"I need you to pretend to be my boyfriend." The words rushed from my mouth as I prepared for impact.

"Are you fucking— Is this for real?" His laugh sliced deeper than the question. "What's your plan here, Baby Blake? You think *pretending* to be your boyfriend is going to make it really happen?" he swore, spinning towards the fire and then back to me again, his body wound so tight I thought he might explode. "*Christ.* Has fame gotten into that pretty little head of yours and made you forget the last time I told you this was *never* happening?"

"Wait, Zach. Just let me explain. It's not what you think," I said, holding my hands up to try and stay the storm. "My manager… says I need a boyfriend."

"Why? You don't seem to have a problem finding those," he bit out, his jaw muscle tensing. "Why does he care? And, more importantly, why would I care?"

A harsh exhale rushed from my lips. "You're right. Why would you when you never did give a damn thing, Zach." *Especially not about how I cried for you.*

I met his hard, glinting stare and forced myself to bite my tongue. Acerbic retorts weren't going to get me what I needed. And I needed this more than I wanted him. *I swear I did.*

One breath.

In for two seconds – *Rep-u* – out for two seconds – *ta-tion.*

"I need you to pretend to be my boyfriend because my reputation is going to shit and my manager thinks that if I go

55

on tour with you and *pretend* to fall for you, it will save my image."

Silence.

So much silence that I began to wonder if I'd said the words or only replayed them in my head.

He let out a tortured laugh, his hands coming up to grip the lip of his hat and bend it in front of his face. Goosebumps erupted over my skin. I knew that laugh. It was the laugh of cruel disbelief when life gives you what you want most, but with a cost that you'll hate yourself for paying later.

I knew because it's what came out of me every time I thought about that night in the treehouse.

"It's just for the next four months until the tour ends," I continued quietly, unable to stand the tense silence any longer. "They just need to see that I am actually capable of being in a normal relationship, that I'm not just dating and dumping guys because I have no heart or whatever it is that they think." *Quit the honest-vomit, Blake.*

Again, I watched my boots move the tiny rocks underneath my feet as the shadows from the fire flickered over them. *Until they didn't.*

Large, hard male. Right in front of me.

Air. Where was the air?

"Why me?" he growled.

All I could see was his eyes and I was afraid that all he could see was my desire.

Because I want you. Because I've always wanted you.

I swallowed, licking my lips once again. "Because it's the only believable option on such short notice," I answered with instead. "You've been Ash's best friend forever so it's plausible I would add your band as my opening act. B-Bruce says that I need to give the public what they want – and what they want is to see me fall in love; he says they won't believe it if it happens with a stranger so quickly." Sucking in air, I realized that I rambled without stopping to breathe. "You can ask Tay - she'll tell you how bad it is."

My eyes fell to the barely visible plaid that covered his chest. I wished I knew what it felt like. I imagined it was as hot and hard as his thigh was that night - *and as hot and hard as his heart.*

"So, you're fucking bribing me with my ticket to fame – to my dream? And the price is that I have to pretend to be your boyfriend?" he ground out.

I nodded, still unable to meet his eyes until unyielding fingers gripped my chin and forced my gaze to his. I swore he looked right into my soul that was engraved with *'Property of Zach Parker.'*

And then my heart stopped when his thumb began to brush over my lower lip. *What was he doing? Why?* Every rub sent sparks right down to my core, like he was rubbing me right between my thighs. The worst part was that he knew what he was doing to me and, just like that night, he did it anyway.

"And how do I know that you aren't going to go and *actually* fall in love with me?" he demanded gratingly.

I caught myself before I flinched at the question. *Painful. Rude.* He wanted assurance that the past wasn't going to repeat itself - that I wasn't going to make a fool out of myself for him again, this time on a *very* public stage.

My nerves steeling, I bristled back against his insinuation. Finally, I'd hit the wall - the edge of the embarrassment I was willing to take over this.

"That was a long time ago, Zach. I was a stupid little girl, as you *well* know. I'm over it. I'm over you," I retorted, trying my best to sound as cold and nonchalant as he did. "*This* is my life now. My career, my music… it's everything. I would hope you would understand and appreciate that enough to know that the situation must be *dire* for me to come to you like this, knowing *full-well* what you would think."

I wanted to pull away, but his grip still wouldn't let me. He still held my face close to his, the rim of his hat shielding us from any light that tried to shine between us.

"Are you sure about that?" The hoarseness of his words brushed over my skin like sandpaper as he came closer. No, not sandpaper. Quicksand. And I was sinking right back into my fifteen-year-old self... and right back into him.

His lips were so close to mine. Another inch - or less - and I could see if his kiss was one more thing to add to the list of his parts that got better with age.

"Because you don't seem sure, *Baby Blake*," he accused angrily, watching as my tongue darted out to lick my lips again. "And I need you to be very fucking sure."

My breath caught, causing my chest to brush against his – my nipples hard and hidden underneath my sweater. His body was hot; his words were cold. I couldn't figure out if I should feel burned or frozen.

He's doing this on purpose, the small voice of my teenage broken heart whispered. *Making a fool of you...*

I surprised myself when I jerked my face free and stepped back, stumbling slightly in my eagerness. He pushed me because he thought I would break. All he wanted was one more piece of evidence that Ash Tyler's little sister - *no matter how famous* - was still pining absurdly for him after all of these years.

"Yes. I'm sure," I managed to insist even though my voice wavered at first, growing stronger as I added, "I'm more likely to fall off stage than I am to fall in love with you," and then grumbled, "And it would probably hurt a helluva lot less, too."

He just laughed like he didn't believe me - and then looked up to the sky like it didn't even matter. Tay was right - Zach wanted this.

I swallowed the bitterly ironic pill that, when I was fifteen, I would have given him the world if he'd just given me the chance and now, I was actually offering it to him to *pretend* to look at me, and it still almost wasn't enough.

Focus on the end game, Blake. Focus on your reputation. It doesn't matter if he wants you; he can save you.

"So, you'll do it?" I asked sharply, like I was expecting nothing less than 'yes' for an answer.

He looked me up and down, resenting me for the opportunity – and for something else that I'd probably never figure out. "You know I don't have a choice. Not when it comes to this," he said tightly. "Fine. I'll do it."

And deep down, I did know. I knew because it was his love of music that had inspired my own. Probably why he ended up being woven into so much of it.

Even though I'd backed him into this corner, I still stared dumbly at him. *Fine?* Was that...it? I'd been prepared to go to war.

"But you're telling Ash," he added, jerking me from my trance. "You're making sure this is alright with him. I don't want there to be *any* confusion as to why I'm agreeing to this."

He always had to twist the knife.

"Of course," I replied with defiant forcefulness. Neither of us had to pretend to like it - for right now, at least. *For tonight.*

Tomorrow, the show would begin.

Feeling the whispers of hurt begin to move through my body, I spun to walk back to the house; I needed to tell Ash and my parents. And then I needed to lock myself in my room with Tay and beg her to tell me again how I was going to do this; ten minutes in his presence had my heart pounding, my body feeling fevered, and my soul yearning for the one man who had proven time and again that he wanted nothing to do with me.

Stopping abruptly, I turned to shoot over my shoulder, "You know," I said, unable to stop the sarcasm from seeping into my voice, "Now, I'm the one who's famous and all, so maybe I should be telling *you* to try not to fall in love with *me*."

Take that, Zach Parker.

My chin rose as I smiled, satisfied with my conversation-ending jab. I should have known that would only make it all the easier for him to knock me right back down.

"Don't worry, Baby Blake," he smirked, and the chill that washed over me had nothing to do with the temperature, "it was never a problem before."

I hated him.

I'd forgotten about that part. I remembered the embarrassment, the hurt, the heartbreak. But in that moment, I relived each and every last rip he'd torn through my stupid teenage heart.*And I hated him all over again.*

***

Zach

'FOUR MONTHS.'

'Pretend boyfriend.'

All I heard was my fucking fantasy.

And my fucking downfall.

I looked like I was listening as she sat her parents and brother down and told them what was happening. I looked like I was watching the way Ash's face twitched in anger, his eyes flicking back and forth between Blake and me. The fact that he was petting Muffin's head, who sat expectantly at his feet, was probably the only thing that kept him from lunging across the room and ripping mine off. And I looked like I watching as Scott and Alison Tyler's faces registered with shock as their daughter told them what she thought she needed to do to get the world to fall back in love with her.

I wasn't. *All I saw was her.*

Beautiful blonde hair that looked like Rumpelstiltskin had fucking spun the gold in it himself. Brilliant blue eyes that made the ocean look like a muddy pond and the sky a faded painting. And even though her sweater did an admirable job at hiding mostly everything else, I still knew what was there. *Like the goddamn sun hidden behind the clouds, she was just waiting to fucking blind me if I didn't stop staring.*

"I don't understand," Alison said, looking from Blake to Taylor like there was a better explanation.

"It's just for a few months, mom. It's not a big deal," she brushed her off, glancing at me as she spoke. "I just wanted you all to know."

I stared back hard, trying to ignore the twitch of my dick at the way even just her lips moving was like watching the prelude to the porno that would play in my mind later as I imagined them wrapped around me.

At least she didn't have on that red lipstick. Seeing that shit on her that last Christmas left me hard for days imagining the red ring of death that she'd leave around the base of my cock. Proof that I'd died from the heaven inside her mouth.

That mouth… I wanted to spend hours with her bottom lip; it had always been slightly fuller, giving her that perfect pout. I'd hoped the top lip would grow into it so I wouldn't feel the perpetual need to suck on the enticing pink flesh. But it didn't. It stayed carved with those perfect arches - the ones that tipped up as if to say that there was a cave of wonders hidden inside waiting for my tongue.

She could never know it, but all I saw was the woman that the tall, lanky, too-trusting-for-her-own-good, Baby Blake had become. All I felt was the way her desire for me still vibrated off of her in waves and my own body strained against my clothes, uncontrolled like a goddamn teenager. All I saw was the indignant anger when I reminded her just how in love with me she'd been, and just how successfully I'd made her believe that I hadn't given a shit.

She was too young then. And Ash's sister. And even those two things almost hadn't been enough to stop me from taking what I'd always felt was mine. I wasn't a jerk... I wasn't an ass... except when it came to her. It helped that wanting what I couldn't have made me irritable beyond all words. I didn't know what else to do when she always stood in front of me wearing her heart on her sleeve; I needed her to hate me.

God only knew why... how... I could have wanted her at fifteen. Back then, she'd really been skin and bones. No curves. No concept of flirtation. But all I saw was beautiful. Her sense of adventure. Her shyness. Her honesty. And the way her big sky-blue eyes always stared at me like I hung the goddamn stars. *But I hadn't hung hers.* I hurt her. I knew everything that she did to try to get my attention and I shot her down.

There were a lot of reasons I fought how I felt about her, but the biggest was that I was only eighteen. There was no fucking way I could feel about her the way that I did. I'd only had a few girlfriends; I had college and a whole fucking life ahead of me; I couldn't find the love of my life in the one girl who'd always been in it.

Ash and I left for school and I hoped the years apart would clarify things, not just for me, but for her, too. I told myself that by the time I graduated, she would have found other guys, dated other guys, and realized that I was just a sorry excuse for a girl-crush. And if she didn't? Well, maybe then it would be ok for us to finally see what was between us.

When you're young, you just run, thinking you can just come back to what you need.

But then her never-fading star shot out of my universe. Never in a million years did I think that Baby Blake would become Blake Tyler: pop star, icon, and arguably the most famous celebrity in the world. Baby Blake who was so goddamn pure, so innocent, so open was now the center of a world that was anything but. Whatever I'd thought or hoped would happen when I came back from college, this card hadn't even been in the deck of options.

So, instead, I came back to her ubiquitous presence and unfailing absence. She was everywhere - the internet, TV, magazine, radio. And not just her songs. I hadn't read all of the tabloids that she mentioned, but I always knew when she was dating someone. The world would never let me forget it. At least when I'd gone to college, she hadn't gotten the play-by-play of my life and relationships. This was my punishment, I reminded myself: to watch from afar as the little girl that I refused to admit that I loved, swiftly and easily made the entire world fall in love with her.

How could they not?

The world was smart where I had been an idiot. So now, I kept my distance and my coldness because I didn't want to be reminded of what I'd given up. *And because of Ash,* I had to keep telling myself.

"Mrs. Tyler, we just need to give the press something to focus on until the tour is done, otherwise, they are just going to continue this negative spiral because it's making them money - not because it's true," Taylor finally spoke, backing up her friend and boss's story.

"Who could actually think that of you though, Blake?" she whispered with astonishment.

Her father spoke before she had a chance to answer. "People who don't know her, Alison."

"And you fucking agreed to this?" Ash's cold voice shot at me.

"Ashton!" his mother exclaimed at his unfiltered expletive.

My hands shoved deeper into my pockets as I leaned against the doorway to their living room. He asked like he would have told me to refuse. He wanted to be angry because it was his sister - *his sister who'd been in love with me for most of her childhood* - but as my friend and as the unofficial manager for ZPP, he knew the only answer was 'yes.'

"You know it's for the best," I said roughly, "for everyone."

"Ash," Blake interrupted with a sigh, stepping into the line of sight between her brother and me. "I need this," she said with a quiet, pleading voice. "I need him to do this."

Growling with his eyes pinned on me, he stood and stalked around his sister, stopping right in my face.

"I want your word right *fucking* now that this is just for show - *for Blake*. I want your word that you won't lay a finger on her unless *explicitly* told to do so for a goddamn camera."

"I promise." I meant it. And I hoped to fucking God I could keep it.

It should be easy, right? Just like it was all those years ago, *to pretend I didn't want her.*

Only now she was twenty-five - *legal* - and much more woman than I could or wanted to ignore. So much so that the rest of my night when I got back to Nashville would be spent with my hand wrapped around my dick, imagining it was those perfectly unproportioned lips sucking me off.

"Good. Because you touch her at any point when it's *not* for the world to see, and you better hope this shit makes you famous enough to need a goddamn body guard because you're going to fucking need it," he threatened with a deadly voice.

I felt his rage as he disappeared out of the house, slamming the door behind him, but there was nothing I could do about it.

She was only partially right when she insisted this would benefit me just as much as her. Yeah, this would be huge name recognition, but ZPP wasn't a nobody. We'd made a name for ourselves, mostly in the country scene and mostly thanks to Ash's phenomenal networking skills. We also had a few crossover singles on our upcoming album that were recorded with Bruno Mars and John Legend, so it was only a matter of time before we were a household name.

No, what it really came down to was that she needed me;

and no matter what I was willing to let her think, she was more important to me than even I wanted to believe.

What I also understood was that in those moments when I'd been inches from those perfectly arched lips of hers, reddened from the cold, moistened by her tongue, I didn't care whether or not this scheme made me famous. I only cared that I'd be able to have her for just a little while.

CHAPTER FIVE

BLAKE

Track 05: Lullaby

*"I thought I came into this with eyes wide open, nothing left to lose.
But, baby, you're the lullaby that brings me back to dreams of you."*

THREE WEEKS LATER

BIG PLANS.
Big stakes.
Big reputation.

"Opening Act Added to *Love Struck* Tour! Who could it be?"

TONIGHT WAS the night - the first show of the US leg of my tour. But even the warmth of Miami at this time of year

66

couldn't shake the chill of nervous anticipation that ran through my body. I flipped back to the previous page in the latest Patterson novel that I was trying to escape into, realizing that I'd been lost in my thoughts.

Player.

Heartless.

Blake the Heartbreaker.

The words played in my head like a broken record. *Heart. Breaks. Her.* Hard to focus on anything else when all I heard was the sound of my reputation screaming and crying as it was dragged through the mud.

I was expecting her, but still the knock on the door made me jump.

"Coming!" I yelled over the edge of the couch.

Grumbling underneath my breath, I pulled myself from the huge plush sectional that graced the living room that was probably larger than my parent's house. I jogged through the penthouse suite that Bruce had reserved for me, passing the full kitchen, full bar, and door to the private freaking sauna, to get to the door. *I really didn't need all this space either.* Not that it wasn't amazing. Or that the floor-to-ceiling windows looking out over the ocean weren't gorgeous. But it was just one more reminder how lonely this life was sometimes – me, in my giant room at the top of the tower, looking out on the world while everyone looked in. They could see me but they never really saw me.

I'd trade high-class for home-y any day.

"Hey," Taylor said a little breathlessly as she came in, dropping her bags on the floor. Due to the last-minute addition to the tour, One Miami was one room short when she'd requested some for the ZPP crew. So, I'd insisted that Tay stay with me and give up her room to whoever needed it.

"You ok?" I asked, watching as she huffed a few breaths, trying to slow herself down.

She was always like this before the show - rushing around

to make sure everything was in order even though it wasn't technically her job. It was even worse today because of ZPP's arrival. We'd been down here for two days already, but Zach, Bobby, Alex, and Ron just got in this afternoon. I'd been in rehearsal, so she'd gone to the airport to pick them up and bring them back here.

"Are those my yoga pants?" I asked, giving her the look. This happened all the time on tour - her stealing my clothes, me stealing hers.

"Sorry," she grinned. "I think I forgot mine at your parents' house."

Taylor had stayed with me the rest of our break. Her parents had moved to Florida after we graduated and their stringent religious beliefs created a divide in their relationship when she began to work for... with... me. I didn't know the last time she'd been to visit them, or the last time they'd called to ask.

She wasn't the type to dwell and I was the type to insist that I'd already adopted her.

"What's up?" I asked, tugging her luggage through the chic dining room and into the master bedroom. "Is everyone settled ok?"

Is he ok? Did he say anything?

After I'd propositioned him (and told my family), he'd disappeared back to Nashville the day after Christmas. It wasn't like I didn't have his phone number or my brother as a means of getting in touch, but I guess I just expected something... *more...* before this whole charade began.

Expectation is the root of all disappointment.

And these roots ran deep.

"Everyone is settled. Zach was all broody, but I'm sure it's because of all the travel and everything," she answered, trying to placate me with a believable story.

"Or because he's being forced to date me," I said wryly.

"Who knew dating a superstar could be such a drag?" I added with a high, breathy voice, pretending to be offended.

"I think he likes it more than he wants to," Tay offered with a grin, throwing open her bag and unloading her toiletries.

"Yeah, right." I rolled my eyes, plopping on the bed. "I can't believe no one knows. As soon as Bruce made the announcement about the opening act, I expected to be mobbed, literally, by people wondering who it is," I mused, staring out at the blue ocean, *really* wanting to go for a swim. "Granted, I haven't checked Instagram yet so I'm sure there are a thousand messages waiting after that cryptic post I made the other day."

I'd gone dark. Like a spy in one of the books that I read. After Levi, not only did I not want to see the media fanfare, I didn't want to be a part of it either so I stopped posting, stopped sharing, and hid. *Even from myself.*

Hard to look at myself in the mirror without imagining a variety of nicknames scrawled across my forehead. *Hard to look at myself and not really start to wonder what was wrong with me.*

Three whole weeks and no one had seen anything from me. Which meant that they were waiting, like vultures, for me to step out into the light tonight. They wanted to see if I was any more broken – like it made a difference; there was no winning with them. And *that* – knowing whatever you do is the *wrong* thing – is the worst feeling in the world.

If I appeared sad and upset – *'Why the long face, Blake? You're the one who broke up with them.'*

If I was strong – *'Blake strikes again and comes out unscathed, ready for the next.'*

Fame was a world built on the sturdy foundations of double standards.

"How would anyone know? You've been off social media since you broke up with Licentious Levi and only reappeared two days ago telling your fans to be prepared. When would anyone have time to suspect?"

"True..." *People were very resourceful though.*

Good at finding truths. Better at finding lies.

"Although, I saw a not inconsequential number of rumors that you'd made up with Levi and that he was going to open your tour."

"Oh my God, seriously?" I groaned. *People were incredible.* For once, I wished I could be *really* honest with my fans about what jerks these guys were.

"Bruce was right, though," she said, grabbing a pair of jeans, white button-down, and her Sperry's out of the suitcase before flipping the lid closed. "He thinks he's going to have to add additional nights to some of the upcoming shows. Everyone is going crazy to know what's going on."

Sighing, I fell back on the bed. "Yeah, well, they should join the club..."

***

HAIR AND MAKE-UP had started an hour ago for me; Tay stopped by to inform me that ZPP was practicing and familiarizing themselves with the venue. My first outfit during the show was a red with gold brocade military jacket and tight white pants that fit well enough to be attractive, but not distasteful.

The best part was the back of the jacket. 'Love Struck' was embroidered in gold with large, flourished letters and a Black Mamba weaving through them. Because when love strikes, it does so with speed and agility and deadly determination. And when it kills you, it does it nice and slow. First, asphyxiation – *taking your ability to speak.* Then, respiratory collapse – *taking your ability to breathe.* And last, cardiovascular collapse – *literally causing your heart to fail you.*

My breath caught in an invisible net in my throat. *Asphyxiation.* It should have been able to get out but it couldn't because he'd taken my ability to speak.

I stared at Zach talking to Bruce and the stage manager. He didn't even notice me, like usual, but I couldn't take my eyes off of him. *Like usual.* He was wearing those painted-on, ripped Diesel jeans - the kind that looked like they'd been purchased with the ten-year-distressed look, only they hadn't.

Like most things that were close to Zach Parker's body for any appreciable amount of time, *the distress came naturally.*

I knew because the rip in the knee was from me. *Yes, only Zach Parker would be wearing a pair of jeans that were easily ten years old because 'if it ain't broke, don't fix it.'* I'd been riding my bike too fast, trying to catch up to him and Ash in the fields between our houses; they'd stopped on the other side of the woods where a huge tree branch had fallen that they wanted to move - and I'd come tearing around the corner, realizing too late what had happened. I slammed on the breaks, my tires skidding in the dirt. Heading right for the branch, Zach quickly yanked me off the bike before I smashed into it and we both fell, tearing his jeans in the process.

Landing on top of him, flush against him, had solidified my need for him. And it had been the beginning of his coldness towards me - just one of the many mortifying moments that had happened that year.

Seriously. I had a spot in the Guinness Book of World Records to prove it.

Topped off with a navy tee covered with a blue and white plaid shirt, his guitar hanging on his back, Zach embodied the hometown-hottie; he looked every part the Southern charmer and childhood friend who was going to sweep in and steal Blake Tyler's heart.

No, heart, it's not really happening. Stop it. We moved on, remember?

"Miss Tyler." Bruce's voice pressed pause on my thoughts.

I shivered as Zach's eyes fell on me. Serene. Unaffected. Utterly blasé and oozing obligation. A flash of something more, but it was gone before I could pick it out.

What was I hoping for? His jaw to drop? *Don't answer that.*

"Bruce. Zach," I greeted them both, turning to Zach to add, "I hope everything in the hotel is ok. You can let Taylor know if you need anything."

"Miss Tyler," Bruce said again, clearing his throat. "I was just explaining to Mr. Parker the logistics of what is going to happen tonight."

"Wonderful," I replied, trying not to let my sarcasm seep too noticeably into my voice.

Bruce didn't notice, but I saw Zach's eyebrow raise slightly at me.

"Blake, you're going to go out and announce Zach and the band," he continued blithely. "Now, remember, I don't want you giving too much away. This needs to be believable - *for your sake.*"

"What exactly are you looking for?" I asked for clarification, because apparently, I was a master of messing these things up.

"Miss Tyler," Bruce looked at me sternly, "your songs, they tell stories, do they not?"

I nodded, brushing a stray piece of hair back up underneath my white fedora.

"Well, think of this tour as one giant story - one giant love song. You cannot walk out there and give the crowd the refrain on the first shot. Tonight is the introduction. They need to see Zach," he motioned to the guitar-wielding god who was standing stock still next to us, "meet him; they need to see what you see and then they need to see how you could fall in love with him."

I gulped, hoping it wasn't audible.

How I could fall in love with him? Easily, I thought. *Easily is the only way I know of.*

Taylor rushed up to us, flushed and flustered; she opened her mouth but quickly shut it again as Bruce continued, "The surprise reveal of an opening act has already gotten their interest peaked, now just give them a small taste. This tour is no longer isolated shows; it is long performance - one that all of those fans out there," he turned and motioned towards where they'd just begun to start letting the crowd enter, "will be following after tonight."

"I understand," I replied softly with a nod, looking to Zach to agree as well. But he didn't. He just stood there looking at me with a blank intensity that had me shifting back and forth between my feet, trying to detour that intensity from dropping straight to my core.

And with that objective and ominous plan, he nodded to the both of us saying, "Let's get this show started," before he walked off yelling for Jenni, his assistant.

"How long?" Zach asked Taylor.

"Fifteen minutes before the show starts. Bruce... wants Blake to go out there first and introduce you, and then the rest of the band will come out."

"I'll let the guys know," he replied and stalked off.

"I..." Tay huffed. "I already told them," she grumbled, turning back to face me with a soft smile. "You good, B?"

Too bad I didn't ask Lin, my hair and makeup magician, to paint a brave face on me; guess I was all on my own for that one.

"Yeah. It'll be fine. Starting slow." I glanced over my shoulder. Through the heavy black curtains, I could see the full stadium, my ears already drowning out the chatter. "They're going to know... as soon as I announce him; they're going to know 'Blake Tyler's next boytoy,'" I said with a low mocking voice.

"Well, he is. Just not in the way they think. So, look at it this way, that means you won't have to do much more than that for tonight." Taylor was always the best at looking on the bright side. A mass of people began to descend on us, signaling that it was show time. Tay wrapped her arms around me quickly, whispering, "May the odds…" It was our 'Hunger Games' half-joke, half-mantra that we muttered before every performance.

"May the odds," I repeated back.

I jumped as Ash slapped his hand on my back, saying with a grin, "Break a leg, sis."

The curtains pulled back. Bright lights. Louder screams.

Only, it wasn't my leg I was worried about breaking out there, *it was my heart.*

Rep-u-ta-tion.

My steps echoed their reminder as I stepped out into the light.

I couldn't stop the smile that spread over my face. Every time I walked out on that stage, I felt like I was flying - soaring. I loved *this.* I loved *them.*

In spite of everything.

In spite of the fact that this stage had become an arena to see if I would come out on top. And in spite of those who loved me, yet loved being entertained more - whether it was by my flight or my fall. Their love could be deceptive, but at the same time so bright that you couldn't see the betrayal it was hiding. Like the sun, it could shine all day, but that didn't mean it would keep me warm.

Rep-u-ta-tion.

The flashing cameras made each step feel like I was walking on a path through thousands of twinkling stars. My smile grew and laughter spilled out of me like soda from a can that had been shaken – bubbling and fizzing overboard because there was too much pressure inside to stop it. It was impossible to see, but I waved anyway. For a few moments, I forgot how they'd deceived me. *And I forgot how I was going to deceive them.*

"Hello, Miami!" It was always strange, hearing myself in my ear and then the almost-echo filter through the stadium. "How are y'all doing tonight?" The crowd went wild.

Stopping in the center of the stage, I adjusted the brim of my fedora, and patiently waited for the noise to start to die down.

"Thank you, guys," I said quietly into the mic. "Thanks for having me here."

The flashing slowed. Everyone was waiting. On the edge of their seats, they wanted my explanation. They wanted to know my surprise. *My secret.*

"So, I wanted to—" I broke off, laughing as someone I heard someone scream '*I love you Blake!*' from somewhere in the crowd on my right. "I love you guys, too." I laughed again. "*So,* I wanted to introduce you to someone very… important… to me."

A flick of my eyes over to the side of the stage revealed Zach, ready and waiting. On stage, I was who I wanted to be. And that person also wanted to be Zach's girl. *So, I let her.*

"I want to introduce you to someone who has been a part of my life for as long as I can remember. He was my neighbor. He is my friend. He helped my brother teach me how to ride a bike - the consequences of which can be seen in the rip on his jeans tonight." I bit my lip as I grinned.

Too easy. It was too easy to be that girl.

It was so quiet in the audience, I could have heard a pin drop from the nosebleeds. Bruce was right. They were all dying to know who he was and what he meant.

I found Zach's eyes watching me – looking *at* me instead of through me. *Remembering.* And my heart picked up its pace. The crowd could have been roaring - I couldn't hear anything except the blood pumping in my ears, a familiar melody that only played when he was around.

I knew I was blushing and I prayed Lin's makeup was doing a good job of hiding it.

"Umm... He also was the one who... inspired me to learn to play guitar," I continued to confess, my voice a little more breathless as it fought its way out over the lump in my throat.

I nodded to him, motioning for him to come out, as I turned back to my fans, giving them my biggest and brightest smile. "So, if you could give a very *warm* welcome to one of my oldest *friends* and someone who is very... special... to me. Zach Parker!"

Now, the crowd went wild. And all I saw was him.

So handsome it hurt.

He walked towards me, his chiseled jawline strong enough to cut through the commotion with the smile that my fifteen-year-old self had hoped to see time and again. It hurt how easily I could believe it knowing it was faked.

ZPP had played a bunch of venues in Nashville, but I knew he'd never played anything like this - tens of thousands of eager and excited eyes on him. The flood of camera flashes lit the sky better than any of the pyrotechnics that I had planned later in show. I saw the way his eyes squinted and smile faltered as he tried to take it all in.

Welcome to my world.

It affected him, but it didn't shake him. I'd come to believe that nothing could shake this man once he'd set his mind to something.

"He and his band, the Zach Parker Project, will be opening for me for the remainder of the tour," I added, hearing how my voice broke with emotion as I spoke. "So, I hope you will show him – them – as much love as you do me."

I watched him soak it all in and shine. His smile grew and mine faltered when he directed it at me.

"Thanks, Blay," he said with a voice that had the perfect, subtly sexy rasp.

The audience melted right along with my insides – piles of

REPUTATION

mush held in by tight pants and the tight red jacket. I'd met tons of models and actors over the last few years (and the media will be happy to tell you just how many of them I'd dated), but none of them had this effect. Zach's casual cool remained unbroken by the pathetic way I crumbled underneath his smile.

In that moment, it hit me exactly what I'd signed myself up for.

"And thank you, Miami, for having us tonight," he drawled, his accent a little more pronounced as he tore his eyes from me, "and letting us play a little for you."

Just like everything else he ever did – he stole the show, *flawlessly*. And they ate him up. Screaming and cheering, his gorgeous smile spreading wider as he waved, his body flexing underneath the lights as he held his guitar steady on his back.

They more than ate him up. He *enchanted* them.

"And yes, Blay——" I shivered at the nickname again, "—is responsible for the rip in these jeans. She's responsible for a lot of things," laughter rippled through the crowd at his wry words. "And I'll let you in on a little secret," he continued conspiratorially, holding his hand up so I couldn't see his delicious mouth move as he spoke, even though he was mic'd and I could hear every word, "I don't know what she's told you, but the missing Christmas cookies every year are because of her, too."

And then that jerk *winked* at them.

My mouth dropped open in guilty shock. "Zach! You can't tell them I steal Santa's cookies," I smacked his arm. "It's not my fault, you guys," I groaned playfully, "If you've ever had those peanut butter ones with the Hershey kiss on top, you know *exactly* why I can't stop myself."

He broke into a smile and actually laughed - *I think* - and then so did I. And it felt as natural as the dawn breaking over the tense darkness that had been perpetually surrounding us for years now.

77

I couldn't move my eyes from his. I should say something. I should get off the stage and let him play. I should do something besides stand there in awe of the smile and laugh that was for me - *even if it might only be fake.* Under the lights, I could believe it was real.

My mouth parted slightly as he stepped closer. He was close, *so close.* And it was like we were back in my parents' yard with only the stars and silence as our company, when in fact, the whole world was watching.

"Thank you, Blake," he said with a low, hoarse voice that I felt echo all around me, "for inviting me to be a part of this with you."

This? Like this fake relationship? The one that felt completely real right now?

I froze. Body. Heart. Breath. As his head dropped towards mine. *He's going to kiss me, I know it. Right in front of all these people. Right when Bruce told us to take it slow.*

I wonder if his kiss be as rough as his voice.

My eyes drifted shut as I tipped into him. I felt his exhale on my skin, harsher than the words and tone he'd just spoken. And then his lips gently pressed down… on my cheek. The touch was soft but the sparks were sharp, shooting like warning flares throughout my body. It took a second to register where he'd kissed me - on that spot that wasn't really on my cheek, but wasn't on my lips either. It was on the in-between - not decidedly romantic, but not far enough away for it to be anything else.

It was just on the edge of being something more.

I fought to not turn my face closer to his. *So close, yet just out of reach.*

And then he was gone.

Story of my life.

As soon as his lips disappeared, the world returned around me - my breathing, the crowd screaming, the lights, *the show.*

"I-I guess I'll let these guys get to it then," I said weakly.

Giving the crowd one more brilliant smile before I walked off stage was one of the hardest things I'd ever done; it was the only time I'd ever faked an emotion for my fans. Everything else out there had been very, *very* real. Too real. Pitifully real.

And they didn't even see. They were enamored Zach and the rest of the Parker Project that joined him on stage, their soulful melodies beginning to float through the air.

I knew from the first note played that I'd be breaking all my rules to be with him.

All the rules to keep me safe.

All the rules to keep me whole.

Tay wrapped her arms around me as soon as I made it off the stage. I hadn't expected it to start this soon. I hadn't even realized that my footing was uneven when it came to Zach Parker, and now I was afraid it was too late. I was already slipping.

CHAPTER SIX

ZACH

I ORDERED A DRINK AND IT WENT DOWN SMOOTH. PRETTY EASY how that one drink then turned into two.

"New Beau for Blake?"

Tonight was supposed to be about me and the boys, celebrating the way we'd killed it last night and tonight – and I was trying so damn hard to keep it that way. Our first major shows had gone off fucking flawlessly and the band was pumped. *Why wouldn't they be?* We'd played some pretty big venues in Nashville but nothing like this. It was incredible. The mass of people. *Tens of thousands.* All there to see *her.*

"New Tour, New Toy! Blake Tyler's New Boyfriend is a Blast from the Past!"

I WASN'T SHOCKED.
She'd always been the brightest goddamn star in the sky.

No matter how I tried to focus on anything else, I kept coming back to her like a fucking forbidden refrain in a song begging to be written.

Her performance was nothing short of amazing. I'd seen videos over the years - it was fucking hard not to; she was literally everywhere I looked. *A reminder of my regrets.* But to see her live had been something else. From the moment she emerged from the jets of red smoke in the center of the stage and proceeded to own every stalking step, every shimmy, and every perfectly timed wink, she'd owned them.

She'd owned me.

And the way she sang... *fuck, the way she sang...* It was more natural than breathing for her. It was no wonder the way she connected with the thousands in the crowd like it was a small gathering of her closest family members.

"Zach, can you believe this?" Ron asked, shoving his phone in my face.

Too close. Too bright. "Christ, what are you talking about?" I rasped as another shot glass appeared in front of me.

"That's from Ash," Bobby, our bassist, said from my other side, raising his matching one before turning back to his and Alex's conversation.

"Our Instagram has shot up five-fucking-thousand followers since we went on last night," Ron replied, pointing to the screen. Ronnie was our drummer and was in charge of all our social media accounts. "I don't even know how many photos we're tagged in." He scrolled through endless photos that the crowd had taken and tagged. "This is huge. Fucking huge, dude."

I tried for a smile; failing miserably, I washed the attempt down with the vodka in front of me. *Fucking Ash.* He knows I hate vodka. One more reminder that this was all just for show.

I didn't know what was worse - having him here or not. He was taking care of a few last things in Nashville before meeting us in Pittsburgh next weekend. With him, the consequences of taking what I wanted stared me in the face, *literally*. Without him, the reward of taking what I wanted was like a damn siren's song, luring me in.

I shouldn't have kissed her last night. A mistake that I barely had been able to hold back from repeating earlier tonight. Technically, it fit with the plan to make *them* believe. What *I* believed though was that I needed to get my shit under control before I did something that I would regret.

It wasn't because I wanted to. It wasn't because when I hugged her on stage tonight, she'd smelled like those damn cookies she loved. The fucking sugar-cookie scent was baked into her skin and all I wanted to do was lick and eat it off of her. It was the most ridiculous feeling: to be surrounded by a mass of people and with just that one breath to feel like it was just her and me. *It wasn't because I wanted her.*

I just needed to stay away from her off-stage, that's what it came down to. *Distance could let my heart grow harder.* I nodded, half-listening to Robbie as he droned on about getting aerial footage of the next show.

And then she walked in.

Like a magnet, my eyes went straight to her, watching as she felt it, too. Pull. Push. Action. Reaction.

My shit was totally not fucking together.

She was in jean shorts that showed off her long – so fucking long – legs. Legs that should have a disclaimer tattooed on them: Warning. May cause extreme muscle reactions if direct exposure occurs. My dick swelled, imagining them wrapped around my waist like lips around a straw – the tight vacuum pulling me in. It made me want to slap another warning label right between her thighs: *Caution. Slippery when wet.* And her cut-off tee? That shit barely hid her tits from—*why the hell was she wearing a bathing suit?* And a baseball cap?

Where the hell was her security?

When I saw her look for me I turned away, signaling to the bartender for another drink. I wondered if she still tasted like cookies. After all these years, I'd never tasted anything so sweet since that night.

"Hey guys! Great show tonight! What an awesome way to start the tour!" Taylor's bubbly voice was the alarm clock going off when you've already been awake for ten minutes.

My body tensed, the alcohol had only started to diminish the adrenaline from the show before she had my heart racing again.

"Did we put on a good enough show, Baby Blake?" I asked dryly, the nickname a defense and reminder of exactly who she was - *who she had to be* - to me.

Blake's baby blues widened at me for a second. Taylor had fallen into conversation with Bobby and Alex, leaving the two of us tensely staring at each other. My jaw ticked as I noticed the way her nipples hardened underneath that t-shirt. *Christ, was she not wearing a bra? What the fuck?* I felt my dick swelling against my jeans. Good fucking thing I was sitting and had no plans to leave.

"You guys were awesome," she answered honestly, her calm face framed by wisps of wavy pale blonde hair that I wanted nothing more than to reach out and tuck behind her ear.

"How was I?" I demanded. I needed to know if she was getting what I was paying for.

Now, she stuttered, "Y-you played great—"

"You know what I mean," I cut her off, the edge in my tone resulting from the impossible hard-on that throbbed painfully in my jeans. A situation that I wouldn't be able to remedy since Ronnie and I were sharing a room and that kid was up until all hours of the night. I wasn't going to jack-off like a damn teenager in the bathroom with him right outside. No fucking way.

"Oh." Her tongue darted out to lick her lips and my cock

83

jumped, wanting the same attention. "Good. I think, good, at least." She shrugged and fuck if my eyes didn't cling to their periphery where her tits rose and fell slightly. "Bruce was gone by the time I got off stage. He has a very particular nightly ritual, but Tay said that social media has been blowing up with a positive response since yesterday."

"You didn't check?" I raised an eyebrow. The way she interacted with her fans, I thought she would have been all over it.

"I did," she admitted softly, adding, "I'm not allowed to check, especially after... recently... until Taylor does. She says I'm too sensitive, so she screens first..." She trailed off, leaning to the side as Alex reached around and handed her a shot. Blake smiled and thanked him.

"Seriously?" I growled at him. A quick glance around felt like every eye - literally - in the place was on her and it wasn't because she was famous. No. No one had even realized that fucking fact yet. They stared because she was gorgeous. And I glared because a twisted part of me roared that she was mine.

Why now?

After all these years. Years that I'd been with other people. *Years that I'd seen her with other guys.* Why. Fucking. Now?

Because now I had the chance to have what I always wanted. *Fate was a fickle bitch.*

"What?" Alex scoffed. "She's legal. And Ash said to buy shots for everyone."

Yeah, fucking doubted that he meant his sister.

I turned to glare at her as she downed the clear liquid. "I deserve to celebrate, too," she retorted, grabbing another one from off the bar and throwing it back - *throwing it in my face -* that she wasn't the 'Baby Blake' that I could boss around anymore.

"You should take it easy there," I bit out. "Have you even eaten?"

Her lips pursed, the second shot not going down as

smoothly as the first. "Yeah, we grabbed McDonald's burgers on the way here."

"Are you kidding?" If that wasn't just asking to be vomited back up, I didn't know what was.

"We were trying to avoid the paparazzi." She shrugged, causing her top to slide dangerously close to the edge of her shoulder. *Fall.* I wanted to see those tits that were taunting me right now.

Because a McHeartattack is so much more preferable.

"Don't you have body guards for that?" I asked, realizing there were still no signs of those huge motherfuckers.

Her eyes glinted deviously, just like all those times that she'd lined Ash's toilet seat with soap, hiding behind the corner in their upstairs hall just waiting for him to sit and slide right off of it. *Fearless.*

"We… may have been trying to avoid them as well." Her careless attitude made my body surge with anger.

Goddammit.

"*Jesus Christ.*" One way or another, this tour was going to kill me. Wiping my hand over my mouth, I swore underneath my breath. She had a fucking death wish. "What is the matter with you? You are—" I cursed again under my breath, glancing around before continuing, "you are *you*. This is Miami. You can't just fucking ditch your security."

"Calm down, *dad.* I told Andrew that he could take the night," she replied with another enticing shrug. "It's just one night. I can be inconspicuous for one night."

Yeah. That was like the sun trying to hide during the day. Impossible.

"You will never be normal, Blake." I was harsh because she never goddamn listened. I ignored my guilt when she winced. I didn't have the flexibility to be the nice guy. Not when she was fucking throwing herself in danger. "I don't care what you told him. I care about what you didn't tell him, which I'm assuming was that you were coming here."

85

"We were just going for a burger and then here to see if you wanted to go to the beach! I figured the four of you was protection enough. Not like some of you weren't football stars or anything…" she retorted with an angry, flustered voice that made me want to kiss some fucking sense into her pretty little head.

The hand that reached out and grabbed her arm, yanking her into me, came from my body but wasn't my own. "Well maybe you could have at least tried a better disguise," I said, nodding to the black leather baseball cap even as my eyes drifted down to her glossy pink lips.

"Yeah? Maybe next time you could let me borrow your asshole one if you can bear to part with it for a few hours." She snatched her arm from my grip. "That disguise seems to be foolproof at keeping people away."

Darting around me, she grabbed Taylor's hand and pulled her out towards the DJ, exclaiming enthusiastically, "Let's dance! I love this song!"

The growl that escaped me was feral, as I watched the two girls escape to the dance floor that flashed like it was testing participants for a seizure disorder. Avicii blared over the speakers, the pulsing of the beat hardly keeping up with the angry drum of my heart.

Alex tried to say something to me, but I couldn't even turn my head. I'd like to believe it was because there were *other* people on the dance floor and I wanted to make sure nothing happened to her.

There were a lot of things I'd like to believe.

My fucking dick screamed that it was because of the way her arms lifted and crossed over her head, pulling her already short top up higher to give glimpses of her pale, flat stomach. Swallow. Swallow. *Fucking swallow.* All my mouth wanted to do was taste it, to bathe that soft skin with my tongue. She would taste like cookies there, too, as I licked and bit my way underneath her shirt. She continued to move and spin like my own personal nymph nightmare that would haunt my hard cock for weeks. And the material clung to her modest tits when she moved like it knew I was watching.

Bathing suits were not supposed to be bras. And friends' little sisters were not supposed to be wet dreams.

I felt my hand flex on my thigh, knowing that they would fit perfectly in my palm. My undefeatable erection throbbed, imagining how I'd be able to cup the entirety of the soft weight in my palm. *I liked the thought of claiming entire parts of her.* As she danced in front of me my fingers itched to hold the bouncing mounds steady for my mouth so I could suck on the hard, outlined peaks right through the thin fabric until they were as red as her goddamn lips.

Biting back a curse, I shifted again in my seat. This was why I stayed away from Blake Tyler.

Because my body needed to have her. But fucking her would fuck everything.

Still, I couldn't look away. The way her hips swayed to the beat had her too-goddamn-short shorts slipping and sliding with every shake. They were too loose and hanging too low on her hips and I began to wonder if she kept moving that way, if it was possible for her to...

My jaw clenched.

Shake them off.

My dick swelled, eager for me to assist her if it wasn't. God, I probably wouldn't even have to unbutton the damn things to get them off. Which was honestly, perfectly fine with me, because right now, ripping them down was even too long a process to get my cock buried inside of her.

The song ended and her arms fell to wrap around Taylor as she laughed. It was a fucking mistake for her to ditch her security - *a dangerous fucking mistake.* But when I saw her smile like that - like for once she could just enjoy being like the rest of us - I understood. As they hugged and half spun on the dance floor, her eyes caught mine and the smile dropped from her face.

Good.

She should think that I'm still upset with her recklessness and not with my own reckless desire.

Caught in my trance, she tugged off her hat to run a hand through her waves of sunshine. *A mistake.*

It might not have been much, but the damn cap had been doing *something.* And as though the curtain had just dropped, some drunk chick down the bar, yelled, "Oh my god! Is that Blake Tyler?"

Like the whole fucking bar couldn't hear her.

I watched her bright lips part, surprise and disbelief registering on her face. In slow motion, she and Taylor looked around, all of us silently praying that no one had heard the obnoxious announcement.

Prayers don't travel as fast as word of a superstar sighting.

Taylor pushed her towards us. The guys and I stood, closing the distance around her, but it wasn't enough. The whole bar drew in like parasitic months to a fruitful flame, asking for autographs, photos, and several obscene requests from the really drunk assholes. Normally, she gave into this shit and probably would have signed bar napkins until the sun came up or until they ran out. But this wasn't a safe space for that.

"You lookin' for a new boytoy, Blake?" Some giant bald guy asked, trying to push through Taylor to get to her. "I'll be your boyfriend for the weekend," he continued to offer with a slur. "I don't mind if you use me, sweets."

Red rage shot through my blood.

Taylor stumbled to the side as he pushed right through her and reached for Blake. I shoved myself in front of the asshole, briefly catching the hurt and concern mingle over Blay's face.

"I think you need to take a step back, jackass," I growled at him. Murder never seemed so possible until that moment.

"Why?" he asked dumbly. "You her latest boyfriend or somethin'? Maybe she'd be interested in two at a time. Be able to move through them a lot faster that way."

I heard her gasp behind me - and that was before my hand shot out and wrapped around this drunk motherfucker's throat.

"Keep talking and the only thing that's going to move a lot faster is my fist through your fucking face." I squeezed for emphasis, enjoying how his face seemed to turn purple for a second. *Throats were a lot softer than footballs.*

He choked and doubled over when I let go and then the crush of people clamoring to get closer pushed him away before I could do more damage.

"I'll be your next boyfriend, Blake. I'll even let you dump me in the morning."

"Let's get the paparazzi in here!"

I watched the fear shudder of her face as the flashes of cell phones now began to distantly register. *Fuck this shit.* I hauled Blake against me and, gripping the back of Bobby's collar to use him as a shield, I pushed us through the crowd and out the door.

Everything had gone from fine to frenzy faster than you could say 'fearless.'

All those photos that had been posted in the last thirty seconds had done the trick. Once outside, we saw a different crowd – one leashed with professional cameras and heading directly towards us.

"Is this what you were hoping for?" I growled at her like it would make the situation better.

Unfortunately, all I could think that there was someone here who didn't like her or her music, who didn't know her but hated her, and decided that tonight was a good time to try to harm her. All I saw was her face as random arms tried to reach through us for her. I hated that she'd put herself in this position. I hated that she thought I could protect her. Mostly, I fucking hated that I would *die* to protect her but it still wouldn't be enough.

"W-we have to get back," Taylor said with a shaky voice. "Let's just call an Uber or something."

"No," I shouted. "Keep moving."

I realized that my grip was biting into the soft skin of Blake's arm. *Good.* I wanted to bite into her. I wanted to punish her for doing this.

We rounded the next corner and I turned to Alex, "The hotel is only a few blocks away. They are going to catch up to us if we have to wait for a car. You guys take Taylor back. Stay on this road and they'll all follow you. I'll cut over another block with Blake and we'll meet you back there."

I didn't wait for any agreement. Reaching up, I yanked the hat off Blake's head and handed it to Taylor, praying that it was enough to confuse the two of them in the dark.

CHAPTER SEVEN

BLAKE

Track 06: Shame on Me
"Fool me once, shame on you.
I knew you were trouble yet twice I fell.
So shame on me now,
I knew you'd pretend not to see me drown."

I NEVER TOOK SHOTS. I'D TAKEN TWO IN THE PAST THIRTY minutes. *Brilliant.*

My head spun like a merry-go-round that was anything but merry as Zach pulled hard on my arm, tearing us away from the rest of the group.

"Christ," I heard him swear as I stumbled into the back of him.

"You're going too fast."

"Do you want to be mobbed by the paparazzi right now?" He sounded so angry. And annoyed. And like he needed to be kissed.

Two drinks and ten years disappeared. I was fifteen again

and he was the gorgeous boy who was treating me like a foolish little girl.

And maybe I was.

I shouldn't have left the hotel without security, but I just wanted to water that seed. I just wanted *one night* where I was off-duty. That feeling was always the worst right after spending time at home and then being thrown back into the twenty-four-seven fame game.

I'd walked off stage to learn that Zach and the band had gone out for pizza and celebratory drinks. Because they could. Because they didn't have to worry about getting mobbed by the press or stalked by sincere and crazy fans alike.

"Zach, I need a break," I pleaded softly, my stomach rolling with the alcohol and the Big Mac – which was turning out to be more like a Big Mistake.

"You can have a break when we get back to the hotel and you are safe," he said roughly, pointing ahead of him to One Miami that was just a block away.

There were no gray areas with him. All black and white. Harsh. Definite. Decisive.

And reading into his protectiveness would have definitely been another mistake. A familiar and harsh one.

Like drinking coffee that's too hot. I got burned every time, but that still didn't stop me from doing it and expecting a different result. Some would remind me that that is the definition of insanity.

I wouldn't disagree.

I'd always been a little crazy when it came to Zach Parker.

I tripped over crack in the sidewalk, stumbling again. "No! Stop!" I insisted, yanking my arm back out of his hand. I took an unsteady step backward and my vision wavered, his harshly handsome, *albeit aggravated*, face coming back into focus.

And then I saw it.

Heard it.

The waves crashing in the darkness just beyond him. *The beach was right there. Completely empty. All mine.*

This was what we'd left the hotel for. I'd bribed Taylor into my plan for burgers and then a stroll on the beach. For the past two days, all I wanted to do was put my toes in the ocean that I could see from my tower – even if it was for just a second.

But being on tour is like driving a Ferrari – everyone loves to look at it all nice and shiny; everyone wishes they could go that fast. What they don't realize is that it doesn't stop to let you out to enjoy the sights that are flying by.

My eyes stuck in his honeyed ones for a split second before I was off. Adrenaline was the only answer for how my feet carried me so surely and steadily across the boardwalk and down the stairs, Zach's heavy footsteps just behind mine.

"*Blake!*" he yelled hoarsely after me.

I ran from him like my life depended on it. *It didn't.* But my sanity did.

The water was so close. I tore off my shirt, turning to throw it back in his face, hoping it would slow him down, only to realize he was right there.

I'd have a better chance of outrunning an airplane than I would him. Or, you know… how much I wanted him.

A strong arm locked around my waist, hauling me back against him - and even my long legs couldn't touch my feet to the ground as he held me like I was nothing more than a ragdoll with my back to his chest.

"What the hell do you think you're doing, Blake?" he demanded in my ear.

I whimpered, "Please, Zach…" In a blurred blink, I'd gone from angry and defiant to sad and lonely, topped with intense longing. "We snuck out so that I could come to the beach," I admitted quietly in defeat. "I just wanted to go in the ocean… once… while we were here. Without the crowds and the people and the *drama.*"

The last thing I needed was another beach trip invaded and then ruined by the press. When I was dating Xavier, we'd gone out to his house in the Hampton's and had been photographed in the ocean. It wouldn't have been so bad if he hadn't insisted on making a fashion statement, wearing an "I *heart* my #Blay" t-shirt. Of course, I thought it was cute at the time. I also thought he was cute at the time. And just like the shirt, he - and all his *feelings* for me - had just been for show.

"Please, can I just touch the water..." I trailed off, no longer caring if he thought I sounded like a whiney, drunk baby. I just wanted to feel something real because everything around me - the show, the fans, the attention, *Zach* - they were all fake. "Just for one minute and then we can go..."

He didn't budge. My chest still heaved from the full-on sprint that I hadn't done in years. Even though I couldn't move, there was no slowing my racing heart - not with him pressed flush against me, his firm fingers gripping into my now-bare stomach locking my hips against his. In the stillness, I listened to the ocean, feeling the crash of each wave in the ragged, humid breaths that he exhaled against my neck.

His body realized just where he had me as his length grew harder against the curve of my ass. Biting my lip, I held back my retraction; I didn't want to go in the ocean anymore. I wanted to stay right here where the desire crashing over us was all too real.

A groan ripped from his chest before I was practically shoved forward.

"Two minutes," came his gruff reply, yanking my shirt from my hand.

If I couldn't drown in him, the ocean was the next best thing.

My shorts dropped into the sand and then with a delirious smile that I could only attribute to the intoxication of freedom, I ran towards the dark, glistening water.

So cold.

Freezing.

Freedom.

I let out a yelp, but didn't stop until the water was up to my chest, the tiny waves cresting just over my shoulders.

That was the thing about the cold - it always brought you back to reality. It made every cell - every molecule - in your body contract with the reminder of life. More and more, I began to feel like I was trapped in my own world and reality orbited around me. I was a fixture in space as the real world - real people and real feelings - circled just out of my reach.

It was beautiful up there. It was breathtaking. It was awe-inspiring to feel like the center of the universe.

But it was lonely.

And sometimes, I didn't want my breath to be taken away. Sometimes, I just wanted to breathe. I wanted to inhale emotions - *good, bad, and ugly.*

Sometimes, I wanted to feel the sting of the cold, real world.

"Blake!"

My eyes jerked open at Zach's voice. If anyone could break through to give me that sting, it was him.

"Come in!" I shot back, knowing I was going to be turned down.

I was surprised his disapproving glare didn't part the seas, demanding my exit, as he stood at the edge of the water, holding my discarded clothes.

Goosebumps ran down over my body, chasing the water from my skin. My nipples poked out against my bikini top, the wet fabric clinging to their upturned peaks. It was even colder getting out of the water, but my body's reaction had nothing to do with the temperature and everything to do with him.

Who needed the sun when those eyes were staring at me like that?

I felt the cold evaporate off of me under the heat of his gaze. He was drunk and hungry. *Ok, maybe not drunk like me, but his guard was momentarily not sky-high.*

I stopped, still standing in the water that was mid-calf.

"Remember the one time you and Ash had a mud fight outside your house?" I asked, the memory suddenly vivid in my mind.

"Blake, we need to go," he said, holding my clothes up.

"Do you remember?"

"Yes, of course I remember. Mud fight. We were boys. We played in dirt," he ground out in annoyance. "Let's go."

His eyes told a different story. *Pure longing.* For me - all length, legs, and pale limbs. He stared at me like I was a nymph or a siren that had just appeared out of the depths of the ocean to draw him to his doom.

And maybe tonight, I would.

"I watched you guys the whole time. You wouldn't let me play because Ash said that mom was going to yell at me if I got any of my clothes dirty."

His jaw ticked as I let out a small laugh - a laugh that was cut short when he spoke again, "So, you went inside, put on your best Sunday dress and then came back out, picked up a huge handful of mud, and to our horror, slathered it all over your front."

I bit my lip, taking another few steps closer to him, but it didn't do anything to stop the smile that spread over my face.

"Then you had no choice but to let me play. I was already a mess," I said triumphantly, reliving that moment of success as though it were yesterday. "In fact, I think you were the first one to tackle me and make *sure* I got exactly what I was asking for."

"What kind of girl wants to be covered in mud?" he growled. "We. Need. To. Go."

The kind of girl that just wanted to play with you.

I bristled at his tone, my next move decided in those last words.

"What kind of *boy* doesn't want to go in the ocean?" I

returned just before I stepped completely out of the water and launched myself at him.

"Blake! What the——" His words cut off with an 'oomph,' my weight knocking the wind from him as we fell into the sand.

In most other worlds, he would have been too big, too strong, and too determined to fall under my sloppy attack. But this - *tonight* - was a rare world. A unique reality where stars walked on Earth and the only thing that made them shine was the electricity in the air between us.

Wonderland.

"Why the hell did you do that?" he grunted, coughing to catch his breath.

I was surprised at the lack of anger in his tone. M*aybe because he was in too much pain*. Belated guilt washed over me. Those shots weren't using training wheels when they took my inhibitions for a ride.

"Payback," I answered with a breathless grin, tacking on, "And I wanted you to come in…" My heart was now racing again. I couldn't look away.

My breasts were small, but even they felt squished in the lack of space between us. I lay sprawled on top of him, one of my hands buried in the sand, the other in his chest. His arms both lay out at his sides and one of his legs rested between my thighs.

"I said I didn't want to," he growled, the vibration I felt all the way down to my core. "And then I said that we needed to go."

It was all well-intentioned - the tone of his voice, the way his free hand slid from the sand, tiny clinging particles pressing into the skin of my waist as he gripped my hip to push me up. *But good intentions don't stand a chance against demanding desire.* Even as he spoke, his eyes drifted down to my mouth, parted and breathing heavily. His hand stilled, his skin just as hot as my own.

I didn't move, taking in every granite-hard and Miami-hot inch of him that lay taut underneath me. Our breaths in sync, I wished he was wearing as little as I was. From the water and my little stunt, my swimsuit had bunched and shifted, revealing far more side-boob and ass than originally advertised. But it was the growing hardness against the top of my left thigh that seared off any last vestige of cold or water from my skin.

I swallowed a small moan as moisture seeped between my thighs. There was no way my bottoms were going to dry anytime soon.

It would be so easy to just slip them...

I bit hard into my lip as my hips unconsciously flexed, rubbing my aching sex against his leg. I gasped - the slight movement causing an avalanche of tension inside of me. Everything was in the extremes tonight.

"Blake," he rasped, his eyelids heavy. "What are you doing?"

"You should have come in," I mumbled. "It might have helped alleviate this." My leg pressed ever so slightly against his arousal and I felt it jerk against his shorts.

The next thing I knew I was pinned beneath him. *I'd have sand in my hair for days after this.* His hips slid and landed right between my legs - right where I needed him.

"Doesn't work that way. Not for you," he admitted with a tortured voice.

My breath tripped and fell out of my lungs like a drunken college girl leaving a frat party would.

I watched regret for his words war with his desire. And that was his seed, I realized. His desire for me. Always drowned out by that unwavering obligation. His fingers flexed into my side and I felt it coming - the shutdown, the push-back.

"We need to go, Baby Blake," he repeated and I wasn't sure for whose benefit. Even the nickname didn't have the usual petulance to it - like he tried, but just couldn't find the feeling to back them up. "Please. I'm trying to keep you safe."

"Doesn't work that way," I whispered raggedly, "Not tonight."

My fingers speared sand through his hair as I pulled my lips up to his - or maybe I pulled his lips down to mine. Either way, it was awkward and clumsy and a little off-center, but eagerness made up for the imperfect execution; I needed to kiss him before he forced me away.

His body jolted against mine like I'd just tased him. I felt him pull back for a split second, but I held on, darting my tongue out along the seam of his lips.

I'd always heard that the tongue is the strongest muscle in the body, but tonight, I believed it because the strength needed to get past Zach's defenses was something I wasn't sure that I possessed. And with just that one touch, all of those stone-cold defenses began to crumble.

The growl that erupted from him seemed inhuman, but I didn't have time to dwell as his mouth claimed mine. Scolding me was typical *from* his mouth, scolding me *with* his mouth wasn't - *but that's what he did.*

Angling his lips, his tongue speared inside searching for mine, seeking to punish it for pushing him over the edge.

There may be a lot of fake things going on between Zach and me for the tour and my reputation, but *this* wasn't one of them.

His mouth tore into mine. Licking, sucking, exploring every corner like it had completely changed in the past ten years. He kissed me like he needed to make up for every day that he hadn't. And he kissed me like he needed to make up for every day in the future that he wouldn't.

My arms wound around his neck, pulling myself tighter to him. Those firm fingers of his cinched into my waist as he rocked his hips into mine. Just once. I gasped as my body shuddered violently. Warmth seeped out from my core with the need to orgasm.

"Is this what you want, Baby Blake?" he rasped into my mouth, rubbing the hard length of his dick against me again.

I whimpered, nodding jerkily as I tried to push back. *I needed more… and I needed it now.*

My hands scored over his shirt. I wanted to feel him. Why was I always the one laid bare - physically and emotionally - in front of him and he always managed to keep all his shields and layers intact?

His mouth was on mine again as the hand on my hip slid higher between us. I tried to force myself from arching against him - *from being that needy* - but I couldn't stop myself as his fingers reached the edge of my suit.

My teeth tugged his lip into my mouth and I sucked hard. It earned me a punishing grind of his ridge into my sex, the material of my suit now rubbing directly on my clit. And then his hand closed over my breast and spots flashed behind my eyes.

"*Fuck.*" I heard his tortured curse as he palmed my flesh. It was followed swiftly by an angry growl before the bunched triangle of fabric was yanked to the side. The large, warm hand that had slung mud at me all those years ago closed over my bare breast and it was more than everything I'd imagined.

"Perfect," he whispered, kneading what was - in my opinion - an all-around-average tit.

I tried to hold onto the word and his voice as he said it. But it was like trying to hold onto the wind.

His mouth trailed along the edge of my jaw, biting and kissing towards my neck. And then his thumb rolled over my nipple before pinching it between his fingers and whatever opinions I had about my boobs were lost.

I rolled my hips against his, blindly searching for what he'd given me all those years ago.

"Zach... please..." I begged. I was so close, but I didn't know how to get there. *I couldn't get there without him.*

"Just let me taste you, Blake, baby," he whispered close to my ear, the switch-up of my nickname melting through my body like fire on ice. "Let me taste you and then I'll take you there."

The half-moan, half-whimper was the best that I could manage as I felt him begin to slide down my body, kissing along the length of my neck as my head pushed back further into the sand. Those fingers pulled on my nipple and my body arched against him, feeling how impossibly hard he'd become against his pants.

Bright flashes appeared behind my eyelids.

God, what was he doing to me?

The flashes appeared again, but this time, the only thing that he did was freeze. My eyes shot open and, like a bucket of ice water had been dumped over us, I realized that the flashes weren't figments of my desire-fragmented mind.

They were camera flashes.

'She's over here!'

'Holy shit! This is going to be great!'

'She's with the opening act!'

The breeze carried their every word over from the boardwalk.

I looked to Zach in horror, every expletive that he didn't say flitting through his eyes. He stayed perfectly still, his hand working swiftly to pull the material of my suit back over my bare breast, lifting off me slightly to make sure that all my necessary parts were covered.

He stood, pulling me up with him so that his back was to the paparazzi, using himself as a shield. He pushed my clothes into my hands, and I quickly yanked them on over my suit.

Even though they'd caught onto our little charade and managed to double back and find us, the cameras stayed on the boardwalk as Zach wrapped his arm around my shoulder and we began to walk swiftly towards the hotel.

I knew from experience that they didn't need to be closer. They had lenses big enough to see the sand particles trapped in my hair – and other unmentionable places – if they wanted to. *And I was sure that they wanted to.*

"Are you happy now?" Zach bit out as we walked swiftly through the lobby.

"I-I'm sorry," I said thickly, trying not to let the tears start to fall.

I had no idea whether or not this was going to be a good or bad thing for the tour, but I had a feeling that this was definitely going to be a bad thing for the two of us.

He punched the elevator button even though the door was already opening.

A really bad thing.

"I told you we had to go. *Fuck,* Blake," he swore running his hand through hair that showed no indication that it had gotten a sand-shampoo. "This was not part of the plan. *Not part of the deal.*"

I winced, not so much at the sting in his words, but at the anger in his eyes. We stared at each other in the reflective metal on the back of the elevator doors as it carried us up to the top.

"It will be ok. It'll be fine," I repeated dumbly, unsure of who I was trying to reassure.

"Will it?" he demanded angrily. "You don't fucking know that. If you knew that, you wouldn't have picked up and discarded your last dozen boyfriends like you were playing a goddamn card game. The whole point of this was to show that you've acquired some semblance of control over your emotions - to give them the fairytale that you seem to think they crave, not just one more fling."

I stared, speechless and suffering at his outburst. I was

surprised he didn't crack his jaw the way he was clenching his teeth.

Ice-cold reality. *Just what I'd asked for.*

"*Even if*—" he broke off with a harsh laugh, "Even if this isn't taken that poorly, do I really have to bring up the fact that having naked photos of you engaged in sexual activity is probably *not* the best way for this fake-fucking-fairytale to break. *Christ*, Ash is going to fucking kill—" He groaned and slammed his fist in the elevator wall behind us, the metal rattling against my back.

"B-but that was real..." I whispered softly. I'd heard the rest of what he'd said, but that last part was the only thing that stuck; what just happened wasn't fake. *It wasn't.*

It was at that moment his eyes tore from mine, glancing down at the floor just as the elevator dinged its arrival.

"No." The doors opened to the floor where his room was, on level below mine. "That was a *mistake.*"

I winced, the words ripping back open one more wound that I thought all these years had finally bypassed. I was wrong. *Raw and wrong.*

And then he walked me to my door, waited until I crossed the threshold, and then retreated before I even had the chance to turn and slam the door in his face.

He always did this so flawlessly - the part where he put another scar on my heart.

CHAPTER EIGHT

BLAKE

Track 07: Lost Cause

*"In that moment, I found who I was.
The very best of me would only ever be
your lost cause."*

9 YEARS AGO

"ZACH."

I stood, nervously wiping my hands on my shorts. I'd been sitting and waiting on the white-washed steps of his front porch for him to get home, refusing to admit that this was slightly stalkerish. He looked like Clark Kent walking towards me – solid and sexy Superman mixed with down-to-Earth farmer - in his ripped jeans and a plain tee stretched over his chest, varsity jacket, and that 'Bama hat on. They'd had a football farewell with the team today; Ash had a dentist appointment afterward which is how I knew that waiting here, patiently *not* stalking Zach's house, would get me a private conversation with him - something that he'd been clearly avoiding like the plague ever since my performance.

I watched as his steps slowed and his eyes narrowed on me. His jaw ticked in annoyance. What was I expecting after the whole graduation party performance last weekend...

Ash had reamed me out later that night for embarrassing the both of them – and myself. *'How could you do that to me? To him.'* He'd made it painfully clear that I was like a little sister to Zach and that he would *never* think of me that way so I should grow up and move on.

I couldn't.

Ash didn't know. He didn't know what I felt. He didn't know about the treehouse.

He didn't know that deep down, Zach had to feel the same.

He had to.

Just like the sun rises and the seasons change.

"What are you doing here, Blake?" he asked tightly, stopping a few feet in front of me.

I tugged my shorts down slightly, hating how I swore I'd stand here confidently and was doing anything but. I bit into my tongue, my teeth searching for the piece of gum that I'd refused to allow myself until I spoke to him.

"I wanted to talk to you," I said, wringing my hands before shoving them in my pockets so that I would stop fidgeting with them.

Ever since prom night, there was something different in the way that he looked. For the longest time, I looked at him as this perfect thing that I'd always want and would never have. Like a yacht. Or a record deal.

"I think you've said enough." Unyielding eyes met mine.

"That's not fair, Zach Parker," I accused with a twinge of hurt in my voice. "I wasn't the only one in the treehouse that night. You knew it was me. And you still stayed. You can't just pretend like you didn't participate - *like you didn't want it, too.*"

His eyes were on fire, but there was nothing warm about his gaze.

"Is this really what you want, right now?" he asked with a strained voice, dropping his backpack onto the ground beside him, his hands resting on his narrow waist. "I've been trying, Blake. I've been trying to stop this as painlessly as possible, but you just. Keep. Pushing. The tree house... then the party... and now, here you are, begging to be fucking crushed."

"No, I'm here because I want you to admit the truth to me," I charged.

"The truth?" he scoffed. "Alright. Let's start with this: do you think I didn't know?"

"I don't understand. Know what?" My forehead scrunched in confusion and my arms folded over my chest.

"Do you think that I don't know about the huge crush you've had on me for basically ever?"

I winced. "N-no... I don't know..."

He stepped closer to me. "Let me walk you through this so that this conversation doesn't have to happen again."

Gulp.

"I've known about your crush; it's been pretty obvious. I kept thinking that as you got older, you'd stop hanging out with us and you'd get over it. But you didn't," he paused, exhaling harshly as he pulled his baseball cap off and ran his hand through his hair. "Then I figured that I'd be moving and you wouldn't have a choice. But then, you hold my prom date hostage in my own—" he broke off, lowering his voice, "—goddamn house. Did you really think I wouldn't know it was you?"

I blinked rapidly trying to coax the tears back into my eyes; only some of them were persuaded. *Stubborn jerks.*

"So then why did you stay?" I asked softly. "I heard you... I felt you. I know you wanted me."

I was like Dory from *Finding Nemo*. Except, instead of swimming, I just *kept pushing*.

"*Christ*, Blake." He let out a harsh laugh. "Let me explain something to you. I'm eighteen years old. My body? It wants to have sex *regardless* of most anything. So yeah, you 'felt' something - but that something wasn't special; *it wasn't for you.*"

I recoiled. I pushed too far and he wasn't going to spare me.

Stupid, Blake. You shouldn't have come here.

"And why did I stay? Because for some screwed-up reason, I thought that maybe if I just got you off, it would get me out of your system."

Tears tracked hotly down my face. I hated him for what he said. I hated him for the lies.

"I d-don't care what you say," I insisted, raising my chin up stubbornly, "I know what I felt and what I felt was real. It's always been real between us, Zach. No matter what you try to tell yourself about that night."

He let out a long, frustrated groan, looking up at the sky before pinning me with a hard stare. I watched him and the battle that was shredding him on the inside. I wished I knew what sides were fighting so I could pick one. Instead, I only got to see which one won.

"Blake, I care about you because you've been like a sister to me for most of my life. I'm sorry if that led to something more for you, but it didn't for me. And even if it did, I'd never in a million years pursue it; Ash would kill me. But this needs to stop. I'm leaving for college and you need to grow up and move on. I'm sorry if what happened led you on, but this... us... is *never* going to happen. *We are never going to be together.*"

Each word was like a bullet to my beaten heart.

He closed the distance between us. My breath came in rapid spurts as I tried to survive his coldness and his closeness.

"Say it," he demanded.

I was trapped. Closing my eyes, I shook my head. I wouldn't - *couldn't.* I had no choice.

"*Say it, baby Blake.*" This time he gripped my chin and

forced me to look at him; he forced me to watch my own heartbreak. *"Say it right now."*

My lip quivered, salty tears leaking into my mouth as the words tasted like acid on my tongue.

"W-we are… never..." I sucked in a sob and he only held my face harder, waiting for the rest of it, "… g-going to be t-together."

I ended with a sob and that only made him angrier. Probably because of the scene I was making on his front lawn.

"Good," he said raggedly, dropping my chin like I was a leper. "Now do whatever you have to do… go write a song about it if that's what it takes to get it through your thick skull."

He stepped around me, walking up the steps. His footsteps stopped, but I didn't turn. With a voice that seemed too soft and too defeated to be the one that would crush my soul, he said over his shoulder, "That night wasn't real, Baby Blake. That night was a mistake."

I was wrong. *So wrong.* He never cared about me. He never wanted me.

All he did was hurt me. If he cared, he wouldn't be doing this.

Screw you, Zach Parker. I don't care if you taught me how to rollerblade or that you took the training wheels off my bike even when Ash said I wasn't ready; I don't care if you helped me with my science homework or always made sure to play 'Happy Birthday' to me on your guitar even when Ash gave you shit for it. I don't care if everyone thinks you are the nice-guy quarterback. You aren't nice – you are a liar.

A redneck, heartbreaker who was really bad at lying.

I *was* going to write a song because the hurt was too much to be contained inside me.

I was going to write a song and then I was going to become famous and forget all about Zach Parker because, *'We were never, ever going to be together.'*

CHAPTER NINE

ZACH

THE PRESS HADN'T SLEPT.

Then again, neither had I.

My phone buzzed on the counter as I poured myself the large cup of coffee that I was going to need to get me through the rest of the day. My temples throbbed as I took a sip of the black liquid. Shit was magic for a hangover but didn't do anything for the ache in my dick.

Last night had been a fucking disaster. The bar. The beach. *Everything.*

Alex was already assed-out by the time I got up to the room. Cold shower and bed was what I needed. Unfortunately, I hadn't been lying when I told Blake that the cold water wasn't how my desire for her worked. I turned that shit to liquid ice and my dick still throbbed just as purple and angrily as when she'd been lying underneath me, all legs and lust, pressing her body up against mine. Touching her breast had been the first hit of a drug that seemed to come from out of this world. All I could think was how easy it would have been to move the lower scrap of her suit over her tight little pussy, unzip my fly, and shove myself inside of her.

And that's exactly what I closed my eyes and thought of as I fisted my harder than steel cock, pumping it two—three times before I came all over the shower wall with a low groan. Yup. Nearing thirty and masturbating like a fucking teenager in the shower to images of the girl I'd grown up with. *Life goals right here.*

Of course, I'd thought about fucking her. I'd thought about fucking her on a regular basis since about the time she turned fifteen and my body told me she was fuckable even though my brain insisted that she wasn't. Sure, it got a lot easier to think of other things when Ash and I moved to Alabama or when I moved back to Nashville. But that's like saying that sometimes it's easier to not focus on breathing. True, but it doesn't change the fact that your body still needs air to survive; it didn't change the fact that my body still needed her.

It didn't change the fact that her brother was still my best friend.

It also didn't change the fact that the more press and popularity ZPP got here, the more sleeping with her would seem no different than any of those other dipshits who'd used her before for her fame.

Guilt… self-loathing… familiar company throughout most of my life, wanting a girl who was at first, a child, but always off-limits in the bro-code.

There are times in life - unavoidable times, really - where in order to be the good guy, you have to be a bad one. I knew how much I hurt her when we were younger - when I told her I didn't want her and that we would never be together. She thought I was ripping through her heart when the truth was that I was carving out my own.

'*Mistake.*'

I was a modern-day Pinocchio with the lies I told her. Only it wasn't my nose that got longer and harder every second that I was in her presence trying to fight the truth about how much I wanted her.

Maybe, I'd told myself back then, *maybe* when I moved back home, if she still had feelings for me, I'd find some way to make Ash ok with it. But the good guy in me wasn't going to take advantage of my friend's little sister. The good guy wasn't going to let my desire take something permanent from her at only fifteen. The good guy in me wasn't going to make promises to her only to leave for four years and expect her to wait. She had so much drive and potential, and the good guy in me knew that she would have put it all on the back burner for a chance at 'us.'

News-fucking-flash. At eighteen, I had no clue what I wanted for my life or my heart. And when I second-guessed football, I second-guessed everything, including my feelings for her. *Christ.* At eighteen the goddamn weatherman had a better chance of predicting what I wanted for my life and we all know how terrible those fuckers are at predicting anything.

Blake Tyler had this funny way about her - an intoxicating blend of incognizant humility. She never really saw just how good she was at something and how much potential she had. Then again, are the stars aware of their own brightness in the dark night?

If we were meant to happen, some time wouldn't make a difference. Of all the options of how the future would play out, this had never been one of them. This life where she was rocketed into a completely different universe and dated guys who were richer than Croesus and looked like they walked out of a Calvin Klein ad…

Everything had changed.

Understatement of my life.

Even just two nights on that stage had increased my respect for her ten-fold. I was a performer; I knew what it took to get out there every night, to put on a smile and a show for fans regardless of personal shit. But the level that she had to do it... *wanted* to do it... *and been doing it* - at was almost nauseating.

For the first time, I saw the toll that it took on her - standing there, in front of the ocean, begging me to let her go in.

You wouldn't fucking think that going to the beach or going for a swim - simple pleasures for most people - would be a big fucking deal. *I hadn't.* That is until your every breath becomes a marketable business transaction. Always being watched and judged for everything she was and everything that she wasn't. The worst part about this whole plan was that fake feelings were the *last* thing I would ever attribute to Blake Tyler - and it was the only thing she stood accused of.

Hell, the damn girl wrote a fucking song and sang it to my face in front of a hundred people because she wanted to show me how real they were.

The world she lived in was beautiful. But like most beautiful things, there was a fucked-up and fickle side that it tried very hard to hide.

So, I let her have her wish - I let her have her real - while I watched from the shore, itching to follow her in, to hold her while the waves rocked us together.

Guilt gnawed at me for how I spoke to her but I'd been so fucking pissed.

I should have pushed her off. I should have stopped it as soon as she tackled me. Or as soon as she kissed me, intoxicating sugar-sweet mixed with the saltiness of the ocean. Hell, I should have stopped it as soon as she began to walk out of the water and I let my eyes drip over her tight, lengthy form, jealous of the water that had the ability to soak right into her. Long legs, the flat plane of her stomach, and then those tits, about to poke a fucking hole through the damn suit, begging to be warmed with my mouth just like the heat of her begged to warm my cock.

I'd sell drugs... *Christ*, I'd sell my goddamn spotless soul to the devil for a taste between her thighs.

But it was the look on her face that got me - the hurricane in those stormy blues; I knew she was coming for me - and I just stood on the beach waiting to be swept away.

I shouldn't have let my desire for her get the better of me... again.

It was my fault that we were there long enough to get caught. But that was only half of it. The other half was the anger imagining just what photos were taken of her and what they revealed. I'd felt a lot of things - a lot of overwhelming things - for Blake up to this point in our lives, but the possessiveness and protectiveness that surged through me was crippling; it had me wanting to charge the boardwalk, grab as many cameras as I could, and throw them all into the ocean along with the necks attached to them. If I hadn't had to shield her, I swear I probably would've done it. If they had put one fucking toe in the sand... My fist flexed around the coffee mug.

My headache had dulled to a distant throb; my dick was just as hard as ever though.

My phone buzzed. All night... all morning... I'd been waiting for this hammer to fall.

Ash was calling.

Nailed.

"Hello?" I answered, but he probably didn't even hear it before he went off.

"*Are you fucking kidding me?*" he yelled. "*I wake up this morning to see you all over my baby sister plastered on every fucking news outlet I come across! What the fuck!*"

I watched how the coffee in my mug rippled as his angry rant vibrated through the phone.

"*I'll fucking kill you.*"

Throwing open my computer, I opened up a browser and began to look at the images of myself gracing every seedy to sincere news website. *Fuck.*

"You done?" I asked when he finally stopped for breath or to see if he'd berated me to death. Probably hoping for the latter.

"Only until you answer."

I cleared my throat. The problem was that I needed a good answer - *and I didn't have one.*

'Just be glad they caught us when they did,' were the words that I had to hold back; I'd been minutes away from fucking his little sister right on the goddamn shore.

I started with the truth - the bar, the 'disguise,' the split-up.

"I knew they were there," I transitioned into the lies, my stomach rolling as I spoke. "I told her to lie... uhh... underneath me, hoping that they wouldn't see a second person. Or at least that they wouldn't be able to see that it was her. They were pretty far away. But they did. And then we didn't want them to think something even worse, so I kissed her." I coughed and ended with, "Because that is the fucking plan, remember? This wasn't my fucking idea. I'm just the one stepping up for ZPP's success. And for your sister's reputation. Unless you don't care about that."

I dumped the rest of the coffee down the drain, my stomach revolting for using Blake against him.

"Yeah, well, looks like a price that you certainly don't mind paying tenfold."

"Whatever, Ash. You know the paparazzi. It's their fucking job to make nothing into something. And if you don't think that they edited and embellished the photos or the story, you're fucking dumb and blind," I countered.

It was the truth. That was their job. Then again, I was looking at the photos and while they'd been edited to make us more visible, if anything, they revealed far less than what was actually happening.

He swore on the other end of the line, taking a moment before he actually spoke to me. "I have to go. I'm at the airport."

"We good?" I asked. The last thing I fucking needed right now was to be at odds with my best friend. Especially when all I could think about was how the hell I was going to make it through the rest of this charade without forcing him to make good on his threats.

"This better be fucking worth it," he replied with a low voice, mirroring my own thoughts. "You touch her for real, though, and I'll fucking kill you."

Click.

Fan-fucking-tastic.

Blake

I WAS LIVING in fifty shades of wrong.

As life happens, you learn to live with pain – mostly of broken hearts – but this… I was asking for it.

I'd gone too far this time.

'ANOTHER FLING FOR BLAKE? The rising star doesn't seem to know how to settle down.'

"I CAN'T DO THIS," I said as soon as Tay walked into the living room.

I saw her step falter in surprise, her eyes widen when she realized I was there.

"W-what? What happened?" she asked with a groan, rubbing her eyes and then her head.

Usually Tay was up well before I was - too many things to

do and not enough time for her organized mess of a mind to do them. Today though, she was struggling and I... well, I'd slept fitfully. Every time I closed my eyes, I was back on the beach, Zach was my sandman taking me further into my dream... until his words turned it into a nightmare.

'It was a mistake.'

"One moment, please," Taylor grumbled, using the Keurig to make herself a coffee before she came and plopped onto the couch next to me. "Ok, what's going on? What happened? I thought you'd be back so much sooner last night. I mean, I just came up here and crashed right away - obviously, those shots did *not* do me any favors." Her stomach grumbled in agreement.

"You're going to kill me," I groaned, my head tipping back against the back edge of the couch.

"What? Why?" Her brow furrowed. "I'm assuming something happened with Zach."

"We ended up on the beach," I began, blowing another bubble in the piece of chewing gum that this morning qualified as breakfast. "And I kissed him."

"Seriously?" she sputtered. "Like for real kissed him or for the cameras?"

I winced. "Well... both." I opened up Facebook on my phone - because, let's face it - everyone was sharing the stories. Handing it to her, I explained as I watched her mouth drop open. "We ended up on the beach and I kissed him for real... and then it ended up on camera."

I watched her eyes scan the headlines, knowing that she was going immediately into damage control mode.

'BLAKE TYLER - A THREE-WEEK break and now she's back on the prowl, this time with her opening act.'

. . .

"PLEASE TELL me it's not that bad," I said softly, pulling my hair back into a messy bun; it hadn't dried right since I'd gone to bed with it wet last night. I felt sand on my scalp in spite of how hard I'd scrubbed to try to get it all out. Just like the memories, I scrubbed and scrubbed and scrubbed, and yet they still lingered in my mind.

"Well…" *Crap.* "It could have been worse."

I blew another bubble, waiting for her to tell me what to do - how we were going to fix it. I took my phone back from her, reading over the painful words again. *How easily they wanted to believe that Zach was just one more notch in my bedpost - and how sensational they thought it was to make it seem like I was incapable of having a real relationship - or real feelings for that matter.*

"Bruce is going to kill me," I groaned, knowing he was going to have a field day with how this turned out.

"Oh, Blake," Tay huffed. "You know the haters are gonna hate."

"Yeah. Hate on me - the player who's just gonna play with all my boytoys." I clicked off the screen, tired of looking at all the eye-catching headlines.

'ZACH PARKER BECOMES Tyler's opening and closing act!'

"JUST SHAKE IT OFF, B and let me handle Bruce," Tay said, reaching out and grabbing my hand. "I want to know what happened - as your *friend,* not as your publicist. You kissed him… and from the looks of these photos, he was definitely kissing you back…"

In a daze, I outlined the events that had transpired the night before.

"What happened?" I repeated. *Foolishness happened.*

Fearlessness happened. I happened. "He did a number on me, but honestly, at this point who's counting?"

She squeezed my fingers and my eyes slid to hers.

"He said it was a mistake, just like before," I ended with a ragged whisper. "I'm such an idiot, thinking that I could do this. I thought it was enough - the time, the space - for me to get over him and my persistent childhood infatuation. Heck, I've dated other guys - *clearly.* How can I still feel this way? How can it still hurt just as much as before?"

She held her cup of coffee out to me. I reached for its warmth and, sticking my gum in the top corner of my cheek, took a sip.

"I don't know, B. I know how you felt about him before. I mean, you grew up with him. This isn't like one of your exes that you knew for maybe a few weeks or a month before you started dating. There's a lot more that's going on and that's rooted so much deeper than you just kissing a guy... it's like Pandora's box. Or, I guess I should say 'Parker's box.'"

I rolled my eyes at her lame but heartwarming levity. *And true.* I'd opened up a whole box of trials and had yet to find out what even half of them were.

She continued, "Time and space don't always make things better. Sometimes, they just give us a reprieve from having to deal with the problem at that moment. Sometimes, they just give us the time to learn and grow to be able to handle the problem when it comes back around."

I nodded and wiped a stray tear from off my face. "I was hoping that it just wouldn't come back around..." I groaned. "It feels like all I've done is remind myself how I haven't learned anything from the first time he broke my heart."

"I don't believe that," she scoffed and gently swatted my arm. "I think that you really haven't seen him in a long time and now, all of a sudden, not only are you on tour with him, seeing him all the time, but you are *publicly* going to be in a relationship with him. That's huge - and a huge reminder of something that you wanted for a long time but never got. Bruce and I may have suggested this as your best - *and possibly only* - option, but that doesn't mean that I thought this was going to be a walk in the park for you."

"What do I do?" I begged her. She always had the answers for everything. All I needed was the answer to this.

"What you know how to do, B. You know how to go on that stage and put on a show. You know how to be yourself for your fans, and right now, that requires you to be the self that wants Zach Parker. It requires you to be the same self that wrote all of these songs about him - the self you channel when you sing them and the self that fades back away when you are done. So, let her indulge. And then let her go."

"How do I not let the lines blur? How do I not get hurt?" My head tipped onto her shoulder as I passed the coffee mug back to her.

"Don't make what happens for the tour become more than it is. This is the second... third... time that he's said this was a mistake. I hate to say it, Blay, but don't be a glutton for punishment. I know the fifteen-year-old-you wants to prove that he wanted you - that he still wants you. But what's that going to cost you to find out? You just can't put yourself in situations where it's easy for the line to get fuzzy - basically any situation that involves you two alone and *without* the cameras."

"It'd be easier if his words matched his actions," I grumbled petulantly.

"We'll keep the contact more structured, more business-like, and planned. Don't worry, B, I got you." Tay hugged me to her side, letting go when her phone began to ring from the other room. "That's probably Bruce. Which means it's time to get up, get yourself together, and show Zach Parker that off that stage, you're no longer the girl whose heart stops for him."

I nodded enthusiastically until she disappeared through

the dining room and back into the bedroom before I let my face fall.

I was afraid it was too late and I didn't want her to hear as I begged my heart to start beating again.

Please, heart, don't turn us into a mistake again.

The saying goes, it's easier to beg for forgiveness than to ask for permission. *Easier for who?* I wondered.

Next time, heart, please ask for my permission before letting Zach break you; you have this depressing habit of tripping and crumbling for him, crawling back to me begging for forgiveness for being so easily fooled.

'Don't blame me,' my heart whispered back, 'love made me crazy.'

I quickly swiped a tear from my cheek.

Please, not again this time.

CHAPTER TEN

BLAKE

Track 08: Jack and Jesus

"I drink you down nice and slow,
Burn my insides like the memory of us.
I'm saying more prayers with you around,
But I can't tell if it's to Jack or Jesus."

THINGS WERE TEETERING. PRECARIOUSLY.

And no, not just my emotions about this whole mess.

People thought big things were hard to move – hard to change. *People were wrong.*

My reputation was big. My reputation was like the Titanic. *The largest ship in the sea.*

'Practically unsinkable.'

Until it wasn't.

'IS THE BLAKE-PARKER PROJECT OVER ALREADY?'

. . .

AFTER LAST WEEKEND IN MIAMI, Bruce insisted that we proceed even more cautiously. *'Too much, too quickly is not believable, Miss Tyler! We. Need. Believable. We. Need. Real.'* I was pretty sure he was having TIAs in between each word as he sputtered them out, dabbing his forehead with the handkerchief that I'd never seen him have to pull from his jacket pocket before.

Fine with me.

I was still hurting - no, reeling - from what had happened between Zach and me. We left the following day for Pittsburgh where the heat from Miami was put on the cooler. Literally. It was freezing in Steel City and I made sure that any conversation - any interaction - with Zach was served on ice.

I smiled and refused to let myself flinch when he gently kissed my cheek for the crowd (who screamed for more). The performance - our performance - was strained and I knew we weren't the only ones who felt it. It was the first time something between us had felt faked.

'Hot and heavy to cold and strained! Another of Blake's boys bites the dust!'

I WANTED to give him a piece of my mind, but I didn't – couldn't – because unfortunately, the only part of me that was currently in pieces to give was my heart. So, for now, silence would have to be my loudest protest. That and the two songs I'd written for my new album, cooped up in my hotel room, and wandering back down a path that left sand in my mind and sadness in my soul.

The press, though, was going crazy. Bi-polar really. But mostly assuming that my date-and-dump habits were still going strong. But there was no going back now.

'Blake Tyler, fast and furious to slow and steady? What is it about Zach Parker?'

TAY MADE me stop checking the quicksand known as social media when I told her that I wasn't going to survive this. Hopefully, at least ZPP would come out whole.

***

"HAPPY BIRTHDAY, RONNIE!" I exclaimed just as Tay and I entered the private area that Ash had reserved in the corner of the Rep Room – a dark and decadent bar downtown. Ron's eyes lit up when he saw us.

I liked Ronnie. I'd say he had the kindest, biggest heart out of all of them. Maybe that's why I was always lulled into conversation with him. I wanted to turn my brother down when he invited us out for celebratory drinks because I didn't want to be around Zach – a feat I'd managed to accomplish for most of the weekend (aside from the being on stage part.) But it wasn't the right thing to do, no matter how Taylor insisted that after a four-hour show followed by a one-hour meet-and-greet, it was ok to say 'no.'

He clicked off his phone and shoved it into his oversized sweatshirt that hung low over pants that looked like they belonged to me. For a country boy, he preferred a slightly more emo look even as the biggest smile crossed his face as he pulled me into a bear hug. "It's your birthday, you should stop working," I teased.

He was always on his phone doing what Tay did for me -

posting, commenting, tagging, and general appraisal of the social network situation.

"I know." He smiled sheepishly and sank back onto the bar stool without reaching for his cell again; I estimated about two minutes before he had it out again and was checking for followers and updates.

"Sis," Ash said and pulled me in for a side hug. "Taylor." His tone slightly harsher to greet her; she barely pulled out a tight smile in response. I was about to ask what the heck was going on, but Alex tugged me to him and began rubbing his fist on my head.

"Seriously!" I groaned.

Ronnie treated me like a friend. But Alex, he and Bobby treated me just like Ash; I might as well have been their sister, too.

"Blake sandwich!" And there was the proof.

Crushed between two men who hadn't played football (but looked like they should have) was just what I wanted to have happen right now. And when I was finally set free, after they had cheered their glasses over my head, I was left to face Zach.

I tried to prepare for this. Black high-waist jeggings, light pink, long-sleeve crop sweater, and tall suede boots. My clothes clung to every length and curve; I wanted to remind him what a *mistake* I was.

Sitting casually at one of the other tables in our corner, my gorgeous country god sat fisting a beer bottle in one hand wearing a Steelers ball cap, his hair peeking out from underneath it. I may have been the famous one, but he was the one who looked like he didn't fit in with his ripped-up jeans and plain tee pulled tight over his muscles as he rested his elbows on the table, perfectly unimpressed with the Rep Room. Not because he thought he was too good for the place, but because he didn't care if they thought it was too good for him. Maybe confidence was what I saw. Assured of who and what he was.

I wanted that.

Every day punched new holes in my self-assurance. I didn't know how much longer that ship had before it sank.

"Baby Blake," he said tightly, eyeing me up and pulling his beer to his mouth. When his full lips closed over the top of the bottle, all I could think about was them closing over me. And my whole body tightened and tingled. His stare glinted with something that I wanted to believe was desire, but could have just been the dim lighting. Still, my nipples hardened against my tight sweater in response.

"Zach." I returned, taking a deep breath, realizing too late that I looked like I was trying to shove my boobs up. Something that I begrudgingly admit to doing many times in the past. *Guilty as charged.*

"Maybe you should put your jacket back on," he said gruffly. "It's cold in here."

I wasn't that cold, but my head ducked down for long enough to see that my tits were about to poke a hole through my shirt. *Forget headlights, my girls had on their high beams.* I quickly crossed my arms over my chest as though that would erase the evidence.

"Does this place serve cake?" I heard Alex ask over the music and crowd that was starting to pick up. "We need to get this kid some cake for his birthday!"

"What flavor you want, Ron?" Bobby's voice boomed. "I'll see what I can do."

"Hey, Blake," I heard Ash's laughing voice and I knew this wasn't going to be good. "Speaking of birthday cake flavors… Remember your fourteenth birthday?"

Nope, this wasn't going to be good.

"Seriously, Ash?" *Why was MY birthday the focus of the night?* Because I was standing with Zach and my brother was still closet-pissed about Miami. There were no cameras and that meant there was no reason for us to interact. I should have been grateful for the interruption, but this was just going to be a humiliation. Another one.

"What? What happened?" Alex asked and Bobby chimed in wanting to know, too.

Taylor shot me a sympathetic look but there was no way she could stop him either.

I could only swallow and stare as my brother revealed yet one more moment in my saga of embarrassed adoration for Zach Parker.

"A week before her birthday, I came downstairs to hear my mom asking what kind of cake she wanted. And you know Blake, she was like, 'Whatever you guys want.' So," he laughed deviously, "I casually mention that Zach is coming over for the family dinner, too, and that he loves key lime pie."

My arms tightened protectively over me like doing so made any difference in stopping this story. Heat rose into my cheeks as Ash continued.

"Wouldn't you know it, dinner rolls around and out comes Key Lime Pie. Now me, I'm dying on the inside as Blake woofs down her slice, at some point asking, with her mouth still full, if Zach is enjoying it. And of course, he's not because Key Lime is disgusting. At that point, I couldn't hold it in. The look on her face - pure confusion until she realized that I'd made the whole thing up."

"Oooo!" Bobby yelled with a lighthearted smile.

"Rookie mistake!" Alex chimed in.

"Whatever." I tried to play it down. It was a stupid prank - the kind of stupid prank that they played on each other all the time and the kind that I'd played on him many times during our childhood, but still; I hated how he always had to bring up stories of all the stupid things I had done because I'd been blinded by the stars in my eyes whenever he was around.

"That's not even the best part," he paused because he was laughing so hard that he had to catch his breath.

"It really is," I interjected. "I think you can stop now."

"C'mon, Blay!" He clapped me on the back and yanked me close. Nope, I wasn't getting any consideration from Ash tonight. "The best part is that, turns out, Blake is allergic to whatever those types of limes are that are used to make it. So that night her face blew up like fuckin' Will Smith in Hitch!"

I rolled my eyes and pulled out of his arms. Walking over towards where Tay and Ronnie were sitting at the perimeter of our little circle at the bar, I flagged the bartender and ordered a Jameson and Ginger Ale. A double.

"You know I'm just teasing you, sis!" I heard him yell to me over the music - and the laughter.

Yeah, I thought, but only to remind Zach how pathetic I was. *Stupid siblings...*

Ignoring him, I spent the next half an hour engrossed in conversation with Ronnie about a new TV show that was based on James Patterson novels - another thing that we had in common. The more the alcohol soaked in, the more my mind could pretend to ignore Zach even if my body couldn't. In fact, it felt like my boobs were locked in a stare-down with him and my sex ached because of it.

I wouldn't say that I was trying to make him jealous because I wasn't actually flirting with Ronnie, but Ronnie was nice and our conversation was comfortable, the way he tried to plot how we could make it onto this TV show as extras. I clung to comfortable like an umbrella in the midst of a hurricane; it wasn't going to be able to save me from the storm, heck, it wasn't even going to keep me dry. But, at least, it felt like I was doing something other than begging to be blown away.

I drank my cocktail quickly enough to take the edge off the situation, but slow enough that it didn't look like I was desperate to get drunk. Slowly but surely, I was able to forget for a moment the mess of emotions that appeared to be permanently tangled.

The next time I looked for Tay, wondering if we should get going, I saw her showing Zach something on her phone and then reaching up to whisper in his ear. There was no reason in the entire world that I had to be jealous, but I was.

Love makes you crazy.

I tore my eyes from them and instead glanced through the curtain that only partially shielded the private room to take stock of the rest of the place. The Rep Room had filled out since we'd arrived. Whether it was just for Ronnie's birthday or because he knew the whole story about Miami, Ash had claimed one of the 'private' rooms at the end of the bar. It was basically just a corner of the space that was semi-shielded from the rest by deep red, sheer curtains. They gave some sense of privacy, but also allowed everyone else to see who was here - which I was sure was great for marketing purposes, judging by all the people who kept snapping photos of me as they walked by.

'Blake Tyler spotted at the Rep Room!' I could see the headlines now. Next week, there wouldn't even be standing room in this place.

Tables that had at first littered the main area were now cleared away leaving a large cushioned seat in the center of the dance floor. I watched as couples filtered to the floor. There was one that mesmerized me - both tall with dark, sultry hair, and Hispanic if I had to guess from their dance skills. 'Despacito' began to play and the way they moved made me feel like I was watching soft porn - but I couldn't look away.

"Blake." I jerked as the shock of his touch on my sleeve exploded through my body. I turned, and from the stony look on Zach's face, realized just how close I'd been leaning next to Ron, both of us trying to look at his phone. "Can I talk to you for a minute?"

I wanted to say no. It was too late, I was too tired, and I'd had too much alcohol.

"Sure."

Typical.

I stood, expecting him to just take a few steps away from the bar, but instead, he began to walk through the curtain. My eyebrows rose in question.

"Let's dance."

My head jerked back to the rest of our group. Ash was watching us but he was also simultaneously in the middle of a heated argument with Taylor - and I had a feeling that it had to do with me.

Swallowing over the dry lump in my throat, I nodded and followed him through the sheer fabric and into the lights.

"Since when do you dance?" I rasped as we weaved through the couples on the floor. Even with the loud music, I could hear the whispers. I saw the looks that they gave me. Some even attempted a photo while they moved.

He stopped just in front of the center seating, melting me with his stare. "Since you needed me to."

I gasped as he pulled me to him and we began to dance.

He was amazing.

I don't know why I thought he'd be anything but. Maybe because I'd never seen him dance. With an ease and agility that I'd only seen on the football field, his body moved against mine and all the alcohol I drank now backfired on me as the heat in my body rose and all the reasons that I was angry at him fell away.

"Were you really allergic to the pie?" he asked softly.

I shuddered and averted my gaze. "Yeah," I answered quietly, keeping my head tilted to the side, trying to look at anyone else but him. "You know me. When I set out to do something embarrassing, I never half-ass it."

His chest rumbled against me as he laughed.

"Just ignore Ash. You know how he is."

I nodded, speechless.

Was he being nice to me? Why was he being nice to me?

Was my brokenness really that obvious?

"For future reference," he leaned in conspiratorially, "my favorite kind of cake is carrot cake." He pulled back to find my eyes again. "Just like yours."

My breath caught. *Don't read into it, Blake.*

Licking my lips, I began, "W-what do you want—" My question was broken off with a surprised inhale as he tugged my body flush against his. I knew it was because of the crowd on the floor and he was moving me out of the way, but it was still no less of a shock to my body. "—to talk about?"

We swayed gently and perfectly in sync. From the outside, it looked calm. Between us though, there was a war being fought in the stillness. His body was impossibly hard against mine. My clothing, that had been chosen for a specific purpose, now betraying me as my nipples hardened. They would have stood out against my thin sweater if my breasts – that were heavy and aching – weren't smashed against his chest. And my jeggings? The thin fabric let me feel every dip and ridge of his body where it was pressed against me. I was surprised he gripped my hips so tightly, knowing that I could feel every inch of his cock thickening.

"Miami." As if our proximity wasn't enough to lure me back to the beach. Memories of that night flooded back - along with the same reaction from my body flooding into my underwear. The heat. The neediness. The desperate plea for release. *All there.* This time, though, when I pressed my hips against him to feel more, he couldn't stop me.

"I heard what you said. We don't have to talk about it," I replied as I licked my lips. They felt chapped, but really they just craved his kiss.

"I'm sorry for what I said."

My feet stumbled at his words. Thankfully, he was holding me so tight that it didn't matter.

"I mean, it was the truth," he continued with a tight rasp.

Why did I even bother to get my hopes up for that split-second? "But I'm sorry for how I said it."

Everything felt fuzzy. Wow, that drink was strong.

Warm and fuzzy.

But not in the cute way. Warm and fuzzy in the way that something was building inside of me, steadily crossing the line from comfortable to uncomfortable. A constant pressure made worse because I could feel it building, instead of it just overtaking me all at once. A slow torture of touch.

"You don't usually apologize to me," I said shakily. "W-what did Taylor say?"

Our skill didn't match that couple who was still somewhere on the dance floor, yet our bodies moved together in the same way that said, in our minds, there were no clothes between us and no people around us.

His forehead dropped to mine. *Burning.* The alcohol. The music. Him. A recipe that baked a release inside each one of my cells. Every brush, every rub, gave my body more of what it was begging for. Good thing my leggings were black because I was soaking through my underwear and they were next in line to be drenched.

My eyes drifted shut, feeling the way his hardening cock began to arch against me. Lost in pleasure. *Lost in him.* My hips rolled against his erection with a mind of their own, needing more but more was always too much.

With a curse, he spun me so that my back was now to him, my ass cradling his hard ridge. One of his hands stayed splayed on my stomach, his thumb inching closer and closer to the underside of my breast. His other hand gripped my waist, attempting to hold my hips steady. Distracted, those fingers teased their way underneath the waistband of my pants.

My head tipped back, savoring each moment that he was touching me. I wanted him to answer my question. I also wanted him to ignore it so that this dangerous dance wouldn't end.

Then an unfamiliar body pressed against my front and my eyes shot open as I gasped. All the desire that had been building in my body now rushed from it like a dam bursting. The moment was broken.

"Any chance I can grab a dance with Blake Tyler?" The drunk, frat guy slurred. Beer in one hand, his other reached for my waist, but was stopped short as Zach grabbed it and twisted it to the side until the man's face contorted with delayed pain.

"Not tonight, buddy."

I was afraid this was going to be like Miami all over again. *I hated this.* I hated how I couldn't just have one moment in public without *crazy* happening.

I saw Andrew begin to move towards the floor. If this guy didn't listen to Zach, Andrew would have him outside, on his ass, and banned from the bar in five minutes flat. Thankfully, the drunk guy backed away with his hands up. "Alright." He shook his head, causing some of his beer to slosh over the side and onto the floor. "Sorry. T-they darrred me," he slurred, looking to the side where his buddies were. "Whateverrr. Y-you're fucking broken anyway," he grumbled and stumbled as he made his way back to his group of snickering friends by the bar. Harmless drunk.

"C'mon, Blake! Let him be the inspiration for your next break-up song!"

"Parker's only going to be good for so many!"

Zach's body turned to granite against me as their words and laughter echoed over the music, heads beginning to turn our way. I winced before I could catch myself. Sticks and stones, they say… But what about words that cut sharper than a knife?

Broken.

Broken Blake.

He spun me back to him, cupping my face. "Don't listen to them. They don't know anything."

"I'm not," I said quickly. Too quickly.

"I know when you're lying, Blay."

"I'm fine. They... have a right to say what they want." And they did. And maybe they had a point.

His jaw clenched. "No, they don't. How can you fucking say that after what that piece of shit just said? It's *me*, Blake. You can rant. You can rage. You can be angry with me."

"I can't be angry!" The words came out more forcefully than I realized. My head darted side-to-side to make sure I wasn't causing more of a scene. "I can't be angry because they are right. I used those break-ups... for inspiration. For lyrics. It's true."

"Blake, that's what we do. We use life. We use our happy and we use our hurts to make something beautiful. Those shitheads have no clue who you are; all they know are the headlines. Your fans – your *Babes* – they know you. They know that what you write comes from all of life: the pieces that ripped you apart and the people that put you back together."

I stared, no longer able to move or speak voluntarily as his words mesmerized me. The way he spoke as he swayed our bodies was hypnotizing, tempting me with what I was afraid to believe.

"Maybe I am broken." The confession mumbled from my lips. With the music, there was no way he could hear what I said and yet somehow, he still knew.

"*Christ.*" His eyes pinned mine. "*You are not broken.*"

I nodded, but trying to swallow down my embarrassment was like trying to force a watermelon down my throat. *Not pretty.*

"But you still don't want me..." Always pushing. The moment was broken anyway.

His mouth thinned, intent on ignoring my accusation. That was the thing about Zach. There were consequences... lines that couldn't be crossed... for those that hurt me. Only, they didn't apply to him.

"You asked for my help, Baby Blake. I'm not going to let you ruin it."

My brow furrowed in confusion as I stared up into his smoldering, golden eyes. Someone bumped into me from behind - the couple that I'd been watching - and shoved me harder against him.

"How am I ruining it?" *Besides by being detrimentally attracted to him?*

"Christ," he swore, locking his arms protectively around me. "You're drunk and you were hanging off of Ronnie. People were starting to notice. If you thought being caught in Miami was bad, imagine the news tomorrow that you've decided to date through every member of the Zach Parker Project."

I froze as I processed his words. Blinking back through snapshots of the night, I knew he was right. I hadn't been thinking.

Why was I never thinking?

One nod turned into several frantic ones and I heard him swear low under his breath. His fingers lifted my chin and I tried to stop my lip from quivering.

He bent his head close to mine. "Blay," he said softly, the word tickling my cheek. "It's going to be ok, ok?"

I licked my lips. "Ok…"

I could have sworn that I heard a growl escape him, but with the music I couldn't be sure. "This is the part where they watch us make up, alright?"

It took a second to register what he said, but then I understood what he was doing. The dance. The apology. It was still all part of the show.

But how did I reconcile the words that came from his mouth with the way his body felt against mine?

"Yeah…" I agreed softly, wondering if he could feel my heart pounding out of my chest. It was trying to make a break for it; I didn't blame it.

He gave me a soft smile - the kind that made my stomach flip - and when his thumb brushed over my lower lip, I realized that he was waiting for me to do the same. Tipping the corners of my mouth up, I nodded slightly into his hand as though I were forgiving him. The moment felt drawn out as I was dimly aware of the variety of cameras, their flashes blending in with the lights from the DJ.

I expected that to be it. I expected him to pull me back to our friends in the corner just like I'd expected him to not be a good dancer.

I expected wrong.

His eyes stayed locked with mine as his lips drifted down - like he'd been trying to keep them afloat for as long as possible. *But you can't tread water forever.*

I didn't breathe until his mouth touched mine, afraid that even just an exhale would push him away. Gently his lips molded to mine. The tip of the iceberg. Only ten percent of the desire that lay beneath the surface.

My body ground against his – and he let it. The desire that had disappeared now returned with a vengeance. But trying to fulfill it was like knocking politely on the door to get into Fort Knox. *No, I would need more weapons than I had right now (or maybe ever) if I was going to break inside of him.*

He kissed me like he rejected me: with practiced ease. *And because he needed to.*

I whimpered when he pulled back.

"Why did you do that?" I begged. He didn't answer me and I followed his eyes to where Tay stood holding my jacket, awkwardly waiting for our moment to end.

He leaned towards her and I heard him say, "She's drunk."

"I am—"

Tay shoved my jacket at me and rolled her eyes at my half-hearted (and slightly slurred) protest. "Yeah, ok, B." She laughed. "I called for the car. Let's get you back to the hotel."

I grumbled as I shoved my arms into my jacket, about to turn and follow her when Zach grabbed my arm. My breath sputtered in surprise when I found his face so temptingly close to mine again.

"Text me so I know you got back ok," he growled, looking around to all of the people watching us.

This wasn't anything like the mob in Miami. Heck, I was walking maybe fifty feet to the car outside, but he stared at me like he was this close to carrying me back to my room himself to make sure I made it there ok.

Protective. Just like a brother, I tried to rationalize.

The warm tingles that gleefully skipped up my spine reminded me that 'rational' and 'Zach Parker' were mutually exclusive.

CHAPTER ELEVEN

BLAKE

Track 09: Sweet Dreams

"I see you. I touch you. I taste you.
Nothing is what it seems.
I want you. You're here. You're mine.
Not even in my sweetest dreams."

I TURNED OVER AGAIN, GROANING LOUDLY INTO MY PILLOW — A process that had now been repeated several times.

Maybe I should try reading again. Or writing new lyrics.

Something.

Anything.

Because lying here, all I focused on was that I couldn't sleep. And I couldn't sleep because of how much I wanted Zach.

I texted him as soon as I walked in the door. Just like he told me to. I also may have asked if he'd made it back ok, too… Not because I was desperate to hold on to whatever had been happening on the dance floor. Of course not. *Superstars don't get desperate.*

A few minutes ago, I saw that he'd finally *read* the text message but still hadn't responded.

So why wasn't he answering?

Maybe something happened.

To a group of five guys, four of whom were or looked like they should have been football players?

It was possible, I argued with myself.

And drunk me was always right.

Or at least she was quicker than rational me, pushing the 'Call' button before I could stop myself.

One ring.

Two.

I clenched my teeth. *He* was the one who told me to text and now, he couldn't even freaking bother to—

"What's wrong?" Zach's deep voice rasped over the phone.

"I... Ahh... Nothing," I sputtered. "I just... I texted you, but you didn't respond."

There was a beat of silence before he spoke again. "You should be sleeping."

"I can't," I whispered honestly.

"Why not?"

I didn't answer. I wasn't ready to admit why I was so restless. I wasn't ready to confess that my entire body still hummed with the thought of his pressed against it. The fire that was lit on the dance floor still kindled through me, sparking and arcing for release.

"You're a good dancer," I said, completely ignoring his question and trying to ignore the ache between my legs.

Silence.

He cleared his throat. "Why can't you sleep, Baby Blake?"

My legs squeezed together begging me to keep my mouth just as shut.

"Because you touched me."

I heard a muffled curse. I was afraid of what might come

next, but I was also excited. There was a danger in telling him something that I shouldn't and that made me hotter. He deserved to hear what he did to me. Especially since I felt what I'd done to him.

"And?"

He was going to make me say it. *Whatever.* I wore embarrassment so well when I was around him.

"And now it aches... I ache. I can't stop thinking about the beach... and if they hadn't found us."

Now, he really did swear.

"Blake..." His voice was so hoarse I wouldn't be surprised if it was rubbing my ear drum raw as he spoke. "I told you that the beach... I made a mistake."

He didn't say it as coldly or as cruelly this time. He said it as though the fact tortured him. *It didn't make it hurt any less, though.*

"I know. But you're not here," I responded. "You can't touch me through the phone. You can't... make a mistake."

Silence.

There was so much silence I thought he'd hung up and I was too drunk and delusional to hear the beeps from the line going dead.

"Are your tits hard like they were earlier for me?"

My eyes widened. *What?* Had... Did he just... Was I dreaming?

"*Are they?*" The hard voice said again.

If it was a dream, it was certainly persistent.

My hand drifted to my right breast even though I didn't need to feel to know that they were.

"I-I was cold."

His deep chuckle echoed through the line. "Baby Blake is a little liar."

My breath rushed out of me.

"You want me to make you feel better? Is that why you called me, Baby Blake?" he growled. "All that dancing made you hot and achy and now you want me to fix it *like it didn't do the same thing to me.*"

I gulped. He was angry. Always angry to hear how I wanted him.

"Yes." It was barely a whisper.

Silence.

My hand still at my breast, I toyed with my nipple like it was a pen I was clicking out of nervousness, each flick causing my legs to squeeze together even tighter.

"Are you wet for me, Blake?" Dream Zach asked.

No Baby. Just Blake. *And pure need.*

Fire licked through my veins because I knew the answer. The heat between my thighs hadn't dulled since I'd left the bar; the alcohol kept it in my system. I shifted in the bed again as my hand slid down to rest on my stomach that was rapidly rising and falling.

"Answer me and I'll make it better," he demanded.

A soft cry escaped me before my tongue mumbled thickly, "Y-yes."

Harsh breaths were the response.

"Touch yourself, Blake." I froze at the command. "Put those fingers of yours down your panties and touch yourself. I want to know just how wet."

I stared up at the ceiling that seemed like it was a million miles away as my fingers crawled beneath my pajama shorts and the elastic of my underwear. I sucked in a quick breath as I slid over the sensitive nub at the top of my slit.

"*How wet?*" he asked again with a low voice.

Would slip-n-slide be an inappropriate answer right now?

I groaned because it was the only thing I could think of.

"Very."

He let out a harsh laugh. "You can do better than that. Tell me how wet."

Well, he asked for it.

I bit back a moan as I pressed my fingers against my slit,

trying ease the throbbing. "W-wet like a slip-n-slide. At a waterpark." His tortured groan made my core spasm and beg for more. "In the middle of a hurricane."

"*Jesus fucking Christ,*" he swore vehemently. "You know how you strum your guitar, Baby Blake? The way your fingers pluck hard over each goddamn note?" *Oh god...* "Well, that's what I want you to do for me right now. I want you to flick over that sweet little clit of yours until it hums."

I moaned. The kind of moan that escapes when it's the dead of winter and you take a sip of hot chocolate that burns your whole mouth yet heats every cell in your body. I was hot and burning as I did what he said. My fingers moved slowly just at first, but then rapidly picked up speed as my body found the path to what it was searching for.

"Stop." The force of his tone jarred me. His voice changed from pissed off and cruel to desperate and demanding.

"*Zach...*" I cried out as my fingers obeyed him.

"Push one finger in. Slowly. Very fucking slowly, Blake." I did as I was told, one finger slipping down from my buzzing clit to my entrance and pushing into myself. "Now you're going to fuck yourself, *Blay,* but not enough to make you come. Because this is how I feel all the damn time around you: close enough to be tortured."

"I-I don't want to torture you," I gasped. "I just want you."

"Fuck." I heard him grunt harder. "Take it out and suck on it."

"W-what?"

"Just—" I heard him suck in a harsh breath, "for once, do what I'm asking you to do, Baby Blake." A million memories of disobedient disasters laced his words.

I did what he asked, but only because I wanted to hear more. Hearing him so close to losing control was as close as

I'd ever come to knowing that Zach Parker had lost anything because of me.

My finger popped out of my mouth and his exhale rushed into the phone.

"That taste should have been mine. Just like everything else about you…" The way he said it, the way need and regret sliced through every word, make me shake. I was forbidden. To him, at least. People said I was damaged. Delicate. Complicated.

They weren't wrong.

Still, he wanted me.

"Three fingers," he ordered. I complied, spreading myself wide with three fingers, the stretch sharp and delicious at the same time. Biting down on my lip, my back arched as I began to slide my fingers in and out, letting my thumb brush over my clit with every penetration.

In between the long spans of incoherent inebriation, where it took all I had to focus on moving my fingers faster and harder towards release, I heard him telling me not to stop, to keep moaning, and that hearing me was like music to his ears. I also heard the hard and heavy grunts and I wondered if he was pleasuring himself, too.

I whimpered. I was closing in on my orgasm and all I wanted to do was chase it. Hunt it. Overtake it. My breath caught as my hand picked up the pace, my fingers finding a rhythm that would carry me all the way.

"*Christ, Blay,*" he growled into my ear. The phone vibrated against my face, my hand was shaking so badly. *He was pleasuring himself.* "You know how bad my dick wants to be inside you? How bad I want to claim you when the world acts like you belong to them?" My lungs weren't functioning. "That's all I think about, Baby Blake. Marking you. Making you mine. Feeling the way that sweet little pussy of yours sings around my cock."

The words were ripped from him like they ripped my

orgasm from me. I convulsed, crying out into my pillow as I felt my body flex around my fingers. Vaguely, I heard a groan come from my phone that had fallen beside me.

All the tension, all the tightness, drained from my body and I could breathe again.

"Zach..." I whispered his name, tapping on the speakerphone button because I didn't trust myself to hold the phone.

Silence.

And then, "Go to sleep, Blake."

In the morning I'd wonder if this was real... and not just one more of my wildest dreams.

Zach

I WAS A FUCKING IDIOT. Christ.

One fucking night and yeah, I could pat myself on the back all I wanted for not touching her like I promised, but that was like making it to a party on time only because I'd run every goddamn stoplight in town. I'd made it, but I'd still broken the law.

I punched the elevator button again, impatient for the damn thing to get back to the lobby.

I'd woken up over an hour ago and after showering off what was left of my jerk-off session from last night, I'd trekked downstairs in search of some strong, black coffee with a side of renewed determination to keep Blake and me strictly business.

I prayed she was too drunk and too tired to remember what I'd told her to do.

143

Slip-n-slide.

I gulped down another sip of coffee letting it burn the hell out of my tongue.

The chime went off just as the doors opened and Taylor came crashing into me.

"Crap!" She dropped her phone and the notepad she'd been staring at. "Sorry, Zach. I-I didn't see you." She bent down to pick up her stuff and spilled more shit from the huge bag she was carrying. "*Shit.*"

I bent down and helped her scoop up the mess. "You alright? You look a little…"

"…Frazzled?" she finished for me with a laugh.

I nodded and shrugged my shoulders.

"Just trying to get everything ready to leave and apparently there was a miscommunication at the hotel in New York about what time we are getting there. And then, she has a whole day free that I have a million people clamoring to schedule up for photos and interviews. The press is up my ass about you two last night - which is good because at least it's not about her talking to Ron - but then I also have Bruce on my ass about scheduling this interview for Blake in Texas—" she barely stopped to gasp in air, before continuing, "And to top it all off, Blake is hungover with a headache from hell, so I'm down here trying to find some Advil or something to help her because she's crawled up in bed, practically in tears. There's no way she can get on the plane like this—"

She broke off because my hands gripped her shoulders and shook her back to the moment because the damn girl looked like she'd lost her mind and her mouth was trying to talk its way into finding it.

"Breathe, Taylor." She blinked up at me, remembering where she was and who she was talking to.

"Sorry, I—"

"Don't apologize," I insisted with a sigh. *Don't do it, Parker.*

Don't fucking do it. "Look. Why don't you do what you have to do and you let me take care of Blake?"

Congratulations to me. I'd just gone from plain horny idiot to certifiable fucking moron.

Even the words leaving my mouth sparked an impossible want

Her eyes widened. "Are you sure?"

I nodded again.

"I... ahh... ok. Thank you." She gave me a small smile and, as much as it was going to kill me to be in the room with Blake after last night, I was glad I offered. "Here's her key. I'll just text her and let her know..."

"No. Just let me handle her, you've got enough going on."

With another mumbled 'thank you' and apology, she took off, on the phone a few seconds later dealing with the first fire on her plate.

***

I DIDN'T KNOCK because I didn't want her to feel like she had to move or worse, wake her if she was sleeping.

Letting myself in, I made for the bedroom.

"Tay?" I heard her strained voice rasp from the room that was shuttered in darkness.

I stood for a moment, waiting for my eyes to adjust to the darkness as I closed the door behind me.

"It's me, Blake," I said quietly.

"Zach?" I heard the rustling of the covers before the nightstand lamp flicked on which was immediately followed by Blake doubling over in the bed, trying to hide from the light. Judging from her cry, it sounded like a hundred knives just stabbed her in the head.

"*Christ,* Blay." Three steps had me by the side of the bed and flicking off the torture device.

Even in the dark, I could see the way she clutched her head, slowly rocking herself. Ripping open the bottle, I dumped four pills into my hand, unscrewed the water bottle with the other, and nudged her shoulder.

"Take these."

She didn't question. She reached for my hands and I gritted my teeth as her touch set my body on fire, knowing where those fingers had been touching last night at my command. I wondered which one had gone in her mouth.

"Thank you," she groaned and sank back down into the bed.

I hated seeing her suffer. And when I had to be the cause, I hated it even more.

And, striving to be the best fucking tortured moron I could be, I walked around to the other side of the bed and slid in next to her.

"What…" she rasped, breaking off as I pulled her soft, warm body against mine. "What are you doing?" Her breath moved unsteadily, just like my heart. "Are you here to yell at me?"

"Yell at you? For what?" I demanded gruffly, continuing before she had a chance to respond. "I'm not here to yell at you, especially not when you are like this."

"What happened last night?"

"Blake…" I trailed off. This was the last thing I wanted to talk about so close to her – and the last thing her head needed.

"Tell me why, Zach," she begged.

My walls, my resistance were being worn down. No. Not worn. Ripped down with violent, determined strokes. I clung to what was left, willing it to be enough. "How long will it take you to learn not to ask questions you don't want the answers to?" I replied gruffly, adding, "Alcohol. That's why."

Alcohol was a good excuse for many things; it was also the wrong one.

"How long will you lie to me?" Her voice was even softer than before. Barely a thread. But it was made out of steel, hard and glinting with the truth.

It was a good thing her eyes were shut and she couldn't see my face. I had enough left in me to create words that were untrue; I didn't have enough left to fake a callous expression to match.

"For as long as it takes for you to believe it." Her body tensed against me. Ever fearless, I sensed as she prepared to fight.

"I'm not here to yell. For once could you—" I broke off, realizing I was about to repeat words that I'd said last night. "Just relax, Blake." This morning wasn't about fighting; it would only make her feel worse and I didn't think either of us could stand that.

Her head insisting that she was in too much pain to argue, she slumped against my chest and I heard her breathing begin to steady.

"Where does it hurt?"

"Head. Everywhere." She shivered and my arm that was around her tightened. *Along with the extremity in my pants.*

Bed. Blake. *Fuck.* There were so many things I'd envisioned around those two words, especially recently. It took me a minute before I could move - or respond - before I made another mistake.

That's how bad it was; she was hungover to the point of migraines and all I wanted to do was strip her down and fuck her until her body felt like it was going to explode for a whole different reason.

But I also wanted to hold her and care for her and take her pain away. *Jekyll and Hyde had nothing on me right now.*

Gently, my fingers trailed up the velvet skin of her arm before moving to the back of her neck. My other hand rose to the top of her head and, at the same time, I began to rub slow circles in both spots, ignoring, with every stroke, the way her body fit perfectly against mine. *The perfect harmony.*

"*Zach...*" she groaned my name and I couldn't stop my hips from shifting underneath her; my name from her lips sounding dangerously close to how it had last night. "That feels... so good..."

"Shh," I said softly, for my sake just as much as hers. "Just let me do this."

Whether she actually listened to me for once or just fell asleep, her breaths turned shallow and her soft curves pressed deeper against me.

I continued to rub her head and neck. I should really get up and leave. I wouldn't though. She felt too good – too right. This was one moment where I didn't have to fight against how I felt – *how right this felt.* Where I didn't have to single-handedly hold up all the walls between us.

This was my goddamn problem.

She thought she'd had me with this stupid arrangement. She thought if the fame wasn't enough, it would be the guilt eating away at me for turning down someone in need who I'd been close to.

Bullshit.

All of it.

I said 'yes' for this moment. I said 'yes' for all these moments - all these *mistakes* - that put me here with her. Because, for a reason I was unwilling to admit to, she was one mistake that I would never learn from. And when it was over – when she was gone – I'd still tell myself that the high was worth the pain.

I tensed when I heard a knock on the door. I had no idea how long we'd been lying there, but apparently our time was up. I assumed it was Taylor, finally finished with her million-and-one to-dos. I wanted to hate her for pulling me from

Blake. *I wanted to hold her forever;* but I should probably be thanking Taylor instead.

Gently shifting her to the bed, I slipped out of it and quietly left the room. Like a starving man forced to walk away from a feast, I took one last regret-laden look at her dark, curled up mass.

I pulled open the door, but it wasn't Taylor waiting on the other side.

"What the fuck are you doing here?"

Ash.

Best friend or not, his casual expression had flipped to explosive anger in the space of a second. He'd kill me - or at least try - if he could read my thoughts. It was a good thing that no matter how long a friendship has gone on, it still didn't guarantee mind-reading capabilities.

"Bringing meds and water to your sister."

He was still tense, like the barest thread was holding him back from letting go. "Why?"

I did my best to meet his stone-cold stare. "I ran into Taylor who was about to have a meltdown in the lobby with all the shit she has to do and she told me Blake didn't make it out unscathed from last night. So, I offered to grab some Advil and bring it up to her."

Not untrue.

He gave me one last hard look like it could break through to what I wasn't saying before he pushed past me into the room.

"Where is she?"

"Sleeping." I nodded to the bedroom.

"Did you go in there?" he demanded.

"Of course, I did. I brought the shit in and made sure that she took some so that her head didn't explode."

He still stared. Maybe he could know what I was thinking. Maybe he did know that the promise that I'd made to not touch her was shaping up to be the only one I'd ever break. *Right after it broke me.*

His shoulders dropped with a loud sigh. "Shit. Sorry." And just as quickly as the anger came, it was gone. "I know. I know you wouldn't... that you're not... It's just so fucking hard to see you two plastered all over the goddamn internet and *not* think that something is really going on."

I didn't say anything because I couldn't. I couldn't add another lie.

"Sometimes, I just want to wring the necks of those shitheads that work for the tabloids." He let out a grating laugh. "Sorry, man. Ronnie asked me to check something on our Instagram and I log in to a feed of photos from you two dancing last night. And then you opened the door... Just fucked with my head there for a minute. Thought you'd been here all night."

I choked and made a weak attempt to turn it into a laugh. *Fuck.*

Clearing my throat, I responded lamely, "Yeah. Well, Taylor saw a bunch of people taking photos of Baby Blake and Ronnie talking. She probably doesn't even remember, but—"

"Yeah," he cut me off with a nod. "I know. It would have been bad. I already got an earful from her this morning."

I believed it. Taylor was in rare form today. Then again, she always seemed to be in rare form around Ash. I pulled my hat off and ran a hand through my hair. Guilt was squeezing my chest and if I stayed any longer I was sure Ash would start to hear my ribs crack.

"Alright. I'm gonna go finish packing."

"Yeah, I should too. I just wanted to check on her." He stepped toward the bedroom door before turning back to me and adding with a voice that, after almost twenty-five years, I knew was still laced with a threat, "Sorry about earlier. I know you'd never actually touch her if it wasn't for this."

My head jerked towards the door and I hoped it looked like a fucking nod because it was all I had.

Once in the elevator, my fist slammed into the wall. *Fucking fuck.*

What the *hell* was I doing? *What the hell had I done?*

I closed my eyes because her face stared at me on the poster that was plastered on the inside of the doors. It didn't make a difference. She was plastered in my mind, too. *Ubiquitous.* Doubts trickled through my blood. *Was resisting her worth it?* Her smile. Her song. The way she moaned my name as she came.

At this point, was resisting her even possible?

I was starting to see the hard truth that it wasn't and I had no idea what the fuck I was going to do.

And certain parts of me had far too many suggestions.

CHAPTER TWELVE

BLAKE

Track 10: Even Keel
"I try to stay steady,
I try to stay stable.
But you crush me like a hurricane."

I AGED TWO YEARS IN THOSE FEW DAYS SINCE WESTERN Pennsylvania when my heart had been patched together all wonky. Like an engine that kept turning over, Zach managed to keep me both at arm's length yet right on the brink of letting whatever was between us roar to life.

There was still uneasiness between us, but the way he held me that morning brought us to an unsteady truce – one that would be easily toppled by any further mention of what happened after we left the Rep Room.

I grabbed a shower right after we checked into our hotel and collapsed onto the bed, towel still wrapped around my hair, and half-asleep even though it was only eight o'clock.

"You better still be awake," Tay admonished, grabbing her

toiletry bag and disappeared back into the bathroom. "I have to talk to you about this weekend. About Zach."

Ugh. No. The last thing I needed was more incentive to have him show up in my dreams.

"Not now," I mumbled against the pillow that I'd already started to drool on. "I'm sleeping."

"Well, then consider this me talking to you in your dreams," she retorted.

"I believe that's called a nightmare," I shot back, smiling as I heard her chuckle.

Too early for bed. Prying my eyes back open, I pushed myself up as Tay walked back into the room with her business face on and the news of what my 'day off' had turned into.

"You know this has to move forward at some point and tomorrow is the perfect opportunity." Her arms folded over her chest like the stern schoolmistress that she was.

I groaned.

"Don't give me that. Things seem to be better after last weekend, right?"

We were in the Big Apple for an extra day before the two scheduled shows - *an extra day that happened to be the day before Valentine's Day.* And apparently, it went without question (at least in Bruce's mind) that it would be a necessary opportunity for Zach and me to be seen out and around the city doing couple-like activities.

"The *whole* day?" I clarified, trying to swallow my apprehensive gasp. I had to stifle my desire to *push...* my desire for him... *for a whole day?* She better be packing extra underwear in my purse for that.

This Valentine's Day was just one giant reminder of all my failed relationships. Spending a whole day with Zach, taunted by how much I wanted him, was bad enough. The fact that it was on Valentine's Day weekend was like rubbing salt in the open would of my heart. Sharp. Painful. I wish I could at least say that it would cleanse it and help it heal, but I knew it wouldn't.

"Blay..." she drawled, giving me the 'you-need-to-do-this' eye. "All in public. All for the cameras. And you'll be all bundled up in the cold - not in some skimpy bikini taking 'Sex on the Beach' way too literally."

"Jerk!" I tossed a pillow at my *best* friend as she disappeared into the bathroom of our suite bowling over with laughter.

At least I was laughing about it now.

I fell back onto the bed. I just wanted to sleep in all day, curled up with my Kindle, and live in a different world - because the two that I was straddling were promising to drive me crazy. But no, it looked like I was waking up to go on a full-on date day with Mr. Heartbreaker himself.

"And he knows about this?" I yelled to her. "That he has to spend Valentine's Day with me? The mother of all relationship-affirming days? Can't we just snap a few staged photos and post them on Instagram?"

Christmas would come quicker than Tay finishing her nighttime facial regimen and I wasn't going to wait for either to come around before finding out.

"Bruce talked to him before he called me. And then I called him to make sure everyone was on the same page. So, yes, he knows and no, we cannot just take photos and pretend like something happened."

Dang. Worth a shot.

"How'd you know I would agree?" I asked, curling into my pillow. "Maybe I already have a date..."

"Nice try, B, but James Patterson is busy tomorrow. I checked. And you've already agreed to this so you don't have a choice." *Alright, valid point.* "Plus, you can't lie to me. I know the part of you that wants to fall for Zach all over again is going crazy for the next step in this charade."

"I thought I was supposed to keep her contained?" I

asked, opening Instagram and scrolling through the fan photos from Pittsburgh, trying to like and comment on as many as I could before I got too tired.

God, it seemed like every picture was of Zach and me dancing at the Rep Room – like a concert hadn't even happened.

"Not in front of the cameras," she returned sweetly. "In front of the cameras, you can listen to the little Bad Blake on your shoulder."

She wasn't on my shoulder though; she was in my head, reminding me of Zach's mouth on mine, the desperate and raw need in his voice when he told me to taste myself, when he confessed to wanting to be inside me when I screamed his name. And she insisted that no matter what words were said, actions make liars out of us all.

"Plus, Zach told me that he was going to take care of the whole day and that he didn't want me to schedule anything. He wouldn't even tell me what his ideas were… which has obviously been really intriguing to me." *I bet it was.* "I mean, it's New York City and all so there is a ton to do, but he seemed like a man with a plan. So, you have to agree for no other reason than I want to know just what he comes up with…"

"Why do I feel like I'm the guinea pig here and you're just itching to see what this whole reputation experiment does to me?"

"Oh, please. Prom King. Football quarterback." She was ticking off all his qualifications on her fingers as she spoke. "Hottest sweetheart within a fifty-mile radius of Franklin, Tennessee. And - according to a verified source - *the best kisser in the world.*" My eyes narrowed as she threw my confession back at me. "I'd have to say that *you're* the lucky one, so you'll have to excuse me if I don't RSVP to this pity party of yours."

I burst out laughing, tossing another pillow at her which she just barely avoided with a shriek.

She wasn't wrong, I thought.

Still.

A Valentine's Day planned by and spent with Zach…

Welcome to New York.

***

"Coffee?"

Maybe it was the fact that I was pretty tired *and* needed coffee, but Zach's southern drawl seemed even thicker than usual. That combined with the way he was leaning his shoulder against the wall in the lobby waiting for me to come down, arms crossed, parka unzipped, henley tucked front and center into his jeans - it all turned my body to mush. *Not a good sign.*

He was flawless. All the time.

Really explained why I struggled to stop myself from falling.

Five minutes into the date day and I was already wondering what possible private places there were where I could try to dry-hump him out of my system. Again.

I fully admit that it was a pathetic goal but Bad Blake liked to set low, relatively achievable standards for herself.

"You could have slept in for longer, Blay," he said with a warm half-smile that was oddly reminiscent of easier times - times when I loved him and he pretended he didn't know.

I shook my head slightly. "Just need some coffee." No matter what Tay said about my makeup this morning, the only thing that would have me glowing was freshly-brewed caffeine running through my veins. "So, where are we headed?" I asked, pulling my hat on over hair that I'd attempted to curl. I gave them until about eleven-forty-five until the curls were completely gone.

She'd been the one to hand me the hat and gloves,

instructing me that I needed to dress warmly today - and insisting just as strongly that she *really* had no idea what Zach had planned. The wool-knit hat had been a birthday gift from Ash last year after he'd come back from Iceland. Complete with the little ball on the top and tassel ties and a set of matching gloves, all my winter T's were crossed and I's were dotted.

I glanced around the lobby of the Plaza, bustling with couples bundled up for the cold, cheeks red and spirits high. We were standing by where their huge Christmas tree resided a month or so ago. The best part was that no one noticed me. No one noticed *Blake Tyler* or southern hunk, Zach Parker of the Parker Project. We were just Blake and Zach - one more couple about to begin the day together.

Couple.

Just outside these walls, Bad Blake, not inside.

Still, a nervous thrill shot up my spine and I wiped my palms on the sides of my legs.

"Can't tell you." He grinned. "It's a surprise."

"Wha—" I broke off. "What do you mean?"

"Calm down, baby Blake," he teased lightly, "We just have to wait for the guys to get back. I sent them on an errand."

Surprises. Valentine's Day. Zach Parker. All the things I liked that I shouldn't.

Bad Blake was having a field day.

"While we wait, let's go downstairs and get you that cup of coffee." He held his arm out. "Unless you want to go to Starbucks."

I shook my head. "Just as long as it's good coffee, it doesn't matter to me."

My coat hid my goosebumps as he touched the back of my elbow, leading me over to the staircase. Below the main lobby was *The Plaza Food Hall* – one of NYC's best hidden secrets, according to Tay. Shop after shop of specialty food: sushi, subs, pizza, chocolate, doughnuts, dumplings, ice cream, cheese and wine - you name it, we walked by it. Most importantly, we ended in line at Billy's Bakery.

My eyes rolled when we got to the counter, but even that not-so-subtle hint wasn't absorbed by Elle, the girl working, who was staring blatantly at Zach with her mouth hanging wide open. Good thing she wasn't making coffee or she would have been drooling right into it.

Only I was allowed to embarrassingly ogle Zach Parker.

"Hey," she said with a low, sexy voice that made me hate her even more.

My voice could do a lot of things. *Obviously.* It was my job. But *that* voice was one I never could seem to master.

"What can I get you?" she continued, batting her eyelashes at Zach like she was trying out for Major League Baseball.

Strangely, this was one of those rare, unicorn situations where I'd gone *unrecognized*. I should have loved it. I should have been jumping in excitement at being mistaken for the normal person that I was.

But, no. Zach went and ruined that, too.

"Two Americanos, please," he replied with a genuine smile. Of course, he'd be nice to her.

I wanted to plaster myself all over him. *Correction: Bad Blake wanted to plaster myself all over him and autograph his forehead so that she knew he was mine.*

"Is there anything else I can get you?" she asked huskily, pushing the tiny laminated menu towards him with both hands...

I bit my lip but it didn't stop the tortured groan from seeping out as the blonde bimbo blatantly pushed her boobs together like they were the daily special.

"Oh. My. God. Elle." An annoyed, flamboyantly shrill voice broke through the incredibly awkward scene. "Good God. If you're going to use your tits to sell things you might as well just go work over in Times Square. *This. Is. The. Plaza.*

And these fine people——" he looked over to us as he spoke, but then did a double take on me.

And my momentary incognito was gone.

He cleared his throat and with a kindness that made me want to jump the counter and kiss him, he continued, "These *fine* people just want their coffee. Not," he paused to wave his arms around in front of her, "whatever else you are trying to give away. Plus, do you have eyes? Can you *see* he is here with someone? I just... I just can't."

And with a final wave of his hand and aggravated sigh, he grabbed the two cups and walked over to the espresso machines, nodding his head for us to follow.

Leaving Embarrassed-Elle sufficiently red-faced, I murmured, "Thank you," to my new favorite barista.

"Oh, please," he said like it was nothing, looking at the cups. "If I had anything to say about it, she would have been gone by now. I swear, the only drink she knows how to sell is a cafe-au-*laid.*"

My hand flew to my mouth as Zach and I broke out laughing.

"Sorry, I'm Claudio, and the only thing that has a filter around here is the coffee machine. Now, what did you want? She didn't write *anything* on these," he huffed.

"After that," I said, wiping tears from my eyes, "just something tall, dark, and strong. *Very* strong."

"Mm mm girl," he drawled out as his eyes flicked up and down over Zach. "I'd say you already got yourself one of those."

And there went all of my hard work on my eyeliner.

While he expertly made our drinks, I reached around for a coffee collar, writing '*You're the best. With love, Blake*' on it.

"*Thank you, Blake. I love you,*" he mouthed when I traded him the signed collar for my cup.

It was only on the way back up the stairs that I realized

he'd written 'tall, dark, and strong' on Zach's coffee with a heart at the end.

"I just tried to call you, Zach," my brother's voice echoed through the space. He and Ronnie stood with their hands clutching at least six white pastry bags.

"Hope you're hungry, Blake!" Ronnie exclaimed with a grin.

"Where were you?" Ash demanded with possessive eyes and a threatening tone.

"Downstairs for coffee while we waited for you," I grumbled; the guy still acted like I was thirteen and needed to hold his hand to walk across the street. "What is all of this?" I reached for one of the bags but Ronnie quickly pulled it back, looking to Zach for permission.

I couldn't see, but I *could* smell; the scent of warm pastry and sugar invaded my nose. Like Christmas cookies and freshly-baked bread were warring to see which could make me drool more.

"Have you ever heard—"

"Nope," Zach cut Ron off and grabbed the two bags from his hand. "Time for us to get going."

"The press won't entertain themselves," Ash grumbled, stepping back and motioning an arm to the front door.

The sting of his words was like a Band-Aid being ripped off. Zach and I had been... fine. *Better than fine, actually.* Sometime between coming downstairs and getting coffee to right now, the fact that it was all for show had been lost in the back of my mind.

"Time to bundle up, Baby Blake," Zach said with a grin. "We've got places to go."

CHAPTER THIRTEEN

ZACH

"MR. PARKER," Bruce Pillars said stiffly as he walked right into my hotel room before being asked. "We need to have a little chat."

"By all means," I stepped back and shut the door.

He looked around the room like he was afraid to touch anything other than the hat and briefcase he'd brought in with him. Shit, I wasn't messy by a long shot, but the way he looked at my sweatshirt that was draped over the couch and the one barstool that was pulled away from the counter... you'd think I was a fucking slob.

"I don't have a lot of time, but I needed to speak with you about tomorrow." He cleared his throat, adjusting the tiny glasses that were dwarfed by the size of his nose. "Blake is in a very perilous position right now. Before the start of the tour, you know how we worked to build the hype surrounding your addition to the tour. Then Miami happened. It could have been a lot... a lot worse. Thankfully, the fans love you, but the press is still searching for that fall – for another break-up; they want her to fall right back into where they want her."

I nodded, folding my arms over my chest. *Was this guy going to tell me something that I didn't know?* He might read the papers, but I held the girl. I held her when they said those things to her face. I held her when she tried to pretend like it didn't hurt. And I held her when she tried to excuse their cruelty, taking the fall for *their* character failures.

"You… you both need to get yourselves together." His tone dropped swiftly and my head tipped back in surprise. "This is a performance - just like every other one you go out and put on each night. Every moment can make or break your career - her career. Let me ask you something. Do you care for Blake?"

"Yes." Without a second thought or hesitation. "Very much," I don't know why I added.

Too much; I cared too much.

"Then you need to put aside the war going on inside your head because everyone can see it in the hot and cold tug-of-war between you two. What they need to see is Blake falling in love with the perfect boyfriend; this on and off thing is worse than a strobe light and more than likely going to give her reputation a scandal-stroke. I don't care what you do when you aren't around her and I don't care what you have to tell yourself in order to do as I'm asking, but if you care about your career or you care about her, you will do this."

I stared in silence. His words were like freezing rain, falling smoothly from his mouth and then stinging with the cold truth when they landed.

"Now then, tomorrow is the day before Valentine's Day; tomorrow is a new day and I need it to be perfect. Tomorrow is the day you start giving her a reason to fall in love with you."

I bit my tongue. She never needed a reason before. Hell,

she'd gone and done it in spite of all the reasons I'd given her not to.

"Of course."

"If you want," he stopped and cleared his throat again, "I can have Miss Hastings prepare a list of activities for you that will keep you sufficiently in public for the majority of the day if—"

"Thank you, Mr. Pillars," I interjected abruptly, "but I can handle wooing Blake." My hand reached for the doorknob even though Bruce had made no move to leave. "After tomorrow, there will be no doubt in the public mind that this is for keeps."

***

I NEEDED that doubt - the doubt in my own mind, the doubt that would keep me from falling just as surely as the damn New Year's Eve ball did every year on the stroke of midnight. I needed that doubt like a drug addict needs Narcan. Yeah, it was painful and it made me angry and perpetually unfulfilled, but it was saving me from the life-threatening addiction I had to Blake Tyler.

And that's what it would become if I let it.

"Can you please tell me where we are going?" She rubbed her hands together before hugging them in over her chest.

"No." I laughed, shaking my head.

New York. February. It was a good thing it was fucking cold outside. Then again, it was the cold that had her bundled up so fucking adorably and her cheeks splashed with pink from the wind. All the layers she wore made me desperate to unwrap them, like the biggest present under the tree on Christmas morning, knowing what was inside was all I'd ever wanted. I wanted to pull her into my arms and warm her from the inside out. Not for the news story. Not for anyone else's benefit but my own because she was mine.

"Fine, well can I at least eat one of whatever is in those bags? It smells so delicious."

"No wonder those Christmas cookies never actually make it until Christmas."

"I still can't believe you told them that…" she grumbled, a shiver springing through her body causing her teeth to chatter for a second.

My jaw ticked as I dove head first into this damned enticing charade and wrapped my arm around her shoulders, pulling her tight to my side. Even in the busy streets, the flutter of camera shutters rang like sirens.

They'd been following us since we left the hotel - parkas on and cameras shielded with bags to protect them from the snow. I had a feeling that Bruce had tipped the press off. No detail left to chance.

"Zach…" she said, eyeing me from under the wool cap that managed to turn her into some sort of sexy snow bunny. *A hat for fuck's sake.* My cock was rock solid over a damn hat. "What are we doing in the park?"

I gave her a devious grin as I led her through the entrance to Central Park. There was still snow on the ground from the Nor'easter last weekend; the flurries today only added to the Winter Wonderland charm.

"Are you…" She trailed off, stopping mid-stride, as her mitten-gloved hands came up over those perfectly arched lips in delight. "Are you… is this for real?"

Her eyes flicked between me and the horse-drawn carriage that was waiting for us. The horse pawed at the ground as the driver turned towards us and tipped his black top hat.

"Are we really going for a carriage ride?" she asked in breathless disbelief.

She loved animals. She always had. I noticed the carriages lined up when we checked in yesterday and after my chat with

Bruce, I knew this was the first stop for the day, confirmed when Taylor said that she didn't think Blake had ever gone on one before.

Oh, I knew how to woo Blake Tyler. Don't you fucking worry about that, Bruce.

I took a step ahead of her and couldn't stop my smile as it spread wide at her unabashed excitement. I didn't give two shits if someone was capturing this moment on camera right now, her excitement was for me alone, and I was going to fucking hold onto it like it was gold. Because, to me, it was.

"I can't believe this," she gushed as we settled into the cushioned seat, mounds of faux-fur blankets heaped on top of us to keep us warm.

"You haven't even gotten the best part," I drawled as the driver signaled the horse to move.

"The food?" she asked, her head spinning to face mine.

I broke out into laughter. Baby Blake was all about her food. Especially sweets.

I opened one of the pastry bags. "Have you ever had a cronut?"

She didn't have to answer 'no.' Confusion quickly became moans of enjoyment as she devoured the love-child of a croissant and a donut. Dominique Ansel was the devil and I was going to tell that fucker to his face if I ever met him. Even though I'd been the one to purchase them, I placed the blame squarely on him as the inventor of the orgasmic treats. Since that's what Blake sounded like as she ate them. *I would know…*

My arm pressed down hard on the blankets trying to ease the strain of my dick against my jeans. You'd think she was naked and touching herself, I was that fucking hard. Shifting in the seat, I opened the other bag and pulled out one of the damn things for myself.

"So, did Tay tell you about these?" she asked with her mouth half-full.

It was a mistake to look at her. It was punishment to watch

the moist pink tip of her tongue dart out to lick every crumb from her reddened lips.

"No," I said gruffly, mostly because I was so damn uncomfortable. "I picked everything for today."

"Oh."

"You don't think I could come up with date activities?"

"N-no," she mumbled, wiping her mouth with a napkin and tossing in back into the empty bag. "I just figured you would ask for help picking out stuff... you know... that I like."

"I know what you like, Blake."

I shouldn't have loved the hopeful fire that warmed her blue eyes. But that fire set off sparks inside of me. Sparks that I rarely allowed myself to feel.

She tore her gaze from mine, color deepening in her cheeks. At least she wasn't going to push it; I guess I should be happy I'd taught her that never ends well.

"So, what happened?" I found myself asking. "With the other guys."

She sighed, relaxing back into the seat. Her head tipped away from me in a heart-wrenching mix of sadness and self-reflection.

I hated the way her face fell further when she realized there was a carriage behind us and a carriage coming the other direction that were filled with paparazzi.

"Ask them." She nodded back over her shoulder.

"I'm asking you."

"I'm bad at love, that's what happened." I watched the way she pulled a smile to her face even as she said it, hearing the cameras flashing, because even a moment of self-reflection couldn't be her own. "You can't blame me for trying... but they can."

I put my arm back around her and she looked up to me with wide eyes.

I hated how I had to bite my cheek until I tasted blood so that I didn't tell her that I pulled her close to comfort her. I pulled her close so that she could feel safe telling me about what happened... So that I didn't tell her that those other guys were fucking tools who didn't know her because I knew her. And I knew that she'd always been mine.

"Liars. Cheaters. Narcissists. *Oh my.*" She sighed, her head falling onto my chest, fitting as though it had been carved right from it. "They were nice when I met them. Obviously. But I guess the *show* was on me."

"They all seemed fake to me," I ground out, annoyed with how much hearing about her failed relationships bothered me.

"Well, I guess I'm just not as smart as you, Mr. Parker," she bristled.

"Comes with age," I said lightly, drawing a small chuckle from her and an eye-roll that I didn't see but knew had happened.

"I just thought they knew what it was like to live lives that tipped between real and fake... that they were guys looking for something real. But I was grasping at straws, hoping they'd be one more tether I could add to the real me."

"*Blay,*" I said hoarsely, trying not to focus on the way she shivered and her cheeks turned pick when I called her that.

There was a beat of silence - maybe like a whole-note's worth - before she spoke again in a low voice as though the wind would take her words and use them against her.

"I know Taylor thinks it's easy for me to differentiate between what happens on stage and off - but it's not. It's lonely up there, Zach. How do I even begin to comprehend how I have to reach inside of me and share some of my most private – sometimes most heartbreaking – emotions over and over again because that's what *makes* the music; it's not the lyrics or the melody. It's the soul. And, at the same time, it's also just a show. The lines get so blurred, I don't even know what they look like anymore. And when I walk off that stage, I walk into a fog unable to see who and what in this world is real. Myself included."

My hand rubbed gently up and down her arm, encouraging her to let me bear some of her burden.

"I love singing and performing. I love my fans. But sometimes, I feel like I'm in an aquarium, drowning behind a layer of glass and people are paying to see it. It hurts to think that they'll be entertained whether I survive or not."

"Your fans love you, Blake," I said with a low, hoarse voice.

"Most of them, yes. But, after all of this, I just can't help but feel like the world is just waiting for me to trip and fall." She paused, her exhale accompanied by a pained laugh. "I don't even know how to explain what it felt like when Tay told me how the press had twisted my last breakup - and how it went viral. There was even a freaking hashtag for 'Blakeup,' I mean, who comes up with this stuff?"

"People are morons," was all I could get out through gritted teeth, wanting to punch each and every fucking person who'd made this gorgeous girl feel guilty for having her heart broken. I wanted to fuck up every person who had broken her heart – including myself.

I couldn't stop myself. I heard her heart and I just wanted to help heal it, if just for a little while. Shoving my anger back down, I reached for something deeper. Something that she didn't know, but that she needed to hear. Something to show her that just because there are people who follow you, doesn't mean it's not ok to get lost once in a while.

There are no roads in life except the ones that you build for yourself. And sometimes, you have to lose your way a little before you know which way you are supposed to go.

"Did you know I almost didn't take the scholarship?" I admitted hoarsely. "I had no idea what I wanted to do with my life senior year. I almost turned Alabama down."

"What? What are you talking about?" Her incredulous face was priceless. "You... you loved football. You loved Alabama. I think that's the only hat you've ever owned."

I knew she'd be surprised. I hadn't talked about it to anyone except Ash and after graduation, well, I doubted he wanted to mention anything about me to his sister.

"I started to realize that football wasn't what I wanted for my life; it was just something that I was good at. And I almost pulled out."

"Then why did you go?"

"Because I didn't know anything else. And I didn't have the confidence to... go against what everyone thought of me – '*Franklin's Football Star.*'" I ended with a slightly mocking tone, adding, "I'd always had this reputation."

"We... they would have supported you, believed in you." She wasn't wrong. But it wasn't about them. It was about believing in myself.

"Blake, your family, your friends, your fans... they all believe in you. None of them doubt who you are or why you dated and broke up with those guys. *They* know who you are. So, for you... for me, too... it's never about them. It's realizing that the only person doubting your character is yourself."

I stared at the old New York buildings that passed along the side of the park. Gorgeous and unassuming. And worth more than I could imagine. *Just like her.*

"Blake, no one... *No. One...* has everything figured out. Not even me. And especially not them—" I nodded to the invisible masses who would judge her.

"Sometimes, I feel like my family - who I only see when I'm home - and Tay, who is half-business and half-not... are all I have to hold onto. Them and my music. And after all of this, I just have to wonder if it's really worth it..." she murmured as she physically deflated against me, like a huge weight was lifted from her shoulders.

I cleared my throat. "It took me a while to decide, but I finally quit football sophomore year to focus on my music... the band. And yeah, people said stuff. But they weren't the people that mattered. People will *always* say shit. People will complain about a rainy day until the sun comes out and then they'll complain that it's too hot. But it was worth it, because it was the real me. Some of us take time... and trials... to realize what we want and to believe in ourselves enough to take it. You can't make everyone happy, Blay. But making yourself happy, *that* you can do and *that* is what we all want to see."

It tore my insides apart hearing her voice thicken as she continued, "I'm trying to be happy. But it's hard when all I can think about is that I'm getting lost in the fake, getting lost in the show. I'm afraid of losing myself."

I tipped her chin towards me, forcing those stormy seas to mine. "Blake, baby," I rasped, my thumb brushing over her lower lip, "you are beautiful and talented and compassionate. You aren't losing yourself. You just care too damn much for people who don't deserve it."

"Zach..." she inhaled my name with a small gasp.

I was saying too much, I knew, but it wasn't enough; it wasn't enough for what she deserved.

"You are the most painfully, annoying, awkward, yet inspiring real person I've ever met. You, who shares personal stories while on stage. You, who runs into the ocean for midnight swims without a care in the world. You, who lit up like a goddamn Christmas tree when you saw the carriage ride. You wear your too-damned-big heart on your sleeve, Blay. So, don't ever mistake your feelings for fake."

My mouth inched closer to hers, our breaths mingling into the fog of desire that already surrounded us.

"They *love* you. Say it."

I watched her throat bob, my lips tingling to touch hers.

"T-they love me," she whispered practically against my mouth.

"Not because you are a pop princess. Not because you entertain them or because it's the cool thing to do. They love you because you bring to their lives – *our lives* – this soft, warm light that reminds us all that it's ok to be human, even if 'human' means mistakes, it also means happy."

"Thank… you," she choked out. My thumb swiped away tears that stained down her porcelain cheeks. "You didn't have… to do this. But thank you."

The pure, soft gratitude in her voice destroyed me. She may be a pop princess, but she was also a warrior. And warriors were only strong when they could recognize their weakness.

"Blake, baby, I will write a goddamn anthem and sing it to you every day and any day to remind you to never doubt yourself again." My eyes drifted to her lips as I added, "Either that or I will fucking kiss you so damn hard your mouth will think twice before it repeats those words again."

Wide eyes, parted lips… she looked like my fucking wet dream. I groaned, my cock stiffening unbearably underneath the layers of blankets, knowing she would taste even better. Forget about blurred lines. I'd just blown so far past the lines that they turned into the horizon behind me.

"I think," she said softly as her tongue licked her lips and my whole body tensed with the restraint it took to not crush my mouth to hers. "I'm done doubting… but I would like that kiss anyway."

I couldn't stop myself if I tried. And I didn't. My lips drifted to hers because at some point, the ocean always meets the shore.

Gently, my mouth pressed against her lips. She was the snowflake on the tip of my tongue. Chilled for a second just before she melted. Swaying into me, her head tilted against my shoulder and her mouth parted.

I captured her sigh. Claimed it. Used it for my own purposes, pushing my tongue into the warm, sweet haven of her mouth; she tasted the kind of sweet that - in all these years - I could never find any other word to describe aside from 'forbidden.'

I wished there weren't a thousand fucking layers between us. I wished it was seventy-five degrees out and she was in that damn bikini. Later, I could be thankful that she wasn't.

Slow. Searching. I licked every inch of her, my cock jealous of the liberties my tongue had. I sucked on her lip, pulling it into my mouth and feeling as her entire body quivered against me. For some, it's a sound or smell; for me, it was tasting the salty insecurity on her tongue that she'd trusted to me that triggered my déjà vu back to the day I should have made her mine. And not just back. Forward. Left. Right. Up. Down.

Alternate realities.

In every instance of space and time, I'd always find her waiting for me and she'd always be mine.

I should stop.

I needed to stop.

My heart was racing, my dick pulsing to be inside of her - any part of her. It was this point where my mind was so fogged with need for something I couldn't have that I did stupid things - that I said stupid things.

I didn't stop. Instead, I explored her mouth like she was my last supper and like I was Judas betraying my heart.

The carriage jolted back, forcing me to break the kiss. Her eyelids drifted open slowly, as though she was coming out of the best dream and was reluctant to wake up.

I slid my hands down from where they'd been cupping her cheeks. Her gloves were still curled into my jacket, no longer trying to pull me closer but refusing to let go.

Her eyes were on me, wondering what just happened. I wished I had an answer for her.

Something very real.

What happens when the road to what's real is impassable?

The jerk of the carriage was the driver forcing the horse backward. Judging by the comfortable stance of the dozen paparazzi several feet away, we'd been in the same spot for awhile and he was trying to do us a favor.

"We should get going, Baby Blake," I said hoarsely, desire still laced through my voice.

Camera shutters fell faster than the snow around us. Her lashes fluttered down, peering out underneath hooded eyes at the crowd that had gathered.

"Yeah," she said softly, the word tearing through me like a dull knife.

I wanted her to know that I would always be here for her, to remind her that who she was was enough; instead, I'd kissed her because what I had would never be enough without her. And now, I'd have to let her believe that was fake, too.

Way to go, Asshole.

I didn't want to move. I didn't want to go on with this. I didn't want to fucking live with everything I ever wanted sitting right in front of me. What I did want was to finally tell her how much I'd always needed her - and how much it had killed me to deny it.

That was the problem with Blake Tyler.

What we had was so damn real that all she could ever be was my fantasy.

CHAPTER FOURTEEN

BLAKE

Track 11: Love Struck

"Like lightning cracks through the sky.
Hot. Bright. Burning. Silent.
Love struck me and I fell."

MY FINGERS RUBBED ABSENTMINDEDLY OVER MY LIPS. PLUMP. Tingling. Slightly chapped. Many words that my lips could be registering except the only thing I felt was Zach.

I was grateful that Lin knew me well enough to hum quietly while she worked on my hair and make-up for tonight's performance because I was too lost in thought to contribute meaningfully to any sort of conversation.

Zach's kiss yesterday had been the best thing to happen to my mouth since chewing gum. And that's why I hadn't indulged my habit since. Odd for me to the point where even Tay made a comment.

Everything about yesterday had been perfect. No. More than that. As far as ideal Valentine's dates go, *yesterday had been a fairytale.* The huge snowflakes falling around us, the carriage ride all bundled up against Zach as he held me... It was out of a dream that I'd had for a very long time.

Who was I kidding? It was still a dream.

What else do you call something that isn't real?

Did I think the kiss was part of his plan? No. Did I know he'd say that it was - or worse, *a mistake?* Yes. And that's why I didn't ask.

I may be slow at it, but I was learning my lesson when it came to Zach Parker.

We left the park with a warm and easy familiarity between us, conversation and chemistry taken down a notch - at least on the outside. It was a step back from the admission of my biggest fears that had seem to come out of nowhere. And it was two steps back from that kiss - a kiss that was as beautiful and brief as a shooting star, leaving me wondering if what I'd just felt was something to wish on or a flicker of something destined to disintegrate.

Oh, that was a good one. I pulled out my phone and opened up the notes app, typing furiously, '*Kisses like shooting stars, if only I could wish on ours. Brightly beautiful. Swiftly gone. Brilliantly burning into flashes of the dawn.*'

The cameras were convenient reminders of the purpose it played.

My heart though was an annoying insistence that it also served a greater purpose.

We'd grabbed sandwiches from a random deli on our way down to his – also secret – afternoon activity: hours spent roaming through Bryant Park's Winter Village. Tiny glass shops littered the walkways of the park, surrounding the giant Christmas tree and ice skating rink. *Winter Wonderland* was what came to mind.

Sure, I wore fancy brands because they sent me stuff or because I was paid to. Most of the time, I passed as much as I could off to Taylor because it was too fancy for me. I loved the soft wool scarves from the third pop-up shop on the right that didn't have a tag, let alone a brand. Zach insisted on buying me one because it was the only outer accessory that I wasn't wearing. I loved the hand-made sterling silver jewelry, set with brightly colored stones in designs that most 'high-fashion' would consider 'highly reproachable.' My stomach twisted when I saw a charm bracelet similar to the one I'd lost on that memorable prom night.

And in spite of the giant sandwich we'd shared, remembering back to the days when we'd split numerous Italian subs while working on the treehouse, we still managed to end up with a cup of Max Brenner's hot chocolate in one hand and Nutella crepes in the other.

Somewhere between Zach's stories about living in Alabama and the ones about all the trouble my brother got into while at college, the press gave up trying to weed through the crowd for any more photos, leaving us to wander in peace.

In a world where days were planned down to the minute to fit everything in, my heart raced with the relaxed spontaneity of what he'd chosen for us to do. It made the date feel more real than any of the other 'real' relationships I'd been in before which was a sad commentary considering that it was purely for show.

Part of me hated that he knew this - whether consciously or unconsciously - that he knew I wanted simple days like this and not the fancy cars or the fancy parties or five-star restaurants or a house in the Hamptons.

Cue Shaina Twain, '*That don't impress me much…*'

Lin's hands in my hair froze. *Crap.* Guess I sang that one out loud.

Shrugging, I gave her a weak smile and she just laughed, shook her head, and went back to work trying to straighten my waves.

I just wanted hot chocolate and carriage rides with someone who wanted to look at the stars instead of using me to become one.

There was a war going on inside of me whether I should be sitting here reliving each and every moment like a love-struck teenager or if I should be focusing on that line that Taylor insists I'm so skilled at drawing.

Real.

Not real.

He loves me.

He loves me not.

***

"Happy Valentine's Day, everyone!" I yelled with a huge smile. I don't know why but every time I went out on stage, I forgot for a second that I was mic'd and felt the need to yell to reach everyone in the crowd. *Like I actually could.*

Good thing my sound crew knew this about me and planned accordingly.

Goosebumps covered my legs underneath the dress I had on. Black tights, black boots, and an off-white dress that looked like a mirror had shattered over it. And that meant that I was cold now, but a few more minutes under these lights - and on stage with Zach - and I'd be warmed right up.

"Thank you—" I paused with a laugh at the classic '*I love you, Blake*' that at least one fan always managed to belt out loud enough to reach the stage. "Thank you... everyone... for deciding to spend your Valentine's Day here with me. Ladies," I continued with a wry voice, "give your man a big kiss right now for bringing y'all here to see me."

I loved these moments when I knew the camera flashes were mostly not for me.

'*What about your man?*' My head jerked to the left as someone yelled.

3... 2... 1... And my face was officially as red as my lips.

'Bring him up there!'

'We want Zach!'

My heart dropped into my stomach. *They knew.* I mean, of course they knew. The photos from yesterday were all over the internet well before we even got back from dinner. By the time I got out of the shower, Taylor already had a press release ready to go and a tweet ready for me to post.

At this point, I didn't know what would be worse, listening to them - or not. I went with *or not.*

"Ok, ok," I said, holding up my hands. "I don't know that he was quite ready for this welcome, but if you could all join me in welcoming my... Zach Parker to the stage—"

The cheers erupted and I couldn't even remember what else I was going to say.

Oh, God.

He looked hot. Hotter than usual hot. Maybe it was the whole Valentine's Day aura. Or maybe it was because I was finally letting myself look at him like he was mine. Tonight, there's no baseball cap. Just the unruly mahogany waves, mostly pushed back from his face (probably from the repetitive run-through with his hand) except for one lock that hung defiantly in front of his forehead. Typical Zach – *mostly* following every rule except in his own way. The dark, fitted jeans were new – and even though they looked amazing, hugging every muscle, I missed the ones that had me ripped and stained into them. The deep red shirt was unfamiliar, too, buttoned-down and straining over his chest before being tucked tightly into his pants. He looked like a magical blend of classy and country that was hot as hell.

I tried to swallow. Twice. I would have had an easier time getting a mouthful of sand down my throat for how dry it was.

His lips broke into a smile and I felt my panties begin to slip...

Correction: Hot as hell now turned into panty-melting. I couldn't look away. My clothes, just like my body, were wholly unprepared for the assault. And this was only the first twenty seconds. They'd have to suck me up out of my puddle of desire by the time the show was done.

Those lips.

Mine tingled with wanting his kiss. His tongue. My breath faltered, oxygen weighed down with desire. And I prayed the crowd was focused on him as I tried to subtly cross my legs. It felt like my desire was literally dripping from me.

Whose freakin' idea was it to have me in a dress tonight? They are fired. I don't care if it was Taylor. F.I.R.E.D.

The ache between my legs was like a base melody playing through every other note of my life. Strumming with a low, soul-wracking hum, a constant reminder of how I wanted our song to end.

"Blake," he rasped. It was a subtle sound - or it would have been if it wasn't magnified through the entire stadium. Like being in a movie theater versus watching TV – the pure sex in his voice became a surround-sound to the cinematic destruction of my body. It literally vibrated through every cell of my body, awakening parts of me that definitely should not be awake on stage.

"Happy Valentine's Day."

I almost laughed. I never thought I'd hear *those* words coming from *that* mouth. It was like getting a phone call that you'd won the lottery – amusingly unbelievable.

"H-happy Valentine's Day," I returned with a strangled voice and a strained smile. *I needed to get off this stage. And maybe get a new pair of underwear.* Talk about wardrobe malfunction; Janet was about to have nothing on me. "Alright, I'll let Zach get to it—"

Giving an awkward wave to the crowd, I was *so* prepared to dart off stage, but I was stopped by a firm grasp on my wrist, spinning me back and trapping me in his stare like a bee in honey.

"Not so fast there, Blay," he said with a mischievous grin. "I have a present for you."

"W-what?" I blubbered. *Boy, this crowd was getting the real Blake Tyler tonight - all awkward and lovestruck.*

I blinked twice and a red rose appeared in front of me.

Now was not the time to lose my voice.

'*Kiss her!*' someone yelled off in the distance.

My fans were not my friends right now. Nope. They were fired, too.

I should have said something to deflect, taken the rose, and walked off stage. *Should've... could've, would've.*

I stared, watching his lips descend on mine until the very last second. And even then, I didn't trust my lips to not make up what they were dying to feel.

And then there was that kiss again. The one that put me back in outer space where all Earth-shattering and cosmic phenomena belonged.

His tongue licked along the seam of my lips, barely waiting for them to part before it darted inside for one more taste like he couldn't help himself. And then he was gone.

Whistles and cheers were the soundtrack to his eyes.

He was enjoying this.

I was afraid I was enjoying it, too.

"So, I got you this rose, even though I think all these great people out here would say that you deserve much more." *Cue cheers of agreement.* "And I would have to agree with them."

This wasn't happening.

It's official. I'd gone crazy. Bat-shit crazy. *Blake. Shit. Crazy.*

This wasn't even real in my wildest dreams.

"So," he drawled, "I know we both kinda have a little thing... like a concert... that we gotta do right now," I felt his grin like he'd smiled it right against the lips of my sex, "but, I was wondering if you'd like to join me for a delicious take-out dinner tonight after the show? I'm told this city has some pretty decent pizza and cheesecake."

His soft, Southern charm was the end of me. The anxiety and uncertainty disappeared and I broke out laughing.

It was too easy to fall for him. And that was when he didn't want anything to do with me. This wasn't a fall. A fall implies an element of unawareness.

I wasn't falling.

I had jumped – *willful, consenting awareness that the landing was going to break me.*

He raised one of those perfect eyebrows and I realized that I'd left him hanging, the entire audience silent.

"Yes. I mean, I'd love to," I gushed out and there was a good chance we could have cancelled the rest of the concert and my fans would have been satisfied. Especially when he then pulled me into his arms, picked me up, and spun me around like I'd seen him do to countless girls in high school, every time wishing it was me.

This time it was.

Crap. Crap. Double-crap.

"I have a request, though," he said softly (which wasn't all that soft when it echoed through the space.) The cheers died down until it felt like a library out there. *Shimmering silence.*

"I thought we could do something a little different - a little special for this crowd tonight."

I held my breath at his suggestion. *What else could we possibly do?*

"I thought we could sing for them. *Together.*"

"A duet?" I squeaked. "W-what song?" My heart was pounding. "You think we should have maybe rehearsed something first?" I whispered, only remembering the audience when they laughed. My smile wavered. Hopefully, at least the mic made it sound like I was being cheeky instead of revealing the butterflies that were all trying to climb back into their cocoons in my stomach.

"You'll know it when you hear it." And then he winked at

me like *that* was supposed to make everything ok. Like charm could make up for preparedness.

He stepped back, taking my hand and pulling me with him so that he could sit on the stool that they always had out for the opening acoustics.

I shivered when his fingers separated from mine, the direct line of heat to my body gone. I rubbed my clammy palms together and then against my nice dress as Zach pulled his guitar around and propped it up on his knee.

My heart screeched to a halt and I glanced at the audience thinking that they had to have heard it.

Singing together – how many more fantasies was I going to have survive?

And then the chords began.

It took all of the first seven in the intro for me to realize what he'd picked. Tears pricked at the corners of my eyes. There are certain songs that are timeless - and not in the sense that they'll be covered for decades, but in the sense that no matter what point in life you hear them, the words always seem to be perfect for that moment in time.

These words were perfect for now. They were also perfect six years ago.

"Stars shining bright above you," I began with a throaty voice that would have made Ella and Adele proud. I stared at his smile, afraid this would all crumble and disappear if I looked away. *"Night breezes seem to whisper, 'I love you.'"*

The look in his eyes faltered. He'd chosen the song though. He'd known I'd have to sing those words to him again.

While I tried to catch my breath - and my heart - from being stolen by him, he took the next line.

"Birds singing in the Sycamore tree, 'Dream a little dream of me.'"

Line by line, note by note, he pulled my shiny broken pieces back to him.

CHAPTER FIFTEEN

ZACH

"I wasn't sure you were serious about this," Blake said quietly when I opened the door.

"Why wouldn't I be?" I raised an eyebrow, stepping back and letting her enter my room first.

She shrugged, her fingers toying with the edge of that shimmering dress that clung to every damn curve of her. It looked good on her; it would look even better off.

I shouldn't have been serious especially after my fucking harebrained decision to ask her to sing 'Dream a Little Dream of Me' with me. I wouldn't take full credit for it. Bruce told me to go out there and do something unexpected and sweet. Singing a duet had been his idea. The song though, had been mine. And dinner? Well that had come from the devil and my dick – wanting more time alone with her. Seeing her standing there though - *in that dress*, red lips and rosy cheeks - it was like a punch to the gut how much I was still craving her kiss; I wanted to linger on her lips until dawn.

I wanted more of yesterday.

"Is Ash ok?" I asked tightly, closing the door behind her.

I knew he'd probably had something to say about it as

183

soon as she walked off stage after our duet. Dinner hadn't been part of the plan.

He didn't like things that weren't part of the plan.

I'd expected shit, but he was gone when ZPP finished and guiltily, I was grateful. Ronnie had given me a half smile and said that Ash had texted him, Bobby, and Alex about meeting for drinks afterward; I wasn't included because I already had 'other' plans.

What the fuck ever.

He'd get over it.

She nodded, adding, "Taylor told him it would be a good follow-up after the show. She... ahh... thinks I should take a photo of our food or something and post it."

My jaw ticked. I hadn't meant for the conversation to turn into how this night was just one more box to be checked off on the Operation-Reputation-Restore to-do list.

"You ordered already?" she turned back to me with wide, hungry eyes.

Too bad mine were only hungry for her.

"I figured you'd be starving by the time you were done, so I wanted to have it ready and waiting. I ordered us Thai. Hope that's ok," I said gruffly, walking around her to start unpacking the food that had been delivered just a few minutes ago. I couldn't stand there and stare at her delectably long body another minute before I ended up laying her out on the table and eating my fill.

"I've never had Thai before," she said, bending over to smell the boxes in front of her.

"Seriously?" I asked, clearing my throat, allowing myself a one-second appetizer to look at the way the dress rode up on her ass. "Well, good thing I ordered basically the whole menu."

"Yeah," she answered quietly with a shy smile, picking up a plate. "Taylor and I usually stick to things we're familiar with. I don't know why. Just easier." Her eyes rose to mine -

which were thankfully no longer lingering where they shouldn't. "So, where do I start?"

"How about this," I offered with a crooked smile, taking her plate from her. "Let me make you a plate."

She licked her lip, releasing her hold. My cock throbbed against the front of these jeans that were way too tight if anyone had cared to ask how I felt about them. *They hadn't.* And they were definitely too fucking tight to be worn in Blake Tyler's presence.

I was going to regret this impromptu dinner date. I was going to regret it like you do one too many drinks at the bar. The problem was I wasn't going to feel that regret until morning, long after I'd already done things that I wanted, but shouldn't.

***

"You think we're out of the woods, yet?" I asked as I poured out two modest glasses of wine. A small celebration of the track her reputation now seemed to be on.

"Honestly, I have no idea if we are in the clear. I'm... obviously... not the best judge of these things. That's what I have Tay for..." she trailed off for a second before her eyes that had been trained on the empty table whipped up to mine and widened as her hand clapped up over her mouth. "Crap!" she exclaimed with muffled distress.

"What? What's wrong?" My heart was in my throat and my hand stopped the wine mid-fill on the second glass.

"I forgot to take the picture and post it." She groaned, pulling her hair back tightly in frustration and then letting it fall in a mess around her face. "Tay is going to kill me; I suck at this whole social media thing."

I laughed, shaking my head, and handing her the wine glass. "Who cares about the photo?"

She took a sip. "Photos or it didn't happen."

My jaw ticked. "What if we go live?"

You wouldn't think that utter confusion could look attractive on someone, but it could; it could look sexy as hell. Especially when all I saw was her hair now slightly messed, her lips no longer stained that deep red, and her body now finally relaxed after we'd spent the past half hour eating and laughing, finding the comfortable zone where we could talk about the past without having to awkwardly avoid where it ultimately led to.

"You've never gone live? Ronnie fucking insists that we do it all the time; he says that that is what people want to see." I dropped back down into the chair, crossing my arms over my chest and looked up at her. "It's just a live stream - a live video. And then people can comment and like it real-time."

She appeared to ponder it for a second, taking another drink of the Cab Sav that I'd poured before giving me a determined nod.

It was the same nod she'd given me when I'd made the mistake of wondering out loud what would happen if we jumped off their parent's deck onto the trampoline, promptly waiting for me to turn my back in search of Ash before she climbed the rail and launched herself onto it.

She'd survived - of course - with a giant squeal and smile.

I, on the other hand, had almost died in that split second when she disappeared over the edge.

"Let's do it!" She reached for her purse, digging inside for her phone.

"Right... now?"

"Isn't that what you just suggested?"

"I mean... that's not what..." I chuckled. What the hell did I really care? I thought as I drained my wine. Especially when she looked much more excited about this than the stupid photo she forgot about.

"Alright, how do I do this?" she asked, shoving her phone in my face.

A few taps and I showed her where the 'Go Live' button was.

"What should I say? What if no one watches?"

The sudden seriousness of her questions and the concern in her eyes had me bursting into laughter. This was the Blake Tyler that the world needed to see. Not the fucking popstar that looked like she had everything. *This* Blake. The one that was nervous and self-conscious, and cared too much about what people she didn't even know thought about her.

The truth is that you can have everything, but still not have everything figured out.

"Guess we'll find out," I said with a devilish grin, hitting the button and dropping the phone into her hands.

I had to give her credit, her transition time from shock to smile was impressive.

"Hi... guys," she said nervously, her gaze slipping to mine, searching for support, and then back to the screen. "Wow... there's a lot of you." *For her, I'm sure there was.* "I've never done this before, so I'm sorry if I mess this up. I wanted to post a food photo from my date tonight, but I was too hungry and ate it all first." She giggled, drinking another sip of the wine that was already starting to have an effect.

Her brilliant blues widened and shot to mine. "What..." Her brow scrunched and before I had a chance to avoid any of it, she stepped towards me and turned, plopping down right into my lap.

She turned to me, startled.

Yeah, you just sat on my lap, Blake, what the hell did you expect to find when you've been parading around in my hotel room in a dress made to be ripped off of you so that I can finally have a taste?

Recovering quickly, she pointed at the screen and asked, "Hold on a sec guys, Zach is teaching me how this works. What are those?"

I grinned. "Those are people liking the video."

"All of them?" she asked, eyes wide in astonishment.

I laughed and nodded my head. "And those are comments coming in."

"Wow, there are a lot of you guys watching. That's so cool! Oh look, questions!"

I looked at the screen, but I was only watching her as she rattled off 'hi' and 'hello' to the slew of people commenting on the stream. We'd be here all night if she kept this up. And she would, too – in order to say 'hi' to each and every one of them.

I sat frozen, partially because moving would make the needy pain in my dick worse and partially because I was star-struck – watching her chat and answer questions like she was talking to her mom instead of hundreds of strangers.

Her hair tickled my nose as she turned to me. "They want to talk to you."

"Me?" I asked, taken aback. "I'm pretty sure they're here for you, Baby Blake."

Pink tinted her cheeks as the world heard me call her that nickname. "They are," she replied, "but they love you, too, with your 'sexy brooding farmboy look.'"

My jaw dropped and she burst out laughing.

"That was a direct quote, I swear!" she insisted, pointing at the screen. "Oh no! It's gone now. Oh, but look, *Krysta* says she wants to ride your tractor." Her hand clapped over her mouth and she doubled over.

"Tractor's full," I grumbled, feeling the way her body shuddered at my words and the way my cock pulsed against her ass. Her eyes met mine on the screen for a split second.

All I could think about was how I was inches – less than inches – from the warm haven between her thighs that my dick wanted to call home. All I could feel was the way she bounced and rubbed on it every time she laughed. *Which was too damn much.*

"I am pretty lucky to have such a handsome date." Her shy happiness was caught on the screen and my stomach tightened.

Her head ducked and a blush crept into her cheeks as she read the responses.

"It's so good to see you happy, Blake!" - Jesse

"Thank you... I'm happy to be happy, too."

Those moments when she thought what was happening between us could be real - they killed me because I thought it, too. And it felt like Edward Scissorhands reached into my gut and went to town.

I couldn't stop myself. *Who could?* She was so warm and open and trusting. The way she still looked at me even after how I'd treated her and the things I'd said should have been proof enough.

I just wanted to give her what she wanted. *What we both wanted.* Just for one night.

"I'd like to add something," I interjected hoarsely, acting rather than thinking as I took her phone and angled it slightly towards me. "I think we all know who the lucky one here is."

My hand tightened on her stomach - below where the camera captured. My fingers brushed over the edges of the design on her dress because the need to touch her was quickly winning out over every sane thought.

Her lips parted into a small 'o' before her teeth sunk into the plump flesh of her lower lip. I raised her palm to my mouth, planting a kiss in the middle of it.

"I think it's time to say 'goodnight,' Baby Blay," I rasped, my eyes locked with hers, neither of us willing to break to look at the camera that was streaming us.

"T-thanks for hanging out, everyone," she said shakily, visibly less composed for the whole world to see.

"See you again tomorrow night, New York!" I added with a half-smile and then clicked off the stream without even looking at the phone. Tomorrow she could go back and watch how her fans had gone nuts to see such a personal glimpse into her life.

Blake stared at me, her eyes heavy with desire. I knew she felt mine. Hell, she could have been the princess with ten mattresses shoved between her and my dick and she still could have felt the damn thing it was so hard, throbbing right in the crevice of her ass.

Cue every lame-ass pun about the (Pop) Princess and my Penis.

This was what tempted her to believe that what was between us was real; I couldn't hide this.

A growl rumbled through me and I broke eye contact. I was going to be that guy if she didn't leave - I was going to be the best-friend's-sister-fucking asshole. I couldn't – *wouldn't* – be that guy.

Clinging to the one last rational thread present in my brain, I forced the hoarse words from my mouth. "Alright, I think we've checked all the boxes that we are supposed to tonight." I felt her flinch. "Maybe it's best if you get going, Blake. It's been a long day."

She turned further in my lap, rubbing her ass all along my arousal in the process. I grit my teeth to stop myself from coming - that's how bad denying myself had been lately.

"No, Zach..." Boldly placing her hand on my chest, right over my pounding heart, she stared at me with those brilliant blues that twinkled with heady anticipation. I watched as her head slowly drifted down to mine and she said softly, "I'm tired of this. I think it's best if we both stay."

Blake

I KNEW I made these same mistakes every time. Bridges were burning, but I never learned. It was moments like this, when those bridges disappeared for a split second, that I knew I did one thing right.

"I think it's best if we both stay."

My breaths were whispers in the air. Silent pleas to not push me away again. Warm entreaties for more of what grounded me and yet made me feel like I could fly.

I was being reckless again. *Fearless.* Practice makes perfect.

I could feel that he wanted me. I could feel his labored breathing against my back, the pounding of his heart against my hand, and the hard ridge of his erection underneath me.

My heart insisted that it had to mean something.

The truth was that could mean nothing.

But my mind was skilled at forgetting to remind me that he was a bad idea.

"Blay..." he said with a strangled voice. "You need to go."

I heard the sound of my voice, asking him again, "Please, stay." Breathing in the spicy and manly scent of him, the next thing I did was reckless, too – with a large dash of stupid. I smiled as my mouth drifted towards those lips that would kiss me and then curse me in the very next second. *Wildest dreams.* Gently, I pressed mine against the tight seam of his, whimpering slightly when he remained unmoving against me.

"Just one taste..." And the blurred, distant line was crossed.

A shudder rippled through him before his hands speared through my hair, tilting my head and claiming my mouth like the night on the beach. There was no one watching here. There was only ever us.

I melted into him as his tongue drove into my mouth, searching for mine. The moment they connected - *sparks flew.* Without breaking contact, I spun to straddle him. My hands roamed everywhere, desperate to touch any part of him. The hands that held my head punishingly under his mouth now slid down to my ass, tugging up my dress to dig into the stocking-covered flesh of my ass and pull me tight against him. My panties were damp; *they had been for a little while.* This made them slip-n-slide soaking.

I rolled my hips against his, gasping against his lips as stars danced through me. Zach growled and bit into my lower lip, tugging it into his mouth. The painful pleasure spurred me on as I chased the sensation of me rubbing against him - feeling the hard ridge of his dick with every move. My underwear was pushed to the side.

"You just can't let this go." His voice was deep and husky, unavoidable frustration dripping from every word and every heavy breath. But he didn't stop, grinding his hips up against my core. "I'm not fucking you, *Blake baby,*" he warned, his lips finding my neck and pressing a hard kiss to the flesh that rippled with the beat of my heart before tacking on, "*Not tonight.*"

"I want you inside of me," I whispered, my voice shaking with a need both so powerful it would scare me later and so essential that speaking it was more necessary than breathing. He already seemed to be a part of everything else about me; this was all that was left.

My slit opened, the pressure now directly on my clit, driving me insane.

"Not here. Not now," he growled back, taking my mouth with punishing force for asking. "*But soon.*" The promise a strangled afterthought as he kissed me deeply.

My eyes rolled back, barely hearing him as lust sizzled like oil on a flame – *burning red.*

I felt it building inside of me, my hips rocking frantically against his as my desire soaked through my underwear and onto his jeans. My fingers clutched into his shirt, feeling my orgasm nearing.

"*Fuck,*" he swore as he lifted me up, carrying me over to the bed and depositing me abruptly on the mattress. Hard eyes pinned me down as he bit out, "Don't move. Otherwise I'll do something that will ruin everything."

My mouth fell open in shock, gasping as my climax screamed and pounded against the door that had been slammed in its face, as he dropped to his knees.

He looked tortured. He was always demanding and sure. The only thing that he was sure of now was that he couldn't stop this any longer.

Need sparked around him like my star had struck him like a comet, splitting him open and releasing glowing, hot lust.

"Pull your dress up." His throat bobbed as I complied.

I tried to keep my head tilted up as my shaking fingers tugged the tight fabric up to my hips, revealing my black boy shorts.

Seconds later, I was bare and Zach was staring between my legs with a possessive hunger that should have been frightening. The equal mix of embarrassment and excitement had my body humming with anticipation.

"You're so damn beautiful like this, *Blakebaby*," he rasped as his eyes drank me in. "Stripped bare, letting me see you without all the armor for the cameras. When you let me see the real you and not just the version the world gets to see, there's nothing I could deny you... there's nothing that could keep me from you."

"Zach!" I inhaled his name harshly, hands gripping into the comforter as the very tip of his finger just brushed over my folds and came away coated with my desire.

Tilting my head up again, I sank into those heady amber eyes.

"I shouldn't be doing this," he muttered even as he opened his mouth and licked my juices from his finger with a groan. Amber turned molten as his hands fell to grip my thighs and force them wide enough for his shoulders. "God, I shouldn't *fucking* be doing this," he repeated the words against my inner thigh, my sex clenching as I felt his lips move over my skin.

My hips shot off the bed when his teeth sunk into my flesh, biting into me so close to where I needed him.

I felt the shudder wrack his body. I felt his breath on my aching sex. I felt every organ in my body stop working as his tongue slid over my slit like it was melting ice cream and he's trying to catch every last creamy drop.

"Jesus Christ, Blake... you taste so fucking... I never imagined..."

I wanted to scream but nothing was working anymore except the parts that he touched.

"I wonder if these lips will sing just as beautifully for me." More desire rushed from my sex. I felt myself clenching fruitlessly, needing his touch.

Everything went black and then white when his mouth closed over my core. Slow. Firm. Demanding. He kissed and licked every inch of me like I was the instrument and his mouth was the master. From my entrance to my clit, his lips explored every place that made my body sizzle and squirm. His tongue seared him into one more piece of me that would end up scarred with his name.

Like he'd designed my body and knew just how to build it up and make it fall apart, he sucked hard on my clit and I cried out, my sex clenching forcefully as cum rushed out begging for the orgasm promised by his beautifully talented lips.

And I didn't - *couldn't* - hold back. My nails scored over and into his back before they dug into his scalp, holding him tighter against me like I was trying to suffocate him between my thighs. *He didn't seem to mind.* In fact, he growled and ate at me even deeper, his finger joining his tongue.

I need this release like I need him. *Unapologetically. Unstoppably.*

Pulling on my swollen clit, his finger curled deep inside me and I was done. I screamed his name, my fingers yanking on his hair as my orgasm ripped through me.

My body had sung for him and he kept his mouth softly covering me until the melody of trembles and moans faded softly into partially sated silence.

Zach

"I've imagined a lot of things, Blake, but not this. I never imagined you'd taste so good," I said with a low voice, still staring at the mind-numbing, cock-throbbing picture in front of me. "Or that you'd come so beautifully."

Blake. In my bed. Dress hiked to her waist. Her slick and shaved *forbidden* pussy laid bare before me, pink and dripping with spit and sex.

I licked my lips on the verge of giving in to losing myself in that all-American honey between her thighs.

Pushing herself up onto her elbows, her glazed eyes met mine and I knew she wanted me to do more than taste her again. But I couldn't. *God,* I couldn't do that to Ash.

My tongue had just broken through every last *bro-code* that existed. Hell, every last fiber of decency and control and respect that I'd prided myself on. Gone.

And I would do it all over again. Just for that taste of the apple in the Garden of Blake.

I stood swiftly, forcing myself a step away from the bed and stumbling in the process.

What had I done?

She sat up, righting her clothing in awkward embarrassment. I wanted to tell her to stop. I wanted to tell her to never be embarrassed in front of me. I wanted to tell her to never hide from me. I wanted to slowly strip every inch

195

of fabric off of her until there was nothing left but the softest skin I'd ever tasted and then I wanted to spend more hours than existed in the day exploring every inch of the body of the woman whose soul I'd known for a long time.

But I couldn't have what I wanted.

So, I didn't move because even too jarring of a breath could incite me to do all the things that I shouldn't.

"I'm sorry," I rasped like it was any sort of excuse for how I was behaving. "*Fuck*, Blay, I'm sorry."

"Don't apologize." Her words were low and strained, adding with an edge, "And *don't* tell me that it was a mistake again." I glimpsed the hurt that crackled like lightning in her eyes before she ducked her head and walked around me.

"Blake," I groaned, wincing as I turned towards her, my jeans digging into my angry cock that was cursing every inch of my self-restraint.

"Don't." She shook her head. "Just. Don't."

I wished I could pretend that I didn't hear the tremble in her voice.

Grabbing her phone and purse from the table, she spun on me, her eyes burning with angry indignation.

"What is the point of all this, Zach?" she demanded. I couldn't even answer before she blurted out, "No. You know what? I don't want to know. I was the one who insisted I stay tonight and that's my fault. You told me to go… I should have listened. Typical, right?" The question punctuated with a harsh laugh. "I was always so bad at listening to you. You'd think after all the scars, I would have learned by now."

I heard the hurt echoing in the hollowness in her voice, like the thought just dawned on her that she only had herself to blame when this was really my fault. After all this time, I'd only gotten worse at resisting her - *and my desire for her had only grown stronger.*

"All I know is that I c-can't do this anymore. There was a

plan. A contract. And we need to stick to it… I need to stick to that."

Resignation.

The last thing I ever expected to hear from Blake Tyler, the girl who'd done everything and anything in her power to do what she wanted - to get what she wanted.

Fearless.

My hands flexed at my sides. I wanted to tell her to keep fighting - that somewhere there would be a way for this to be ok. I didn't want to stick to the fucking plan. I didn't want to stick to my principles. I didn't want to stick to anything. But that was who I was - who I was raised to be. And I wasn't going to take advantage of the fact that I was wooing a girl who was already prone to falling, regardless of how real it felt for me.

And I wasn't going to break my promise to her brother.

Or break it any further, at least.

"You're right," I agreed with a tight nod even though the words felt like the worst betrayal I'd ever committed. "I will do better," I swore quietly.

For her sake and mine, I better.

Otherwise, the only thing I'd be breaking was her heart – if I hadn't already.

The silence was a deafening truce between us.

"See you tomorrow." She walked to the door, pausing to tip her head slightly back over her shoulder, adding, "On stage."

I remained frozen in place until the door clicked shut behind her. Dropping to my knees where I'd just been, I pounded my fist into the bed.

Fuck. This. Shit. Fuck it.

Closing my eyes, I refused to let her go. I saw her lying here, naked and open for me, as I fumbled to unzip the pair of jeans that I was going to fucking burn after tonight. Pulling out my demanding erection, I pumped my fist, still smelling her desire… tasting her sweetness…

I remembered the way her needy off-limits pussy clenched around my finger as she exploded under my tongue, gushing her desire into my mouth. With a strangled grunt, I pulled my undershirt up over the head of my dick just as I came.

"*Fuck,*" My cum soaked through my shirt; it was release but it wasn't enough.

I needed to resist her. At all costs. Even if it meant I needed to be put in a fucking straightjacket around her.

Stripping down, I made my way into the bathroom and flipped on the shower.

Just a few more weeks… I stepped into the warm stream, closing my eyes, and running the water through my hair

Her heartbroken face flashed in front of me.

You might be able to resist her body, my traitorous body taunted, *but you won't be able to resist her heart.*

CHAPTER SIXTEEN

BLAKE

Track 12: Star-crossed

"I'd like to think our love was written in the stars.
No matter what happened, never a shadow of a doubt.
Now I know that whatever was written, whatever was felt.
Could have been. Should have been. Now crossed out."

GROANING, I PULLED MYSELF FROM BED AS I HEARD TAYLOR enter my bedroom. She'd let herself into my suite a half an hour ago to wake me up, leaving me to lie lazily in the plush bed, my muscles sore and stiff from yesterday – my heart used and bruised from this entire tour.

I couldn't be mad at Zach. *Ok, I could.* But what was the point? I'd asked for the letdown. In fact, I think at some moments during that evening (the thought of which still making my body warm and needy) I even begged.

If crazy was doing the same thing over and over again expecting a different result, then torture is doing the same thing over and over again knowing things will never change.

Maybe it wasn't just torture. Maybe it was just pure insanity.

Either way, I'd numbly come to accept that night that no matter how far I pushed him, he would never fall. He might trip. He might stumble. But his loyalty and steadfast determination was a foundation buried so far beneath the surface that I'd sooner dig to China than be able to get through it.

According to Google, I figured I was past the 'anger' stage of grief and steadily moving into bargaining. Mostly because I swore to myself… to Taylor… to God… that this wasn't going to happen again. I swore that I would listen to my head and finish the tour the way I was supposed to just as long as my heart wasn't broken anymore. *And it was a deal.*

So, when we'd landed yesterday in Austin and had most of the morning to give the world a 'show' before the concert began, I went into the prospect with a calm resignation to be kind and *not* careless. And because it was Texas, I suggested that we go for a trail ride. *(Not because I'd been craving something that reminded me of the carriage ride in New York.)*

Taylor researched a local horseback riding barn that was just outside of the city - Maverick Trail Rides. Zach picked up our rental - a Jeep Wrangler - and we'd been off to our latest adventure. Tay made sure to post a photo to my Instagram when we landed, tagging the barn we were headed to - a one-hundred-percent guarantee for a full parking lot of paparazzi when we arrived.

Thankfully, none of them were brave enough to actually follow us on horseback. Instead, they pulled out fancy lenses that looked like they could have captured my face if I'd decided to go for a hike on the moon and followed us at a distance.

The day was beautiful. Our guide, Danny, was really funny and the kind of nice that made light of the fact that she had a superstar on one of her horses - even taking us on detours when we ended up on roads that were littered with those same cars from the parking lot. I smiled and thanked her even though avoiding the cameras defeated the official purpose of why we were there. But I couldn't tell her that.

The *unofficial* purpose was written in a code of secret smiles and laughter between Zach and me as we tried to control the animals beneath us who had minds of their own. The ride was laced with moments where he forgot to keep me at arm's distance and I forgot to keep him at least a heartbreak away.

Luna, my horse, was a pig in another life and kept veering off or jerking her head to try and eat some grass. Zach's mount, on the other hand, Troy, wanted nothing more than to bite Luna's ass the entire ride. And it didn't matter how many times I slowed to let him pass me, somehow, he and Troy would always end up behind me again.

The Texas sun was warm, but not as hot as Zach's hard stare as he watched me ride. I shifted in the Western saddle, letting it rub against me in ways that it wasn't intended to and imagining it was him moving beneath me... all the while knowing his heady gaze was because he saw what I was doing - letting each roll of my hips against the pummel of the saddle press against my ache. And he knew it was because of him.

I suffered with the memories that were still all over me like a wine-stained dress that I couldn't wear anymore. Meanwhile, he'd kept to his word because that was the role he played best: the admirable asshole. Cool and collected, he became the perfect boyfriend when the world was watching. In private, it felt like there were still worlds between us.

Those lips of his though... they'd taken on a whole new meaning in my life. Until this point, they'd been the bearers of nicknames and taunts, they'd brought trials of pleasure followed by the verdict of heartbreak, and they'd been the unattainable goal - the end zone that my lips would never reach.

But now... I shivered and clenched my thighs tight

together as I felt a rush of hot moisture between them. Now they'd transformed into exquisite destruction. Biting my lip, I let myself drift back to New York and the memory of his mouth devouring every inch of my desperate sex.

Deal. Remember the deal.

"Blay."

My eyes shot open as Taylor stood in the doorway with her arms over her chest.

"Sorry," I mumbled guiltily, throwing the covers off my now-steaming body. "My body doesn't want to move after yesterday."

Even though the trail ride was only ninety minutes, add on to that the show that followed complete with dancing and jumping, and it was the perfect recipe for legs that were at the same time too stiff to want to move and so weak they felt like jello when I tried.

"Sounds like you should grab a hot shower before we have to leave," she said, walking into the adjoining bath and turning on the water before I could think about responding that a *cold* shower might be more in order.

"When do we have to go?" I asked hoarsely as I wobbled over to her. "And what's on the schedule today?"

"Ahh... well..." she stuttered and stopped me in my tracks.

"Tay..." I eyed her, too sore to handle any suspense.

"You have a radio interview this morning with Austin Live." The announcement came out in a rush.

"Oh. That's fine," I said moving past her and grunting with every effort I made to strip.

"They called this morning though."

"About what?" I shut the shower door behind me and stepped into the hot stream, quickly cranking the dial down to cool.

"Well, they want to interview you and Zach."

"What?" I asked, whipping the door open and sticking my half-drenched head back out.

"Bruce already told them 'absolutely.'" She gave me a pleading 'don't shoot the messenger' look along with a shrug that said 'out of my hands.'

Of course he did.

A half-groan, half-whimper escaped as I hung my head in defeat. It was one thing to act like we were dating and fake (*but not really*) smiles and stares, maybe a kiss here or there, for the cameras; it was a whole different beast to *talk* about our relationship and about each other.

"It'll be fine, B," Tay tried to reassure me as I shut myself back into my watery confinement. "You guys have a ton of actual memories to draw from. And it's not like anyone except the radio host - DJ Dave - can see you."

I grabbed my cookie-scented soap, the kind that even had a recipe on the bottle, and squirted it angrily onto the washcloth. "What if our stories don't match?" *We needed to get our story straight.* I huffed quietly at the moment when an interview began to feel like a trial.

"Take turns answering."

"What if Zach says the wrong thing? He's... He's never liked me the way that I liked him. What if he isn't convincing?"

"Then just do most of the talking," she replied. "You were the original subject of the interview anyway. I'm sure the guy is just going to ask Zach like one or two questions and then forget about him; you are still the star of the show."

I let the water run directly over my face, hoping it would wash away my anxiety over how things never seemed to go according to plan when it came to Zach. I had a feeling that this was going to be no exception.

"How could I forget?" I grumbled.

♪♫♪

Zach

FOR SOMEONE who sang in front of tens of thousands of people on a regular basis, Baby Blake looked like the picture of a Nervous Nelly as DJ Dave, the six-foot-two bald body-builder who was either eating weights for breakfast or on a steady supply of steroids, led us into the recording room. If the Rock had a twin – a twin who was slightly bigger and slightly more tatted – DJ Dave would be him.

I tried not to laugh as Blay sat in the seat and immediately began fidgeting with her hands in her lap. *Talk about giving away that there was something more to our story.* Right after she'd just spent the last twenty minutes in the car, breathless and blabbing about all the things I could and couldn't say in front of this guy - *like I hadn't known her her whole fucking life and desired her for half of it.*

"Alright guys," DJ Dave said with giant white smile. "I just have to go check one thing and then I'll be back. We go live in five." And with a rock-on hand sign, he strolled back out of the room, leaving the two of us alone for a minute.

"You're going to eat right through your lip, Baby Blake."

Immediately, her mouth parted and she licked over where she'd been about to wound herself.

"Remember, just let me do most of the talking," she muttered.

I chuckled, "Whatever you say."

"Seriously, Zach."

"I am being serious." I threw up my hands. "Speaking of

being serious… I *seriously* think that DJ Dave's teeth probably glow in the dark."

"Zach!" she exclaimed and turned to glare at me even though I could see her trying to fight her smile that said she completely agreed with my assessment; the man's teeth were *blindingly* white. "He can probably hear you."

I laughed, prompting her to groan and bow her head.

With her hair pulled up in a ponytail, all I could focus on was the slender column of her neck sloping down to her shoulders that were partially bare from the one-shouldered top she had on. Before I could stop myself, my hand rose, my fingers brushing lightly on her exposed back.

She shivered but didn't say anything.

I should have been happy. I should have been fucking elated the way she'd stopped pushing. Like New York had finally pushed her too far. And like an asshole, I wanted her back. I was fighting to find something that would convince my stupid goddamn head that I deserved to be with her. And that I wasn't scum for what it would do to my friendship with Ash.

They trailed up to her neck and then began to knead into the taut muscles. Resting her chin on her hands, she let out the most fucking torturous little moans and sighs like she was purposely trying to see just how fucking little she had to do to get me off.

"Y-you don't have to do this…" she finally said with a soft voice. "They can't see us."

"I know, Baby Blake. I know."

That was the whole point.

Most things I wanted to do to her were things that shouldn't be seen.

***

.   .   .

"So, are you happy with how the tour is going so far?" DJ Dave asked.

He'd been steadily talking to Blake for the past twenty minutes with a few unimportant questions thrown my way - mostly about ZPP.

She'd remained tense when he came back in the room even though the smile on her face told the world a different story. So, I kept my hand on her back, rubbing slow soothing circles along the edge of her shirt, enjoying the spark every time my fingers brushed over her skin.

When the red 'Live' light illuminated, I slid my hand to hers, prying her tightly gripped fingers apart and threading mine into them.

Distantly, I heard her words, but what I was really listening to was her body - the way her chest rose and fell (more rapidly when he was about to ask another question), the way her pulse sped underneath my fingers when they rubbed the back of her hand, and the way she licked her lips every time DJ Dave said my name.

"Alright." Mr. Glow-in-the-Dark-Teeth said as he turned to me; Blay's hand squeezed mine hard. "So, Zach. I think we are all dying to know some details about the two of you - lifelong friends that fate has now brought together in a different way."

If he only knew.

"What is your first memory of Blake?"

Easy.

I grinned and I heard her groan beside me. "What?" I said turning to her. "I didn't even answer him yet."

"I know, but I know what you're going to say and it's embarrassing."

"Oh, really? I don't think that you do."

"Of course, I do. I was there," she insisted. "You're going to tell him about the eggs."

DJ Dave laughed and reminded the two of us that we

weren't alone. Blake's cheeks turned a version of pink that perfectly matched her shirt. My dick wondered if it matched her nipples underneath, too.

I winked at her and began my story. "The first memory I have of Blake is the day that her family moved to Franklin." Out of my periphery, I saw the way her brow furrowed adorably because she clearly didn't remember. She'd been eight at the time.

"My parents and I walked over to their house to welcome them to the neighborhood - a neighborhood that consisted of now our *two* families and a variety of farm animals. I met her parents and her brother, Ash, who was eleven - the same age as me - but there was only mention of Blake who'd apparently cried the entire morning and stormed up to her new room the second they'd arrived."

"Fast forward to that night. I'm climbing into bed and a light outside my window catches my eye. I figured it was just from their house; I wasn't used to any light coming from that direction. So, I look out and see a few lights on in their house, but before I look away, I see another light roaming in the field - *a flashlight.*"

Blake's eyes widened; she was remembering.

"I get dressed or whatever and run out there. Low and behold, it's the little sister - Blake. And she's lugging a rolling backpack with a huge image of a golden retriever on it behind her. Long story short, I introduce myself and all that - she wasn't too impressed at the time. So, I ask her what she's doing and she tells me that she's running back to Nashville to be with her friends - specifically her friend Layla and Layla's puppy, Oreo. Honestly, it seemed like she was more upset about leaving the dog than her friend, but who am I to say for sure?" I let out a soft chuckle as Blake playfully swatted my arm. "Naturally, I ask her how she knows that she's going in the right direction and, staring at me with fiery blue eyes, she replies that she is following the

North Star because she knows that Nashville was north of where we were."

"Smart," DJ Dave interjected with a grin.

"Right. So, I realize that I have a small problem on my hands because this little spark over here is determined to walk her way back to Nashville. By herself. In the dark. Obviously, the first thing that I say is that she can't run away; she lives here. And that her parents and brother will be really sad."

"What did you say, Blake?" The DJ asked Blake, clearly wanting her to get a word in on this story.

"I-I think I might have said that I didn't care. That he couldn't stop me." She laughed and buried her face in her hands.

"To which I said 'Fine' but that I was going with her." She nodded, agreeing with me. "A few steps later, I dramatically let out a sigh and pretend like I'm saying to myself, 'I'm going to miss you, Cookie.' You're probably wondering who Cookie is – well, so did Blake. So, I told her that Cookie was my family's border collie. That stopped her in her tracks. You should have seen how wide her eyes went when she clarified *'You have a dog?'*"

"Oh my God! I do remember this!" she exclaimed next to me.

With a smile, I continued, "So, I told her that I do - or did. Not anymore because she was making me leave him to go to Nashville with her."

"I told you, you didn't have to come," she interrupted.

"And I replied that she was stuck with me whether she liked it or not *but* at least if she stayed here, she'd get to meet Cookie and be her friend, too." I shot Blay a smile before I ended with, "And that was the first time I met her. I'd say she's been stuck with me ever since."

DJ Dave laughed and the look on his face was the one that everyone listening probably had - the one that recognized something real when they saw it. My smile flickered because it was real - but that didn't mean I could have it. *Or keep it.*

"Wow!" he exclaimed. "What a story. What. A. Story. That's awesome, you two. I'm sure all your fans listening, Blake, are going crazy over this. I'm also pretty sure that we want to know the eggs story."

Blake groaned and rolled her eyes.

Figuring it would take up some time that would otherwise be spent on questions that would be too probing for comfort, I appeased him, recounting the time I'd shown Blake our chicken coop. She hadn't realized that the eggs weren't fertilized and would never become baby chicks. So, later that night, I'd caught her, with her Easter basket no less, trying to smuggle out all of the eggs in an attempt to 'save' the chicks.

That one had DJ Dave doubling over in a fit of laughter for a good minute and a half before he finally started to breathe again.

"Alright, I know our time is almost up. I just have one more question for you Zach, since time seems to have gotten away from me."

Both Blake and I tensed, knowing whatever was coming was what we'd been dreading.

"How did you know?" he asked. "How did you know that what you felt for Blake was more than friendship - and dare I say love?"

Fuck.

And even though we'd managed to escape a shitload of potentially problematic questions, damn DJ Dave really knocked them all out of the park with this last one.

Blake didn't blush this time. No. All the color drained out of her face. Even though she probably wanted to try to take the reins away from me on this one, she couldn't; she sat frozen.

"That's a good question," I said, buying myself some time. I glanced over to girl who I hadn't been able to shake after all these years, the one who'd grown around my bones, onto my mind, and into my heart.

With a sigh, I answered hoarsely, "Dave, let me ask you something. The breath you just took, do you remember taking it?"

He looked at me like I had three heads, but after a moment of stuttering, answered hesitantly, "Uh," he stuttered. "I mean, no. I guess not."

"Exactly. You don't focus on breathing. It just happens," I continued. "You don't see it. You don't smell it or taste it as the air is going in. The only reason you know it must have happened is because of the effect it causes; it's only after the fact, it's only when I ask you, that you know you breathed in order to live." I paused, pulling my hand from Blake's to adjust my hat. I couldn't look at her. I couldn't look at her because she'd know that I was telling the truth.

"I can't tell you how I knew or when I knew that I wanted to be with her because I couldn't see it coming. Or smell it. Or taste it. All I knew was that at some point I'd breathed her in and now I needed her to stay alive."

Blake

"Why did you say that?" The words rushed from my mouth as I grabbed onto Zach's arm and pulled him to stop before we reached the car.

He spun to face me with the chiseled, hard expression that had been carved onto his face as soon as the interview ended. "Because he asked the question," he barely replied through lips that were pulled taut in an angry line.

"Did... did you mean it?" I whispered, my hand dropping from his arm as he stepped closer to me.

I couldn't believe what I'd heard. *Neither could DJ Dave for that matter.* That question was going to end us – I was sure of it. All I could hope was that Zach could come up with another cute story that would appease rather than answer the incredibly personal question.

But what had come out... What it sounded like he meant... *How could I believe that?* Not after what happened in New York. Not after he'd told me (more or less) that whatever he felt for me was a mistake - *that I would always just be a mistake. Blake the Mistake.*

Mistake Blake.

How could you *not* believe it? My heart argued.

"Zach..." I whispered, licking my lips as I tipped my head up to his. He was so close, but not close enough. Our chests touched as our lungs fought for the same *'oxygen'* between us, his head dipped towards mine and I thought he was going to kiss me. I thought he was going to show me that it was true.

What he said... Well, I wouldn't have ever thought to put it that way. No. If I'd been given the chance to answer, I would have said that I knew I loved Zach from the moment I realized that it was only he who seemed to have the missing pieces to my heart.

Unfortunately, I was still learning that the only reason he had those pieces was because he was the one who'd broken it in the first place.

His nose nuzzled mine and the battle that fought inside of him was both frustrating and familiar.

Fight for me, heart, I tried to breathe into his, knowing this wasn't part of my deal; *I was now bargaining with the wrong person.* Still, I pleaded to the part of him that wanted me. The part that kissed and touched me even when he knew that he shouldn't - even when it made him a traitor. It was the part that healed the hurt and warmed the coldness that he'd left in me.

"Did you mean it?" I asked again, so tempted to kiss him

So close. So close to everything.

"I meant..." he paused, his nostrils flaring with angry breaths. Whatever he'd been about to say was going to add to my missing parts; I could see it happening right in front of me. "I meant what I said about sticking to the contract. To our plan. I said what I had to."

To end the conversation? Or to tell the truth?

"Which is why *this*," his mouth captured mine in what would look like a gentle kiss but felt like his lips were holding the bull back from the fight, ready at any moment to break free and devour me, "is just for them," he finished as his lips turned up in a small, fake smile.

The heat from his touch dissipated and I didn't have to turn my head to know that the cameras had gathered to capture the two of us after what was sure to be reported as a 'sensational' interview sealed with a kiss.

He turned and walked to the car leaving me to try and find balance between the intense high I'd been at to the extreme low that he'd pulled me to. I glanced behind me, half expecting there to be a trail of broken pieces of my heart behind me as I followed him.

I hated the way he could just stand there, a breathtaking model of devastating dissonance, as he held the door open for me like a gentleman while breaking my heart like a scoundrel.

CHAPTER 17
BLAKE

Track 13: Homesick

*"Every little moment with you is every little reason
why it feels like half my heart is missing.
If home is where the heart is,
then I'm homesick for you."*

2 Weeks later

I blew another bubble, the popping of it like a soundtrack to
my nervous tick as I waited to take the stage in Santa Clara,
wishing I could turn and run as fast as I could into the ocean
instead.

Not really. But sort of.

"Love is in the air (literally!) for Blake Tyler!"

AFTER TEXAS, we'd flown to Vegas for three shows at the Aria. California was this weekend and next, then onto Denver. Show after show. Kiss after kiss. *Lie after lie.*

"Dinner, Carriage rides, Duets… This popstar's very own fairytale is unfolding right before our eyes!"

ZACH WAS that sensation in my life where I couldn't tell whether he was hot or cold, real or fake – all I knew was that he burned. After that interview, it felt like everything changed even though everything stayed the same. *Don't ask how that is possible, but it is.*

Case-in-point: our day trip in Vegas. We'd taken a break from the commotion on the Strip to head out to the Hoover Dam. I'd gone from laughing so hard that I cried, trying to get away from the spray that would turn my hair into a frizzy mess, to warm and tingly when Zach pulled me close.

I could have spent forever standing there in the mist with his arms wrapped around me, his hands stuffed in my jacket pockets. That moment, when I tilted my head up and Zach looked at me like I was all he wanted before bending down to kiss me, still replayed in my head like the end of a Hallmark movie.

Even though I knew that the gesture was staged for the slew of curious eyes fixed on us, the kiss sent electricity up and down my spine, making my heart beat erratically. It. Was. Real. What we had was unstoppable, no matter what my mind argued – *or tried to bargain away.*

The cameras that accompanied every excursion were the devils on my shoulder flashing reminders that it felt that way because it was supposed to look that way.

Emotions are the worst indicators of reality.

Their insistence became louder every day. Especially when we'd managed to keep to the pact we'd made in his hotel room. Translation: we hadn't been completely alone since Valentine's Day.

I'd come to the conclusion that we were living in this sort of Wonderland - *where it was never worse, but never better.*

"Ready, B?" Tay came up to me, holding out a tissue in front of my face for me to spit my gum into.

"Yeah," I answered with a sigh.

"Just a few more weeks, ok?" She gave me an encouraging smile that I attempted to return. "Things are going really well. I know I keep telling you that but, seriously, it couldn't be going any better."

"Blake Tyler finally catches her perfect guy! (After throwing back all the rest of them!)"

HER HAND RUBBED COMFORTINGLY over my back.

"Easy for you to say when your childhood obsession isn't being dangled in front of your face every night." My joke fell flat. Jokes that aren't really jokes tend to do that.

"It could be worse." I groaned, knowing she was definitely going to find something to make me count my blessings. "I could have told you that you needed to date Stevie Cunningham."

I laughed and playfully smacked her arm. Let's just say Stevie Cunningham was one of those kids who hadn't figured out personal hygiene by the time high school rolled around, but was still convinced he was hot shit; there wasn't a week that went by that he didn't ask Taylor out, whisper that she was secretly his girlfriend, or try to corner her in the hall to get her number.

She was right, it could be much worse.

Then again, there was no way in hell that I'd ever be in danger of falling in love with Stevie Cunningham.

My heart may be going haywire with all of the mixed signals that it was getting, but my reputation was steadily thriving. And that was the whole point of this stupid thing. I should be happy.

Be happy, stupid heart.

The day we'd spent out together had jump started it, but it was the interview that cemented that this was something different for Blake Tyler - that this love was real.

They had no idea.

Since then, duets had been a requirement for each show. Not always something slow and steady. Last weekend, we even had the other ZPP guys come out and perform 'Life is a Highway' with us. It was new and fun and our chemistry on stage was almost as good as it was off.

Tonight was my night to choose. With the way my insides were being twisted in every direction and after my phone call with my parents last night, I'd opted for 'Home' by Michael Bublé. I laughed and made sure there was a smile on my face as I spoke because I didn't want them to hear my worry and my hurt.

"Just remember, B, don't cross the line," Tay added as I stared out onto the stage where the lights were flickering, indicating that the show was going to start soon.

She didn't know it, but I'd come to realize that there *was* a line between Zach and me, only it didn't separate us; it was the line in the chorus that sang, '*I've been loving you for such a long, long time.*'

It was a line that would only ever lead me directly to him.

I jumped when an arm came around my shoulder. *Not Zach;* my body always knew when he was close.

"You good, Blay?" I tilted my face to see my brother's brown eyes narrowing on me with concern.

He looked like he stepped out of a J. Crew ad with his khakis and blazer, stylishly calm and collected. His face told a different story. I saw how he pushed Zach away after New York - cold and curt to his oldest and best friend. And I saw how it affected Zach; he tried to play it off like Ash was just busy and dealing with a lot of inquires for ZPP to perform since they'd become insta-famous.

It was a lie.

Ash hated seeing Zach and me together - even when he knew it was faked.

And with me, my brother had become even more protective - always stepping in to do anything that Zach might offer or ask to do. Holding the door. Making sure to bring me water when I walked off stage. He only let Zach near me when absolutely necessary. It was a complete one-eighty from when we were younger - even after the whole graduation party incident - he never cared to leave the two of us alone.

"Great," I answered with a forced smile.

"Over halfway done. Then this shit will be over. Done and gone."

I winced at the hard edge in his voice. He rubbed his hand over his mouth and I could have sworn it was to cover a curse. Then with a nod to no one, he walked away and left me with only one mind-numbing, heart-stopping, soul-crushing thought: *What was going to happen when this was over?*

Like lightning, it only took one brilliant crack for my calm and sanity to burst into flames.

When this was over... and Zach was gone.

My mind spun like a top out of control. He'd be gone. Everything would go back to the way it was. Everything except my heart. My brother's statement burned away all of my excuses and rationalizations.

I'd fallen in love with Zach Parker, again.

Or, more depressingly, maybe I just realized that I'd never really gotten back up from the first time I fell.

I choked, trying to suck in air that felt like was vanishing. I focused on my breath. I focused on the thing I needed to survive. *Zach was right.* I didn't know the moment I'd fallen in love with him; all I felt now was that the only thing that was keeping me alive was being ripped from me.

Tay quickly handed me the water bottle she'd been carrying, looking at me with concern.

"Sorry. Thanks," I said, replacing the cap. "Let's get this show on the road."

Buttoning my blazer, I squared my shoulders, shoving all of my painfully conflicting emotions back down deep inside the little cage I'd had to build for them - a task I'd perfected over these past few weeks.

I put on the sparkling smile that my adoring fans were expecting to see and walked out onto the stage like the show wasn't going to cost me another piece of my heart.

***

SMILE AND WAVE. Just smile and wave.

Step after step, all of me threatened to fall apart as the edge of the stage seemed to get farther and farther away. *Rep-u-ta-tion.* I was tied together with that smile but I was rapidly coming undone. I made it to side and out of the lights, stalked by hollers and cheers for another encore, and my shoulders completely collapsed.

I felt the lyrics to 'Home' right down to my bones earlier and they'd echoed in the space for the rest of the performance; that was me - surrounded by a million people and yet I still felt all alone.

I felt like I was living someone else's life - the fairytale the world thought I had - the one where Blake Tyler actually gets what she wants.

I needed to get out of here.

"Hey! Blake, are you ok? What's wrong?" Taylor pushed through the group of people that always surrounded me when I walked off stage - to take off the mic, hand me water, etc. "*Go*," she said forcefully and they all dispersed.

"I just need to get out of here. It's... hot," I said thickly. "I-I feel like I can't breathe."

She tugged off the blazer I had on, leaving me in just the white cowl-neck shirt and black jeans. "Alright, let me go grab our things and then we'll leave. How does some In-and-Out and Netflix sound? Good, yeah?" she asked as she squeezed my arm, directing me away from the stage before she disappeared down the hall.

Most days, Tay knew me better than anyone. But today, I felt like I didn't even know myself.

"Blake?" He always found me at my weakest. Or maybe I always found him when I needed him.

My crossed arms unraveled as I spun to face the man who didn't want my heart.

He stalked over to me, his hands gripping into my shoulders. "What the hell happened? What's wrong?" he asked as he tipped my face to his.

"Nothing." I turned my chin from his grasp. I couldn't look at him right now. I felt like I was in the middle of the desert, starved of water for days, and I couldn't tell if what was in front of me was really what could save my life or if it was just another mirage.

"Bullshit," he growled. "More bullshit than the time you lied to your mom about knowing the truth about Santa Claus because you didn't want to get Ash and me in trouble for telling you."

I gulped and shifted nervously. I was a horrible liar.

"I-I just need to get out of here. I can't breathe—"

Was I having a panic attack?
Right in front of him?
Seriously?

I could hear the blood pounding in my ears. My head felt weightless as it tried to free itself from my body that was weighed down with utter brokenness. Embarrassment made it worse. *God, where was Tay?*

"Ok! I have all our—" Taylor cut off, stopping abruptly in the hall when she saw Zach and me, looking between the two of us.

"I'll take that," Zach said, grabbing my favorite worn L.L. Bean bag from her hand. "Let's go."

He grabbed my hand and I stumbled.

"Wait, where are you going?" Tay asked following us out towards the parking lot.

"I'm taking her someplace where she can relax," he said gruffly, opening the passenger door of his rental mustang and ushering me inside.

I was in a fog - throat, tongue, thoughts - everything was heavy and thick and I felt like I was suffocating.

"Alright." I heard Tay's worried response. "Let me know if you need anything."

"Thanks." The door shut next to me but I could still hear the last thing that he said. "Tell Ash she's with you. Sick. Please."

***

"WHERE ARE WE GOING?" I managed to ask, a few minutes into the drive. My legs were pulled up onto the seat, my heels from the show discarded on the floor of the car.

"You'll know when we get there," was the only response that I got.

Another few miles weaving through city streets and I had my answer. *The beach.*

Zach pulled in and drove to the far end of the lot. Not that it mattered. No one was here this late at night anyway.

"Alright, Baby Blake, let's go."

I stood too quickly, blood rushing to my head and I felt my knees give way.

"Christ," he swore, hoisting me up into his arms.

Like I weighed no more than a football, he carried me over the sand, heading straight for the water's edge.

And he didn't stop there.

He kicked off his shoes and then, clothes and all, he carried me into the chilled waves that soothingly lapped the shore.

"What are you doing? We have clothes on!" I cried out as we went deeper, the water now at his waist and coming quickly for me.

"Going for a swim." And then my legs dropped, splashing into the sea. "I think they'll dry."

I gasped as the cold soaked them, but Zach still held me safely tight against his chest. I knew he was trying to put me at ease, but my stomach was already in knots from the show - knots that seemed impossible to disentangle.

"Jerk," I shot at him, wrapping my legs around his waist and holding myself tightly to his chest for warmth if nothing else.

He just chuckled.

We just stood there for a minute and he made no move to release me. He didn't ask questions. He didn't demand to know what happened. He just let me anchor to him and allow the waves to rock my emotions back to some sort of equilibrium.

"I can't do this, Zach," I whispered softly, the words finally finding their way to the surface.

"Can't do what, Blay?" The soft rasp in his voice sent

shivers to all the parts of me that got me in trouble. "The tour?"

The tour.

I ducked my head and the tears let loose. He probably thought I was crazy - a simple question turned me into a sob fest, but I couldn't stop. My whole body heaved in the water against him as sobs shook my body.

"Blake, baby," he hushed, holding me - rocking me. "It's alright. I got you. It's all going to be alright."

Seconds were stained with tears as I cried into the corner of his neck, my arms wound tightly around him. *Delicate. Protected.* How I felt in his arms broke me further. I couldn't continue to pretend like my feelings for him were just for show; it was like trying to hide the fact that my heart was beating - at some point, trying to hide it was going to destroy me.

"I just want to… need to know… is it killing you like it's killing me?"

"Oh Blay," he said gently, pushing my now-damp hair away from my ear to whisper soothingly, "It's just a few more weeks. Then they'll forget about everything that came before. People like to throw rocks at things that shine."

He didn't know. He didn't understand. And I couldn't find the words to make him.

"Blake," his fingers on my face tightened and his demanding stare intensified. "Listen to me. *Forget* about the cameras. Reality isn't in a static image or a tagline. *The cameras are liars* - liars because they stop time, which cannot be stopped; liars because they show everything in focus when nothing is *ever* in focus. You can't see the real you through a lens so let the drama queens find their fix somewhere else. This system is built in such a way that the truth doesn't always win out. But your fans will still be there and they will still love you."

I shook my head against his shoulder.

"They don't know me, Zach. I barely know me." Tears clogged my throat. It was all too much. Constantly surrounded and yet I still felt all alone.

"What do you need me to do?" He pulled back and brushed the hair away from my face, searching for my eyes that I wouldn't give him. I shook against him – from the cold or the sobs building inside, I couldn't tell. "Shh…" he whispered with the waves. "I'm here. When you lose where you came from, *I'll be here*. When you forget the way to go, *I'll be here*. And when you feel like no one is standing beside you, *I'll be here*. Just be still, *Blakebaby*. I'm here. I've got you. Just tell me what you need."

I sobbed for what seemed like no reason and every reason at the same time. I wished I could tell him what to do. I wished I could give an order and it would appear - just like anything else in my life could. I could ask for Mariska Hartigay to show up in my room tomorrow to film an episode of *Law & Order* and *someone* would make it happen. But I couldn't ask for Zach Parker's heart.

"I can't, Zach. I can't do us." My lip quivered. "Maybe they're all right. Maybe I'm not capable of a relationship." A pitiful laugh escaped me. "At this point, I'm not even capable of a fake one apparently. I thought after all this time I could, but there is no faking it for me. You're the song that's inside of my soul. And I've tried, Zach, I've tried to re-write it over and over again. But what I feel for you doesn't change; the notes are notched into my bones."

I felt his body tense against me, but the water was a safe space. It would wash all my star-crossed heartache away.

"Blake…"

I quickly pressed on before he - or the more circumspect side of me - had me swallowing my words once again.

"This was a mistake," I continued. "But I didn't know. I didn't know what you were."

"And what's that?"

I blinked twice as though it should have been obvious. "The piece that makes me... me. I think that... I'm only me when I'm with you." I swallowed. "But I'm not really with you. Which means that I can never really be me. And *that* is why I can't do this." My words picked up steam - or maybe it was only the emotions behind them. "With you, I forget about the cameras. I forget that this is all part of an act. I forget that I'm supposed to be a different person just because they see me. I forget because I want to be with you - *I want you to be mine.*" I paused to swallow over the lump in my throat, hoping that the water splashed on my face camouflaged the tears. "But then you strike a chord that stops everything and reminds me that none of this is real - just like the rest of my *glamorous* life."

"Blake..." I could hear the weight in his voice, but I couldn't hold it in any longer. He could pretend like there was nothing to talk about between us, but I couldn't.

I wouldn't.

"N-no," I insisted, whipping my head side to side. "I thought I'd be ok with it, but I'd rather not have you at all, than have *this* where I question everything I've ever felt about you. I'd rather have *nothing*, Zach, than feel like I'm losing *everything*."

It came out in a rush. Was it a mistake that I said all that? *Probably.* Because I knew that this tie between us was delicate. But this was what was in my head. *And in my heart.*

"Blake, stop," he gritted out through clenched teeth and I could practically hear another reprimand coming.

"No. We should go." I started to move, frantic to get away from my downfall. "You don't have to do this. I'll be fine. We should go."

Denial. I could live in denial for a few more weeks after I cried out the rest of my heart and soul tonight.

"We're not going anywhere," he said harshly, yanking me

hard against his chest, water splashing between us as my hips jerked into his.

He was hard. I could feel his length between us. I'd felt it from the moment he picked me up earlier. But I'd learned to stop believing that it was going to change anything between us.

Some things run deeper than desire.

"Why?" I demanded, unable to stifle a sob. "So you can tell me to suck it up? To 'stop whining, Baby Blake'? Or maybe just to remind me that wanting me is just for show - or better yet that it's a mistake? I-I can't hear it again. I can't—"

Hard, unyielding lips crashed down on mine, halting my hysterics. One arm locked around my waist, the other speared through my hair, angling my head so his tongue could claim every inch of my mouth and force those words right back down my throat.

Hot. Possessive. Punishing.

I hated how nothing about his desire felt faked. *I loved how nothing about his desire felt faked.*

Our mouths moved together like a duet that only we knew how to sing. High and low. Fast, then slow. The rest of the world drained into black and white, but this... *us...* we were singing in color.

His arms pulled me tighter against him, barely leaving room for any water to fill between us. And still, I wanted to be closer. I wanted to mold into him... seep into his pores... so that it would be impossible for him to let me go - or push me away. My tongue shoved against his, begging for more - pleading for his marks. And he gave them to me. Nipping, sucking, stroking, he covered the entire scale of sins that only he could inflict on my mouth.

My body burned. I waited for the water that lapped against us to start hissing and turn into smoke at any moment. The ocean was becoming our own personal hot tub, heated by our desire that seeped into it.

Why was I not stopping this? I know I should except it's all I've ever wanted.

I liked (too much) the way he was everything I ever wanted.

I knew I should stop it. I was here because I wanted to stop it. But I couldn't. *It's only going to feel good tonight and then the heartache hangover in the morning is going to break me.* He'll break my heart and I'll only have myself to blame. I've seen this story play out before because it's *my* story. This is *my* heartbreak song on repeat and yet for some reason, every time the damn thing comes on, I sing along like *this time* it's going to change its tune.

His hips began to rock into mine. His erection rubbed against my sex in slow motion as the water displaced. I was wet. Everything. Everywhere. *Because of him.*

"Blake," he said with a deep voice, tugging my lower lip into his mouth and sucking on it like I was his favorite candy. "I want you. *Fuck, I've always wanted you.*"

I shook my head, unwilling to believe it, but he covered my lips again, not giving me any other choice.

"Yes. You." He forced my gaze to his and I lost myself in those starry eyes that were sparkling up my darkest night. "You aren't a mistake. You are perfect, *Blakebaby*. And I've wanted you for as long as I've denied it."

Goosebumps rained down over my skin, his words igniting heat low in my stomach. My heart tripped and sputtered as it tried to catch up with what he said. *Was I dreaming?*

I should push him away. I should walk - *run* - away.

But he was quicksand.

"None of this is fake, right here." His hand slid down, fingers gripping my chin firmly. "Nothing between us has ever been fake." He gently kissed my lips. "Hidden." *Kiss.* "Denied." *Kiss.* "Avoided." *Harder kiss.* "But the feelings behind it all haven't changed - *they've always been real.*"

His thumb rubbed over my lip that dropped open, wanting to believe what I was hearing.

"W-what are you saying?" I whispered like he'd drugged me with the truth. "Why are you saying it?"

"I tried. I swear I tried for your sake. And for Ash's." A tortured strain entered his voice. "I tried to stay away. I tried to keep my promise. But I want you. And I knew from the first goddamn note we played that I'd be breaking all my rules to be with you." *Was I dreaming?* "I can't... I won't... continue to watch the light in your eyes when you're with me fade as soon as you think it's just one more performance - that I don't walk away from you each and every goddamn time hating myself."

His harsh laugh rumbled against me. "Like I haven't needed to jack off like a fucking teenager every night since Miami because I want you so badly that I can taste that sweet pussy of yours on my tongue." His fingers flexed into me.

I bit my lip as a small whimper escaped my mouth, my hips subconsciously rocking against his hard length.

"Like I haven't continued fighting this battle even though the war was already won."

"Then why would you say those things?" I asked hoarsely, crippling fear of the past repeating itself cluttering my desire. "Why would you make me believe you didn't?"

His hand cupped the side of cheek. "For all the wrong fucking reasons, *Blakebaby*."

I shivered again at the nickname that strummed on a string directly attached to my heart.

"Against the law. Against the bro code. Against my promise to your brother," he continued, and I watched his face darken, plagued by the thoughts that whispered betrayal.

"Zach—"

He pressed a hard kiss to my lips. "No, Blay. You aren't alone. I thought if I denied it for long enough, it would become true. But all it's done is become torture. And I won't do it anymore." His breath caressed my cheek. "I'm here... I'm here, baby, and I can't do this anymore either. I won't keep lying that every touch – every word – is feigned when the truth is that every piece of it is coming from a part of my heart that I've tried to stop from beating. But I can't, Blay. I can't because *you* are the beat in my heart."

I felt every word and every inch of him as it seeped into me. Like the wet clothes clinging desperately to my skin, I clung to him. My teeth sank into my lip to hold my breath, unwilling to let this moment go.

This was the moment I'd been waiting for my whole life - the moment when the god finally seduced me. And I couldn't decide if it was really a choice - this getting swept away?

"What are we doing?" I finally whispered. My only motivation for breaking the magic of being swallowed up by star-reflecting waves was to go wherever he would take me.

"I'm going to do what I should have done a long time ago."

His stare was hungry and determined and a thrill ran through my body, knowing that this was a look I'd never seen before except in my dreams.

"And what's that?" I don't know why I asked. He was so close and all I wanted was to taste his mouth again.

"Make this real. Make *us* real... Make you mine." He leaned in and brushed his lips to mine, his breath hot against my skin.

Thank goodness for strong water and strong arms to keep me afloat.

"And you, Baby Blake," he continued with a slight grin, "are going to let me."

"Oh, I am?" I asked, wishing it came out feistier and less breathless - *but beggars can't be choosers.* "And why would I do that?"

"Because now that I have you, I won't let you go," he said with a soft, bewildered possessiveness that dug right into the deepest, most vulnerable part of me that had loved him since I knew what love was. Whatever he meant, whatever this was, it was sincere.

Any other thoughts I had were drowned out by the desire

screaming through my veins. My world had begun to feel like a black and white movie until now when he kissed me and held me close; it had been monochromatic misery until he painted me golden.

Heaven help me now.

CHAPTER 18
ZACH

I BIT INTO MY CHEEK, TRYING TO STOP MYSELF FROM SMILING at the way she fidgeted in the passenger seat as I drove us back to the hotel. She thought there was still time for me to change my mind; it was written all over her face. The thing was, I'd been going in the wrong direction for nine fucking years. Changing my mind would be like throwing myself back into oncoming traffic.

If I could even make it that far.

All of this silence and patience... desire and anticipation... My body was shaking, trying to hold back from her.

Her squirming was only part of the reason my eyes had trouble staying focused on the road. Her fancy shirt was molded to her breasts and her nipples were hard and poking against the wet fabric. I thought of Miami and how I was a fucking idiot for waiting so long to taste them. Her dark jeans were tight when she'd been on stage, now they looked like they were spray-painted on and *fuck* if my dick didn't jump at the thought of peeling them off.

I shifted in my seat to adjust my obnoxious fucking

erection, my jeans draining more water into the seat with the movement. *Good thing this was a rental.*

Throwing the car in park in front of the hotel, I reached behind her for my jacket that I'd tossed in the backseat earlier and held it in front of her.

"I'll ruin it," she said, looking from the navy sport coat back to me with concern.

"Blay," I said tightly. "Your nipples are about to cut right through your shirt and while I'm dying over here, painfully enjoying the sight for the entire damn drive, there is no way in hell I'm letting anyone else - *or any cameras* - see what's mine."

Fuck if I haven't wanted to call her that since I was too young to know everything that it could mean.

A second later the jacket was on and she was tucked underneath my arm as we quickly navigated the lobby, catching only a few curious stares but no cameras.

The doors didn't shut fast enough before I had her up against the back wall of the elevator, my lips crushed to hers, searching for the warm sweetness that I was ravenous for. She whimpered - a sound that did to my dick what the bell did for Pavlov's dogs. I shifted against her, needing more contact, and rode my knee up between her legs. Her needy pussy immediately started grinding against me.

The elevator music that hummed in the background was just as ridiculous a soundtrack to the demanding kiss and unabashed dry-humping as Christmas carols playing during a porno.

Ding. Time's up.

Grabbing her hand, I pulled her towards my room enjoying the rosy tint to her cheeks and the deep blue desire crashing in her eyes.

2202.

2204.

2208. Finally.

Kicking the door shut behind us, I hauled her back into

my arms. Desperate. After so long. Finally getting everything I wanted.

Wrapping my hand around her neck, I pulled her lips just to mine. I wanted her. *All of her.* Every moan. Every touch. Every cry. Every shade of red she turned when she came. Screw the past and screw Ash. Even if this ruined our friendship - *even if this ruined me* - I needed to be with her. *Inside of her.* I needed to claim every last inch of Blake Tyler for myself.

"Are you sure?" I growled into her mouth, our heavy breaths mingling in the fraction of a space between us.

"I feel like I should be asking you that," she murmured. "I've been ready for nine years."

I bit her lip for reminding me just what a fucking moron I was and then crushed my lips over hers. My hand pulled her tighter against my mouth, allowing my tongue deeper inside her sweet warmth to feel every inch. Her hips rocked against mine, silent praise and pleas for giving her what she needed as I licked and stroked into her.

"Jesus, Blay, I want you so bad," I panted, pulling back from her.

I watched the bone-chilling fear flash over her features and I knew she thought this was going to be a repeat of the other night.

"If I don't make an attempt now to get us towards the bed, I'm going to end up fucking you against the door," I groaned, taking her hand as the color returned to her cheeks in full force.

"And if I said I wasn't opposed to that?" she murmured as I led her through the spacious, elegantly furnished suite that was reserved for me.

When I'd checked in yesterday, it had just been another fancy-ass hotel room. Tonight, I was glad that it was the nicest fucking hotel room I'd even seen because I'd been waiting a decade for this moment - and she had, too; everything should be perfect.

Opening one of the doors that partitioned the bedroom from the living space, I pulled her ahead of me, following behind as our shoes squished on the carpet.

"I'd tell you that I am." I stopped her in front of the bed, turning her to face me. "There's no way that after waiting this long I'm not going to properly savor every forbidden inch of you in a bed."

My hand dropped hers to unbutton my shirt that clung to my chest. The hunger in her eyes as I pulled the damp fabric off of me made it hard for me to force myself into going slow.

With a wet plop, my shirt dropped to the floor and a second later, Blake closed the distance I'd created, her hands planting firmly on my chest. Clenching my teeth, I tried to restrain myself as her fingers grazed over my skin, tracing along my collarbone, down over my chest, along the flexed ridges of my abs. Her touch drove me insane. I handcuffed her wrists with my fingers before they went any further.

"My turn."

I grabbed the bottom of her shirt and, like I was unwrapping the only Christmas gift I'd ever wanted, peeled it up and over her head and let it fall next to mine. My teeth ground together, seeing her small tits that were pushed up and together by the plain black bra she was wearing. *They were perfect.* I reached behind her, tracing up her spine and not missing the way it made her chest jump as her breath caught in her throat. When the clasp released, I tugged the straps from her shoulders and let the last barrier fall away.

She swayed towards me, craving my touch. And I wanted to touch. Hell, I wanted to touch and taste and fuck the perky pink tits that taunted me. But first, I just wanted to savor this moment of being mesmerized.

"I've imagined your breasts so many ways, Blay. So many

233

ways… So many times…" I broke off, my voice choked. "I always knew they'd be beautiful. But I had no idea."

In a trance, my hand raised to grab one rosy nipple between my fingers and tugged. Her whole body shook as pleasure rippled through it and, gripping her upper arms, I pushed her back until her knees hit the bed, forcing her to sit.

Her legs spread immediately as I knelt in front of her.

This was what I'd always wanted but never could take.

My hands slid to her waist, holding her perfectly still so I could lean forward and flick one nipple with my tongue. Her gasp was like music to my ears - the beginning of a song that I was going to play over and over again.

Cupping the soft weight toward my mouth with one hand, the other slid around to support her back. With the growl of a man who'd been starved for almost a fucking decade, my lips closed over the taut peak.

Silken and sweet. Jesus, she tasted like everything I could ever want.

Slow, I instructed myself as I let my tongue swirl over and around her flesh, trying to focus on her little mewls of pleasure and *not* on how my dick was about to explode in my pants.

I had control - but there wasn't much of it left.

I sucked hard on her tit and she cried out, her hands digging into my scalp to pull my mouth tighter to her. I took my time turning every inch of that breast pink before turning my attentions to the next. By the time I was done - or I was forced to be done because my cock was so swollen in my wet jeans that circulation was being lost - she was gasping my name; if I didn't stop now, she'd orgasm without me. *Without me inside her.*

And that wasn't happening again. *No. Fucking. Way.*

"I could spend days on your beautiful breasts, *Blaybaby. Days…"* I rasped as I pushed her back onto the bed, admiring my handiwork on her red, swollen nipples. They were vibrant red tattoos of how delicious she tasted.

"Zach, please," she whimpered, writhing on the comforter like she was lying on a bed of flames.

My fingers dug into her hips, pushing her into the mattress for a split second before I flicked open her jeans, hooked onto the waistband, and unpainted the denim from her skin, taking her underwear right along with them. Pink porcelain greeted me, still cool to the touch as I tossed the last of her clothes to my side.

"Just one taste." She was watching with wide eyes, propped up on her elbows. I rubbed my hand over my eyes, like I couldn't believe what I was seeing - that I was seeing her, spread wide in front of me, her slick pussy begging to be filled. "So beautiful, Blay. So wet."

This was what my dreams were made of. My little runaway with her pink sex dripping and clenching for me.

I sighed, running my hands up her thighs and then letting one finger drift along her wet slit. She shivered on the bed as I leaned in, inhaling the scent of her that was only for me. Holding her legs wide for me, I groaned pressing my tongue flat against the base of her pussy and letting it run slowly up to the velvet bud between her folds, taking every drop of her with me as I went.

I knew she didn't have long as I slipped one finger inside her passage, feeling the way her muscles flexed around my finger. A second slow lick was accompanied by a second finger inside of her. And then I went three for three.

Stretched.

Perfect.

Forcing my tongue away from her drugged sweetness, I pulled back and stood to strip off the rest of my clothes, my eyes never leaving hers.

Small hands covered mine. "Let me." Hungry eyes looked up to mine as her tongue darted out over her lower lip which was even fuller because I'd been making her bite it.

Fuck.

My body vibrating, I clenched my jaw as she undid the zipper on my jeans, stifling a groan at the pressure against my cock. I saw stars when she tugged the waist down over my massive erection and dragged my jeans to my ankles. My cock was red, angry, and throbbing as it bobbed heavily right in front of her face. I watched the subtle widening of her eyes and the lick of that damn lip. She wanted to taste me. To suck me. And fuck if I didn't want to shove my dick down that pretty little throat of hers and watch those red lips leave streaks down my shaft.

Christ. I tried to inhale. *I didn't think I'd ever been this hard.*

Never one to be subtle about what she wanted - especially when it came to me - I watched her slim fingers wrap around me and pull me towards her mouth. My hips jerked and I quickly unpeeled her hand from my length before she found herself with a face full of cum.

"Next time, *Blakebaby*," I growled and pushed her back onto the bed.

If I survived this time.

Climbing between her thighs felt like coming home - if home was a place I'd dreamt about but never been. My thick arousal lay wedged against her hot core. Throbbing. Demanding. Leaking with raging desire. I couldn't stop myself from rubbing against her, craving the wet friction of her body.

"Please tell me you're on the pill." Her throat bobbed as she swallowed, nodding as her knees rose on either side of my hips, landing me further encased by her slick folds. "I've never had sex... unprotected... before," I ground out, my vision going white as her heat soaked me, "but I can't stand the thought of not feeling you tonight."

She whimpered. "I know, Zach. I know…" Wrapping her legs around my waist, she moaned, "I need you inside me."

Hungry lips sought mine. I gave her the kiss she was searching for – the one that sealed this, and us – the one that made this for keeps.

I positioned my tip at her entrance, letting her desire drench me.

"*Blakebaby...*" I groaned as I pushed inside of her impossibly tight core.

Hot velvet gripped my cock. Heaven. Hell. *Hers.* Inch by torturous inch, I slid inside her and her small gasps had the power to end me. I refused to release her gaze. Watching the way her lip quivered, the way her breath struggled, as I spread her muscles and stretched them wide to accommodate me was hypnotic. Sparks marched down my spine, demanding my surrender to the need to slam inside of her and take what I'd dreamt of for years.

But she was too perfect for that.

Tonight was too important for that.

"You ok?" I could barely focus on her as I pushed the last inch of my dick into her unbelievable pussy, dying little by little in the hot vise around me.

"Yeah," she exhaled and shifted underneath me, her muscles rippling around mine.

"*Fuck,*" I swore at the mind-numbing sensation. *Nine years. Nine fucking years.* I felt like pleasure had been boiled down and cut like the finest drug before it was injected in almost-fatal amounts back into my veins. Groaning, I sunk my teeth into the side of her neck desperately trying to hold on as I began the torturous pull back out of her.

"You can... go faster." Her long legs wrapped around me. I froze, the head of my dick just inside her entrance.

"*Christ, Blay,* I want to go more than faster, *but I don't want to hurt you.*" My arms shook as I rested my weight on them, trying to keep myself from ramming into her.

Her head turned towards mine and she said with a soft, throaty whisper, "I need you to go faster." She arched against me, her legs giving me no retreat, and I sank swiftly back into her heaven.

There she was, the girl who would smear mud all over her Sunday-best to get what she wanted.

And fuck if I didn't want to give it to her.

She gasped at the barely-familiar invasion – the kind that said I filled her perfectly and that she was desperate for more.

A growl tore from my chest as my mouth captured hers. Pushing my tongue roughly inside her lips, I drove my cock into her just like she wanted – faster and unforgivingly. Her hands ran frantically over my body, gripping and scratching, needing more.

I couldn't think. All I knew was that I needed more of the friction of her body around mine as I pounded into her. And my Blay was right there with me, meeting each grinding thrust, panting and moaning with each unyielding assault.

Our hips slapping together sounded like a fucking slow clap leading up to the most incredible moment of my life. *Faster and faster. Louder and louder.* I heard each time I slid into her sopping wet pussy and more of her desire leaked between us

I felt her orgasm build - a sensation that would have been lost with a fucking condom. Her muscles quivered, her legs opening wider, demanding that I drive deeper inside her, hitting that tender spot with each stroke.

"Come for me, baby," I grunted into her lips.

Her whole body tensed and arched as she screamed my name. Her orgasm crashed through her, making her needy sex jerk and clench greedily around my cock. Her scream – like a fucking siren's song – pulled me to my little death.

"Blay…" Her name spilled from my lips as I exploded inside her. My release erupted long and hard as I filled her with my cum.

Mine.

Goodbye, Press.

Goodbye, Fans.

Goodbye, World.

Blake Tyler was mine.

I collapsed onto her, our bodies quaking together, aftershocks rushing over us in tandem. I kissed along her jaw, burying into her neck and breathing in deep. Cookies. And sex. *Both sweet and delicious.* Her fingers trailed up and brushed gently along my cheek, like she couldn't believe it either.

"Part of me wants to tell you that I never knew it could be like that," I said, my voice barely even a whisper, afraid to let the force of my emotions show. "The other part tells me that I always knew it would be like that with you."

I felt her swallow, her heartbeat picking up pace underneath me. "Me, too."

CHAPTER 19
BLAKE

Track 14: Beautiful

"Keep me safe. Keep me warm.
Bring me back through the storm.
Love is patient. Love is kind.
Love is beautiful when it's with you."

I DIDN'T WANT TO MOVE IN CASE THIS WAS ALL A DREAM; I wasn't ready to wake up. My body still hummed with release. Lying here, fading in and out of reality, my heart swelled with the love I could no longer deny.

I blinked a few times, testing out whether or not everything would disappear with each one.

Nope - still Zach. Still here.

Still mine.

A soft cry escaped when I felt him start to move, slowly pulling out of me and lifting off my chest.

"I know, *Blaybaby*," he said hoarsely, "but we should shower."

"I don't want to move." I turned into the covers.

Zach chuckled as he grabbed my ankle and tugged. "Trust me, I don't want you to move from my bed either, but we need to shower and get some sleep. You'll need to get back to your room early in the morning," adding with a heavier tone, "We can't risk Ash finding out this way. I need to be the one to tell him. He deserves that much at least."

Icy hot fear. It climbed like poison ivy through my veins, sucking the life from a love that had just begun to bloom.

I shivered at the mention of my brother's name, a strained ball of anxiety forming inside my belly. *Of course, we'd have to tell him.* I tried to find the rational part of me that should have known this was coming. The blissful bubble that I'd been living in the past few hours now dissolved, leaving the repercussions of what we'd done in its wake. We'd just started down a slope that was treacherous. *My wildest dream, dangerous.*

I tugged the comforter up to my chest, an uneasy feeling creeping over me. It was too easy. This. *Us.* And it was too tenuous. What Zach said earlier in the ocean tried to latch onto my heart, but it was too scarred for it to take hold. Instead, fear gripped me that one word from my brother would have Zach walking away from me again. Alone. Broken. *Just like the last time.*

Swallowing over the lump, I wondered how to convince Zach to hold off on telling my brother so I could hold onto this perfect for a little while longer.

My body stirred as I watched Zach's *really* nice ass walk into the bathroom, but not before I'd gotten one last look at his massive erection that had just destroyed my body in ways that I didn't think I wanted to survive. The shower turned on and a second later, his sex-tousled waves appeared in the doorframe, raising an eyebrow at me. '*You coming?*' it said.

With a grumble, I slid from the bed, enjoying the embers in his eyes as I walked by him with what I hoped was a saunter, stepping into the large open rain shower and underneath the warm stream.

"Hey!" A large hand had swiped the shampoo just as I went to reach for it.

"I'll do it," he replied with a sexy grin.

My nipples tightened as he squirted shampoo into his hands before unceremoniously slopping it onto my head with a chuckle.

"You are terrible at this." I laughed.

But then his magic fingers began to rub and that laugh quickly disappeared, replaced by unstoppable tiny mewls as he massaged my scalp.

"You were saying?" he rasped and my body turned to mush all over again.

I didn't even care to respond, it felt so good. I swayed against him, hearing the soft hiss as my stomach brushed against the tip of his cock that hadn't completely softened.

"Can I ask you something?" I whispered.

"Sure," he answered, but then turned me underneath the water to wash the suds from my head.

Rubbing the water away from my face, I stepped out and let him take his turn.

"When did you know it was me?" I wondered out of nowhere.

No. Not nowhere. The question came out of the girl who'd never stopped loving him.

He didn't open his eyes, asking through tight lips, "What do you mean?"

"In the treehouse."

Every nerve in my body was like a livewire - hot and ready to ignite; this was the first time that night was ever mentioned between us.

His gaze caught my eyes and my breath. Unsteadily, my lungs tried to fight through to hear his answer.

"As soon as I heard your footsteps in the woods."

My mouth fell. *What?*

"What... You mean you knew the whole time?" I asked incredulously.

My mind played back through every piece of that night.

"Blay," he chuckled, pulling me flush against him, the warm water raining down in between us. "How could I not?" My stomach flipped. "How could I not recognize the footsteps that I'd heard so many times crunching along the same path? Do you know how many times Alexa would have been cursing me trying to navigate through those woods? I would never have heard the end of it - and probably for good reason."

He did have a point.

"I knew you were up to something. You were quiet and distant. Pretending to do homework while you listened to your brother and me talk."

Wow, the teenage mind really does have a distorted sense of reality.

His fingers brushed under my chin, tipping my face up to his. "And I could be stuck in a windowless room on the darkest night, but you, I will always know. I will always see... *I will always find you.*"

My eyes fluttered shut as his lips touched mine. I sighed and swayed into him, wanting more. *Needing more.*

I heard the small whimpers for a few seconds before I realized that they were coming from me as he gently toyed with my lips. "You're like the North Star, Baby Blake; no matter where I steer, I somehow always get led straight back to you."

"Zach..." I whispered in a daze. He wrapped one arm around my waist to steady me - a good thing since I wasn't sure my legs could hold me after that.

This time when he kissed me, he meant business. He barely pressed his tongue against my lips before they gave way. The shower got hotter.

"*Fuck,* I want you again," he growled.

I wrapped my arms around his neck and rolled my hips against his very hard length that was trapped between us.

"You can have me again." I bit onto his lower lip and sucked it into my mouth, releasing it with a loud pop. "You can have me any time you want."

"I don't want to hurt you." His hoarse whisper tore at me, the raw desire fighting against the man who did his damnedest to always do the right thing.

"It only hurts when I know you want me and you still pull away," I said softly, peering up at him underneath my eyelids. "I've waited a long time for this night; the least you could do is make it up to me." The tease came out a little too breathlessly - a desperate attempt to distract from the rational little devil standing on my heart, reminding me of the past.

His forehead dropped to mine, a soft laugh rushing from his lips.

"Anything for you, *Blakebaby.*"

I smiled along with my heart as he kissed me, feeling his grin spread against my lips. "Just remember though, tomorrow when it's uncomfortable to walk out onto that stage, you were the one that asked for it. Just remember, when you see me walking towards you and you sit down on the stool for our little duet and it pushes against your sore and swollen pussy - you asked for it. And when you sing…" He broke off with a chuckle. "When you sing, just remember all the notes my dick made that beautifully famous voice of yours hit tonight as I stretched you and filled you with my cum."

So bad. *So good.* Funny how his words did *unspeakable* things to my body.

Heat tingled through every molecule of every cell. I could hardly breathe I needed him so badly. My core throbbed, begging to be used in the way that he promised. I felt his arousal lengthen between us, thick and throbbing. I let out a soft moan as my heart picked up its pace, knowing that he was going to be inside me again.

Insatiable. Needy. Unashamed.

He flipped me around with a grunt as my ass pressed

against his erection. My hands reached out to steady myself on the tile, gasping as the cold seeped into my fingertips. I felt his breath on my neck as both hands reached around to cup my breasts, tugging my nipples between his fingers.

One hand dipped down over my stomach between my thighs, my legs instinctively spreading to give him better access to my aching sex. The first brush of his fingers over my tender clit sent sharp sparks through my body. A brief pain quickly turned to exquisite pleasure as the pad of his thumb flicked back and forth over me, driving me insane.

"Bend."

He didn't have to tell me twice.

Cupping my sex, he dipped a finger inside of me, a brief warning of what was coming. Angling my hips back against him, I felt the head of his cock brush my clenching hole. I don't know what I was expecting, but it wasn't for his fingers to stay teasing me as he slammed into me from behind, forcing a small yelp from me.

"Still so damn tight." I loved hearing him without any control. "You feel perfect, you know that?" He stayed completely still, shoved so far inside of me I knew he was pushing against something that he probably shouldn't. But I loved the feel of it - the feel of him buried deep, so deep he could become a part of me.

I bit my cheek, tasting blood. Everything that he did and said made me want to come. My body raged for another release.

"You know how badly I wanted this that night?"

I tried to keep breathing even though it felt like my insides were ripping themselves apart.

Still, he continued to speak, knowing that the words were doing just as much, if not more for my arousal than his dick was pressing gently against the spot inside of me that would give me my orgasm.

"I regretted going out to the treehouse because I wasn't

feeling it. I almost left. And then I heard your footsteps. *Fuck.* Your untouched tits. The way you rubbed your sweet virgin pussy against my leg, leaking your desire through your underwear. I wanted to do this." He pulled out and slammed back into me. My arms shook, bracing against the wall as I cried out. "I wanted to claim you then. I wanted to feel you squeeze my cock like you are right now." His fingers flicked over my clit again and my muscles responded, trying to clench around his massive length.

"Fuck how I wanted this..." He slid out and thrust in again but this time couldn't bring himself to stop.

If I wasn't crazed for release, I might have cried. Maybe I was crying - the fifteen-year-old version of me finally hearing from his lips the truth of how he felt that night - but with the shower I would never know.

"*Oh, Zach,*" I moaned as he hit my sweet spot over and over again, each time rubbing my clit.

It felt like my body was being pulled in two different directions that magically led to the same place - a place that only he knew the way to. It was like he knew the workings of my body just as well as if he'd been fine tuning it for the past six years.

He drove into me and with a pinch on my clit, I screamed into the tiled room, my body exploding inside and out. My hips jerked back against him, his hands now grasping my hips as he thrust into me a few more times before I heard his strangled groan and felt another wave of warmth deep inside me as he came.

My breath fogged the gray-blue tile in front of my feet. Everything I saw was a fog, all I could do was feel - feel the way he rode out my orgasm and his, feel the way that my core still clenched around his length that pumped out his desire with long, heavy pulses into my core, murky white droplets now landing on the shower floor as he overfilled my body.

"It's always going to be like that, isn't it?" he rasped, gently kissing my back.

I moaned in agreement and then in loss as I felt him slide slowly out of me.

"It's always going to be like that." No longer a question, he promised it as he turned and wrapped me in his arms.

It wasn't until I could start to feel the water on my skin again that we moved and finished the shower that we'd started.

***

"Zach," I said hesitantly when he handed me a towel to dry.

His curious gaze met mine, waiting for what I was about to say. My stomach clenched at how gorgeous he was, naked with tiny rivulets of water running down over the hard planes of his muscles.

"I... I don't want to tell Ash yet." His expression hardened. I knew he wasn't going to be happy about that. "I just..." I ducked my head, focusing on drying my legs as I spoke again. "I think we should wait until the tour is done. It's only a few more weeks."

"You want us to lie to him for weeks?" His tone was flat with displeasure.

"Well..." I bit my lip. "Or we could just... not do this again until we are back home."

His face grew even darker at that, his lip curling slightly as what I'm pretty sure was a growl came from his chest.

"Is that what you want?"

"No!" I said quickly - too quickly - my head falling to wrap my towel around me. When I looked back up, he was right in front of me, his hands waiting to cup my face and hold my eyes to his molten ones.

"Good. Because I don't think that's possible," he rasped, the gold in his eyes glinting with anger. "I told you, Blay, now that I have you, there's no way in hell I'm letting you go."

"Ok... well you're just going to have to hold on quietly because I'm not ready to tell my brother." I was determined. Fear made me that way.

I figured if I just had some time... if we just had some time first... then it wouldn't matter what Ash said in anger - because it was a safe bet that he was going to be livid; it wouldn't matter because by then Zach would know that we are meant to be, no matter what my brother said.

I saw his jaw muscle flex before he agreed. "Fine. But as soon as the tour is over."

Standing up on tip-toe, I kissed him again.

"Now lose the towel Baby Blake," he demanded as he tugged at the edge I'd tucked in. "I think I still have some making up to do before I have to sneak you back to your own room."

I grinned. Shimmying my body slightly, I sent the towel whooshing down to the floor and walked back into his arms.

CHAPTER 20
ZACH

9 YEARS AGO

"WHAT THE HELL WAS THAT?" I heard the rage brimming in his voice, desperate to spill into a physical fight.

I couldn't believe she fucking did that in front of everyone. Especially Ash.

I opened the door into his house and stalked inside.

"Zach!" A hard grip dug into my bicep as he whipped me around to face him just as the screen door slammed shut. I'd been trying to get us as far away from the crowd as possible before we had this discussion. "What. The. Fuck. Was. That." Ash was one of those that had a long fuse but a very big bomb at the end of it, especially when it came to anything involving Blake.

"Does it look like I have any fucking clue?" I met his stare, daring him to contradict me. "You think I would actually know she planned on singing a damn song to me?" I asked harshly as I yanked my arm from his grip and headed down the hall into the kitchen - and farther away from all the guests outside.

At least that part was true. I had no idea she was going to go and do this. Then again, the second she took the stage clutching her damn guitar, I had a feeling it wasn't going to end well. I did have an idea why she'd written the song; a small idea that might have to do with the way I'd encouraged her to ride my leg the other night. My dick twitched remembering the way she came and the wet mark that remained stained on my pants after I'd forced her to leave.

Guilt had been slowly gnawing at me since then. No, that was a fucking lie, too. Guilt had been gnawing at me from the second that I started seeing Blake as anything but a little girl and my best friend's little sister. Guilt for how my eyes lingered too long as she sauntered around me when Ash wasn't looking. (Her tight little shorts and sad excuses for shirts hadn't helped either; they made me horny and that made me irritable.) Guilt for how I closed my eyes at night and her sunshine hair lit up my mind, her porcelain skin glimmering underneath my imagined touch, and her pink pouty lips. Guilt for how my favorite hobby became recalling every blush I'd caused her in embarrassment and every moan that slipped from those lips when she tasted her favorite cookies, meshing memories together to form my own little movie as I let my hand grip my dick and fist myself until I came hard and gasping underneath my sheets.

I wasn't the type of person who had this problem. I was the kid who, when I was told not to do something, not to touch something, I listened and didn't question or complain. (Ash was the complete opposite and I was forever making amends for his breaking the rules.) But with Blake, I couldn't listen and all my body did was complain.

It turned me into a cold and curt person that I didn't recognize but it was my only recourse - it was the only thing I could do to make me feel like I wasn't betraying my longest friendship.

But then the treehouse had happened.

That was the night I could no longer talk myself into believing that I was only attracted to her because she kept trying to flirt with me. No. I wanted Blake Tyler like fire wants kindling and like lightening searches for water. I wanted her because I needed her to ignite me.

I'd avoided her at all costs since that night to the point where I was even starting to get curious looks from Ash as to why I never wanted to hang at his house.

"Well it sure as shit sounded like you should have an idea," he growled at me, eyes glinting.

I clenched my teeth, pulling my cap off my head and slamming it on my parent's kitchen countertop - the momentary safe haven.

Blake was reckless; I should have anticipated that she would do something like this. Maybe if I hadn't been so cold. Maybe if I had just talked to her and explained instead of lashing out in unfulfilled sexual frustration… maybe she wouldn't have turned this into a show. But how did I explain something like this? *How did I explain something to her when I couldn't even wrap my own fucking head around it?*

Time slowed as my mind raced, choosing my next words carefully. "I knew she had a crush on me. But you fucking knew that, too."

It was pretty damn obvious the way she was flirting all the time.

"Of course, I knew about the damn crush. God, the way she stares at you sometimes is laughable and disgusting at the same time."

I twitched, hating how he was talking about Blake – hating that my body hummed every time she looked at me like that.

He swore underneath his breath. "You don't fucking write and perform a song about a crush, Zach." He pounded his fist into the counter before stepping just inches from my face. "I swear to God, if there's something going on between you and my sister—"

251

I knew he'd kill me right there and then if I told him what had happened and I can't say that I would blame him. I wasn't a bad guy. I wasn't a player. But that kind of shit didn't matter to Ash. Loyalty mattered to Ash. Family mattered to Ash. I was like a brother to him and 'Thou shalt not touch my sister' was a commandment written in stone. The truth about Blake and me would have betrayed them both. So, I cut him off before he said something that would force me to lie.

"The only thing going on between Blake and me is the fact that I've been trying to avoid her."

His eyes narrowed, inspecting my words, looking for the faintest hint of something - *anything* - that might suggest that there *was* more to the story.

"Well, that is true," he begrudgingly admitted through clenched teeth.

It was true. Why it was true though…

A second later, he stepped back and I could breathe again. Running a hand through the bleach-blonde hair that he shared with Blake, he paced a few steps before turning to me again.

"Zach." His eyes were still sharp, searching for any sign of weakness in my story. "I swear, if you ever touch Blake - if you *ever* even look at her like she's been looking at you, we are done. Fucking. Done. Touching her will end this friendship and then I will end you."

It wasn't so much of a nod as it was a way for me to get away from his stare that I was afraid could see right into the darkest part of my heart that wanted to touch and take every inch of her, regardless of his threat.

"Do you understand me?" He pressed with a low voice.

"Yeah, man," I answered sharply, starting to walk past him. "We should get back outside before this becomes more of a shit show."

Again, his grip dug into my arm. "I want your word."

It doesn't matter, I told myself. I was going to be leaving for college. She was young. By the time I came back she probably wouldn't even remember me, let alone still want me. And by then, hopefully I would feel the same.

Still, the next words that came out of my mouth felt like lies in the making. But what choice did I have except hope that they never had the chance to bloom?

"I swear I won't touch her, Ash," I spat as though I was offended that he'd forced me to say the words. Really, I was pissed at myself because even though there was no proof, no evidence, and no indication, there was a single silent thread of doubt that tied the two of us together.

For Ash, doubt that I was telling the truth.

For me, doubt that I could keep my promise.

CHAPTER 21
BLAKE

Track 15: Tread Carefully
"Watch my step.
Don't let this slip away.
Tread carefully,
It's only my whole heart on the line anyway."

LOVING HIM WAS DANGEROUS.
Loving him was passionate.
Loving him was fearless.
Loving him was burning red.

"Blake Tyler delivers near-perfect show in Bay Area arena!"

I SKIPPED off the elevator back to my room like I was Dorothy who'd just found the Wizard and a way home. Even the keycard ding was like music to my ears. When I spun into my room though, my feet tripped over themselves when I found Tay sitting on the edge of my bed.

"Hey," I croaked out, dropping my shoes onto the floor.

"Were you with Zach... the whole night?" She looked down in her lap, her phone screen flashing for a second before she turned it back off and stood.

Guilty.

I ducked my head remembering that I had seen a slew of messages from her late last night - *early this morning* - when I'd set two alarms to wake Zach and me so that I could get back to my room before dawn. I'd been sore and exhausted and, honestly, too desperate to be curled back in his arms that I hadn't thought about answering her; *it had been really late anyways.*

"I'm so sorry, Tay. I-I saw your messages but it was late. I didn't want to wake you." I fumbled miserably with the hem of my *very* wrinkled shirt, hating the look of hurt and concern on her face.

"I've been worried sick." Her lip quivered and her hand immediately raised to her mouth.

"Oh, Tay," I gushed and closed the space between us, enveloping her in a giant hug. As soon as my arms went around her, her shoulders shook with sobs. "I'm so sorry. I didn't realize. I... I thought you knew I'd be with Zach... that he would take care of me."

I bit my lip thinking of *all* the ways that he had.

"I-I was so worried," she repeated, wobbly. "I thought he'd bring you back... earlier... and then I ran into your brother in the hallway—"

Oh no.

"What did he say?" I tried to keep the panic from seeping out as I pulled back from her, keeping my hands on her shoulders. "What did you say?"

"He asked where you were, of course." Her strained laugh

did nothing for the knots in my stomach. "I'd told him earlier, when I went to grab your stuff from the dressing room, that we were just going to hang out and watch movies in your room. So, it made no sense why I was on the way to my room."

"Did you tell him?" I gulped, struggling to get air past my lips.

"No!" she exclaimed, a slightly insulted look crossing her face. "I-I told him that I came down to grab you some Nyquil because you weren't feeling well." Her gaze became even more tortured. "I lied to him, B. I lied to him about you and then I had to convince him *not* to come check on you because it might be contagious or something."

More tears fell from her eyes and for the first time, I saw hard evidence of something that had always nagged in the back of my mind - the idea that Tay might have a thing for my brother. Every once in a while, the thought occurred to me, but like Ash, she'd been like a part of my family for so long, I just assumed that something like that couldn't be.

And in doing so maybe I'd been even blinder than Ash.

"I lied to him about his sister and his best friend." Her hands came up, forcing mine back down to my sides, so that she could rub her temples. "So I stayed locked in here all night, half-expecting him to burst through the door any minute and realize that you weren't here - *and neither is Zach.* And you know your brother, B. You know he'd shoot the messenger."

I grabbed her hands and clasped them to me. "Tay, I'm *so* sorry. I promise you this will never happen again. I will never put you in this situation again, ok? I was just so… lost… and then Zach found me and everything else just faded away." I sighed. "It's not an excuse; it's just the truth."

She nodded taking a steadying breath.

"I'm sorry," I repeated again softly.

With an attempt at a smile, she hugged me quickly and

said, "It's fine. Sorry for freaking out. You know what not-knowing and not being organized and having all the answers does to my anxiety. And the thought of having to explain it to Ash…"

"Yeah." I pulled back from her and glanced down at myself. "Although, I probably shouldn't have hugged you. My clothes are full of sand."

Her eyebrows shot up. "Just what the heck did you do last night?" She looked me up and down and I tried - *but not really* - to bite back a grin.

Reaching for her hand, I pulled her unceremoniously behind me as I headed for the bathroom, needing one more shower after Zach kept me in bed after my alarm for *'just five more minutes.'* You wouldn't think that would be enough time for anything impressive to happen. *You'd be wrong.*

It was debatable whether or not it was the story or my shower that made the bathroom steam, but as I scrubbed down I told Tay everything that had happened from the beach to his room to his confession. I even peered out to see the look on her face when I told her that he'd known it was me the entire time in the treehouse.

"I can't believe it!" She gasped. "I mean I can. But good thing I'm hearing about this now. If I knew this when I ran into Ash… I mean, he had no reason to doubt me last night and I still had to wet a washcloth with cold water and plaster it to my forehead for a minute when I got back to the room."

I shut the shower door again, gnawing on my lip. The warm fizzles that spread through my body when I looked down and saw all the little red marks - tattoos from my night with Zach - quickly faded away when Tay brought my brother back up.

I was the too-trusting one. Obviously - the way I'd been lulled into all of my previous relationships. Ash was my opposite. He had a select group of friends in high school because he didn't trust anyone enough to let them in close.

Guilty until proven innocent. Zach was like a brother to him, but I *was* his sister and he'd grown up believing what our dad said in partial jest: that *'no one will ever be good enough for our Blake.'*

"I'm still in shock, B. You and Zach. After all this time." I grabbed the towel off the door and stepped out of the shower, rubbing myself dry. "And it was really that good? I mean, it's been a while since Xavier…"

I grimaced. It was like I'd completely forgotten any other guy that I'd had sex with. Contrary to my relationship track-record, I hadn't *slept* with all of them. Xavier had been almost a year ago. And Levi? I guess a part of me knew that I should be waiting to take that step no matter how much the other part of me threw myself at him because I was trying to prove something to myself and the world – that a guy could actually want me for me.

I gave her a look, but it was my blush that did me in. I'd spared her the details the first time around, just trying to get out the basics of how my world had been turned completely on its head - *or its heart* - in the past twelve hours. With a wicked grin, I gave her *some* of the delicious details - most of the ones that would explain why it hurt to move certain ways right now.

"Well, that should make the rest of the tour a little easier, since you're *really* dating him now, right?" She moved to the side as I wrapped my towel around me and reached for the hairdryer. Rehearsal was at ten. We were going to be cutting it close.

A huge smile exploded over my face and I squealed a 'yes.'

But then my face fell and I muttered, "No."

"What do you mean?"

"For all intents and purposes, it's still a show between us."

"Because of Ash…" She trailed off knowingly before her eyes narrowed. "Wait, was that your idea or his?"

I jerked back slightly. "Mine… why?" She shook her head. "Uh, uh. No way. Spill. What are you thinking?"

"Nothing, B. I just don't want you to get hurt, that's all. You know how you are when it comes to Zach…"

"And how's that?" I asked softly.

"Well… you just tend to jump without looking and then fall…" I recoiled as her words sliced through me. She planted her hands on the side of my arms. "Blay. You know I'm happy for you. I - of all people - know what it's like to want someone who doesn't want you and I also know how long you've lived with that for him."

"But…" I prompted, knowing there was always a 'but.'

"I don't want you to get hurt. There's… a lot… riding on this situation and not just for you, but for him. I know everything that he's put you through and I just want you have a sliver of caution, that's all."

I wanted to be mad at her for saying it but I couldn't because she was right. It's not that I didn't believe what he said or what he felt for me; I just wasn't sure that it was enough.

She squeezed my fingers, bringing my focus back to her. "Zach is the most loyal person I've ever met. I mean, it's no wonder he's Ash's best friend. But he is loyal to a fault. He will put other people's feelings ahead of his own - like when he asked Alexa to prom even though he didn't really like her. Like when he didn't call you out in public for the whole graduation party thing because he didn't want to create tension between anyone. I mean, the whole reason that he signed up for this tour was to help you."

She put up her hand when I went to interject. "I know what you're going to say and maybe… maybe him wanting you played a role and maybe the opportunity for ZPP played a role. But look in the mirror and ask yourself, if you took away all of that, would he have still agreed?"

My head ducked down. He would have. He would have agreed to help me without being invited on tour and without wanting me. Taylor was right; Zach put others' wants before his own. Others wouldn't want us to be together. *And I was his own.*

"I'll be careful," I promised, turning away from her towards the mirror to finish with my hair. "And hopefully, when the tour is over and we tell Ash, he'll prove us all wrong."

She rolled her eyes, knowing just as well as I did how unlikely that would be. "That's another thing," she added. "If you are keeping this from him until then, you need to be *much* more careful. No more randomly disappearing, leaving me in the dark as to where you are going and when you'll be back and still expecting me to cover for you. I… don't have a leg to stand on with your brother."

She laughed nervously. *There was definitely something there.* But the look on her face told me if I asked about it right now, I'd be met with cold, hard denial.

"I know, I know. We will be more careful." I gave her a promising smile.

She pursed her lips like she didn't believe me and then turned to leave the room with a low grumble. "I'll believe it when I see it."

"We will!" I yelled after her with a laugh, turning back to my untamed hair.

CHAPTER 22
BLAKE

Track 16: Reckless

"Faster. Higher. Together we have more than nine lives.
Love is the kind of reckless you'll never believe you won't survive."

I COULDN'T HELP BUT CHUCKLE AT BOTH HOW RIGHT AND HOW utterly wrong the press always managed to be about my life. At least the headlines were all overwhelmingly positive now. Badmouth anything about me or Zach and one of *Blake's Babe Squad* would rip you to pieces… for today at least. Tomorrow could be a whole different story.

"From duets to live streams, Blake Tyler shares unique glimpse into her first serious relationship and WOWS her fans!"

I JUMPED as the door to my dressing room opened and slammed shut, the lock clicking as an afterthought. My phone fell from my hand, slipping between the seat cushion and arm of the chair that I'd been curled up in. Tay always made sure I had a 'writing chair' on every set so that I could feel cozy as I worked on songs for my next album. There was a vanity to my left, a small, red velvet sofa to my right, flanked by a mini-fridge on one end and a dressing rack on the other.

I really didn't need anything fancy. The only thing I really cared about in the room was the guitar that was currently on my lap.

And the Zach in the doorframe.

My eyes slid up from my guitar and the new song that I'd been writing and matching chords – 'Finally Ours' – to find my gaze captured by the very man who inspired it.

"Hey, beautiful," Zach rasped, a sexy 'you're mine now' grin gracing the classic lines of his face.

Since last weekend, we'd (barely) managed to keep our distance while 'at work' - barely managed to keep up the façade that in private we were making all too real. During the week was easier. The beach. The Griffith Observatory. Joshua Tree National Park. We went exploring with our little posse of paparazzi and instead of feeling laden with anxiety that I was faking a story and burying my feelings, I felt free - free to be happy with the one who held my heart. And that, I wanted the world to see.

"Everyone is falling in love with Blake and Zach!"

LAST NIGHT, I'd slipped into Zach's room after Tay fell asleep and we stayed up watching *The Hunger Games* series most of the night.

Ok… we stayed up doing other things most of the night, but the movies were still playing in the background.

"What are you doing here?" I asked breathlessly, flipping the notebook closed before he could see the verse that I'd been writing. The affronted look on his face had me taking stock of what I'd just said. Shaking my head, I ran a hand through my hair. "Sorry. I just… wasn't expecting you."

"I know." He closed the distance between us. "But I needed to see you."

Especially before and after the shows (and around Ash), we tried to keep our distance. Probably a slight over-correction but I was too afraid of ruining the beginning of our love story.

"Oh yeah?" I licked my lips and stood, setting Marty (my Martin acoustic guitar) down on the chair behind me.

His hands cupped my face and before I could protest, his lips were on mine. I tried to shove the piece of gum that I'd been chewing up into the side of my cheek, but I wasn't fast enough. His tongue swooped in and pulled the now flavorless wad into his mouth.

Pulling back, he smiled at me, the piece of gum held between his front teeth. Reaching up he plucked it from his mouth and tossed it into the trash can on the other side of us.

"Stop chewing gum," he said with a low voice as that hand gripped my chin, his thumb brushing languorously over my lower lip.

"Why?"

"Because I get jealous of anything that gets to spend so much time inside your mouth."

A small groan escaped as moisture rushed between my thighs before I could even think. It was so lame. If I had heard him say this to any other girl I would have pointed a finger at him and burst out laughing. But he was saying it to me. And because he said it to me, it made all the sore parts of my body come to attention, craving more abuse.

The match had been struck. And before I could get any

words out of my parted mouth, he chuckled huskily and slipped his tongue back inside and locked my mouth back to his. Sparklers flared inside my body as I opened for him, letting in the demanding force of his tongue. The kiss turned heavy in a way that it seemed even Zach wasn't prepared for. His arms locking around my waist, his arousal dug into my stomach as I wound my arms around his neck.

Stroking and sucking, my body melted from his kiss. I squeezed my thighs together, the ache quickly turning unbearable.

"What was that for?" I whispered between heaving, gasping breaths when he finally pulled back.

"I missed you." My heart skipped a beat. "And now I need you."

My eyes flicked to the door. "Anyone could come in."

Translation: *What if Ash comes waltzing in?*

"I locked it." One large hand slid from my back up underneath my t-shirt to close over my breast.

"What if someone knocks?" All of Tay's warnings echoed in my head. This was definitely not being careful. Yeah, there was still time before the show started and yeah, it was unlikely that someone would bother me while I was songwriting.

But it still wasn't careful.

Tugging my bra down so that it pushed my breast right up into his hand, his fingers pinched my nipple and the fireworks that exploded inside me blew up all thoughts of carefulness into bright, colorful fragments of need that rained down on every cell of my body.

I felt the wall against my back and the wall of Zach against my front, hard and hot, his V-neck tee tight over his chest. I instinctively locked one ankle around his leg, letting his hips fall further into the cradle of mine. I arched against him, suddenly desperate for him to be inside me.

"Too loud," he grumbled and I gasped as he hoisted me

up, holding me with one arm as the other moved Marty from the chair I'd been sitting in.

"Careful!" I exclaimed and Zach arched an eyebrow at me as he gently propped my instrument against the side of the huge brown leather armchair.

Zach took Marty's seat and he became mine. Straddling him in the huge armchair, my gym shorts rode up high on my thighs. My breath caught at how gorgeous he was staring up at me. I reached up and tugged the baseball cap off his head, letting it fall to the ground.

"Careful!" he said, teasing me with a wink.

"I missed you," I confessed, rubbing myself against him.

"I missed you too, Blakebaby." His hands found the edge of my tee and lifted it up over my head. "I couldn't wait until later."

A shiver climbed up my spine. More words I thought I'd never hear from him.

"I'm not complaining," I said with a throaty voice that I seemed to have acquired only recently. *Only for him.*

"You should be... how many times I had you last night," he said even as his hands drifted around my back to unclasp my bra. "I should at least have given you until tonight."

"I don't want you to," I arched my breasts into his hands.

I didn't want him to question it. I wanted him. And I wanted him to take me just as much as he wanted to. We'd have to work on that.

"Good." The word was borderline an inarticulate growl as he tipped his head forward and tugged my nipple into his mouth.

I closed my eyes and gave into the magic of his mouth. I shouldn't have been surprised that every time was like this. Maybe it was all in my head because I'd built up this fantasy for so long.

No. I believed with my whole heart that there was

something much more to it than that. There was more to the longing, the need, and the indescribable pull between us.

My hips began to rock against his length on their own accord, trying to put pressure on that sensitive spot that craved it again. I'd never been this greedy for sex before. *I'd never had a reason to be.*

"Fuck," he said, licking across the tip of my breast as his hand delved beneath my shorts and panties.

I gasped as the pads of his fingers slid over my clit down to my entrance.

"You're already so wet, Blakebaby." His teeth gently closed over my nipple, sucking hard with a groan.

"I want you inside me," I said softly, still afraid that someone might actually hear my desperate admission.

"Soon. You're not ready." He smiled as he moved to my other breast to torture me, refusing to oblige my request.

"Zach," I bit out between moans as he licked and sucked my nipple until it was bright red and begging for more. "I want to ride you. I want your dick inside me."

I shivered at the coarseness of my own words. Thankfully, my body was already so flushed with desire that the slight embarrassment didn't make much of a difference.

"Christ, Blay." He pulled back, his hands standing me up for a second to tear down my track shorts and underwear. I barely stepped out of them before he had me back on top of him.

I moaned at the feel of his jeans against my bare clit, unable to stop myself from massaging against them.

"You like leaving your mark on these jeans, don't you, Baby Blay?" he taunted me with dark desire burning in his eyes.

"Y-yes."

"Maybe I should let you come all over them." His hands returned to my breasts, kneading and tugging them until my nails were digging into the firm bulk of his shoulders. "Like you did to my pants that night."

I gasped loudly, on the edge of the release I longed for but that still evaded me as the present meshed with the past.

"God, I remember how you rolled against me, just like you're doing now," he grated out through clenched teeth. His hands slid and gripped my hips, stopping me from moving. "I wanted to strip you bare. I wanted to play with your flat tits. And then I wanted to ram myself inside your tight virgin pussy."

I whimpered, fighting against his hold, needing to press and rub and ease the fit inside my body.

"So do it now," I pleaded, resorting to circling my groin the best I could.

"You're not ready." Fingers slipped down between us, the pad of his thumb rolling over my clit. I bucked against him and cried out.

With a curse, he yanked my mouth down to his, covering it and any other sounds that might be tempted to escape. I was free to move against him and my core sought out his fingers like they were the antidote to this pleasurable poison.

His fingers searched and slipped inside me, but it wasn't enough. Reaching between us, I undid his jeans, pulling his pulsing erection out. I scooted closer to it and in return, Zach curled his fingers inside me, knocking me off balance with a wave of unfiltered need. Hard and heavy in my hand, I fisted his arousal firmly, pumping up and down, watching the redish-purple head become even larger.

"Zach..." I murmured his name just as he withdrew his fingers from me, as though reading my thoughts.

Dragging myself up, I positioned my soaking slit over him and sunk down onto his hard length. Maybe I wasn't ready for him, the way my muscles protested at the large invasion, trying to spread themselves wide enough to let him inside. But that only made me want him more - the way I could feel every fiber stretch as his cock speared deeper inside.

I forced my eyes to stay open, trained on his face as it contorted with pleasure.

"So tight, Baby Blake." The barest sheen of sweat graced his face as he tried to keep it under control. "Fuck..." he drawled out as I slid down the last two inches in a rush, sinking him completely up against my womb. Enchanting eyes met mine and his hands held onto my hips, locking us for just a moment in the most perfect definition of ours. "It's like every time your body molds just for me. Like you were molded just for me."

My core clenched around him, loving his words that made me frantic to move. His hold released, freeing me to search for the orgasm that taunted my every cell. Sliding up and down his long length, I threw my head back, moaning softly with each impale. One hand guided the rhythm of my hips, the other slid up over my stomach to lift my breast to his mouth. He latched onto my nipple, tugging on it each time I rose up to his tip and rammed all the way down onto his base.

I lost myself in every sensation overwhelming me. I lost myself in him. With him inside me, my body began to sing that song of my soul, rising higher and higher, until the edge was in sight. Zach shifted ever so slightly in the seat so when I sank down the last time, he struck me deeper than he'd ever been. His head hit the most sensitive spot inside of me with that stroke and released the orgasm that had been bouncing around inside my body, turning my body into a needy version of a pinball machine.

I screamed but it was swallowed by Zach's mouth as my sex convulsed around him. He took over, thrusting up into my shuddering passage two more times before a groan ripped from his chest and the hot rush of his climax erupted inside me as I milked him.

Our staccato breaths dotted the air as our hips slowly ground to a halt, goosebumps slowly covering my skin.

My eyes blinked open, meeting his gaze. And then a giggle escaped me.

And then another.

And then he was grinning with me, pulling me into his arms and holding me close. In that moment there was no worry, no stage, no crowd, no reputation, and no brother. There was just us and happiness.

My forehead dropped to his and his lips reached up and pressed a quick, hard kiss to mine. "You should probably get back to work," he rasped even as he tightened his embrace.

"You probably shouldn't have been the one distracting me," I retorted, clenching around him once more, feeling him swell again in response.

A new spark lit the dark desire that was still brimming in his eyes, but we both knew we'd already borrowed too much on this time.

"You mean you can't write lyrics like this?" His grin wavered as he helped me slowly lift my hips up and off of him. "I was just giving you some inspiration."

With a glance at the door, I quickly cleaned myself up, watching Zach do the same before tucking his still-erect dick back into his jeans. I bit my lip. It was a challenge - one that I was looking forward to besting later tonight when I snuck back up to his room.

"You should know by now that you're already most of my inspiration," I replied wryly. There was no point in hiding or lying about it now. He was the inspiration that had started it all.

Picking my bra up from the floor, I rose back up to find him in front of me, his fingers tipping my chin up. "I don't want to be most, Baby Blake. I want to be your all."

My breath caught.

I loved Zach Parker.

The thought hit me like a getaway car - fast and crazed, driving off furiously into the sunset with my stolen heart.

The door handle jiggled and all my thoughts were wiped white with fear as I tried to swallow down the acid in my throat. Three sharp knocks followed and my heart held off on beating the entire time as I fumbled to get my bra on, Zach stepping around in front of me in case whoever it was decided to bust down the door.

"B? You in there?"

I breathed again when I heard Tay's voice coming from the other side.

"One sec!" I yelled, tugging my t-shirt on over my head in a flurry and rushing to the door.

"Blay—" I ignored Zach's voice as I pulled the door open.

I plastered a smile on my face, breathing heavily as I met her hazel stare.

"Hey, why was your door—" she broke off seeing Zach behind me. Her eyes did a shuffle between the two of us. "Oh. I see. I can come—"

"What's going on here?" Both of our wide eyes skidded to Ash who'd rounded the corner and placed his hand on the doorframe.

"Nothing," we both said in awkward unison.

A perfectly arched eyebrow that matched my own rose as he looked between us and then peered into the room. His face shadowed as soon as he saw Zach. "What the hell are you doing here?"

I felt Zach's presence as he came up behind me, resting one hand on the other side of the door frame. I coughed to hide my reaction when his other hand came to rest reassuringly on my back; he stood too close to me for Ash to be able to see that that hand was anywhere other than in the pocket of his jeans. I tried to keep my face blank as I slid my gaze up to his face that calmly met my brother's accusing stare.

"Just running through our duet for the night really quick," he said casually. "These things seem to go better when we go at it at least once before the show."

Blood rushed from my head at his words. He was toying with me. I swayed back against his hand.

"Yeah? What are you singing?" He was searching and the flush I felt deepening on my face wasn't helping.

"Umbrella." I heard the small smile in his voice before I felt Zach look down at me. "Isn't that right, Baby Blake?"

Seriously? Rihanna? My thoughts were mirrored by my brother's expression.

"Yeah," I answered, reserving my tight smile for Zach. "It was my night to pick. I guess I was thinking that we should try something a bit edgier."

Or several things.

"Alright," Zach continued before Ash had a chance to respond. "Gonna go let the guys know. See you out there."

He made sure to brush his hand over my ass as he moved through the doorway and nonchalantly strolled through our little pow-wow towards the other dressing rooms like there hadn't been anything going on.

He was good at this - making people believe what he needed them to so as not to hurt them.

And that scared me a little.

A second later, Ash gave up his witch hunt and with a nod to the two of us, jogged down the hall after his friend, leaving Tay and me to ourselves.

She pressed her hands to my chest and pushed me back into the room, shutting the door behind me.

"Are you serious, B?" she asked in an aggravated whisper, her hands flailing.

"I know," I groaned, burying my face in my hands.

"Do you know what would have happened had it been him knocking on your door instead of me? If he had gotten here first?"

271

Yeah, I did. It was why my heart was still racing.

"I know but——"

"No buts. I'm not joking. Either you tell Ash or you do a better job at not getting busted."

I pointed to the door as though my brother was still standing there. "He had no idea! He always looks at us like that. I'll agree that we need to be more careful but I think we handled that pretty smoothly."

Her arms crossed over her chest and she looked at me with amused eyes.

"What?"

"Your shirt's on inside out, B."

CHAPTER 23
BLAKE

Track 17: All I Need is You
"The world is new.
All I need is you, three chords,
And a tune."

RECKLESS. DANGEROUS.
Like skydiving without a second parachute.
This love was treacherous.
But nothing safe was worth the ride.

"Even high in the mountains, Blake Tyler forms intimate bond
with fans, bringing them further into *Lovestruck* romance!"

I TRIED to listen to Tay's warning. Zach and I even talked about it and agreed that we needed to keep the mind-blowing sex to nights when and where we knew it was safe. But then he would look at me on stage like I was the only star in his sky and before I knew it we were ducking out of dinners and conversations, meeting frantically in hallways or elevators or behind the band's instrument cases. Touching. Kissing. Loving.

What started out as a simple tune, quickly became a melody layered with walks on the beach, sneaking out late, and soul-stealing kisses that transformed it into our song.

"I feel like I can still smell the weed," I teased as we climbed the final flight of stairs towards the Red Rocks stage. We'd finished our show here at the Amphitheater a few hours earlier, the open venue echoing out into the red-glazed Colorado mountains. Zach had warned me - and he'd been right - about the heady marijuana scent that clung in the air. Thankfully, it was less now that the crowds were gone.

We headed back to the hotel in Denver as planned, changed, and then Zach texted me to bring a light jacket and meet him in the lobby in ten minutes. Yoga pants, lace bralette, and a loose crop top were a quick and sexy choice, my whole body anxious to know what he had in store.

Imagine my surprise when (after a thigh-squeezing make-out session in the car) we drove back out to the stage that we'd just left about an hour earlier.

With the lights off, it almost—

"Reminds you of home doesn't it?" My head tipped back towards him as we strolled lazily through the open-air theatre, sparks flying through my body as he read my mind and his knowing eyes made my belly clench.

"With the lights off, yeah," I agreed with a sigh.

It's funny how some things look one way under the lights and feel completely different outside of them. Like two sides of the same coin.

Like Zach and me.

It was called Red Rocks for a reason; the stage was nestled among jutting red-orange sandstone formations, named Creation Rock, Ship Rock, and Stage Rock. (We'd gotten a brief tour of Red Rocks Park earlier before the show.) Even now, just with the moonlight, the entire place was still vibrant, still burning.

This time, I walked along the seating area that was littered with screaming fans only a few hours ago. A few rows up from the stage, I turned to look at it, barely illuminated and only the shadows putting on a show.

In the distance, I could see Denver sparkling on the horizon, buzzing and still alive. Even though we were only a few miles away, it felt like so much further because of the vast peacefulness of the park.

The air was washed clean from the scent of weed with the freshness of the full moon. I breathed deeply, soaking it all in. This was a rare view for me: no fans, no lights, no camera - and looking *at* the stage instead of out from it.

"Why did you bring me back here?" My eyes were still locked on the empty platform as he trailed a finger along my shoulder and down the back of my arm.

He climbed down to the next row of benches, heading for the stage. "Beautiful. Secluded," he answered, pausing to look back at me. "Sometimes it's a good reminder," he nodded to the stage before hoisting himself up onto it, "that it's just metal and wood." He stomped on the platform. "That even though it can feel like a whole different world up here, it's not. And you don't need to try to be anything more than who you are or anyone besides yourself to step onto it."

My arms hugged my chest as his words soaked in. Over the past year before this leg of the tour, I'd been slowly losing myself. Step by step. Until that day when Tay told me that my reputation was tanking. It stopped me in my tracks and when I looked back, I couldn't even see the path that I'd come from; I couldn't see how to get back to myself.

There are many excuses for how I got there: trying to please everyone (which is immeasurably harder when 'everyone' includes millions of fans), seeing the world as I wanted it and not as it was... and then believing I could *will* that world into existence. Not so unlike my sixteen-year-old self who thought she could trick the boy who'd grown up with her into thinking she was someone else, the self that thought a song would change his mind.

Excuses.

The reason I was lost was because I was trying to find *him*.

My gorgeous god.

From his rejection, I'd developed the bad habit of *needing* to please even at my own expense. From his memory, I searched for him in every guy that I met. I looked for forever in guys that were *clearly* only about the moment - *and their moment in the spotlight*. And from his presence, I was finding my way back.

I still didn't feel right going out on stage and fooling the crowd with something that was real. *Not that they would ever know.*

But I would.

And I was the type of girl who sang her heart on her sleeve because it wasn't right to hold those kinds of things in. Through everything, it was my fans that had kept me going. Their love. Their encouragement. Their support. As the world tried to tear me down, they stood around me and in return? I lied to them.

And that needed to change. Which meant I needed to talk to my brother.

But not tonight.

I made my way towards the stage, watching Zach as he slowly spun, looking up at the stars that turned the night into an endless diamond sky. His head tipped down to me just as I wrapped my arms around his waist.

I still felt a pinch of anxiety every time that I was the first to initiate any intimacy, afraid that he was going to pull back and push me away. *But he didn't.* The instinctive thought barely formed before his hands cupped my face, tilting it to the side so that his lips could kiss along my cheek.

I mewled like a content kitten, sighing into the embrace. "It's a beautiful night out. All the stars... that's what reminds me of home."

He stared at me – the intensity hitching my breath. "Of all the stars in the sky, *Blakebaby*, you're the only one I've ever wished for," he whispered.

My heart felt like it was performing a drumroll in my chest, *'Introducing the most perfect man of all time...'* it announced.

My mouth parted, but no words came out. How could there? How could there be any response that would be *enough?*

I caught his grin just before he kissed me softly, his tongue slipping between my lips, grazing too quickly over the edges of my teeth and meeting the tip of my tongue before it was gone. "Will you sing for me?" he murmured, sucking gently on my lower lip.

I moaned and tightened myself against him, needing to be flush against his hardness. "You know I can't stop myself," I said breathlessly. "My body only knows how to sing for you." I rolled my hips against his and shuddered, feeling his long, hard length against my stomach; it had been there since our lusty kiss in the car and still it grew thicker as I stayed pressed against him, trying to ease the ball of tension that rolled through every inch of my sex.

He smiled against my mouth. Actually, he laughed a little and I pulled back, my eyebrows scrunching up at him.

"I know that, babe," he rasped, dropping a kiss on my nose. "I want you to sing for me though. With these lips." He kissed my mouth quickly.

My face flushed, realizing he hadn't been implying anything sexual; he actually wanted me to sing for him.

Amused by my expression, his chest rumbled against my heavy breasts. I tried to pull back, embarrassed, but his arms locked around my back, caging me to him.

"Don't worry," he promised, "I'll let your other lips sing for me soon." The red in my face deepened as the glint in his eyes shimmered devilishly. "I'll even let them use my dick as their microphone."

I choked on my breath as warmth rushed into my panties. At this rate, I wasn't going to be able to find my voice to sing for him.

"I can't believe—" I began to sputter before his mouth covered mine in a hard kiss, silencing me.

"Sing for me." It wasn't a question this time.

"I sang for you earlier when we were on stage," I insisted, my words losing steam. My breath backfired sharply into my lungs when one of his hands slid up underneath my shirt to cup my breast. My eyes drifted shut as he toyed with its hard peak through the lace.

The echo of my moan was the applause he deserved for the way he played with my breasts. I could write an album - *maybe two* - on all the things his touch on my nipples did to my body. I wouldn't though. God only knew what *that* would do to my reputation.

Was he sure he wanted me to sing for him? Because I wasn't going to be able to do it like this...

"I want you to sing *the* song."

My eyes flew open. The fire in my skin now felt like I was being raked over the coals. I shifted uncomfortably, pulling back from him.

No. No, no, no, my mind unwilling to relive the pain of the past insisted.

"My song," he insisted. Meanwhile, my traitorous body screamed *yes* as his fingers rubbed and tugged the fabric of my bra over my painfully aroused nipple, turning the undergarment from tempting into torture device in the beat of a quarter-note.

I moaned, my head falling forward onto his shoulder. *Dammit.* I'd do anything he said if he said it with his hands.

And then his touch was gone, the night chill washing over me.

"Zach!" I gasped at the loss.

He grinned roguishly at me, dropping a kiss on my nose before stepping back just a few feet from me and sitting on the floor of the stage, unrelenting eyes staring up at me and the stars.

"Sing it for me, Baby Blake. Just one more time…"

"Why?" I sounded desperate, begging him to retract his request.

Even with how we felt about each other… with what we now were… I still knew that the song from graduation would open so many old wounds that I'd rather just forget.

He stared at me for a long moment, heavy emotions rolling through his eyes and washing over me. Desire. Need. Regret. *Love.*

We hadn't said it to each other, but like any great melody, love wasn't something that needed words, love was something that hums its way into your heart and gets stuck there, playing mesmerizingly over and over again because you just can't get it out of your mind… body… or soul. *And you don't want to.*

"I want to hear you sing it for me again. Now. So I can finally listen to it without having to hide how it makes me feel." His voice broke and I realized how important this was to him; I realized how important making that day up to me was for him. "I want you to sing it for me so I can give you the response I should have nine years ago - the one that came from my heart."

I swallowed, my arms holding my stomach so that I didn't rush over to him, fall onto my knees, and blurt out just how much I loved him. (Also, so that I didn't vomit from nervousness.) For a second, I panicked, thinking that I'd forgotten the words.

A thought almost as foolish as the one about how I was over my feelings for him.

And then my mouth opened and, for the second time in my life, I sang like my heart depended on it.

"In your eyes, I am the sunrise.
Always there and taken for granted."

The first lines wavered. No mic. No sound system. Not even Marty to strum along with me.

"In your eyes, I am the sunrise.
Easily ignored, too familiar to be enchanting."

All acoustic. All authentic.

"Here I am, day after day.
My heart, it rises for you."

All my heart. All my soul.

"So, don't walk away,
My heart, it rises for you."

All of me.

His stare was glued to me as he stood and stepped towards me. My voice wavered but I kept singing as he got closer, his face ragged with emotion.

"Don't turn me away.
My heart, it rises for you."

It's amazing how a song... a lyric... *that melody*... can take you back to a moment in time. The specific moment when the crowd of family and friends disappeared from my vision. When I could feel each ray of the summer sun beating on my skin, highlighting the racing of my heart as my gaze locked with his.

It didn't matter that his beautiful eyes were the most familiar sight of my entire life; they were the only future that I wanted to look into. They grounded me and made me feel like I was flying all at the same time.

"Don't turn me into a sad little story:
And leave the mess of my heart
That had the nerve to adore you."

The last came out as a throaty, raw plea that would have made Adele proud.

Pure and utterly frightening silence surrounded us again. Heavy breaths the only reminder that time was still moving around us even if our love stood still.

"Beautiful." His hands gently cupped my face, thumbs swiping lightly over my cheeks, wiping away the overflow of my emotions.

Sometimes words are enough. Sometimes words set to music are enough. But other times, what you feel for someone can't be written or sung. This was one of those other times; the syllables and songs were nothing but drops in the emotional ocean, lost in the powerful waves that swallowed them whole.

For years I'd written about this man, but the only music that could ever convey what was between us were the beats from our hearts, the rising and falling scales of inhales and exhales, and the lyrics that my body sang from only his touch.

This love was the most beautiful thing I'd ever heard.

And I broke down. Tears that had been streaming down my face since the last verse, now flooded with new. He pulled me tight to him, raining kisses down on my hair and face. "I'm so sorry, *Blakebaby*. I'm so sorry I hurt you."

I pulled back so I could look at him again. "It's ok." My weak and watery smile probably suggested differently.

"I didn't deserve you… I don't deserve you," he whispered hoarsely, his voice torn up by the ragged emotions that had been locked away for so long. "I was stupid… *so fucking stupid.*"

"Zach…" I whispered his name, my lips searching for his.

Obliging me, his mouth slanted over mine. His kiss was demanding yet gentle, like a rip current, pulling me with a dangerous force that could only be felt underneath the calm waves. His tongue slid between my lips, searching and stroking mine. He explored every corner and licked every crevice of my teeth like he wanted to taste whatever remained of his song.

I sighed, slowly blinking up at him when his mouth pulled back slightly.

"That is what I wanted to do," he began softly. "When you finished singing that day. I wanted to walk up on stage and kiss you like this - like I'd been dying to ever since the day you fell off your bike and onto me – the day you forced me to realize that you had breasts and long, *long* legs... and that you were no longer a little girl."

"You did?" I asked dumbly simply because I just wanted to hear him say it again. Correction. The fifteen-year-old me that had been suffering inside wanted to hear him say it again because she never thought this moment would come.

He nodded, his thumb brushing over my cheek. "And then," he continued, "I wanted to look into these shining, midnight-blue eyes and tell you that, all this time, I've loved you in secret."

My heart exploded - like a star or an asteroid that finally collides with something greater than itself. A million little pieces fragmented around a love that was greater than our past, greater than our pain, greater than this ruse, and greater than my reputation.

"And I loved you without reason," I confessed. "My heart has always been yours."

The stakes were high, but I'd waited long enough for this moment where this love was ours.

And seventeen years after the day when I learned that sometimes losing something can be the best thing, I also learned that a heart exploding is *vastly* different from a heart breaking even though they both ended in pieces. That's what the stars were in the sky - shining bits of my heart that couldn't hold together with the love I felt for him, shimmering in their splendor.

My heart beat out of my chest. My soul shone through my eyes.

Blissful and utterly petrified. Completely and desperately frightened of what can happen when you finally have everything that you want. His lip twitched, only inches from mine. His body solid and burning against mine, his arousal creating a permanent hollow in my stomach, his intoxicating blend of pure male and potent desire invading every pore, his lips touched mine before he mouthed, "*Blakebaby,* I don't deserve your heart, but it's the best thing that's ever been mine."

I moaned into the kiss. Some love stories might picture this kiss as the epitome of sweet and loving. Not ours. Ours was hot and needy. Our love was raw laced with ravenous. I was on fire as his hips ground against me, still seeing stars even though my eyes were closed. My whole body salivated for more of this friction.

My arms locked around his neck and I climbed him like ivy around the thickest, hardest… hottest tree. I needed all of him and I needed him now.

I needed to replace the last bit of that memory with this - with Zach taking my willing heart and my needy body.

He groaned into my mouth as I rolled my core against his erection, quickly losing my mind as the friction set off warning flares everywhere in my body.

I barely caught his curse before my back was flat against the floor I'd been standing on hours ago, Zach jamming his arousal against where I wanted him.

"*Zach…*" I breathed.

He reared back and I choked, thinking he was going to leave us both hanging.

His stare was love and desire that mingled predatorily.

With a sexy smirk, he said hoarsely, "As much as I love the

yoga pants, Baby Blake, all I want you wearing right now is starlight."

He took his good 'ol torturous time, first pulling my shoes off. Then, leaning over me, tugging my shirt up over my head before reaching one hand under my arched back and deftly unhooking my bra, my breasts spilled from the lace. I watched the battle inside him play across his face as he stared at my swollen and needy tits. My chest rose and fell unsteadily, so desperate to be touched by him. And then I watched the moment he lost, his mouth swooping down and latching on to one taut peak.

Laving over the bud, his hand cupped and kneaded my other breast. I writhed on the floor, racing towards the pleasure he teased me with as my orgasm stayed just ahead of me out of reach. My hips arched, searching for his hard cock to rub against. *Hell, I would have even settled for a leg. A thigh. A hand. Anything.*

But he didn't give in. No. He stayed and proceeded to bite and suck my other breast while I whimpered, feeling like I was reaching for the moon - right there but so far out of reach.

With a pop and a grin, he released my nipple, looking up at me from underneath hooded eyes. His golden gaze pinned mine as he continued what he started - undressing me completely, my yoga pants and underwear gone in one smooth motion.

Then his eyes roamed and mine trailed along. My nipples were rosy red and glistening in the moonlight, my stomach quivered as pent up desire made my body twitch uncontrollably.

His eyes flicked to the empty seats. "I wonder how many fans picture you naked when you're up on stage."

"I-I think," I said with a weak voice, "that I'm the one who's supposed to picture them naked."

"Do you?" He raised an eyebrow.

"No!"

He nodded, his eyes flicking back to me, drifting down until I felt his stare on my sex.

"I picture you naked," he continued with a sexy smirk, his hand that was resting on my knee slowly drifting down the inside of my thigh.

I bit my lip, feeling my sex clench, needing him to get to there faster.

"O-on stage?" The words just left my mouth when I felt one finger slide down my slit. My hips jerked up but his finger pulled away.

"*Everywhere.*" His expression darkened as he lifted that finger to his mouth and sucked.

"*Zach…*" I pleaded.

"Now I don't have to picture it; now, I can *remember* it," he growled. "Naked. On stage. This perfect pussy wet and ready for me."

I couldn't even get out a 'yes' before he pushed two fingers inside of me. One hand planted on my hips, pinning them to the floor as his other hand worked its magic. I whimpered and cried for more of his touch, but he wanted to watch. He stayed kneeling above me as his fingers pushed in and out of my slick channel, his palm rubbing over my clit.

My heels dug into the stage, trying to push myself up harder against his hand. He wouldn't let me, but he gave me what I needed. In and out, he hit the same spot every time. And when I reached the point where my breath was gasping in but not releasing out, he curled his fingers hard into that sweet spot and I exploded. His hand couldn't control my hips that were powered with my climax as they jerked against him.

"Wow…" The word rushed out, hardly even sounding like me.

I heard his tight chuckle. "We're not done yet."

Goosebumps washed over my body. "No?" I swallowed hard watching him begin to lie down between my shaking legs.

285

"You should know, Blakebaby," he blew over my swollen folds, the warm heat of his breath making my inner muscles clench greedily for more, "every song has at least three refrains."

My brain processed his words in staccatoed syllables while my body interpreted them as whole notes. I cried out as his tongue flattened at the base of my sex, sliding all the way up to swirl around my clit.

"And my name on your lips as you come is your refrain."

I shoved my fingers through his hair, grateful that he hadn't worn his iconic baseball cap. Threading through the locks, I tugged harshly, partly as punishment for torture and partly because my sex was desperate to feel his tongue.

I felt the warm rush of air from his laugh before his mouth sank down over me. There was no more teasing. I felt it in the way his fingers dug into my hips, the way his body felt tight and on edge between my legs, and the fury with which he shoved his tongue inside my passage - he was close to losing control.

There was a brand-new Blake Tyler song being sung from this stage right now - one that would never come out the exact same again. Moans spiraled from my mouth as his tongue drove into me over and over again, the firm velvet rubbing against my muscles and licking my juices from them.

My head ground back into the hard wood of the stage and the stars in the sky mixed with the ones in my head as Zach sucked hard on my clit and my climax rocketed through me.

"*Fuck.*" The word was a Band-Aid over my pulsing sex.

I lay limply as he pushed himself up and ripped his shirt off over his head. I wasn't sure if I had limbs anymore. Or if they worked.

One part of me still worked; still throbbing, my core clenched as I watched Zach unzip and chuck off his jeans and boxer briefs. I swallowed the pool of saliva that collected in my mouth seeing his long erection jutting out from his hips.

I was about to have sex. On stage. Under the stars.
With Zach Parker.

I may be a popstar, but I never thought I'd be classified under this type of exhibitionism.

I let those thoughts drown me for a second, my gaze held captive by his, and wondered how this dream turned out to be a reality.

He knelt back down between my thigh, his hands shoving them wide. Desire rushed from my core as he stared at me. He loved to do that, I'd learned over the past few weeks - to stare and take a moment to appreciate my sex spread wide for him. He liked to watch as it made me hot and impatiently horny. He liked to watch me squirm and my pussy drip in anticipation.

Leaning back over me, his mouth took mine with long slow strokes of his tongue. I felt him prod at my entrance that was gasping for him. Supporting himself on both hands, his hips flexed and pushed the blunt head of his arousal just inside of me.

Don't get me wrong - I loved his fingers and his tongue.

But this fullness and the need for it was what drove me out of my mind.

"I'll never get tired of being inside you." His lips etched over mine as he slid all the way home.

A silent, strangled gasp escaped my mouth before he swallowed it. I was still reeling from the last two 'refrains,' my core sensitive and used, but still he took. And I willingly gave.

I arched my hips, needing him to move faster. I inhaled his growl before the moment of sweetness was over and he slammed into me. The amphitheater was perfect for resonating the sound of our flesh frantically slapping together, the moans and grunts of desperate need in a delicate situation.

For the first time in my entire life, I was on a stage and not putting on a show for the rest of the world.

At least I hoped I wasn't.

This moment was just for me - *and all for us.*

I felt it coming. Every muscle fiber tensed like I was preparing to take the biggest hit of my life. I braced myself as my pulse quickened like a drumroll for desire.

Zach had brought me here - he'd taken a situation so public and turned it perfectly private. He'd taken the Blake the world knew and grounded her to the Blake that I *was.*

"*Blakebaby,*" his hoarseness drifted into my mind. "*I love you.*"

The dam broke.

My orgasm crashed around me, the potential of it held back for so long behind the wall of words that hadn't been spoken until this moment.

My fellow stars now knew to whom I'd hitched my shine as I screamed his name. My body clenched around him, pulling him deeper and harder inside of me. I felt his low drawn-out groan before I heard it. I felt the way his body shuddered. I felt every push and pulse of his dick against my muscles. And I felt the hot jets of his release soak into every part of my body.

We gasped for air like it was going out of style - chests rising and falling together in an angry tug of war for the limited space between us. I didn't want to move. *I never wanted to move.*

"Holy shit, Blay."

I tried to laugh but he was heavy lying on me so it just sounded like I was gasping for air.

"*Fuck.*" He pushed up and stared down at me. "Sorry."

I stared up at him, wondering again how all of this could be real.

"Say it again," I whispered.

"I'm sorry," he repeated before kissing my nose with a grin.

"Not that part." I rolled my eyes because he was doing this on purpose. "The part where you said that you loved me."

The grin fell away, replaced with a look that burned red - red with desire and possession and untouchable love.

"I love you, Blakebaby." The words felt incredible - better than the shows and the fans and the Grammys and the fame. The words filled me. *He* completed me.

I licked my lip, soaking in every millisecond before speaking. "I love you, too, Zach." The faintest hint of a smile tried to break through the heaviness of what those words meant to him.

Unspoken. Unreasonable. *Untouchable, this love of ours.*

He kissed me again softly, sealing in the words that couldn't be unsaid, before he pushed off and rolled to the side, leaving us both lying there, on the Red Rocks stage, looking up at the stars. They winked at me in my flickering vision, knowing that what I'd found down here was worth the fall.

Good or bad, I always knew this love would leave a permanent mark, but tonight, our love was glowing in the dark.

Letting it go free, I never thought I'd feel this way again, *but this love came back to me.*

CHAPTER 24
ZACH

I HAD A BAD FEELING ABOUT THIS.

Blay and I spent our few free hours touring Minneapolis - visiting Paisley Park, exploring the skywalks; tonight was our only show in the city, so we tried to make the most of it. Every second with her, I regretted every second I fought to be without. I wouldn't make that mistake again. And I was going to work damn fucking hard to make up for it.

I just got out of the shower and picked up my phone, expecting to see an adorable text waiting for me from my girl - and there was - but there was also one from Ash with a room number and the word 'Now.'

To say our relationship had been strained ever since Colorado - hell, even since Cali - was putting it fucking mildly. I knew he didn't liked the situation from the start and I knew that it had gotten worse as more time passed and more photos were taken, more stories printed; we'd given them a fairytale and it looked damn believable.

Because now they were true.

But he didn't know that.

Seeing the text stopped me in my tracks, cold sweeping over me as I thought more about it. He'd barely said two words to me since Colorado except about the band or the show. And that didn't sit well with me as I tugged a tee over my head, reaching for my worn-out jeans.

It didn't sit well with me at all.

I couldn't stop myself from thinking that I'd been right - that we should have told him right away. The thought gnawed at me like a dog with a bone. I didn't like being the bone. I didn't like the feeling that whatever I was about to walk into was going to rip me apart.

BLAKE

Want to come warm up with me before the show? ;)

I GROANED as my cock swelled in my pants; it was habit and excitement that made me read her text right away when I should have ignored it. Warming up before the show had nothing to do with our voices or the music. It had become our thing - these stolen moments, tiptoeing on the edge of being found out. We couldn't keep our hands off of one another. Hell, I'd forced my body to resist her for a decade. Now, it needed to be paid back what it was due. *With interest.* But I think there was also a part of us that *did* want to be caught - not all the time, but just one time - there was a part of us that didn't want to keep the truth of us hidden anymore.

It was like being given the most fucking incredible gift in the entire world and not being able to share it. Not only that, but the continued thought that possessing that gift was somehow wrong of us.

And it wasn't wrong.

We weren't wrong.

We were everything that was right.

. . .

291

ZACH

I can't. I have to go talk to Ash.

I DEBATED whether or not to tell her he texted at all, but in the end, keeping it from her wasn't an option. Plus, she needed to know that it was only something serious that could keep me from her right now.

BLAKE

Everything ok?

ZACH

I'm sure it's just about the band. We haven't had a whole lot of time to talk about what's next for us.

I SENT the message hoping it would calm the both of us.

It was Ash's room number in the text; he was on the same floor as mine but just at the end of the hall on the other side of the elevators. The bright purple of the carpet and vibrant patterns on the walls only made the approach more unnerving.

I knocked swiftly, barely catching my surprise when Bruce opened the door. A split second later I met Ash's gaze in the background. Dark. Brooding.

"Please, come in, Mr. Parker."

I stepped inside the suite that was essentially identical to mine. The purple from the hall carried into the space but in a much lesser quantity, substituted with orange and silver designs instead.

Ash was sprawled on the chair next to the couch in the sitting room that adjoined the bedroom. *The same chair that I'd been sitting in the night before while his little sister rode my dick, her breasts bouncing in my face.*

My head ducked for a moment. *Fuck. Pull your shit together, Parker.*

"What's going on?" I asked, stepping farther into the room.

"Please, take a seat," Bruce said, motioning to the couch.

Ash still hadn't said a word.

"Is someone going to tell me what the fuck is going on?" It looked like someone had died - someone Ash hated, the way his expression was pitch black and blank – like black steel. The look was so eerily calm that if someone hadn't already died, they were about to.

"Yes." Bruce raised a hand and cleared his throat into his fist. "We've asked you here because there's a problem."

"What do you mean? Problem with what?"

"With Blake. With the plan."

My heart thumped in my chest like a gavel coming down to announce my guilt.

"Mr. Tyler," he continued with a flick of his narrowed eyes over to Ash, "has been contacted by some members of the press. They've found out that this whole thing is a sham."

"What? How the fuck did that happen?" I dropped onto the couch, yanking off my hat and pulling my hair back from my face.

Not what I was expecting to hear. And nowhere in the realm of what I thought was possible. *Very* few people knew that this had all been for show. There was no way they could have found out unless someone *told* them.

My mind raced through and dodged thoughts like they were linebackers on a football field as I tried to find my way to a solution that kept Blake safely in my arms.

"The point is that we don't have a lot of time. They are threatening to go public with this information." He cleared his throat again, holding up his finger like there was more. *Of course there was fucking more.* "Let me rephrase. They are going to publish this story one way or another. They've given us the night in case *we* want to be the ones to break the news to the public."

I squinted at him. "Awfully fucking considerate of them…"

Something wasn't right here.

I looked to Ash but his eyes were still on Bruce - *ignoring me* - with the slightest hint of a smile on his face, like he was just waiting for what the man was going to say next.

"So… how do we tell them? What do we do?" What else could I ask? I wasn't about to blurt out that it was now the truth and we could tell them that - *not without Blake's permission.*

"We aren't going to tell them," he informed me.

"Excuse me?"

"You are going to break up with her."

The world came to a screeching halt. *I couldn't have heard him right.*

If I was surprised before, well this… this took the fucking cake on that.

This was like sophomore year in college when we'd played Alabama. Ash had thrown me the ball - a perfect pass; I had everything lined up - the catch, the landing, the path to the end zone. *Perfect.* I caught the football, my feet touched the ground, and as I turned and pushed off, I ran into a mammoth of a man. I don't know if it was the angle, the momentum, or if he was just *that* large, but I bounced right the fuck off of him, falling back to the ground - at least that's what I assume. As soon as I hit him, I remember the shock registering through my body but then my world went black.

This was like that. Solid. Out of nowhere. Knocking me back.

The only consciousness I had was that I was about to lose her.

"I don't understand," I rasped, trying to grasp onto the

straws of rationality that screamed at me: *They don't know that what you have is real!*

"I've been discussing with Mr. Tyler and we feel that this is the best way to handle the situation," he replied calmly; I tried not to blame him as he didn't realize he was asking me to carefully and purposely slice my chest open and take out my heart.

"Why? Won't they just publish it anyway?"

"Unlikely. How would that look?" And here began the reasoning. "Blake Tyler gets her heart broken and the press insists that it was all fake? That would be like them publishing a video of the reporter kicking a puppy, Mr. Parker. They want a good story; they don't want to destroy their career; they don't even want to destroy her. They want a sensation and a broken heart is more sensational than fake news."

I couldn't believe what I was hearing.

"In fact, I think this will turn out even better than the original plan. It's one thing to prove that Miss Tyler does have a heart, but to show it being broken? I can't think of anything better to garner more sympathy or support."

This was so fucked up.

"Wait. What do you mean 'show it being broken?'"

And then for the first time in the past fifteen minutes, Ash spoke. "You're going to break up with her on stage tonight and then ZPP is going to leave the tour."

"No." The word left my mouth like air left my lungs. *Without thought.* "No fucking way."

"Why, Zach?" He questioned, raising an eyebrow at me. "Why would that be a problem? You'll have saved Blake's rep and ZPP's popularity is off the charts. *Isn't that what you're here for?*"

I glared at him, wondering if he knew – not just what happened, but what he was asking me to do. He dared me. The fucker was daring me to rage that I was in love with his sister and there was no fucking way that I'd publicly break her heart.

My fists flexed. I wanted to. Every cell of my body itched to.

Every breath I took geared me for the fight of my life - the fight for my heart.

But then Bruce spoke again.

"Mr. Parker," he said, but I still didn't take my eyes from Ash. "I'm sure that you've seen the stories that have been written about the two of you recently. I'm also sure that being a young, impressionable girl that there is a chance that Miss Tyler may have developed some slight feelings for you. However, if you were to think about the consequences if you do *not* do this, I believe, knowing how close you are to, well, the whole family, you will understand that this is the right course."

"Oh I will?" I ground out, vibrating with the need to hit something – *anything* – within reach.

"Miss Tyler has been *falsely* accused of many things in the recent past - the whole reason we are in this situation. The press has tried to portray her as flighty and uncaring and heartless - unable to keep a boyfriend because she doesn't care. If they publish this story and reveal that the only relationship that has truly seemed real to the world is the one that was faked, she will never recover from that; her reputation will never recover."

I hated him. I hated Bruce Pillars with his pinched eyes and wiry glasses. I hated him for his schemes and the way he directed Blake's life like she was just a pawn instead of a person. Mostly, though, I hated him because what he said dug its claws into my mind and whispered how it was the truth.

"For all these momentary issues," he continued, rubbing his hands together, "Miss Tyler is the most... the best... singer... performer, I've ever had the pleasure of working with - and I don't mean that because of how popular she is or how much money that she makes. I mean that because she truly cares about her fans and how they see her. Every album, every show, she gets up there and she gives them *all* of her. It's rare, in this world that is overrun with the weeds of falseness, to find someone who continues to be so true."

My throat tightened. Of all the things he could be saying, I wasn't expecting this. I still hated him for what he was asking me to do, but my anger at *him* was quickly falling like sand through my grasp.

"She is a role model to so many. She is truly a light shining brightly in this messy, *very messy*, night. And for as much as they love her, she also loves them. She does this *for them*. She has blossomed into the person she is *for them.*"

I tore my eyes from Ash, finally raising them to Bruce who stood there no longer with the calm composure of an agent, but with the rare trace of emotion on his face that validated every word of praise that he spoke.

"If this story runs, Mr. Parker, all of that will be gone. You and I both know that we all thought this plan was for the best at the time - because we thought it was the only way to show everyone the part of Miss Tyler's heart that gives easily and freely, to give them proof of what they should already know. If they find out that in order to do that, we had to give them something false, they will crucify her. No. Matter. What."

I fought against the words, swinging to hit them away as they flew at me. But it wasn't enough. I was overwhelmed by them and their stupid fucking truth. The press would eat her alive for doing this. They fed on scandal, fed on it like they'd been starved of food for years. They were gluttons. They were rabid. They would devour this until there was nothing left to her, let alone her reputation. And for a scandal like this, their memory was long. It would forever be a lingering taste on their tongue, easily and expertly able to be recalled at a moment's notice.

And Blake, with her heart that was far too big to fit on any sleeve, would be crushed. *And I would be responsible.*

Like a crack of thunder, what I needed to do crashed and boomed inside my mind.

"What do I need to do?" I rasped hoarsely, keeping my eyes trained on Bruce. In my periphery, I saw the small beginning of a satisfied smile tip Ash's expression.

And even if we told them the truth? We'd still have to admit that the truth started as a lie – a lie that would still do her in.

I listened numbly. Words were spoken and just directly absorbed, not heard.

"She can't know, Mr. Parker." The phrase was repeated numerous times. "It needs to look as real as possible. Mr. Tyler has already booked the band flights back to Nashville tonight. The quicker you are gone, the less chance for questions."

I stood abruptly. I didn't need to hear this anymore. I knew what I had to do. *I fucking hated what I had to do.*

And, just like nine years ago, I was going to do the right thing. I hated how the right thing always meant I had to hurt her for her own good. For a brief, moronic second I thought about just telling her - talking to her about it. And maybe if I didn't know her like I did, I would've. *But she'd give it all up for me.* She'd tell me she didn't give a shit about what anyone said or wrote. '*Who reads those things anyway?*'

She would lie.

And I couldn't live with myself knowing that I'd been responsible for her fall. She was too damn bright for that.

"Mr. Pillars." With a curt nod to the empty space between Ash and him, I stalked towards the door.

Before I could open it, Ash's palm held it shut. My head jerked, meeting the cold stare of my oldest, best friend.

"You. Promised."

Two words lifted the fog.

Ash knew.

298

When… how… it didn't matter. What mattered was that he knew which could only mean one thing.

"You looked me in the face and swore you Wouldn't. Touch. Her." He snarled. I wanted to punch him for what he'd done, but I realized that's exactly what he wanted: a reason to fight me. "You're lucky you agreed tonight otherwise I would have fucking ruined you. Now get the fuck out of my sight and away from my fucking sister."

"Is that what this is about?" I demanded, my voice cutting like steel. "Punishing me? Then do it. Punish *me*. I deserve it. I broke my fucking promise but I think love is a damn good reason. You want to hurt me? Go right ahead. I deserve it. And I'll take it, for her."

He sneered. "Tempting. But I don't need to hit you to hurt you. Actually, as much as I want to, *not* kicking the shit out of you is going to make this hurt you more, so that's what I'm going to do."

He reached and yanked the door open.

"One day you'll realize that we didn't do this to hurt you," I said with a low voice. I may have submitted for Blake's sake, but that sure as fuck didn't mean that I was going to do it quietly, especially if this was all because of *him*. "Right before you realize what a fucking piece of shit you are for doing this to her. Again. For making me break her heart. For her. For you. *Again.*"

I watched pure rage vibrate through him and I felt pity almost as much as anger. Ash was my best friend. He was there for me through everything - high school, football, college, ZPP. He was like a brother to me. And that meant I knew better than anyone just how deeply rooted this sense of loyalty ran. I tried to make him see over the years what it had cost him - friends, girlfriends - but he couldn't… wouldn't. Now it was going to cost him our friendship and I had a sinking feeling it was going to cost him his sister.

"You know what Ash? Nine years ago, I chose to stab

myself in the heart rather than stab you in the back. You'd think that by now you'd realize that I wouldn't have fucking done this if I didn't love her with every goddamn breath in my bones." I watched his nostrils flare and I knew I'd struck a nerve. "I hope this was worth it. I hope your pride was worth it."

Ash didn't care what this did to Blake. He thought she'd survive my leaving her just like the last time. *But last time wasn't like this time.* The last time I hadn't known that she was all I needed.

It was when I punched the elevator button, needing to get outside and get some air, that I realized I'd been holding my breath, knowing that letting it go meant time was ticking closer to the moment when I had to break my girl's heart – and my own.

At this point it didn't matter what the truth was - whether Ash had made up the entire thing about the press knowing or whether he'd convinced Bruce that this was the only way to resolve it. I wasn't willing to risk it - everything that she'd worked so hard for. *I wasn't worth it.*

She was going to hate me.

I was going to hate me.

But at least they would still love her and still look at her as though she were made of pure starlight.

***

My hat was so twisted in my hands, it should have broken by now.

I watched her. Watched her as she stared blankly out at the stage, like she somehow knew it was the fucking plank she was about to walk onto - a plank that I was going to push her off of.

My fingers were still chilled from walking outside for the past half hour. After that meeting, I needed to get out of there. I needed to think. And I needed to make sure that I didn't run into her because she made me fucking weak. One look. One word. And I knew I would give in. Touching her would convince me to say to hell with her career - *her life* - and take everything that she was and keep it for myself. *Nine years of starvation had turned me into a selfish, greedy bastard.* I'd prided myself on always doing the right thing. With her, the lines blurred on whether it was the right thing - or just the right thing *for me.*

Two roads. One destination: losing Blake. *There was no good option.* At least if I was the one to break it off, she wouldn't lose any more face in front of the world. At least I'd be able to give her that.

The thought that I knew we should have told Ash was no consolation now; that fucker would have thought we'd betrayed him no matter how or when he found it.

It was the one thing that had surprised me though - I thought I'd care more about what Ash thought. He was my fucking best friend, I should care if I'd hurt him. But if I did, it was nothing compared to what I felt for his sister.

Again, I felt like kicking myself for running from her all this time.

My Blake. *My North Star.*

And then I heard it. The crowd chanting for her, begging her to come on stage. She didn't realize it - too lost in thought - but an unconscious smile appeared on her face hearing them; they lit her soul.

I wouldn't take this away from her.

I wasn't worth it.

CHAPTER 25
BLAKE

Track 18: Falling Stars

"Speeding. Burning. I never learn.
I wonder, can I wish on my own falling star?
Because wherever I fall, I hope it's where you are."

STIFLING ANXIETY. NOT THE 'I'M-ABOUT-TO-GO-ON-STAGE' butterflies. No, this was the nervousness that rubbed like sandpaper over every inch of my skin, taking my calm and rational layers with it.

It was *fine* that I hadn't heard from Zach since he'd gone to meet with my brother.

I was *sure* it was about ZPP.

So sure.

Just like I'd been sure about Xavier. And Levi.

I'd been so sure about them.

Until I wasn't. And then the uncertainty invaded my insides like poisonous weed, growing, climbing, tightening... consuming. And that's what I felt now. The thickness in my throat that I kept trying to swallow as I tried to talk to Tay like nothing was wrong.

"You ok, B?" She adjusted my black sequin party-looking dress, tucking the cord of my mic down the back.

"Just nervous." My eyes focus on the two stools on stage. I would be out there in five and I hadn't seen Zach yet – which wasn't the norm.

"Not the normal nervous. If you were normal nervous, you'd be smacking on a piece of gum right now." She came around me and crossed her arms over her chest.

"Nothing." I ducked my head, glancing around - *looking for him* - before I confessed miserably, "I-I just wanted to see Zach before the show but he couldn't because he was meeting with Ash. I'm just... worried. Maybe Zach was right. Maybe we should have told him."

My lower lip replaced the gum I didn't have.

"Oh?" Her brow scrunched. "Stop chewing on your lip. You're eating away the red." She pulled out the rouge lipstick that Lin had put on me from her pocket and dabbed some where I'd rubbed it off. "You know, I saw Ash a little earlier, but he said he was meeting with Bruce..."

My eyebrows rose. *Well, that was news.* I rubbed my freshly-coated lips together.

"I doubt that if he knew, he'd confront Zach in front of Bruce, don't you?"

Logical. Rational.

I absorbed her words, willing them to dampen my racing heart.

"You're right." I shook my head. "I'm sure you're right."

The stagehand pulled back the curtain. "May the odds..." I heard her whisper as my smile – the one that belonged to them found its place on my face.

Rep-u-ta-tion.

The echo followed me out on stage. Even amidst the screaming crowd, my doubts droned louder.

"*Hello, Minnesota!*"

No matter what was going on inside, their energy always fueled my smile. I welcomed them. Thanked them. Joked with them. All my usual manner of finding my comfort zone in front of thousands of people. All the while my eyes darted to the side of the stage.

Eventually, the words left my lips because they were rehearsed; they were expected; they were everything that was my life.

"Ladies and Gentlemen, if you could give a big 'ol Minnesota welcome to my… breathtaking… boyfriend - and the leader of the opening act - Zach Parker!"

The crowd went wild.

Seconds felt stagnant as I stood up there alone. Waiting. Petrified.

I turned to stare at the side of the stage, a familiar line of faces watching me, but there was still one missing.

And that was the moment I knew.

At least my brain did. My heart still lagged behind, weighed down with hope that had been bloated by love over the past many weeks.

I gasped for air, hoping the mic wasn't picking up on my slow death - as though it wasn't written all over my face that was projected all around the stadium. I took one step towards the side, about to mumble something to the crowd when I saw him.

His eyes were sharp - hardened honey; they were the amber that preserved the fossils of his feelings about me from the start, the feelings that put loyalty before love. *Every. Single. Soul-crushing. Time.*

I took steps back as he walked towards me, the crowd cheering again unknowing that they were chanting for my demise. My thighs hit the back of the stool and I was forced to stop and wait as he descended on me. The hard line of his jaw told me everything I needed to know about how unshakably determined he was.

"Zach…" I murmured when he stopped in front of me. "Please don't do this," I mouthed desperately.

Everything around us vanished - just like it always did. It was just him and me. Our world. *Our wondrous world.*

"Blake, I'm sorry," he said clearly, succinctly. Like he was telling me it was sixty-two degrees outside.

And it was in slow-motion – standing there in my black party dress, red lipstick, with everyone and no one to impress – that I lost him – one more time to match all the times I'd loved him.

Zach lit a fire inside of me, a fire that burned so hot and so bright, I swore my love for him would melt me from the inside out. Now, he was dousing it. There was no warmth left in him, only a cold callousness. Nowhere and nothing ever made me feel as hot as Zach did… or as cold, the way he blew through my hollow heart like an arctic wind; I'd never be anywhere as cold as him.

"I can't do this anymore, Blake." I choked as the lies I'd easily swallowed, the ones of love and forever, now came back up with a vengeance. "I'm sorry. It's over."

He was saying it but it didn't feel real; it felt like he said sorry just for show.

I stood speechless. Agape. Destroyed. Derailed.

There were no words left. For nine years almost everything I'd spoken, written, or sung had been about this man and now, that well of words was dry.

What do you say when you've lived through this experience so many times that you've exhausted all heart? When you've replayed the tape so many times that you've destroyed it?

What do you say when tears are streaming down your face in front of the entire world?

And what did I do when the one who meant the most to me is the one - the only one whose ever had enough of me to break my heart - is walking away from everything that we had?

The alternate, yet equally true reality crashes down on me: *Zach Parker broke up with me in front of the whole world.*

At least he did it *before* I sang for him this time, I thought, looking down and seeing the droplets splatter on the stage floor. You know the pain is bad when the tears are hot – little drops of scalding sadness to seep into the cracks of my heart and burn away the nerve endings that are too frayed to fight.

This time, as he walked off stage to the gasps of shock from the crowd, he took my whole broken heart with him. This time, he'd left me with nothing.

Nothing but them.

I turned to the crowd. My fans. Those whose love gave me the courage to stand on this stage time and again and share my heart with them.

Even if I could, there was no point in going after Zach. In fact, I didn't want to leave this stage. This stage was the only thing holding me together. *They* were the only thing holding me together as I quickly became undone.

I was the idiot. *I knew from the start that this was the type of thing that was either going to be forever or go down in flames.*

Spoiler alert: Smoke alarms were going off everywhere. Sprinklers were next. No firemen in sight.

My hand shook as I pulled the stool to me, lifting myself up onto it as I tried to find the right words to continue.

What was I supposed to say?

'Ladies and Gentlemen, I give you Zach Parker, the one man who has taught me many things, but nothing as well as how to make a fool out of myself for him.'

No.

I pulled Marty onto my lap, my fingers wiping the tears that landed on my guitar.

"I don't know what to say right now," I admitted quietly, scanning the arena quickly before looking down again. I took a chance - a shot. I know they think that I'm bulletproof, but I'm not. I listened to the hushed murmurs and whispers; I listened to them wondering what had just happened.

I was a paper airplane flying in a hurricane.

And then I heard it.

'We love you, Blake!'

'We're here for you!'

Tears overflowed from my eyes, dripping down over the knuckles of my hand that was clapped over my mouth.

'He doesn't deserve you!'

'And he wears stupid hats!'

My shoulders shook with a half-sob, half-laugh. I was in shock, I knew. *I also loved those stupid hats.* But that wasn't important. The words kept coming - not from me, but from them. Encouragement. Love. Support.

I didn't deserve it, but they did for me what my music had done for them. I ripped myself apart to give them words that would make them strong. Tonight, they didn't ask of me. They gave.

They screamed and cheered so my small sobs wouldn't be heard. They chanted and sang so I could have a moment to find my voice through the pain. They fought to give me strength.

Mesmerized, I thought, this was it… *I had fallen.*

But then they turned the flashlights on their phones on, a million twinkling lights suddenly shining in my view, and the craziest sense of peace washed over me. It's these dark moments, in the darkest of nights, that produced the brightest stars. *They were my stars.* I was in awe of *their* glowing love. I was blinded by *their* shimmering support.

I had reached for the moon and it landed me here, among them.

Even though I didn't have the right words to say, I knew what needed to be sung. Just like every other time Zach had done a number on my stupidly forgiving and needy heart, I dug deep for the lyrics to songs from my debut album, *Heart Break* - lyrics I'd written about him the very first time he'd broken me.

It was time to let my music do the talking – *the healing.*

Heartbreak was my national anthem and for the next four hours, I sat on that stool and sang it proudly. Alone. With only Marty to accompany me. I opened back up that diary of intense emotions and romantic mishaps and I relived them all so that the hurt had somewhere to go.

A diary that should have come with the subtitle: In Memory of Zach Parker.

I confessed to them the truth about all of this time I'd been wasting, hoping he would come around - how I gave out chances like they were free samples and all he ever did was throw them away.

I admitted to them that I'd needed him like a heartbeat. And then I assured them that this was the last straw because I didn't want to hurt anymore.

Finally, I swore to them - to them and myself - that we were never. *Ever.* Getting back together. How did I know that? Because he'd convinced me that what he felt was real, when in fact it was a lie. *It was a show.*

I'd known all this time that we'd been walking a fragile line. It was strained but it was *strong;* I never thought I'd see it break.

And because of that, I could never believe any more words that came from his mouth - even if those words were 'I'm sorry.'

So, I sang because that's what I do. *Because that's who I am.* And that's the only place that I find solace. I sang and sang until I'd forgotten about our beautiful, magic love. I sang until all that was left was more wrecked memories of this sad, tragic affair. Some time in the future, I'd use them to build the walls of my castle higher - so high that even those reaching for the stars would be discouraged from trying to climb it. The walls would protect me, *the Queen of Broken Hearts.*

And then I walked off that stage the same way I'd started this tour - swearing that I'd never let myself fall for Zach Parker again.

And haunted by something that keeps me holding on to nothing.

***

"WHAT DO YOU NEED, B? Let me get you something," Taylor insisted, pacing nervously in her hotel room.

I'd had the strength to walk off stage last night, but, just like I knew would happen, as soon as the strength and the energy of the crowd was gone, I sublimated.

Not crumbled. Not shattered. *Sublimated.*

A fancy word for turning from solid into vapor - *into nothing.*

All of the hurt and pain that had been building and bubbling against the cage that the show had held in, turned me from whole into a blank space.

I remembered Tay's face as she tried to hold it together so that she could hold me together. I remembered going to her hotel room and her helping me into bed. I remembered the pain in my chest, my stomach… all of me… the whole time. I remembered how I cried because I couldn't escape it.

And I remembered Zach walking away. *Always walking away.*

'I can't do this anymore.' 'It's over.' 'I'm sorry.' The memory of those harsh, burning words worked to cauterize every injury caused from my heartbreak. The pain was excruciating. But it was the only way to stop the bleeding: to hurt so much that it singed my heart shut.

"B?" Her hand rested on my foot, drawing my focus back to her. "Tell me what to do."

She was desperate to help, but I was beyond helping.

"Take me home."

It was an easy request. We were leaving today for Nashville and then I had two weeks off before the final show of the tour, which meant that I had this week and the next to figure out how I was going to walk back out on that stage with a smile on my face like the entire world hadn't been witness to the most painful moment of my entire life.

"I went and packed all your stuff from your room. I have it here and all ready to go."

"What time is it?" I wondered out loud. She pulled out her phone to check and I saw her eyes widen and face scrunch as she swiped through notification after notification. "Almost eleven."

I groaned, pulling the covers up higher on my face and reaching for a tissue. "I want you to make them forget about me."

"Who?"

"The world." I didn't want to be a star. I didn't want everyone to watch my fall.

'Blake Tyler's heart broken on tour!'

"Oh, B…"

"What are they saying?" I don't know why but I wanted to know. *Needed* to know. I held out my hand when she looked like she didn't want to tell me. I was too fragile for her to fight me on it though.

'Blake Tyler forms unique bond with fans after Zach Parker breaks up with her on stage!'

"OVERWHELMINGLY SUPPORTIVE," she said softly as I continued to swipe through the trending posts, my stomach clenching tighter with each one that showed photos of Zach and me on stage - of my face when Zach walked off. "They can't believe what happened to you - that he would do that. And your reaction..." She sighed. "That entire crowds' hearts broke for you last night, Blay. Every. Single. One."

'Crowd Consoles Broken Blake at Minneapolis Show!'

I CLICKED off her phone and tossed it onto the bed in her direction before wiping my eyes. My pillow was still damp from last night.

"Glad to know," I said thickly, hating how the tears demanded their turn to speak, "that the price of a spotless reputation around here is one perfectly good heart."

I knew this was going to happen. I knew he was trouble when I walked into this fire - and still, I went willingly. *Shame on me now.*

"Let's go home, B." She sat down next to me and bent over to awkwardly hug me again. "We'll find a way through this, ok? You are going to be fine," she whispered. "I know it doesn't feel like it, but your heart is far too big for a jerk like Zach Parker to have broken it."

I didn't move, mostly because I was pinned beneath the covers but also because I couldn't. Tears leaked down my cheek, the lie detectors of my silent agreement. *She was wrong.* It didn't matter how big my heart was, what mattered was that I'd signed every square inch of it over to Zach.

Shame. On. Me. Now.

. . .

311

***

I was just tugging on a sweater when there was a sharp knock at the door. Stupid heart jumped.

Even Tay darted a wondering glance at me before she took charge and went to open the door. I couldn't stop my feet as they padded towards the muffled voices that were growing louder.

It's not him.

Still, my heart fell when I rounded the corner and saw Ash standing in the doorway. Ever the contradiction, his eyes flicked to mine a swirl of defiance and repentance.

And like a lightbulb flicking on, I *knew* that my brother had something to do with this.

"What. Did. You. Do?" I demanded, my finger pointing obnoxiously at him as I strode closer.

His eyes widened. Yeah, I'm sure I was a sight with my red eyes, red nose, coming at him like a raging red balloon. Seeing that he wasn't getting Broken Blake right now, his expression hardened.

"I didn't do anything," he ground out, stepping just inside the room. "But I could ask you the same thing, Baby Blake." He taunted me with my nickname from Zach. "What did you do? Or should I say *who* have you done?"

"You're an ass, you know that? My personal life is none of your business!" I accused, jabbing a finger into his hard chest, wincing as it bent back uncomfortably.

"It is when you're *fucking* my best friend!" he said through clenched teeth, his eyes flaring.

He knew. I knew that he knew. But to hear it from his mouth was like the final nail in the coffin.

"How did you know?" I needed to know how long the rage had been burning inside of him.

His jaw ticked. I wondered if he would keep it from me. "I

saw you come out of the hotel together in Denver. I watched you get into the car."

I swallowed, remembering what had happened right *after* we got in the car to drive back out to Red Rocks.

"What does it matter?"

"It matters because he fucking promised he'd never touch you. That lying motherfucker promised me. And then he *touched* you; he goddamn *touched* my baby sister."

I saw all the things that were admirable about my brother and how - like most things in life - when pushed to the extreme, they become a flaw. Protectiveness over me to the point where he would destroy a friendship that he'd had for almost his whole life, to the point where he couldn't see that he was protecting me from happiness. And loyalty to those he cares about - a select few - and in a way that he expected returned - a way that Zach had violated.

I let out a groan of frustration, seeing red. "I'm not a baby! I'm twenty-five, Ash. Twenty. Five. And he can be your best friend and my boyfriend! I don't understand why that's so difficult a concept for you to grasp."

"Because!" He roared at me, letting loose. "Because you fucking lose yourself. Did you forget that I was there? Our *entire* childhood I watched as you traipsed after us, hoping that he'd give you a second look? I saw the way you dressed up when he was coming over. The way you borrowed mom's make-up to put on for his birthday and Christmas Eve. I knew it was always you always stealing his t-shirts that got left at the house."

My mouth went dry as my heart thundered with each footstep that led me back to the past.

"You made a goddamn fool out of yourself, Blake. I don't think I need to remind you about graduation." His words took what was left of me and ground it into nothing. "Back then, you were a kid and I figured you'd grow out of it before it mattered. But then you didn't."

Tears had begun to stream down my face again.

He swore harshly and speared his hands through his hair like he wasn't the one who'd just ruined everything.

"Do you think you'd be here right now?" He held his arms wide. "Do you think you'd have all this and be where you are had Zach given you the time of day? Let me spoil it for you, you wouldn't. You were meant to do greater things greater than dating the boy on the football team. Around him, Blay, you don't even see yourself. Maybe the limelight has blinded you, but I see *you* out there on stage. I see the way this brings you to life. And whether you want to admit it or not, you'd throw that all away for him. *You'd throw yourself away for him.*"

I laughed.

It was one of those laughs that was hard and painful and should have been given a different name other than what it was because there was nothing light or happy about it.

What was it with the men in my life sacrificing me in my name? And then not noticing until it's too late to do anything?

This was my life. Never simple. Never easy.

Never a clean heartbreak.

No one here to save me.

The laughter didn't stop. Tears fell along with it - and not because I was laughing too hard. Ash and Tay both stared like I was going crazy. *That's what happens when you stay in Wonderland too long.*

"I hate to break it to you, big brother," I said with the sharpest edge I could manage. "But what you see isn't reality. I lose myself in this life. I feel too much. I care too much. I give too much. And I *love* it. But it makes me lose the parts that still need to feel and care and give back to myself. Zach helps me find that. *That* is why I cling to him. Every day I feel like I'm a kite flying too high, pulled this way and that by the winds of the world - 'smile,' 'sing,' 'fall in love,' 'but don't do it too quickly'... Sure, those winds can lift me up - but they can also kill me in the end. And Zach... He. Holds. Me. Steady. He grounds me. He cares for me. He finds me when I've lost myself."

The expression on his face changed just as quickly as those tropical storms that appear at the shore from out of nowhere. He'd come here dark and vengeful - and just as quickly, the clouds that had been blinding him cleared and the anger washed away.

"Never mind." I let out with a huff - too emotionless to continue, too tired of feeling to even want to. "I didn't do this to hurt you. I can't help the fact that he's what inspires me - that he's what saves me. Maybe I won't need him anymore, now that I don't have a heart."

"Blay…" he ground out my name, whether it was to scold me or apologize, I'd never know.

"Don't, Ash. You've done enough," I cut him off as Tay stepped between us. "Now that that is cleared up and my life seems to be back on the track *you* feel is the right one, I'm going to go crash and burn."

I turned and walked back into the bedroom, slamming the door behind me. Tay could hold her own out there with my brother. She'd have my back even if it was hard to recognize the way it was so full of holes.

CHAPTER 26
BLAKE

Track 19: Take the Fall

"Love is two parts: me and you.
One part to give it all.
The other part to take the fall."

I LOVED NIGHTS LIKE THIS IN FRANKLIN. NOT BECAUSE OF HOW I felt. No. Heartbroken nights were the most painful kind - and a pretty prevalent kind at that when I was here. No, the nights when it was silent and clear. The slight chill sent me curling tighter into my fuzzy jacket as I lay in the hammock out back. My mom had turned on the porch light fifteen minutes ago when she finally got tired of watching me from the window, waiting and worrying for me to come back inside and go to bed; there was nothing they could do for me.

I wanted to stay here. I wanted to go back to being grounded - to being able to look up at the stars and appreciate their beauty instead of empathizing with their shimmering pain. I didn't want to go back up there. I didn't want to go back up to be stared at and used by the press for my heartbreak to make them millions. Like the moon, they took my light… they took it and reflected it to make them shine.

"Millions rally around Blake Tyler after her authentic, heart-wrenching concert of strength in Minnesota!"
"We all thought Zach Parker was the one!"

I TAPPED my pen on the notebook that sat empty in my lap. The last time he'd broken my heart, the words had come easily. This time, my heart still echoed with nothing but the hollowness of a black hole.

"Blake Tyler was love-struck-out on her Lovestruck tour. What will happen in Nashville?"

MORE TEARS SLIPPED from my eyes and I wished they'd turn into words instead of useless blobs of wetness on my sweatshirt.

Why did he do this? Why was I not enough?

It was the million-dollar, million-star, mystery of life question. It chanted in my head every moment since that show. A sick and twisted taunt mingled with a healthy dose of 'I-told-you-so' deja-vu.

Why did I fall for it?

That was the real question. How did I end up back here? In the hammock. Wallowing. Lost. Crying because Zach Parker had turned my love for him back in my face. At least last time the rejection had been private; this time, the whole world had front row seats to the concert of my crumbling heart.

I was a wreck and he was the wrecking ball.

An aggravated and strangled yell escaped me as I stood, tossing my notebook and pen onto the fabric. Arms over my chest, I looked back at my parent's house. There were still lights on which meant I wasn't going back inside. I couldn't bear any more questions, let alone reassurances that everything was going to be ok.

I spun in the other direction, hating what I was faced with.

The treehouse.

Maybe Ash was right. I did lose myself when it came to Zach.

Wiping my cheeks with my sweatshirt sleeves, I crossed my arms over my chest, a sudden spark of determination flaring inside me. My heart might have been broken but I wasn't. I was angry - angry at how quickly I'd let myself fall back into old habits, how quickly I'd let myself fall back in love with him, and how devastatingly quickly I'd crumbled.

Next I knew, my feet were crunching over the newly growing weeds and branches on the forest floor as I made my way to the treehouse. I hadn't been back here since that night. I refused. It had been too painful at first and then I was away so much that it didn't matter. When I was here, it was just another place to remind me how foolish I was with my heart.

Blake Tyler never learns. That should have been the headline. Maybe I should have Tay see if we can get that one out there. Or how about, *'Blake Tyler on a permanent heart break until further notice.'*

I laughed because what else do you do when something hurts too much?

A drop of water landed on the tip of my nose. It took another two for me to realize that these were actually from the sky and not from my eyes.

The rungs of the ladder shifted slightly under my weight

and I wondered if anyone had been up here since that night. Hoisting myself through the entry, I stood in the empty room. It seemed much smaller than I remembered. Maybe it was just the significance of the memories that it held that made me remember it bigger.

Walking to the window, the wood of the awning creaked as I forced it up and locked it into place. My hands came to rest on the cool wood and I drew the long deeps breaths like I'd learned in the yoga class Tay dragged me to on Wednesday.

I blinked slowly, staring into the star-speckled night, listening to the steadily increasing raindrops on the tin roof. Or maybe they were raining on me. I sure felt like I'd turned into the tin man, desperate for a working heart.

What was I doing here?

Sometimes, things happen in life that shake you... that break you a little bit. It's hard to go back to the scene of the crime, but even after all this time, time was taking its sweet old time erasing him. Maybe I thought that coming here would help. A burial of sorts to the old Blake. There would still be scars, I knew; this love had left permanent marks.

My phone buzzed and I pulled it out to make sure it wasn't my mom freaking out or Ash trying to talk to me again.

'Please just leave me alone,' I'd said to him in an eerie monotone, glazed eyes meeting his as we boarded the flight home. Ash was the instigator, dousing me with gasoline before Zach had lit the match. I could see how he regretted our argument and what he said; the look in his eyes was the same look he'd had when he realized what telling me the truth about Santa Claus had done.

He'd been annoyed that Zach continued to play along when I was younger and still believed. He sat me down, insisting that I couldn't hang out with them if I still believed in Santa. And then he told me the truth about the fat man in the suit. I, of course, played it cool - like the truth hadn't put a giant crack in my childhood. But it was on Christmas morning, when he watched as I picked up one gift after another, looking at the stickers that said 'From Santa' on them, and realized what he'd really done. Sure, he'd given me the truth, helped me grow up a little - but he'd also stolen the magic.

Whatever he'd said to Zach, he thought he was doing me a favor. His eyes as they took me in, all bruised and broken, told me he now saw that all he'd done was take more magic from me again.

I refused to talk to him after that. Wednesday was the last day he bothered coming to the house - probably because Tay had taken it upon herself to give him an earful, ending with, *'So loyal, huh, Ash?'*

I let out a sigh. *Speaking of.* It was Taylor who was calling me.

She was visiting her cousin in Nashville - a planned get-together otherwise I had no doubt she would have been glued to my side all day, just like she had been every day for the past week. Movies. Spa days. Yoga. All-you-can-eat Chinese take-out. I secretly wondered if she thought all that high cholesterol would fill in the cracks of my broken heart.

It wasn't fool-proof. I'd had plenty of meltdowns, but I would have melted down had she *not* been by my side.

I silenced the call.

Sorry, Tay. The old Blake can't come to the phone right now.

A drop of water landed on the screen and I immediately looked up, thinking that the roof was somehow leaking - but no, just tears.

Loving Zach had been like driving a Ferrari the wrong way down a one-way street. Exhilarating. Passionate. And sure to end suddenly. *Painfully.*

It was everything about this moment. The silence. The stars. The rain on the roof. It was the train that ran off its tracks. I was hanging up the life that I'd dreamt up and that we'd never get back.

It was sad. Beautiful. *Tragic.*

"Blake?"

I whipped around, my heart going into overdrive.

Blinking several times, I stared at Zach, standing a few feet in front of me. Instinctively, I raised my hands and wiped my eyes again, convinced that he was a mirage in the middle of my desperate desert.

"Zach?" I rasped. "What are you doing here?"

It only took me another second to see my answer: he'd come wearing his best apology. Too bad all I could think about was how many times I'd had to watch him leave.

"I need to talk to you." His face was partially in shadow, but I saw the pain glinting in his eyes. *Or maybe that was just mirrored from my own.*

"What more could you have to say that I haven't heard before?" I offered quietly.

His jaw ticked and I knew I'd hit a nerve.

"Blake, I need to talk to you. I need to explain what happened," he insisted, taking a step towards me. I retreated, bumping back into the wall, my hand going to the sill of the open window. "Please."

"How can you do this?" *I didn't want to know the answer.* My head flew side to side furiously. "No." *I couldn't go through this again.* "No, Zach." He stepped closer again and my body lit up like a runway, ready for take-off. "I can't do this again." I put my hand up, my head turning away as I searched for strength; I might as well have been looking for water in the desert.

"No, Blake." His hands clasped my arms. I froze, slowly turning up to his face; he looked watery through my tears. "It's not what I made you think. I gave you the wrong idea. On purpose, but wrong. So wrong, *Blakebaby.*"

My throat seized on a sob. I'd barely pulled myself back

together this week. Imagine you had a jar of sand and it spilled. Well, trying to put back every grain of sand would have been much more manageable a task than putting myself back to rights. His palms cupped my face and I realized that I'd still been shaking my head 'no' - a silent plea to not do this to me again.

"He said they were going to ruin you," Zach admitted with a low, tortured voice. "He said the press found out about our plan and that they were going to publish it; the story would have destroyed you. Even if we came out with the truth, no one would have believed us."

"I would have… I would have believed in us because for me, it's always been you."

"Blake," he groaned, thumbs wiping away my tears. "I couldn't do that to you. I couldn't let you take the fall. You're too bright, *Blakebaby*, and the world needs your light."

"But I needed you." The words felt foreign, like I was talking about a girl I used to know. "And now, I need to not."

He swore under his breath, the warmth brushing across my face. "I need you, Blay. And I fucked up. I tried to be unselfish. I thought I needed to put you and everything that you've accomplished before what I wanted. Just like all those years ago when I put your future and your brother before how I felt. I'm a slow fucking learner, babe." He let out a soft chuckle. "Too many hard hits in football or something like that. But I'm here. I'm here and I've finally fucking learned that how I feel for you can't be ignored."

His words echoed inside the empty space in my chest where my heart had been.

His hoarse voice crept over me again. "What we have is written in the stars - and I won't let anything or anyone cross them again."

A soft, sad laugh escaped me.

"Don't you get it, Zach?" I whispered. "I know… I knew… that what you said wasn't how you really felt. But even though you knew that, you said it anyway." His jaw clenched.

"I don't care what you think - or what Ash or Bruce said - you've been up there, you've *seen* them. I would have survived whatever was written. *We would have survived.*"

"I didn't want you to feel like I'd forced you into sacrificing all of this…"

"So, you thought you'd fall on the sword instead? The worst part is, Zach, every time you think you're sacrificing yourself for me… the reality is that you're just sacrificing me." I wasn't trying to twist the knife, but he had no idea what he'd put me through. "And this time, it was for the whole world to see." A sob wracked my chest.

"Blake, *please.*"

I felt his fingers tighten ever so slightly on my face as his whole body tensed in frustration. He was saying all the right words. It was just too late.

"This is the last time, Zach," I said quietly. I was defeated, but I didn't care. *It's only by starting from the bottom that I could rebuild myself whole again, piece by shattered piece.* "This is the last time you tell me that I've got it all wrong, the last time I tell you that it's been you all along. This is the last time I let you in."

Pain seared across his face before his lips descended on mine with pleading desperation. I kissed him back. Opening and letting his tongue sweep inside, I sighed, tasting how his addictive sweetness became tainted with the salt from my tears. I knew he thought that this kiss could change things - *could change my mind.* Nine years ago, I had thought that the night in the treehouse could change how he saw me.

But just because I could jump out this window right now and spend a moment suspended in the air didn't mean that I could fly.

And for a long time, with Zach, I believed that I could. *Lesson learned.*

"I'm sorry, Zach," I mouthed against his lips just as they separated from mine. "I can't say I'll forgive you and risk another goodbye."

I hated hurting him. If I thought that being with Zach was only possible in my wildest dreams, then this - right here, right now - where I was the one pushing him away was a complete alternate reality.

Right before his eyes, I was breaking. This was no longer about the past. There were no more reasons why.

"This is the last time… I won't let you hurt me anymore." I pulled my face from his hands - and he let me, because he knew better than anyone that when push comes to shove, I will follow my feelings every time - whether they lead me to make a fool out of myself for him or they pull me away.

He stood, an immovable statue, turned to stone by my words. I stepped around him towards the exit as I wiped my face with the ends of my sleeves, not bothering to hide my sobs anymore. It was fitting, I thought, that the story of us had started and now ended in this treehouse.

As I brushed past him, the rain on the roof was like a small army of applause, a watery ovation for the first time I'd had the courage to walk away from what my heart so detrimentally needed.

CHAPTER 27
BLAKE

Track 20: Clarity
"Love is insanity.
Insanity gives me clarity."

"I'm not going to lie, B," Tay said with disbelief ringing clearly in her voice. "Even I might have forgiven him... and I'm not the one who's been in love with him for over a decade."

I knew she wasn't trying to make me second-guess (or in this case, millionth-guess) the decision I'd made on Saturday when Zach had surprised me in the treehouse. It was her blunt honesty that had kept us friends all this time, especially in times like this.

"He'll always think that *something* - my future, my brother, my job - will trump how I feel about him. I can't... stay... with someone who thinks it's easier to give up on me and us every time. Even if his intentions are good."

She stared long and hard at me as we sat in my parents' kitchen, the backdoor open, the perfectly cool beginning-of-summer breeze blowing through the screen door. Max lay snoozing just inside the door; Muffin was currently curled up by Tay's feet.

"I know. It's just crazy. All of it."

"It was a mistake," I said quietly. "This whole thing." She winced, so I quickly added, "It's not your fault, Tay. I went along with it. I agreed with it. I had lost myself."

"What are you talking about?"

"They were right. The press. What they wrote about."

She gasped and pointed a scolding finger at me. "Bite your tongue, lady."

"I'm serious." I ate another bite of watermelon that my mom had cut up and left in the fridge for us. "I mean, they were all narcissistic jerks. But I was also lost and spiraling." I sighed. "Last year, when Matt and I fought that last time about how he was nasty and distant to me because of how famous I was… when I told him I was breaking up with him, he said, *'Go right ahead. You'll never find someone to love you. You live in a fantasy world, Blake Tyler. And anyone you date will just be falling in love with the fantasy of you.'*" I rattled off the words that had been embedded deep inside my brain a year and a half ago.

"Oh, B…" I hadn't told her. I hadn't realized how they'd affected me until I'd embarked on this whole heartbreaking charade.

Swallowing the last bite of watermelon along with the tears the admission had cost me, I continued, "It hurt when he said that, but I'm just starting to realize how much. Everyone after that - Xavier, Levi - I was blind to who they really were because I wanted to prove him wrong; I wanted to prove the words wrong. Deep down, I was scared he was right. So, I jumped into relationships that I should have questioned from the start. I looked past things that should have been obvious. I was desperate, Tay, to find someone who was real."

Looking up from the empty bowl, I saw the tears running down her face.

"And then, right in the middle of something that was designed to be fake from the start, I found *him*. And myself." I handed her a tissue and then took one for myself. "I didn't know what to expect after Christmas and after what you told me the media had been spreading. But I shouldn't have worried. I shouldn't have doubted myself."

"I'm sorry—"

I waved her off because the last thing this was was her fault. "Every word. Every song. Every show… I go out there and I sing *exactly* what is on my mind and in my heart and my fans know that. The people who love and support me *know* that. They know that because they know me. The media doesn't. And their pens may be swords, but at some point, they'll realize their shields are only made of paper – and the truth will cut them down quick. The people who are willing to believe the fake stories that are in the news are *not* the people who care about me."

I was shaking, every cell itching with the intense truth in my words. I had been lost. I wasn't anymore.

"I am where I am for a reason." I was no longer crying. For the first time in a week and a half, the semblance of strength flickered in my muscles. The whisper of a beat fluttered in my heart. "My fans love me *for a reason*. I don't give them fake. I give them heart-wrenching real. I give them mistakes. I give them embarrassing emotions of a stupid lovesick girl who sang a song for a stupid stubborn boy. *I give them me*."

I gasped in air, realizing that I must not have been breathing the entire time I climbed up onto my self-assured soapbox.

"You give them magic," she said with a watery smile.

"No, I give them real – but in this world, sometimes being real is all it takes to be magic… which is why I have to tell them."

The smile fell from her face faster than Janet Jackson's wardrobe malfunction as she let out a strangled, "What?"

"I'm going to tell them," I repeated, knowing this was going to give her a heart attack.

"But... after everything..." she stuttered. I'd known her for long enough to see this coming. "Bruce is *not* going to be happy."

"I know. But it's not because of Bruce that my fans love me," I replied ruefully. "And I've thought about it a lot. Just like I've thought about Zach a lot. But I need to do what is right for my soul - and that means being honest about everything. Maybe the truth will be the thing that finally frees me."

Her eyes narrowed and she stared at me for a questionable number of seconds. This was what happened when a thought struck her - a realization - that she was working through the best way to tell me.

Maybe she was going to try to convince me against this.

I gritted my teeth, prepared to stand my ground. After Minnesota and seeing how my fans had been there for me as my heart was literally broken in two on stage in front of them (not to mention all the outpouring of love and support since), they deserved the truth from me.

"And what about being honest with yourself?" she asked with a calm insightfulness that unnerved me.

"What do you mean?"

"What about admitting to the truth that you are still in love with Zach?"

My mouth opened and shut, heat rising to my cheeks. *I couldn't deny it.*

"I-I'm sure part of me will always love him." I shrugged it off.

"No, Blay." She shook her head. "I'm not talking about that childhood part. I'm talking about the woman who fell head over heels for the country football star-slash-singer with the horrible choice in hats. I know it's easy to think that you kept it a secret from everyone these past few months. But I didn't need to know the truth to be able to see it." Her hand came up to halt me as my mouth opened again. "And I *have* seen you with other guys so don't even think of trying to tell me that this is how you are with all of them."

"It was a show…" I grumbled reluctantly; it was all I had left.

A shiver ran up my spine. "You can't fake magic," she replied with a low, steady voice. "Only real love shines with that."

I stared down at the counter, knowing that I'd begun to cling to certain hard truths about this entire situation and chosen to ignore other ones.

"I sent him away, Tay," I whispered. "I told him this was the last time I'd love him."

Next I knew her arms were around me. "So just apologize and tell him that you are a big fat liar. That's what he did, isn't it?"

A thick laugh escaped me. "Yeah, but I never thought that what he said was the truth. I made him believe me because I wanted to believe me."

"Just say you're sorry. He loves you. He will forgive you. Heck, he probably still just wants you to forgive him!"

"Yeah… Band-Aids don't fix bullet holes." I huffed, quickly swiping tears from my face. "Have you… heard from him?"

Ugh, I'd been doing so well with keeping my wonderings to myself.

It had taken everything in me not to ask anyone anything about him – and every time I didn't, I almost did.

"No, I haven't, but…" she trailed off just as the screen door opened and my brother came in.

I glared at him for a second before glancing to Tay. The way she was chewing a hole through her lip said that she'd known he was coming. I no longer had my shield.

"Can we talk?" Ash's voice rasped into the heavy silence.

"I thought you said everything that you needed to before we left Minnesota." I tried to keep my tone level but I couldn't help the words. He'd hurt me. Almost as much as Zach had.

His jaw ticked and I waited for the sharp rebuttal, but he looked to Taylor who sent him a hard, unwavering stare almost like she was reining in his anger.

"I didn't. I'd like to talk to you." *Interesting.* "Please."

How had he'd managed to convince her of that?

"B, I'm going to run to the store and grab some more tea. If that's ok..." Typical Taylor wouldn't actually leave if I didn't want her to.

"Yeah," I sighed. "It's fine."

"You need anything?" She hopped down from the stool and I answered in the negative; I probably could have used something, but I was more interested in the way that Ash was watching her than anything.

"How about you, Ash?" she asked him with the hint of a quiver in her voice that only a lifelong friend could detect.

His head jerked in a no and then that steely stare remained locked on her until the front door clicked shut.

***

"Blake," he addressed me with steady, concerned eyes.

"Ash."

The sibling stare-down was going strong. But then my brother uncharacteristically broke, running a hand through his hair and nodding over to the family room that sat attached to the kitchen, separated by a round morning room table.

"Can we sit?"

He took the loveseat and I took the chair - the same seats that we'd chosen since we were kids. *Usually Zach sat beside him on the couch. And then they'd toss pillows at me in the middle of a scary movie to make me scream.*

I blinked back the memories.

"Why are you here, Ash?"

"To make things right," he answered hoarsely and on his face, I saw the kid who realized that his loyalty and protectiveness had gone too far.

I paused, debating what to say, what to offer. Pulling my knees up under me, I let out a long sigh and said, "I know… you were trying to look out for me."

"Fuck, Blay, it's more than that. God, I don't even know where to begin. I should have come to you. I was just… so fucking livid… when I saw the two of you sucking face in the car. I even looked for the fucking cameras." He paused to let out a hard laugh. "I looked because I thought that there had to be a good reason. Turns out there was a good reason, just not one good enough for me."

I winced, chewing on the inside of my cheek because I was craving gum for my nervous tick.

"Sorry." He pinched the bridge of his nose. "I'm just… having a hard time with this. Obviously."

"Well, you don't have to worry any more. Zach and I are over," I offered, hoping it would ease some of the demons he was wrestling with.

"That's not… what I want for you," he said tightly, pinning my gaze. "Unless it's really what you want. I know that you probably know, but dad would kill me if I just sat here and blankly apologized for everything instead of acknowledging exactly what the apology is for."

It was one of the house rules growing up - if you were going to apologize, you couldn't just mumble off an 'I'm sorry'; admitting to what you'd done wrong was part of the process of doing what's right.

"I'm sorry because I led Bruce and Zach to believe that there was a threat that the press was going to find out about the charade. I'm sorry because I suggested to Bruce that the cleanest way to handle it was to have you break up. I insisted that the only way it was going to look real was without you knowing ahead of time because you had a crush on Zach…" He trailed off, not needing to elaborate any more on that.

"Ash…" I said softly, groaning as Muffin, who'd just realized that Tay had left, trotted over and hopped up onto my lap.

"Just let me finish, Blay," he begged, pulling at his hair so hard I thought he was going to rip a chunk out. "That's not even the fucking worst of it. I mean maybe for you it is, but for me, I'm such an fucking asshole for what I said to you."

My throat felt like someone was blowing a balloon up inside of it.

"I just… I don't know. I don't even know what the fuck my problem is. I guess because Zach has been like a brother to me… and you're my sister. I remember when you had a crush on him in high school and I was so pissed because I thought it was going to ruin everything; I thought it was going to ruin our friendship. And you are my *baby sister*… I couldn't stomach him touching my baby sister."

"Ash," I chuckled, "you know I've dated people. It *is* what got me into this whole mess."

"I know but even though it's all over the news, that's what makes it seem not real. It makes it seem like it's not you. But when I saw you and Zach together, it was too real for comfort and I… Well, I went about it the wrong fucking way."

"You were right though, I do have a tendency to forget about everything else when all I can see is him. I don't know if it's right or wrong, good or bad, but my love for him makes me crazy," I admitted softly, refusing to put that sentence in the past tense.

He gave me a crooked smile. "Yeah, well, if it doesn't, you aren't doing it right."

I raised an eyebrow at him, wondering exactly how and why he could be speaking from experience.

Shaking my head, I spoke, "It's ok, Ash. I should have told you. I should have... Zach wanted to... I just thought everything with the tour and then because things were so delicate between him and me. I don't know... I guess I just wanted to hold onto it for a little while longer before I shared."

"I'm sorry, Blay."

Lifting Muffin and putting him on the floor, I plopped down onto the couch next to him. Sinking into the well-worn leather, I wrapped my arms around him.

"It's ok." Forgiveness was freeing. "It doesn't really matter anymore anyway."

He pulled back from me. "It should."

"No. And I just heard it from Tay, I don't want to hear it from you, too. It's just not meant to be between Zach and me."

"Bullshit," he snorted.

"Excuse me?" I reared back. "A week ago, you literally sabotaged our relationship and now you're telling me that I should be fighting for it?" I laughed at the irony even though he didn't seem to find it amusing; *sometimes, you have to laugh just so that you don't cry.*

"Blay, he fucking broke up with you because I made him - because I told him your career would go down the fucking tubes if he didn't."

"I know that! But he didn't come to me. He didn't talk to me. After every stupid and foolish thing I've done to show him how much I care about him, he still thinks it's not enough to be worth the fight." I hugged myself, really not wanting to argue with my brother over this.

"He fucked up. It's what we do. And then we grovel and fix that shit. It's the fucking circle of life, sis."

I couldn't stop myself from smiling, hating and loving the hope he gave me.

I kept telling myself that the truth was finally going to free me. The truth was that freedom was nothing but missing *him*.

"This is my life, Ash. The lights, the people, the real stories, and the fake news… Sometimes it's a fantasy; sometimes, it's a fight. I can't be in a relationship with someone who *might* be more concerned about what the world wants of me than what I want. At the end of the day, I'd rather go to sleep at night with the man I love and our future in front of me than with the world and their whims behind me."

"He's not going to let you go," he grumbled. "As much as I'm still not too fucking pleased about it."

I patted his arm. "I didn't give him much of a choice."

Laughing, he stood, waking Muffin from his nap. "He may love you, but you're still Baby Blake; one way or another, you still do what we want you to." His tease was laced with truth as I stuck my tongue out at him playfully.

"I'm going to head out," he said over his shoulder, strolling towards the back door.

"You don't want to wait for Tay to get back? We're just going to hang and watch a movie."

A shadow crossed over his face. "Nah. Maybe next time."

CHAPTER 28
ZACH

I WAS DETERMINED. PERSISTENT. *RELENTLESS.*

I wasn't going to let Blake go and I didn't give two fucks what she had to say about it. I knew she loved me. I knew she wanted to be with me, too. *I could fucking taste it on her.*

So, I was going to persist until she was fucking mine.

I'd been knocked down and knocked out in football plenty of times. I knew that mind-numbing sense of shock and confusion and head-splitting pain. *This was nothing like that.* After that night in the treehouse when she left me, I felt like I was being plowed into by a linebacker with every goddamn beat of my heart - knocked down again and again.

But if she thought I'd been stubborn and determined to *not* want her all those years ago, she had a whole other thing coming now - *now that I knew what could be.*

My head jerked towards the door to my studio apartment in Nashville as someone banged loudly on the door. *Probably Ron or Alex.*

I'd hardly talked to the band after we'd dropped everything and disappeared from Minnesota. I think they knew that some shit had gone down. They didn't ask. And truthfully, they had every right to know that ZPP had hit a slight dip in popularity from my cruel break-up with the world's pop princess.

I should have looked before I yanked open the door, seeing familiar blond hair and blue eyes staring back. Too bad it wasn't the sibling that I cared about getting forgiveness from.

"What do you want?" I asked Ash tightly, preparing myself for a fight.

"Can I come in?" he asked casually, leaning against the doorframe.

"Depends." My eyes narrowed on my former friend. "I think you can punch me just as well from out here. Not in the mood to have to clean blood up off the carpet."

His mouth tipped up just a fraction in a smirk. "I'm not here to punch you. I'm over that phase."

I stepped back. "I'm surprised I made it through unscathed..."

"Someone had to tie me down," he quipped.

"Oh yeah? And who was that?" I asked as Ash walked into my place like this was any other day *before* I fucked his sister and he'd forced me to break her heart.

"Doesn't matter." He strolled over to my Ikea dining table, sprawling into one of the chairs. "I'm here to talk about Blay, not me."

My body immediately tensed. "Then you've come for nothing because I don't give a shit anymore what you think. I did what you said and I have never regretted anything more in my entire life. Your sister means the world to me - and instead of showing her that, instead of giving her what she deserves - I told her that what the world thought was more important than how I felt. And it was my fucking choice to listen to you, but if you think I'm going to do it again, you are a fucking moron."

He gave me a blank, bored stare and I almost wished he was here to punch me so I could swing one back at him.

"You done?"

I crossed my arms over my chest, intrigued. "Yeah."

"Good. Because I'm not here to do any of that shit. I'm here because I wanted to tell you that I was wrong."

"Seriously? Ashton Tyler admitting fault?"

"Yeah," he sneered at me. "Go call your fucking paparazzi and let them take a photo so it will last longer."

I laughed as I walked into the kitchen to grab a bottle of water out of the fridge. "Want one?"

"I think I need something a little stronger." He eyed my Glenfiddich on the counter.

I filled a glass with ice and poured him two fingers, setting it on the table next to him, and waited for him to explain himself.

He took his time taking a sip and savoring it before he spoke again. "I'm here to help you fix our mistakes." I continued to stare, unsure and unwilling to believe him. "I'm here to help you fucking fix shit with Blake."

"Seriously?"

"No, I'm really just here for the whiskey," he scoffed, rolling his eyes like they were trying to shake off my idiocy for asking. "Yeah, I'm fucking serious."

There was only one question I needed the answer to. "Why?"

His eyes deepened to black and blue as his jaw ticked in annoyance. *Yeah, well, if you want to help me fucking fix it, you are going to have to fucking convince me that you are really here to do that.* Ash downed the rest of the whiskey before he responded.

"Because, as much as it's still fucking disgusting to me, you two are meant for each other. I saw it. The whole world fucking saw it. I just couldn't see the forest through the trees."

"She doesn't think so." I crossed my arms. "How do you know?"

Part of me really wanted to know. Part of me just really wanted to torture him for the shit he had pulled.

"Because you both love each other. Do you really want me

to spell it out? No one would have believed this whole charade if there hadn't been some truth in it. And they certainly wouldn't have gone ape-shit over it if the charade hadn't actually been the truth. You both love each other. In the way that my sister can't seem to stop herself from writing or singing about... In the way that still really makes me want to haul off and punch you every so often."

I laughed, giving him a slight nod and giving up on my questions.

"I'm sorry, Ash. I didn't plan on falling in love with her." I let out a sigh. "I didn't plan on breaking my promise to you."

He waved me off. "Don't. I was a dick for making you promise that in the first place. And if anyone was going to punch somebody out there," he nodded towards the door, "it should have been you punching me for how I backed you into a corner. I was a fucking insane, protective asshole."

"Agreed."

Bending forward, he rested his elbows on his knees, propping his chin on top of his clasped hands. "Alright, you done with the third degree? Pretty sure there are better fucking ways to spend our time - like trying to show my sister that she's being an idiot."

"Not sure that's quite the vibe I'm going for."

"You're right. You're both idiots."

I cut him off, "I actually have a plan. And now that you're here... well, let's just say I could use you."

"Of course, you could," he replied confidently. "When have you ever come up with a good plan that didn't involve me?"

"Dick."

He stood, extending a hand. "We good?"

I pretended to eye him up for a second. "If I get her back," I taunted even as I clasped his hand and pulled him in for a hug.

"You'll get her back," he replied. "I give her props for

standing up to you, but let's face it, you're the one thing she's never been able to resist."

"And she's the one thing that I never want to let go," I said with an even tone, making sure I held his stare. This was one promise I didn't want him to mistake; this was one promise I was never going to break.

"Alright, let's get this show started then. What's the plan?"

I grinned and went to grab another glass. Even though my chest was still sore, knowing I had my best friend on my side gave me hope.

I was going to show Blake Tyler that she was my world - *the rest of the world be damned.*

CHAPTER 29

BLAKE

Track 21: Open Book

"You said my cover told you everything,
but you couldn't have been more wrong.
You said I lied and cheated, all for the story,
The truth is I've been an open book all along."

"THANK YOU, NASHVILLE!" I YELLED TO THE CROWD AND EVEN
with the mic, it was still drowned out by their screams. "It's so
good to be back home."

My smile was so big that it hurt. But it was a good hurt
compared to the other kinds I'd been experiencing these past
two weeks. I waved and scanned the crowd, catching my
parents and Ash in the front row. Right next to my mom was
my aunt and my three cousins. And then I winced, thankfully
only slightly, seeing Zach's parents there, too, right next
to Ash.

"So, we didn't get to chat yet," I began, acknowledging
that I'd come out on stage and begun with three songs back-
to-back from my *Heart Break* album without really saying

much. It had been my idea, my way of giving me some time to steel my nerves for what I planned. I'd also chosen the three songs that should be listed under 'Related Resources' when it came to Zach Parker; they were all about him: 'Treehouse,' 'Sixteen,' and 'Retched Romeo.'

Tay was right, Bruce wasn't pleased when I told him what I needed to do, but he also wasn't completely opposed. I think after the last show, he realized just how far my fans were willing to go for me - how much they cared – and that if I thought this was the right thing to do, so would they.

I grabbed the stool that they had set out and pulled it a few inches closer to the front of the stage, smiling as I heard my name being cheered from various locations in the arena.

Climbing onto it, I sighed and crossed my legs. "I'm sure I don't need to tell you what happened at my last show." Holding my hand up to the side of my mouth, I pretended to whisper, "If you don't know, I'd rather not relive it so just ask Google while I ramble here for a few minutes."

'We love you, Blake.'

I smiled.

Deep breaths. Be strong. Be courageous. Be honest.

"I do, however, have a confession." I bit my lip. "I have something to tell you that I am so deeply sorry for."

If the world stopping ever made a sound, I was sure it was this one: the collective catch of seventy-thousand breaths.

"It's kind of a long story. One that can mostly be summed up by saying that I haven't had the best luck with love. Especially very recently." My lips tipped up in a wry smile.

'Me too!'

'Boys suck!'

'Your songs are exactly how we feel!'

And then I laughed at myself. At how sad a *lovestruck* girl I could be. But there was a smile in there, too, because I wasn't alone. And with that comfort, I sat up straighter, brushed my hair back from my face, and had a heart-to-heart with seventy-thousand of my closest friends.

"There are some people that would have you think that I actually *like* going through boyfriends faster than Kleenex during allergy season and that this is all a game to me." I cleared my throat. "I'd like to break it to them… it's not a game; I'm only human – and that's an FYI not an FYE. So, I'd like to set the record straight tonight." I shifted in my seat, setting Marty - my shield - down and propping him against the stool. "The heart is a funny thing. A puzzle. And, maybe like some of you, I've been searching for the missing piece. Ok, I'll be honest, I've been trying to jam anything that looks like it might fit into there."

More laughter rippled in waves from the crowd.

"I've never been good at puzzles," I muttered sheepishly, drawing more laughs from them. "Have you ever liked someone and been afraid that they won't love you for you? That they're with you for some *other* reason?"

Overwhelming shouts agreed with me. My 'other reasons' might be more complex or more obvious than theirs, but they weren't different.

"Glad I'm not alone in that," I said softly. "So, I was searching and I made some bad choices - choices that, because of all this," I spread my arms wide to indicate the lights and the fame, "seemed much more sensational to describe as heartless rather than hurting. Imagine your latest break-up… what happened… whose decision it was… and then imagine that it was written as the complete opposite. *Welcome to my life.*"

I let out that hard laugh again, unable to stop myself, and said, "You know, they tell me that I'm lucky up here all dolled up and dazzling, but really I'm just confused because I don't feel pretty or worthy – I just feel used."

"So that leads me to my confession. My apology." I stood, too antsy to stay seated, and walked to the edge of the stage.

"It may or may not come as a surprise that most of the songs from my *Heart Break* album were written about Zach Parker. The truth is I've been in love with Zach for most of my life. *The truth is that my heart has been his to break for a very long time because love is a ruthless game – where in order to win, you have to lose.* And this love is the kind that you fall into until it hurts or bleeds, but never fades with time."

They were the truest words that had ever come off of this stage - and I'd sung most of my heart out to these people. But this. This was the kind of personal that most stars tried to keep under wraps because some part of your life deserved to only belong to you. I didn't disagree. But I'd also lied to them which, for me, meant that they deserved this at least – the missing piece of my heart. Honest. Raw. Unfiltered. Unembellished.

I choked after speaking, surprised by the rush of tears that flooded my eyes and crept over the edge.

I still loved Zach and I'd sent him away.

Maybe there was still a way to fix that; I couldn't be sure. All that I could be sure of right now was what I was about to do.

That truth burned so brightly that it should have lit up the entire stadium even as all the lights on the stage went off.

Wait, what?

What was happening?

I whipped around, trying to look to the side of the stage and see if there was anyone who could tell me what was going on. The power hadn't gone out - I could still see some dim lights in the stadium seating. It was only the stage that had gone completely dark.

"I'm so—" I broke off, realizing that my mic wasn't working either. "Can you—" I tried again, but I doubted that even the people in the front row could hear me talking over the general gasps and wondering rumbles of the crowd.

I stumbled backward, tripping into the stool. I felt Marty

begin to fall and it was a miracle that I reached out and was able to grab him before he crashed to the ground. I bit into my lower lip hard. *What was going on?*

I just needed to tell them.

I could hear the words I'd recited, the confession that was written with every beat of my heart, screaming in my head:

"The press doesn't want my broken parts; they want to turn them into permanent scars. Over the past several months, their harsh words have cut me down. But you guys, your love and support was like a flood, drowning them out. This is me. Broken. Bruised. Brave. Blake. I'm sorry for what I did, but I'm not sorry for who I am because it's who I'm meant to be."

My catharsis was withheld and now it burned in my throat like bile unwilling to go back down inside; the truth needed to come out.

Breathe, Blake.

It was probably less than a minute that everything had gone dark and I felt paralyzed but it felt like much longer.

There was nothing on the stage right now between me and the side. I was sure that if I walked in that direction, I'd run into someone who could tell me what the heck had just happened.

"Sorry for the interruption."

I froze at the voice that was not mine booming out into the audience, the goosebumps echoing the ripples in my heart. I waited - holding my breath like every other spectator in the crowd for him to speak again.

Zach.

Zach

I watched her from the sidelines, shadows shuddering in the dark. It had taken a fuckton of bribes and convincing to be able to pull this shit off - especially since Blay had decided to alter this show for her own purposes, too. Ash had gotten me a copy of the set-list and timing and it was just a miracle that he'd decided to ask Tay for it because she'd been one of the few who had the updated version.

Clearly, Baby Blake was planning something for her fans, something that she didn't want getting out before the show.

As soon as I watched her walk on stage and perform those songs that were tattooed on my memory as a melodic reminder of what I'd done to her, I knew what she was thinking.

Good thing I'd already been one step ahead.

I let her talk to them, waiting for the right moment to give Ash the signal to shut down the stage lights, putting most of the venue into a blackout. I'd almost missed that fucking moment because she admitted to tens of thousands of people that she loved me and the only thing I could hear - think - acknowledge - was that She. Loved. Me.

After it all, she still loved me.

I had no plans to leave this stage tonight without her by my side, but I sure as shit felt a whole lot more confident in what I was about to do.

"This wasn't part of the schedule," I drawled, hearing the half-smile in my voice. As I walked out onto the stage, Ash had them bring the lights back on low, keeping a soft spotlight on me. "So, I apologize for stealing the show."

She knew it was me.

They figured it out as soon as they saw me take off one of the hats they so vocally disapproved of.

'Jerk!'

'Asshole!'

'Get off the stage! Boooo!'

I was officially being booed while on stage. *First time for everything.*

"I know, I know," I said, holding up a hand like I was trying to wave defeat. "I'm a dick. But trust me, you're going to want to hear what I have to say."

Crickets.

I'd never heard silence quite this loud.

I turned to face Blake who was standing there with her mouth wide open - an image that I'd save for later.

"What are you doing here?" I read her lips as they mouthed the question. Her mic was still off – I'd made sure of that.

I stared at her for a second, taking in her straight hair, cut off shorts, black boots, and plaid shirt. *This* was the Blake that I knew - not the one covered in sequins and sparkles, but the one that was homegrown honey. *All natural sweetness.* It looked like Nashville was getting full-fledged Baby Blake tonight.

"I'm here for you," I told her, refusing to let her look away from me. *I was here for her and I would fight for her because I was never fucking letting her go again.*

'*Yeah, sure you are!*'

'*Don't fall for it, Blake!*'

I gritted my teeth, instantly willing to gut anyone who told her to stay away from me.

"I know Blake just told you how she's loved me forever. Well, I need to be honest with you, too... I've loved her for longer." That shut them up. "You're probably wondering then, how I could do what I did?" I asked rhetorically, letting my hat fall from my hand. "You see, Blake's problem is that her heart is too big. She loved me when I didn't deserve it. And my fault was always that I was convinced I didn't deserve it. I thought I was falling on my own sword the day I decided that I wouldn't let her sacrifice the things I knew meant the world to her - her family, her career, her fans - for me."

"Zach..." I turned my head to see Blake at my side,

staring at me wide-eyed, wondering if I was really going to do this.

"The truth is, ladies and gentlemen, that for the past five months, we haven't really been dating."

I could see the shock as it rippled through the crowd, suspense and anticipation clogging the air. We both looked out at the dimly lit crowd, half-expecting a riot to start at my confession. But they waited.

"Blake came to me over Christmas and asked me to be her fake boyfriend to help get the press to leave her alone, to help stop them from rubbing her heartbreaks in her face." I tore my eyes from them because they didn't fucking matter; I'd let *them* matter for too long when she was the only one I should have been focused on. "That may upset some of you. But you should also know that even though our relationship may not have been real, our love always was."

The angle of the low lights was just enough to reflect off the tears I saw begin to collect in her eyes. Like a reflex, my fingers itched to wipe them away.

"I broke up with her because I was afraid that information was going to be published and would damage her career. Again, I acted like a fucking - *sorry* - idiot, believing that I wasn't enough to fill this beautiful woman's Texas-sized heart." Her hands rose to cup over her mouth and wipe the wetness from her face. "I care about what happens to your reputation, Baby Blake, but after losing you, that's nothing compared to how much I care about what happens to your heart."

The 'awws' that echoed through the crowd would have been made me laugh if I wasn't ripping my heart from my chest to give this woman the apology that she deserved.

"Zach, I—" she started as she stepped towards me.

I held up a hand and kept talking. "You gave me your heart nine years ago, Blakebaby, and I've done a shit job of taking care of it. I've bruised it. I've scarred it. I've broken it.

All in an attempt to give it back to you. But just like the night I met you, when I wasn't going to let you go anywhere - run anywhere - without me, your heart wouldn't let me go. I still don't think I deserve it. The only thing that's changed is that now I don't give a fuck whether I do or don't; *it's mine.* And I'm here tonight to tell you that there's no way in hell you're getting it back."

Her hand pressed against her lips that I was pretty sure she was going to bite right through in an attempt to not start sobbing. Tears ran down her face like drops of disbelief. I couldn't help but smile because I was nowhere near fucking done. No, when I was done there was going to be no one on the goddamn planet who would ever question how much I loved this woman and what I would risk to keep her.

"This is me, Blay, all of me standing here in front of you, swallowing my stubborn pride, and saying that I'm sorry for that night. This is me telling you that I can't live without you any longer. And I hope that having all of me will be enough." I stepped barely an inch away from her. All I wanted her to be able to see was me. "Because without you, *Blakebaby,* I'm a melody living in a world that can't hear sound."

And that was what broke her last bar of restraint; she let out a strangled sob and with a curse because I couldn't stop myself, I pulled her hard against my chest, unable to keep my hands off of her any longer.

And then her head tipped up to mine and she murmured loud enough for only me to hear, "Zach, the shine of the thousands of spotlights and all the stars in the darkest of night skies – all of this will never be enough for me. Without you, the rest of it will never be enough. You are all I need."

"I'm so fucking sorry, baby," I choked out as she dove into my chest again.

The cheers and sighs faded into the background as I held my girl, feeling her body shake against me. Part of me knew that she was mine, the other part still held onto her like my life depended on it.

And it did.

A short second later she pulled back, wiping her face and darting her eyes to the stunned crowd and back to me.

"I-I'm sorry," she said with a wobbly voice. "I-I'm a mess."

'You're beautiful!'

'Forgive him!'

Her words had echoed softly through my mic.

I chuckled. "You're not a mess, Blay. You are the most headstrong, awkward, and captivating kind of beautiful." I could see the way my words made her want to break down again. And if she did? So be it. She deserved to hear every fucking phrase. She deserved to be worshipped on stage... in private... every damn second of every damn day.

'Listen to him!'

"Your beautiful is made up of starlight and wishes and magic - the type of magic that foolish men like me run away from... and then run back to when it's too late."

Her lower lip quivered so badly I wanted to bite it just to keep it steady.

"Am I too late, Blakebaby?" I whispered quietly.

'No!'

'Tell him he's not!'

'Kiss him!'

Smiles broke on both of our faces at the last one. Talk about having a commentary accompany one of the most important moments of our lives. I didn't care. I would have yelled it from the fucking mountaintops if that's what it took to make her mine.

"You're not too late," she said with a watery smile. "I miss you too much to be mad anymore."

The lights came back on with a flood. Unnecessary. The smiles that broke on our faces could have lit the whole damn stadium.

"I love you, *Blakebaby*. Always."

"I've always loved you, Zach," she returned as she wrapped her arms around my neck.

At that point, the crowd had ceased to exist. It was just her and me. Against the world. For the world. It didn't matter – we'd create a brand new world.

My forehead rested on hers, losing myself in those brilliant blues before I claimed her lips, kissing her like I should have in Minnesota - and ten years ago. *This* was the fairytale kiss. And it wasn't because there were people or cameras watching - in fact, it was in spite of those things. For the first time, they knew what they saw was for real.

It was only when the chanting of '*Blake and Zach*' gained full steam - and when Ash flicked the lights (because even though he knew how we felt didn't mean he was ready for *this* to be paraded in front of his face) that it registered that we were still in front of the crowd.

"Sorry," I rasped hoarsely. "I got a little carried away there."

Her red lips widened into an even bigger smile. That was my girl. Wearing her heart on her sleeve... shirt... shoes... and smile.

"You're my North Star, *Blakebaby*. No matter what happens or where I go, I always find my way back to you."

"Seriously?" she whimpered before she sobbed again. "They're all seeing me ugly cry!"

Laughter rippled through the crowd as she playfully used my shirt to wipe her face.

'*We love you, Blake!*'

I laughed. "Well, there's more coming."

Palms against my chest, she pushed back. "Are you joking? I'm a mess!"

"Blay," I cupped her face, "I have almost ten years of things built up inside of me that I should have done and should have said. The best I can do is have someone bring you out a box of tissues because I'm not done with you yet."

She groaned as the crowd went wild. *At least I had them on my side.*

I stepped back and faced the stands. "I apologize for taking up so much of the show you came to see, but I'm not sorry," I said with a devilish grin. "Now, y'all came to hear Blake sing - and you will - but first, I have a song that I want to sing for her."

"Oh, God. I think I need to sit down." We all laughed, hearing her mumbled complaint. Apparently, Ash had her mic turned back on low.

I thanked one of the stage hands who ran out with my guitar and a second stool for me to sit. A few quick strums to verify that it was tuned and ready (like I hadn't checked ten times before coming out here), I looked over my shoulder.

"This ones for you, babe."

And then I played. Familiar chords. A familiar tune. She knew what was coming... because she was the one who wrote it.

"In my eyes, you are the sunrise.
Bound to my blood and always on my mind."

Even though I took some liberties with the lyrics, this time it was my turn to sing my heart for her.

"In my eyes, you are the sunrise.
Effortless captivating, too enchanting to be mine.
Here I am, day after day.
My heart, it rises for you.
So, please always stay,
My heart, it rises for you.
Say you'll be mine, Blay.
My heart, it rises for you.
And I know for me, it's always you.
Please don't leave the mess of this man
With the heart that adores you."

My heart pounded as the last chord faded into silence. It wasn't blood, but Blake that pumped through my veins. And then she was in my arms again.

Fearless.

Forever.

Mine.

CHAPTER 30
BLAKE

Track 22: Fairytales

"Some say fairytales are unbelievable,
But I'd ask them if they've ever met you."

"ARE YOU SERIOUS RIGHT NOW?" I LAUGHED, HALF BREATHLESS as I jogged trying to keep up with him. "*This* is where we rushed back to?"

He shot me that smirk over his shoulder - the one that had turned my insides to mush since I was fifteen. *The one that said he had plans and that I was a part of them.*

I shook my head as we slowed through the brush, coming to a stop at the base of our old treehouse. *Back to the beginning.*

We'd finished the show - a show that had been the perfect ending to the tour and a perfect beginning for us: surrounded by love and a couple thousand fans. It didn't matter how long it had been or how many people were watching - surrounded by a sea of stars and stares, all I would ever see is him.

'Blake Tyler takes ownership of past break-ups in heartwarming concert confession.'
'Blake Tyler gives the best concert of her career, complete with a happily-ever-after finale!'

ASH WAS RIGHT. There was a part of me that was blind when it came to Zach - blind to fear and anxiety, blind to pressure and popularity, blind to anything but love.

The crowd... my fans... the world... finally got what they'd been looking for - and so did I - something true in a world that too often was filled with frauds. *A love story.*

Whatever I'd done... whatever he'd done... it was forgiven for love. Because if there is one thing in this world that everyone understands, it's that love isn't perfect, but it's worth it.

I hoped that one day Ash would meet someone who showed him how that was never a bad thing.

The second the lights had gone dark to a crowd cheering for us to give them 'one more kiss,' he'd tugged me off stage and out to the car, flooring it to get back here. No one seemed to mind. I'd see my family in the morning.

This is what it should have been ten years ago - the two of us sneaking out here because what we had was written in the stars.

"Why are we here?" I asked again as Zach began to climb the ladder.

He didn't answer me.

But when I got to the top, I forgot I'd even asked.

Zach stood in the middle of the room on top of a makeshift bed, not so dissimilar from the one that had been up here *that* night. Candles lined the three walls, flickering in the cool summer night breeze that blew through the open window.

It wasn't fancy cars or a fancy restaurant with fancy clothes and *fake* feelings.

It was simple. It was subtle. *It was us.*

"Is this real?" I whispered, unable to take my eyes off of him. He'd shucked his shirt on the drive here, leaving only the tee he was wearing underneath, partially tucked into the front of his jeans that sat low enough on his hips to make me squirm. And the way the light rolled over his body in waves made me desperate for the touch that I'd been craving throughout the entire show.

"I have something for you," he rasped even as he stared at me hungrily.

"This… is beautiful, Zach," I replied, looking around again, this time breathing in the warm vanilla from the candles and the way it mixed with the earthy forest scent. "How did you… Who…"

He grinned. "I got everything ready. Taylor left the show early to light the candles. But this isn't the surprise."

I gaped. *Was the man trying to give me a heart attack?*

"What else could there possibly be?" I asked incredulously. "First, you commandeer my show and force me to forgive you." His stomach flexed as he laughed and I realized that my teasing had done anything but lighten the situation. "And… and then you whisk me off stage to come here…"

He stepped towards me, his hands reaching for my hips as he tugged me to him. "I know it's not the Plaza. And I know it's not the perfect beaches of California or the wide-open, star-lit freedom of Colorado, but—"

"*It's perfect,*" I finished, stepping onto the small mattress and wrapping my arms around his neck.

"Blake…" he growled my name before his lips crashed onto mine, kissing me hard.

Two weeks.

Too long.

His tongue touched the seam of my lips just as they

opened for him, letting him inside. *Why does wanting him always feel like the first time?* I let out a moan as he sucked on my tongue before tugging my shirt from my shorts, unbuttoning it and forcing it off my arms. My jeans and underwear were gone before I could catch my breath.

I needed him.

There's something else he brought me here for, but the desire between us was too hot and desperate to contain. Like a spark in the middle of the dry forests of California - this wildfire needed to run its course.

His hands gripped my ass and lifted me, my legs wrapping around his waist pushing his thick length against me. I rolled my hips against him and he groaned.

"Do you even know what you are searching for, *Blakebaby?*"

With every word he erased the parts about this place that had broken my heart. With every word, he gave me the pieces back one by one.

"Yes," I whispered against his lips as he lay me down on the mattress. "You." I bit his lower lip and the growl that erupted from his chest was lethal with lust.

One hand cupped my breast as his mouth slid down to claim the other. He tongued my nipple into his mouth, drawing on it with steady pulls that had my hips thrusting up against him in tandem.

Releasing my breast with a loud pop, he kissed a path down my stomach, nipping at the soft flesh near my belly button. I felt the warmth of his breath trickle down over my core and my body clenched in anticipation.

"*Zach...*" I pleaded.

His fingers skated down to dig into my thighs, spreading them wide to accommodate his shoulders.

"Let me see how you shine," he demanded as he spread my legs wide, baring my sex to him. "For me, Baby Blake?" He blew a soft breath over my aching pussy.

"Only for you," I said in a breathless voice.

With a hungry moan, his lips pressed to my core and my body jerked up against him as sparks flared. The movement spurred him on. With my lips spread wide, he flattened his tongue over me, licking from my entrance all the way to my clit with the Goldilocks amount of pressure.

"Honey…" he growled against me, making me shake with need.

My fingers searched for his head and clenched into his hair, pulling him against me.

"Please," I moaned.

I felt his body tense against mine. He loved what he did to me. And I loved what my begging did to him.

Every time he touched me, my response felt the same, but different; each time felt new. It was like when I sang any of my songs; they were the same chords and the same lyrics, but they never came out *exactly* like the last time.

I gasped as his tongue pushed inside of me again and again as his thumb slid back over my clit. Everything blurred like I have no contacts in; the candles in the room look like giant yellow halos, magical yellow balls that make this feel even more like a fantasy. My moans mingled with the sounds coming from between my legs. Later, I would add it to the list of embarrassing things that I'd done in front of him. Later, I would realize that I still didn't care.

I could feel the way his mouth smiled against my sex and he groaned each time I pressed up into him, more of my desire gushing against him that he greedily sucked up; it was the hottest thing I'd ever heard. Those groans ripped me apart as the lights in the room melted into a giant blur and I shattered underneath him.

Gasping and shaking, I was completely undone. By tonight. By him. By everything.

I felt the soft, quick presses of his lips against the insides of my thighs before my vision focused again on him as he stood. Tugging off the rest of his clothes, he stood there, looking down on me - sprawled out, flushing, and dripping; he looked down on me like the god he was.

I gulped, watching him lick the rest of me off of his lips. My eyes drifted further south. The candles let me see the fine sheen of sweat over every inch of his body that I knew so well yet was still discovering. My greedy perusal halted when I got to his erection hanging thick and heavy between his legs, pointing directly at me. One of these days I would taste the sweet saltiness of him on my tongue. But not tonight.

"This was all I wanted that night," he rasped, his hand gripping his cock. "All I wanted was you. Here. Sprawled out with your long legs spread open for me."

My hips arched, wanting exactly that.

He dropped to his knees, leaning on one hand over me.

I lost myself in those eyes - golden, just like his heart. "I love you, *Blakebaby,*" he said with a thick voice. "You don't even understand how much. You couldn't."

"I love you." My hand came up to cup the side of his face, pulling his lips down to mine. "And I think I could... but I'd prefer that you show me."

He chuckled against my mouth, deep and full of promise.

"Anything for you."

His mouth ravaged mine. I tasted myself on his tongue and that only made me hotter. But he was just as crazed. Before my hips could grind up against his, I felt the head of his cock at my entrance, slipping it back and forth over my entrance and my clit, coating it with my juices. My core clenched as he pressed against my entrance.

I stopped breathing as he sunk his thickness all the way inside of me, wanting to feel nothing - not even the air I needed to survive - except for the way his arousal pushed apart my tense, needy muscles to find the deepest place inside me.

He froze and we both just *felt... lived...* that moment. It was the pause - the inhale - before the beat dropped. And then, with an angry growl, he took what we both needed. Sliding back out he thrust into me again. The old mattress squeaked underneath us as our hips slammed together.

His mouth left mine and I didn't complain when he began kissing and sucking on my neck. The stars that I always stared up at exploded in my vision as I came, the world falling away beneath me. Zach's hoarse yell came a split second after I felt the rush of his heat filling up my passage, coating me and marking me as his forever.

Even through turbulent breaths, he didn't stop kissing me: along my jaw, down my neck, tracing my collarbone. Tender, yet possessive.

I may be a face that the entire world knows, but I belong to him.

Slipping out of me, he gently cleaned us both before pulling me tight to him. I curled into his side, searching to be closer to him: the only place that ever felt like home. His hand around me gently stroked my back. I could stay here forever.

"Did you bring a blanket?" I asked, hearing how my voice had dropped a notch from being completely and totally sated. *From pure bliss.*

I began to sit up when his arms cinched around me.

"Wait," he said softly, reaching for my left wrist. "I need this for a second."

My brow furrowed. My eyes darted down to my hand and then back up to his intense gaze.

"I should have given this to you a long time ago," he began hoarsely, leaning over to feel for his jeans, digging around for something in them before he came back to me. I wasn't prepared for what was in his hand when it opened. I balked. I gaped. And then I broke into tears.

"I should have returned it to you." He turned my wrist, gently laying the charm bracelet that I thought I'd lost almost a decade ago on a night that was so similar yet so different than this one. "I found it after you'd gone, but I couldn't bring myself to give it back. Especially not after the graduation party."

He stared, focused on the task of locking the clasp and securing the piece around my wrist.

"I pushed so hard and then this was all I had left of you to hold on to."

"Y-you kept it?" I stuttered, a disgusting mess of tears and tremors.

He nodded, his thumb rubbing over the inside of my wrist, moving the guitar charm back and forth.

"I kept it... for a lot of reasons. The first one that I told myself was that it was a reminder of exactly why I couldn't have you; Ash gave it to you and I promised him..." He let out a clipped laugh. "I told myself a lot of things, most of which weren't the truth. The truth is that I loved you and I left you and I held onto this, hoping that you'd hold onto me until I came home. And then you let the world fall in love with you. So, I held onto it, like somehow... someway... it meant that I had a part of you that no one else had."

"You do," I insisted, grabbing his hand and pulling it to my mouth. "You always did."

Tears overflowed down my cheeks, his hands quickly moving to brush them away. I pressed my hand to his chest, right above his heart and whispered, "So you're not just saying all this so that I make you famous?"

Half-joking. Half past fears.

"Are you sure you're not just doing all this to save your reputation?" he teased back, drawing a small laugh from me. His head tipped down to mine, kissing my hands that clasped his. "I never cared about reaching for the moon, *Blakebaby.*" His lips inched closer and brushed over mine. "Not when I can spend my life with you underneath the stars."

I let out the girly, sixteen-year-old giggle that I'd been saving for a very long time before I pressed my lips to his. My eyes drifted shut with a smile still on my face. That was the thing about love, you could have everything in the world, but without a heart, it all added up to nothing. This love... our love... was real.

"I love you," my heart whispered to his.

"I love you, too, Blakebaby."

Today was a fairytale.

EPILOGUE
BLAKE

Bonus Track: Forever
"I would gladly lose myself in love. In you.
Because that's where I find me.
I realized the fall no longer matters
when forever is staring back at me."

'Blake finally finds Happily-Ever-After with Zach Parker!'

BLISS. THE KIND THAT MAKES YOU TINGLY AND LAUGH FOR NO reason or every reason. That was my life now – every moment of it. *With him.*

We were snuggled up on the back deck to our farmhouse. Zach had wrapped a blanket around my shoulders insisting that there was a chill in the air and he didn't want either of his girls getting cold. We sat on the rocking swing, me wedged between his legs, lying back against his chest, his arms holding me tight against him as his hands rubbed lazily over my swollen stomach, our little girl resting peacefully (for the moment) against my bladder.

In the distance was the (second) treehouse that we'd built together when we bought the property two months after the Lovestruck tour ended a year and a half ago. That treehouse had seen a lot of things since then.

We made music in that treehouse. We made love in that treehouse. And we'd made the promise of forever when Zach proposed to me on a star-encrusted August night last summer.

"How long will you want me?" I'd teased him softly.

"Forever. As long as you'll have me." And then he'd dropped down on one knee.

So many tears had been shed in that small space, but they'd been happy tears; they'd been tears because I never knew I could be this happy.

There are girls that will plan forever in order to have the perfect wedding. And then there was me. I planned the wedding for a perfect forever - which meant becoming Zach's wife as soon as I could.

During the Lovestruck tour and the few weeks following it, I'd written more songs than I could produce on a single album. With Zach's help - and a fair number of planned duets - I narrowed it down and managed to finish recording my next album, *Forever*, the day before he proposed. *I had a feeling that wasn't a coincidence either.*

The album released in the fall and the tour? Well, it was going to start the new year. And that's when I figured, what better way to start Forever than with forever? So, in Zach's parents' barn that was covered with snow, decked to the nines with enough twinkle light to make Clark Griswold jealous, my dad walked me down the aisle to the love of my entire life with Ash standing by his side.

Shivering and sublimely happy, we said I do in the place where we'd argued 'I don't' for so many years - 'I don't want her,' 'I don't love him,' 'I don't care if this hurts her,' 'I don't care if I never see him again.'

Karma. Fate. I didn't care what it was called as long as it meant forever.

"How long will I be with you?" I tipped my head up and asked quietly as we held each other during our reception and watched our close family and friends dance and drink and celebrate our love.

He kissed my nose and replied, "As long as the sea is destined to wash against the sand."

After our honeymoon on a secluded island where the sea was ours and clothing was completely optional, we started the Forever tour as husband and wife, sharing our fairy tale with a few hundred-thousand of my closest friends. ZPP opened and Zach became a permanent part of my show - and the crowds loved it and us.

There were no more rumors. No more falling reputations. There was nothing that could break what we had after all we'd been through.

In fact, halfway through the tour, something happened that made us even stronger.

Did I mention that our honeymoon was clothes and birth control-free?

With four months left to the tour, we found out that we were pregnant. I stared at that little blue strip like it was telling me that I'd won another Grammy. And Zach? My eyes welled with tears remembering the way he'd crushed me to him, kissing me, then pulled my shirt off of me to kiss and whisper to my stomach. Happy excitement quickly turned to relentless desire as his kisses drifted lower with that devilish smirk that said he was about to try to get me more pregnant just to be sure – if such a thing were possible, he would have accomplished it.

"How long will you need me?" I whispered much later against his lips, his cock still buried and pulsing inside of me, our bodies sticky with sweat and satisfied love.

"*Mmm,*" *he groaned and flexed his hips, letting me know that it looked like he was going to keep 'needing' me all night.*

"*How long?*" *I said just before I bit his lip.*

"*I guess…*" *He pretended to think. "I guess for as long as the sun still rises in the morning.*"

We'd kept the news to ourselves until just before the last few shows, deciding to do one of our popular livestream videos to let all our fans know the happy news. Pink and blue balloons littered the remaining concert. Happy, adoring fans sent us cards and gifts; *I'd never felt more loved.*

We found out we were having a girl the day before our final show in Nashville. And with what may go down as the most publicized gender-reveal in history, the Forever tour ended with a series of pink fireworks sparkling into the summer sky.

We were still writing. We were still going to be recording. But touring? I wasn't sure when our next concert would be. And as much as I loved seeing and singing for my fans, there are some things in life that are just more important, I thought, looking down at my modestly swollen stomach. I smiled to myself and sighed.

"Is she moving?" Zach quickly asked, always ready at the drop of a hat to worry about me or our baby.

"Just a little… right up into my ribs," I answered with a small groan, shifting against him. "What are you thinking about?"

"How much I love you, *Blakebaby*" he whispered gently against my mouth.

"How long?" I breathed back, slowly blinking my eyes open so I could lose them in his.

"How long will I love you?" He waited for my nod before his mouth thinned with pure focus - because simple words were not enough for Zach. Not when it came to me. And then his eyes flicked up towards the most perfectly clear, star-studded night. "As long as there are stars above you."

I was melting. "*Zach*…"

"Even longer if I can," he added with a rasp, brushing a finger over my lip before kissing me gently… reverently.

The End of all Endings.

Want Ash and Taylor's story? REDEMPTION is available now.

OTHER WORKS BY DR. REBECCA SHARP

Carmel Cove

Beholden

Bespoken

Besotted

Befallen

Beloved

Covington Security

Betrayed

Bribed

Beguiled

Burned

Branded

Broken

Believed

Bargained

Reynolds Protective

Archer

Hunter

Gunner

Ranger

The Odyssey Duet

The Fall of Troy
The Judgment of Paris

The Sacred Duet

The Gargoyle and the Gypsy

Country Love Collection

Tequila
Ready to Run
Fastest Girl in Town
Last Name
I'll Be Your Santa Tonight
Michigan for the Winter
Remember Arizona
Ex To See
A Cowboy for Christmas

The Winter Games

Up in the Air
On the Edge
Enjoy the Ride
In Too Deep
Over the Top

The Gentlemen's Guild

The Artist's Touch
The Sculptor's Seduction
The Painter's Passion

Passion & Perseverance Trilogy

(A Pride and Prejudice Retelling)

First Impressions
Second Chances
Third Time is the Charm

Standalones

Reputation
Redemption
Revolution: A Driven World Novel
Hypothetically

Want to #staysharp with everything that's coming?
Join my newsletter!

ACKNOWLEDGMENTS

To my husband – You are the best thing that's ever been mine. The stakes are high, the water's rough, but this love is ours. Allways.

To my sister – Thank you for always going over a thousand different versions of my covers and helping me pick the best one and then make it better. Love you.

To R.S. – I'm now just realizing that we have the same initials so people are going to think that I'm thanking myself here, but I'm not lol. Thank you for putting so much effort and detail into making sure that my books are perfect when they reach my readers.

To my Blogging Babes – Ari, Kassa, Alicia, Shelly, Mackenzie, Ally, Elizabeth, and the numerous other bloggers that I'm forgetting but who have graciously and enthusiastically supported me on this journey. You make my heart so full.

To my Sharpies – Thank you for putting up with all my secretive teasers that I couldn't hold back any longer but couldn't give any details about.

To Kassa and Lisa – Thank you for your honest and invaluable feedback, support, and just general laughs and loves.

To my readers – This is all for you. Thank you for being the unshakable force behind this journey.

And to Taylor Swift – For obvious reasons, you should be thanked twice. You should be thanked more than twice. THANK YOU for never letting the hate get to you. Thank you for being a class act. And thank you for music that touches so many of us.

ABOUT THE AUTHOR

Rebecca Sharp is a contemporary romance author of over thirty published novels and dentist living in PA with her amazing husband, affectionately referred to as Mr. GQ.

She writes a wide variety of contemporary romance. From new adult to extreme sports romance, forbidden romance to romantic comedies, her books will always give you strong heroines, hot alphas, unique love stories, and always a happily ever after. When she's not writing or seeing patients, she loves to travel with her husband, snowboard, and cook.

She loves to hear from readers. You can find her on Facebook, Instagram, and Goodreads. And, of course, you can email her directly at author@drrebeccasharp.com.

If you want to be emailed with exclusive cover reveals, upcoming book news, etc. you can sign up for her mailing list on her website: www.drrebeccasharp.com

Happy reading!

xx

Rebecca